BATTLEFIELDS
OF NORTHERN FRANCE AND THE LOW COUNTRIES

BATTLEFIELDS
OF NORTHERN FRANCE AND THE LOW COUNTRIES
MICHAEL GLOVER

MICHAEL JOSEPH LIMITED LONDON

First published in Great Britain by
Michael Joseph Limited
27 Wrights Lane London
W8 5TZ 1987

British Library Cataloguing in
Publication Data

Glover, Michael, 1922
Battlefields of Northern France
and the Low Countries
1 Battlefields-Benelux Countries
Guide-books
2 Benelux Countries-Description
and Travel-Guide-books
3 Battlefields-France-Guide-books
4 France-Description and Travel
-1975-Guide-books
I. Title 914.4'04838 · DC45

Battlefields of Northern France
and the Low Countries
was conceived and edited by
Thames Head
Avening Tetbury Gloucestershire
Great Britain

Editorial and Marketing
Martin Marix Evans

Design and Production
David Playne

Designers
Tina Carter and Mike Seaton

Design Assistants
**Heather Church David Ganderton
Nick Allen Jane Moody
Melanie Williams Richard Murphy
Lynda Marmont**

Editor **Gill Davies**

Consultant Editor **Leo Cooper**

Co-ordinator **Lois Wigens**

Typeset in ITC Benguiat on Scantext
by Thames Head ·

Printed by New Interlitho, Milan, Italy

WAR CEMETERIES AND MEMORIALS

The Commonwealth War Graves
Commission maintains hundreds of
cemeteries where may be found the
graves of men and women of the
Commonwealth forces who died in
two World Wars. Those who died but
whose graves could not be found
are commemorated on memorials
built by the Commission.

Lists of these cemeteries and
memorials are obtainable from:

2 Marlow Road,
Maidenhead,
Berkshire, SL6 7DX
Telephone (0628) 34221

Rue Angele Richard Beaurains,
F62012 Arras Cedex
France
Telephone Arras (21) 23 03 24

Elverdingestraat 82, B-8900 Ieper
(Ypres), Belgium
Telephone Ieper (057) 20 01 18
or (057) 20 57 18

Details of the location of a specific
grave or memorial can also be
obtained; the name, initials and
service particulars of the deceased
should be included with any such
request. Special editions of the
Michelin Road Maps (sheets 51,
52 and 53) can be supplied by the
Commission, who have also erected
green and white road signs *in situ*
to help direct the visitor.

KEY FOR BATTLE PLANS

Railway ·····················

River

Canal

Road

PICTURE CREDITS

ABBREVIATIONS

ANZAC Australia and New Zealand Army Corps

AOC Air Officer Commanding

AVRE Armoured Vehicle, Royal Engineers

BEF British Expeditionary Force (1914-18 and 1939-40)

DD Duplex Drive (that is driven by either tracks or propellers)

DLI Durham Light Infantry

DUKW Amphibious six-wheeled truck (the acronym is the project designation, used by the manufacturer, which was adopted because it was appropriate)

GOC General Officer Commanding

HQ Headquarters

KOSLI King's Own Shropshire Light Infantry

KRRC King's Royal Rifle Corps

OBLI Oxfordshire and Buckinghamshire Light Infantry

Para Parachute Battalion, Army Air Corps (later Parachute Regiment)

PIAT Projector Infantry Anti-Tank

QVR Queen Victoria Rifles, KRRC

RAF Royal Air Force, previously Royal Flying Corps (RFC)

RASC Royal Army Service Corps

RCT Regimental Combat Team, US equivalent of a British brigade group, that is, three or four infantry battalions with supporting arms such as tanks and artillery

RE Royal Engineers

RHLI Royal Hamilton Light Infantry

RM Royal Marines

RN Royal Navy

RTR Royal Tank Regiment (previously Royal Tank Corps)

RWF Royal Welch Fusiliers

US United States (of America)

VC Victoria Cross

CODE WORDS

DYNAMO Naval operation for the evacuation from Dunkirk, 1940

FORTITUDE Cover plan for OVERLORD (q.v.) 1944

GARDEN Offensive by XXX Corps into Holland, 1944
See also MARKET

GOLD Western British landing beach in NEPTUNE (q.v.)

HERBSTNEBEL German offensive in the Ardennes 1944

See also *WACHT AM RHEIN*

HILLMAN German strongpoint in Colleviiie-sur-Orne and Bénouville, north of Caen. Its companion fort was MORRIS

JUBILEE Raid on Dieppe, 1942

JUNO Canadian landing beach in NEPTUNE (q.v.)

MAGIC US operation for breaking Japanese codes

MARKET Airborne operation to seize bridges between Belgian frontier and Arnhem. In co-operation with GARDEN it became known as MARKET-GARDEN

MORRIS See HILLMAN above

MULBERRY Artificial harbours off Normandy Coast, 1944

NEPTUNE Landing in Normandy, 1944

OMAHA Eastern American landing beach in NEPTUNE (q.v.)

OVERLORD Allied campaign in north-west Europe, 1944-45

PHOENIX Concrete caissons used in MULBERRY (q.v.)

RUTTER Projected raid on Dieppe, superseded by JUBILEE (q.v.) 1942

SWORD Eastern British landing beach in NEPTUNE (q.v.)

ULTRA Intelligence gained from the reading of the German Enigma code

UTAH Western American landing beach in NEPTUNE (q.v.)

WACHT AM RHEIN German plan for the offensive in the Ardennes. Changed to *HERBSTNEBEL* on 2 December 1944

HOW TO USE THIS BOOK

Battlefields of Northern France and the Low Countries has been created to fill the gap between the tourist guide book and the historical account, to create a link between the map and the events which took place there. Armed with modern route maps of the areas to be visited and this book, the traveller will be better able to discover the past. To augment the lively text describing the battles, the following travel aids are provided:

1 A general 'overview' illustration of the countryside in which the action took place, with key towns and locations marked, to which the road map can be related (see, for example, page 10).

2 A small map relating major roads to the battlefield area, and information on selected places to be visited in the area (see, for example, page 27).

3 In the 'touring routes' section, suggested itineraries specially prepared by the Automobile Association for these books (pages 230 to 237).

In a book of this size, it is necessary to be selective and inevitably some sites, monuments and museums of interest have been omitted. The information given here, however, provides a good foundation upon which to base a visit. Add to this the help of Tourist Information offices and local people, some further specialized reading (see page 238), as well as those happy personal discoveries, and exploring history will prove a delight.

INTRODUCTION 8

1 ARNHEM: OPERATION MARKET-GARDEN 1944 10

2 BASTOGNE AND THE ARDENNES 1944-45 26

3 CALAIS AND DUNKIRK 1940 44

4 CAMBRAI 1917 62

5 CHÂTEAU-THIERRY 1918 76

6 CRÉCY 1346 AND AGINCOURT 1415 84

7 NORMANDY AND OPERATION NEPTUNE 1944 100

8 SEDAN 1870 120

9 DIEPPE 1942 130

10 THE SOMME 1916 AND 1918 146

11 VIMY RIDGE 1917 178

12 VERDUN 1916 188

13 YPRES 1914 AND 1917 198

14 WATERLOO 1815 220

TOURING ROUTES 230

FURTHER READING 238

INDEX 239

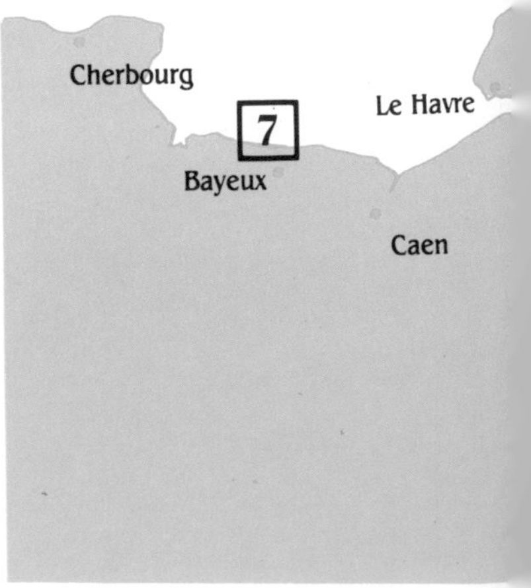

Cherbourg

7

Bayeux

Le Havre

Caen

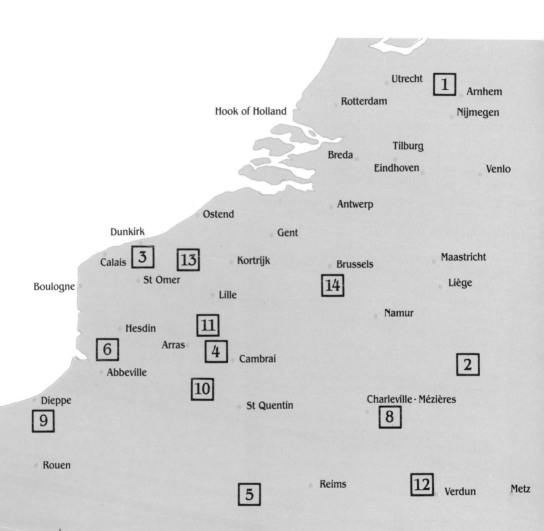

INTRODUCTION

MANY, PERHAPS MOST, GUIDES to battlefields concentrate on the visible memorabilia, the monuments, the cemeteries and the museums. Indeed, these have a great fascination of their own, many being impressive, some intensely moving and a few, notably the huge Ossuaire at Verdun, bloodchilling in their starkness and their implications. Yet by definition all such memorabilia are extraneous to the battles they commemorate since these things were not actually there at the time.

What I have tried to do in this book is to explain just why and how the battles were fought and what actually happened there. The readers I have had chiefly in mind are travellers on their way to other destinations who, without being specialists, have an interest in military history and find themselves with a few hours to spare. In addition those who may be visiting the graves of their forbears could be interested in discovering what their relatives were doing when they were killed.

France and the Low Countries are liberally sown with battlefields - it is not for nothing that the area was known as the Cockpit of Europe - and only a few can be described in a book of this size. The criterion for inclusion has been the importance of the action and the survival, at least in part, of the ground on which it was fought. Mons is a Battle Honour as proud as any in the British Army but there is little point in visiting it since even in 1914 it was a built-up industrialized area and has since been so reconstructed as to be unrecognizable. Naturally some battlefields have been mutilated over the decades. Towns expand - Arras and Dunkirk are good examples - and even away from built-up areas, motorways are built. The ground over which the tanks advanced towards Cambrai on 20 November 1917 now contains the intersection of two autoroutes.

The memorials themselves can hinder the imagination attempting to picture the ground as it was at the time. It requires an effort of will to look at Vimy Ridge and ignore the fine Canadian Memorial on the highest point. Waterloo is an extreme case. In the 1820s the ground held by Wellington's right centre was changed out of all recognition by the construction of the Lion Mound as a tribute to the gallantry of the Netherlands troops in the 1815 campaign. For anyone wanting an overview of almost the entire battlefield the Lion Mound is the obvious place to go but it was not there at the time of the battle and no one could have had that all-embracing view. If Wellington had been able to stand on the summit and watch the movements of the French troops he may well have fought the battle differently. What commanders know, either by sight or through messages, about what their troops are doing is a vital factor in any battle. To continue the Waterloo example, it is worth going to La Belle Alliance to realize just how little Napoleon, who spent much of the battle there, can have known of what was happening on much of his front.

Some of the battles included were fought on a vast scale. The 1916 offensive on the Somme covered over a hundred square miles and lasted four and a half months. To comprehend such a struggle would take weeks of visiting and reading. In such cases I have narrowed the focus to concentrate on an assimilable area for a limited period. Thus for the Somme I have chosen the village of La Boisselle and its immediate surroundings to serve as an epitome for the whole of the fifteen-mile front on which so many men went to their deaths in the doomed attack on 1 July 1916. Quite apart from the crater of the great mine, it is not difficult to imagine how the Tynesiders and their comrades of 34th Division went slowly forward in succeeding waves in open order across the shallow valley to the village. Looking back from the village it is equally easy to see how clearly they must have appeared in the sights of the German machine gunners as the sun came up.

Each battle is dealt with in three different ways. First comes a narrative telling how an action came to be fought in that particular place, what the generals intended, what actually happened and what, if anything, was achieved. This is supplemented by a guide to the ground showing how the battle was fought and how it looks today. Also included are directions for reaching the site and, where appropriate, particulars of what facilities are available. The third part consists of shorter pieces. Some of these are intended to show what it was like to be in that particular battle, some with the tactics and weapons concerned, some on nearby places of military interest, such as battles fought in other wars.

The overall aim of this guide is to help the reader to understand what it was like to take part in the battles described. To derive the fullest value it is important to try to share the thoughts of the soldier at all levels. It is not too difficult to imagine how a regimental soldier felt as he marched or rode forward into a hail of arrows, or musketry, or machine-gun fire. What is much more important is to enter the mind of the generals responsible for launching them into the attack. In particular it is essential to discard the manufactured myths which hold that most generals, especially British generals in 1914-18, were moronic butchers. Faced with unprecedented and largely insoluble problems, they did their best to win wars which the politicians were unwilling to end by other means. Many generals made many mistakes but it ill becomes politicians and armchair historians to censure them unless they could, or can, make practical proposals as to how the job might have been done better.

There are a few points on which some explanation may be useful. In order to distinguish between bodies of troops of various sizes I have used different types of numerals, thus:

> Third Army (or Army Group)
> III Corps
> 3rd Division
> 3 Brigade (or equivalent)
> 3/Battalion (or equivalent)

The British and Empire or Commonwealth armies used the term 'brigade' to denote a tactical formation of two, three or four units of battalion size. Most other armies call such a formation a regiment. In British usage a regiment is a battalion-size unit of armoured vehicles or artillery. In British infantry a regiment is a non-tactical grouping of battalions. To complicate matters further the Rifle Brigade is a regiment (in the infantry sense) as is the King's Royal Rifle Corps.

I have at times used the word 'British' to embrace all the nations of the Empire or Commonwealth. The evidence suggests that the soldiers of Australia, Canada and New Zealand were content, even proud, to be called British until about the middle of the First World War when their own prowess in the field, at a time when the troops from the British Isles were inevitably decreasing in quality, gave them a growing sense of separate nationality. If my use of the blanket term 'British' offends any reader from the Commonwealth I can only apologise and point out that, particularly in French and German usage, Australians, Canadians, New Zealanders, South Africans and soldiers from the Indian sub-continent, to say nothing of Irish, Scots and Welsh, are almost invariably referred to as English.

I must acknowledge my appreciation of Tonie and Valmai Holt who helped to develop the concept of this guide. My thanks are due to John Sutherell, to my brother Colin Glover for help, advice and information in various forms and to Dr Wilma George of Lady Margaret Hall, who primed me on the history of ostriches. The staffs of the Ministry of Defence Library, in particular John Andrews and Judith Blacklaw, and the London Library have, as always, been both helpful and forbearing. I owe a special debt of gratitude to Leo Cooper for his support and sustenance and, as in all my books, I depended wholly on Daphne, my wife, who kept the whole show on the road.

Michael Glover
March 1987

Road to Ede

Ginkel Heath

Johanna Hoeve

Dropping Zone

ARNHEM

Den Brink

Oosterbeek

Lower Rhine

Elden

Driel

The approach between the Belgian frontier and Arnhem is almost uniformly flat and is intersected with six major and many minor waterways. Off the road innumerable small dikes make movement in vehicles, even tanks, impossible

DP

DP

River Waal

Nijmegen

0 1 2 3   6

10   Kilometres

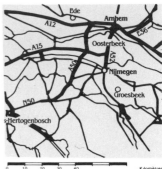

DP

ARNHEM
AND OPERATION MARKET-GARDEN
6 JUNE 1944

In Britain the epic fight of 1st Airborne Division at Arnhem tends to be thought of as a separate action. In fact it was only a part of a much larger operation spread over more than fifty miles and involving far larger forces than a single division. It was, moreover, Hitler's last victory and one he should never have been given the chance to win. It was the end-product of inter-allied rivalries and, above all of the arrogance and vanity of the newly promoted Field Marshal Montgomery.

In the late summer of 1944 the allies found themselves the victims of their own success. The breakout from the immediate beachhead in Normandy had been slower than anticipated; the final result had been an advance far faster than even the most optimistic had calculated with the consequence that there was a desperate shortage of supplies of all kinds. It had been reckoned that the armies would reach the line of the Seine on D+90, 4 September, and that by that time the ports of western France would have been in allied hands for seven weeks, being by then restored to working order and available to import stores from America. In fact by 4 September the great ports of Brittany and the Loire were, with the minor exception of St Malo, still held by the Germans while American divisions were operating beyond Verdun and the British had reached Brussels and Antwerp. Although Cherbourg had begun to receive cargoes on 16 July it was as yet working far below its capacity and the bulk of the stores required still had to be brought ashore through the bridgehead and transported to the fighting troops by truck. Another consequence of the rapid and unexpected advance was that the senior command of the allied armies became permeated with the idea that the German armies were irretrievably broken and that one final push would end the war.

Eindhoven, Nijmegen and Arnhem/Oosterbeek offer ample accommodation; from here all the landing sites and approaches can be visited. Oosterbeek is the place with most to see as it was central to the 1944 action. Travel there on the Utrechtstraat road rather than the motorway, so as to pass through many of the landing fields (the Airborne Monument is on the edge of these). Once in Oosterbeek, go to the excellent Hartenstein Airborne Museum which houses many exhibits, audio-visual presentations and dioramas of the battle, and alone would justify the journey! It is open every day (except Christmas and New Year's Day): Sundays and holidays 12.00-17.00; Monday to Saturday 11.00-17.00 hours. Visit too the Tafelberg Hotel - where Marshal Model saw the landings and which represented the emergency hospital in the film *A Bridge Too Far*.

The main road from the Belgian frontier near Neerpelt through Eindhoven, Zon, Veghel, Grave, Nijmegen, Elder and Elst follows the route of the British advance along a road they were seldom able to leave, however narrow and exposed it became. The John Frost Bridge in Arnhem has been rebuilt to the original plans but in 1944 the housetops would have reached its approaches. Small houses by St Elizabeth Hospital were the scene of bitter fighting. There are modern buildings here now, and more under construction.

Above all else the allies needed a great port in working order and none could have served their purpose better than Antwerp which 11th Armoured Division captured on 4 September with its installations undamaged. Unfortunately it was quite useless since it can only be approached through an estuary fifty miles long which is dominated by the island of Walcheren and the isthmus of South Beveland - both of which were firmly held by the enemy. Not that this state of affairs was irreparable. A comparatively short, and at the time practicable, further advance into North Brabant would have sealed off the Germans on the north of the estuary and made their position untenable. Unfortunately Montgomery, who had more grandiose schemes, halted the thrust northward and gave orders that his army 'will advance eastward ... from the general line Brussels-Antwerp'. This decision was, in Montgomery's post-war words, 'a bad mistake' and meant that Antwerp was not in fact open for shipping until 28 November. Meanwhile all allied operations were in a logistic strait-jacket.

If the enemy was as weak as was being assumed, sufficient supplies could be scraped together to permit one major thrust to be made across the Rhine and into Germany but to mount this would have meant the halting of all other operations. In the existing state of relations between the American and British commands the decision as to who was to undertake such a thrust posed an insoluble problem. The Americans had more troops on the Continent and public opinion in the States would have been outraged if their armies had been halted while the British won the war. On the other hand Montgomery was the most experienced and possibly the best allied general - though his constant assertion of his opinion on this subject had managed to antagonize all the American commanders from Eisenhower downwards. Faced with the choice between Bradley's all-American Twelfth Army Group or Montgomery's Anglo-Canadian Twenty-First Army Group to strike the knock-out blow, Eisenhower, and who shall blame him, compromised and opted for a temporary priority to Montgomery. This decision was immediately nullified when General Patton committed his Third Army to an unauthorized offensive with the tacit approval of Bradley. Montgomery did obtain some additional supplies but the main result of Eisenhower's decision was to give him the use of the only powerful uncommitted force of allied troops, First Allied Airborne Army (which Bradley did not want because he mistrusted airborne operations). They had the advantage that they would be able to go into battle without imposing additional strain on the allied lines of communications through France.

Montgomery's plan was to seize a bridge over the Rhine and then swing round to encircle the Ruhrland. There were only two bridges over the great river in front of his Army Group - Arnhem and, fifty miles upstream, Wesel. The latter had many advantages since it was closer to the Ruhr and there was one less major water obstacle between it and the existing front. If Arnhem was *A Bridge Too Far,* Wesel was one bridge less. General Dempsey, commanding British Second Army, and most of Montgomery's staff favoured going for Wesel. The air commanders favoured Arnhem and the Field Marshal agreed with them, possibly because if he struck too far on his right he might have to share the bridgehead with the Americans.*

IWM   IWM

(LEFT) General Omar N. Bradley, commanding Twelfth US Army Group. He found it increasingly difficult both to work with Montgomery and to control his own fiery subordinate, General Patton.

(RIGHT) Field Marshal Sir Bernard Montgomery, the most successful allied commander but one who was too arrogant to work comfortably with allies. Though normally cautious he was capable of great rashness.

---

* Such perversity is almost unbelievable but it is fair to add that many of the American generals behaved quite as badly, to say nothing of General Mark Clark's sabotage of the allied plan on the advance to Rome.

vehic...
front of one...

*Allied airborne landings,
September 1944*

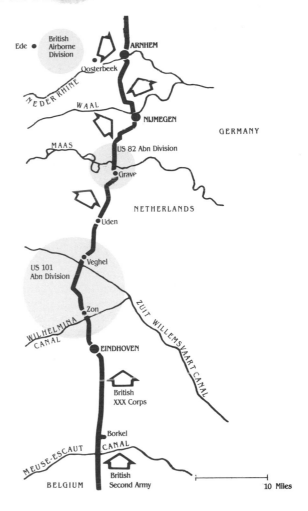

Ede •

British
Airborne
Division

ARNHEM

Oosterbeek

NEDER RHINE

WAAL

NIJMEGEN

GERMANY

MAAS

US 82 Abn Division

Grave

NETHERLANDS

Uden

Veghel

US 101
Abn Division

ZUIT WILLEMSVAART CANAL

Zon

WILHELMINA
CANAL

EINDHOVEN

British
XXX Corps

Borkel

MEUSE-ESCAUT CANAL

BELGIUM

British
Second Army

10 Miles

objectives but ~~~~~
and dropping zones for those who we
arrive on the second and third days. In addition
the fears of the air commanders and the shortage of aircraft forbade any attempt to drop
troops on their objectives. In each case the
landing grounds selected were some distance
from the objectives and, in the case of the
bridges, not at both ends of them.

It was basic to the conception of *MARKET-
GARDEN* that only total success would serve.
Unless the armour was able to advance over
Arnhem bridge the operation would be a failure
since there was no useful purpose to be served
in seizing Eindhoven, Nijmegen or any other
intermediate town. This merely emphasized
the risky nature of the project, a long advance
over a single road picketed by an inadequate
number of troops, however well trained and
determined. The only possible justification for
attempting it would have been certain knowledge that the enemy was in total disarray and it
was known at Twenty First Army Group that this
was no longer the case. By the end of the first
week of September General Student's First
Parachute Army was, although its name was
something of an exaggeration, putting up a
stern defence on the Meuse-Escaut Canal and,
far more sinister, reports came in that 9th and
10th SS Panzer Divisions were rapidly refitting
in the Arnhem area and had already received
new and powerful tanks.

USAF

14

In the week before the attack was launched Montgomery was told by his own Intelligence staff, by Eisenhower's headquarters, by the Dutch Resistance and from the decyphering of ULTRA that these divisions were nearby. He refused to take these reports seriously and did not pass them to the Airborne Corps. In fact, Lieutenant-General F.A.M. Browning, who commanded the corps, was given the same information by one of his Intelligence Officers and decided not only to ignore it but to discard the officer who gave it to him.

D-Day, Sunday 17 September, was gloriously fine and was heralded with raids made by a thousand Flying Fortresses on known anti-aircraft gun batteries in the *MARKET-GARDEN* area while fighter bombers attacked German barracks and defences in the immediate areas of the planned drops. From 10.25 am onwards 1,534 transport aircraft, 491 of them towing gliders, started to take off from twenty-two English airfields in two streams. Above them flew in relays more than a thousand British and American fighters but not a single German aircraft put in an appearance although thirty-four planes were brought down by anti-aircraft fire and three hundred more were damaged. For one reason and another, forty-six gliders had to slip their tows before reaching their targets, thirty-five of them before even crossing the Dutch coast.

82nd (US) Division started landing around Grave at 12.30 pm, and 1st (British) near Arnhem ten minutes later. 101st (US) Division began to touch down in the Eindhoven-Veghel area at 1 pm, and an hour later a heavy barrage was opened on the defences facing the Neerpelt bridgehead. At 2.35 pm, 2/ and 3/Irish Guards (the former being armoured) started for the north.

Ahead of them rocket-firing Typhoons of the RAF attempted to clear a strip extending one thousand yards on either side of the road. In contrast to the chaotic airborne operation in Sicily a year earlier, the airborne troops landed, almost without exception, just where they were intended to. Surprise was complete, so complete that Field Marshal Model, in command of the German Army Group B, was lunching unconcernedly in the Tafelberg Hotel within sight of the British landing.

Dakotas dropping parachutists during Operation MARKET.

17 September 1944. Parachutists landing to the west of Wolfezen. Gliders of the airlanding brigade are already on the ground.

IWM

IWM

1st Airborne had as their dropping zone the open heathland (now just beyond the motorway) seven miles west of Arnhem bridge and, leaving 1 Airlanding Brigade to guard that area, Major-General R.E. Urquhart sent 1 Parachute Brigade to seize the road bridge. From the start things went wrong. Only 2/Parachute Battalion reached the bridge and they were quickly surrounded - although with a single six-pounder anti-tank gun and some PIATs* they succeeded in destroying eleven German armoured cars which tried to cross the bridge from the south. 2/Parachute Battalion had no chance of reaching the southern end of the bridge.

Not only was the opposition stronger than had been expected but, thanks to the loss, damage and the inadequacy of most of the sets, radio communication broke down almost completely. Thus Urquhart could not get in touch with the fighting troops, could not report to the main army, could not call for air support and could not advise where supply drops should be made. On the following day, in an attempt to find out what was going on, Urquhart went forward to 3/Para in Oosterbeek and, becoming involved in close fighting, was penned up in a house for twenty-four hours during which he was unable to control his division.

Meanwhile, some twenty miles or so to the south of Arnhem, 82nd Division had a rather more successful day on 17 September. They succeeded in seizing the bridge at Grave, one of the few at which parachutists had been landed at both ends, and secured a bridge, off the main route, over the Maas-Waal Canal at Heuman. They also took possession of the high ground near Groesbeek which was a vital flank guard against any counter-attacks coming from the Reichswald Forest. Unfortunately, because only seven thousand men could be landed that day, there were insufficient available to mount more than probing attacks towards Nijmegen bridge.

A dozen miles beyond the southern end of 82nd Division's operations, 101st dropped successfully and acquired about as much of their fifteen-mile area of responsibility as could have been expected. They secured the bridge over the Dommel near St Oedenrode and the two bridges (canal and river) near Veghel but although they secured both ends of the bridge at Zon before nightfall, the Germans managed to blow the bridge itself.

The XXX Corps attack on which, in the long run, everything depended went very poorly. The folly of trying to advance along a single road was underlined early on when anti-tank guns and *panzerfausts* (infantry anti-tank rockets) blocked the road with burning tanks. It took another strafe from the Typhoons and an infantry attack to clear the way. By nightfall the

Maj-Gen. R.E. Urquhart, commanding 1st Airborne Division, outside his headquarters at Oosterbeek in September 1944.

IWM

The Airborne Memorial on Ginkel Heath (Dropping Zone Y).

DP

advance had covered less than eight miles. Next day they were able to join with 101st Division and go through Eindhoven but when they reached the blown bridge at Zon there was another serious hold-up while the sappers and bridging equipment was brought to the head of the column and it was not until 6.15 am, on 19 September, that the advance could start again. More than forty hours had passed since the first parachutists had been dropped and XXX Corps still had forty-five miles to cover before they reached Arnhem.

* PIAT stands for Projector Infantry Anti-Tank, a spring-operated weapon which could throw a bomb weighing $2\frac{1}{2}$ pounds. It was able to pierce tank armour at up to about 100 yards and was useful against houses at three times that range. Weighing $34\frac{1}{2}$ pounds, it was a cumbersome weapon which could be dangerous to the firer.

Fog over southern England delayed the airborne reinforcements on 18 September. 82nd Division had to fight hard to keep open the landing ground so that its glider-borne component could land during the afternoon and this meant that there were still insufficient troops to mount a serious attack on Nijmegen. Here the defenders were being reinforced by armour from the Arnhem area which, since 2/Para still held the north end of Arnhem bridge, had laboriously to be ferried across the Lower Rhine. 2/Para, however, was inevitably a wasting asset and the rest of 1st Airborne Division's prime task was to break through to them. This was made no easier by the delay in landing 4 Parachute Brigade which did not start arriving until 1 pm. Meanwhile their dropping zone had still to be held by most of the Airlanding Brigade and an attack eastward by 3/Para was halted short of St Elizabeth's Hospital.

Reinforced by 1/Para, they found it was possible to get past the hospital but could go no further and by that time neither battalion was strong enough for decisive offensive action. However in the early hours of 19 September they managed another advance which reached within half a mile of the bridge before they were fought to a standstill. 4 Parachute Brigade sent two battalions round the north of the town but they were stopped east of Johanna Hoeve where the enemy were firmly established.

Sherman tank at Oosterbeek Museum. The Sherman was the workhorse of the allied armoured division but was no serious match for the larger German tanks.

DP

Early on 19 September 2/South Staffords continued the advance beyond the hospital with 11/Para in support. They made some progress but were heavily counter-attacked by tanks and, running out of PIAT ammunition, were finally broken, the tanks continuing to catch 11/Para unprepared and on the move. By afternoon the South Staffs with the three parachute battalions (1, 3 and 11) were fighting a defensive action in the eastern houses of Oosterbeek, their total strength 420 men.

By this time Urquhart had escaped from his accidental confinement and was trying to get a grip on the battle, ordering his two remaining parachute battalions to come south of the railway and attack along the river bank. It was a difficult withdrawal and in the middle of it the glider-borne element of the Polish brigade landed between the opposing sides, losing all their heavy equipment and many of their personnel. At the same time a large supply drop, which was flown in with incredible gallantry and heavy loss, fell straight into the hands of the Germans. The lack of wireless communication at this stage of the operation meant that 1st Airborne had been unable to warn the RAF that the pre-arranged dropping zone was now out of their control.

DP

German anti-tank gun, 75mm PaK40, capable of piercing 66mm of armoured plate at 2,000 yards. The wheels have been removed.

Near the bridge 2/Para clung grimly on to a shrinking number of houses but the Germans, unable to evict them by infantry and tank attacks, started methodically to demolish the houses which they held by artillery fire supported by air attack although one Focke-Wulf hit the twin spires of St Walpurgis Church and crashed. The drop of the Polish parachutists, planned to take place at the south of Arnhem bridge, had to be cancelled owing to bad weather.

To the south of Arnhem, the landing of 101st Division's glider brigade proved highly expensive, seventeen aircraft being lost

German paratroops on the fringe of the British perimeter: 'the situation in Arnhem is grave'.

and forty-two gliders landing in German-held territory. Otherwise things went rather better in the south. Guards Armoured joined up with 82nd Division and were able, by way of Heuman, to reach the southern out-skirts of Nijmegen before dark. They were, however, extremely vulnerable to attacks on the flanks of the long thin corridor they had driven, and behind them British tanks and US paratroopers had a hard fight to pre-serve the rebuilt bridge at Zon from a German drive. This was the day when the first messages (passed on the artillery net) began to trickle through from the Arnhem area. It was learned that the bridge was still intact and that 2/Para was still in its vicinity though it was believed to have lost control of it (in fact they blocked the bridge until late on 20 September). It was also learned that the rest of the division was belea-guered in Oosterbeek. Early the following morning there came a request that the dropping zone (DZ) of the Polish parachutists should be changed to the area of Driel, on the south bank of the river opposite Oosterbeek.

Wednesday, 20 September, saw a spectacular triumph at Nijmegen. It took the whole of the morning to winkle the Germans out of their posi-tions on the approach to the bridge but that afternoon witnessed two of the greatest feats of arms of the whole battle. 3/504 Parachute Infantry crossed the fast-flowing Waal a mile downstream from the bridges. Using British canvas assault boats - a difficult craft to handle which they had never previously used - and paddling with their rifle butts, they went across in two waves under a hail of fire from small arms and 20mm can-non. Despite supporting fire from tank guns and Typhoons, they suffered fifty per cent casualties but they kept going, established a bridgehead and pushed eastward to the railway bridge. Meanwhile four tanks of 2/Grenadier Guards, led by Sergeant Robinson and commanded by Captain Lord Carrington (later Foreign Secretary and Secretary General of NATO) crashed across the road bridge, knocking out an 88mm gun which was trained on the roadway. Behind them came Lieutenant Tony Jones, Royal Engineers, in an unarmoured vehicle, who made safe the German demolition charges. By nightfall the leading tanks had reached the point just beyond the bridge where the road and railway met.

The face of battle: Utrecht Street after the British had failed to force their way along it.

On the morning of 21 September, it was found to be impossible to force an armoured division up the road from Nijmegen to Arnhem. The road was raised on an embankment and tanks on it were an easy prey to 88mm guns. An infantry division was called forward - 43rd (Wessex) - but they had to fight their way forward past the thirty-mile column of vehicles in the rear of the Guards.

Meanwhile at Arnhem the situation was deteriorating rapidly. 2/Para, its colonel disabled and half its strength lost, was forced to surrender as the few buildings it still occupied burned around them. The rest of the division tirelessly fought to preserve a diminishing perimeter in Oosterbeek. The Polish Parachute Brigade were prevented by bad weather from taking off in the morning and then had a disastrous flight. Only 53 out of 110 transport aircraft arrived over the dropping zone and only 750 men could be assembled on the ground at Driel - and even then there was little they could do to help the defence of Oosterbeek since they had no assault boats. On the following day they were joined by some armoured cars from the Household Cavalry who managed to find a way across country to them. That day a German counter-attack blocked the XXX Corps axis between Veghel and Uden and it was not until 24 September that joint British and American forces were able to re-open this vital supply link.

The fight went on until 25 September. 1st Airborne became even more constricted in its defensive perimeter, German counter-attacks continued to threaten and occasionally break the vulnerable supply line which stretched back into Belgium. 43rd Division managed with difficulty to join the Poles around Driel and to support themselves on an improvised track, under observed German artillery fire, across the flat, ditch-intersected land. A few hundred Poles and some of 4/Dorset crossed the river in assault boats to reinforce the airborne survivors. Nothing could be done to force the main advance beyond the village of Elst. That day the decision to withdraw was made and during the night, D+8, the remnant of 1st Airborne was successfully withdrawn, the airborne gunners forming the rearguard and destroying their 75mm howitzers before withdrawing to the boats. The Germans were left with 6,450 prisoners (1,700 of them wounded) and 1,500 dead.

(TOP) Infantryman making a dash across the opening of Nieuwe Plein.

(BOTTOM) German assault gun being camouflaged at the corner of Nieuwe Plein.

B

B

Caught in the crossfire. A German ambulance - part of a convoy carrying wounded - which was destroyed.

Germans infiltrating Oosterbeek in an attempt to break into 1st Airborne Division's final perimeter.

'For you the war is over.' British prisoners being marched away from Oosterbeek. In almost all cases the Germans treated those they captured with humanity and respect.

B

B

IWM

1st Airborne Division was destroyed but that was not the total of the butcher's bill. The two US airborne divisions suffered 3,500 casualties and XXX Corps 3,700; and 658 allied aircrew were lost - to say nothing of 261 aircraft destroyed and 1,438 damaged. All that was gained was a long, vulnerable and useless salient and the loss to the Germans of 3,300 men, of whom a third were killed. The courage and endurance of everyone engaged - British, American, Polish, German and, in particular, the members of the Dutch Resistance - should not blind anyone to the fact that *MARKET-GARDEN* was a disastrous failure. What is worse is that it was a predictable failure - to undertake an advance over sixty-four miles of a single road, crossing six major and many minor water obstacles, would be a highly speculative enterprise at the best of times.

A Bridge Too Far. The road bridge at Arnhem (since replaced). The picture was taken on the day after 2/Para Battalion was rounded up and the roadway had just been cleared of wrecked vehicles.

To attempt it with little more than half the transport aircraft required and with those same aircraft instructed to land their loads in inconvenient places could only make the attempt foolhardy. It might have been justified if the enemy was on the point of collapse but a fortnight before the attack was launched it was clear that the Germans had steadied themselves, and a week before it was certain that, with two armoured divisions in the vicinity, opposition would be tough if not overwhelming and the chances of success infinitesimal.

Two days before D-Day Eisenhower, originally a supporter of *MARKET-GARDEN*, was so convinced that it had become impracticable that he sent his chief of staff, Lieutenant-General Bedell Smith, to dissuade Montgomery from undertaking it. As Bedell Smith said, '*I tried to stop him but I got nowhere*'. Montgomery was determined to demonstrate that he was the greatest general in the world. He had been stung by accusations that he had been over-cautious in the Normandy campaign and he was set on showing that he could take risks which would enable him to administer the *coup de grâce* to the German armies with his own troops and by his own skill. Fifteen thousand allied casualties was a high price to pay to prove that he was wrong.

IWM

TO WAR IN A PLYWOOD BOX

MOST people when considering an airborne operation think principally of parachutists drifting down to the ground and tend to forget that in World War II about a third of the attackers travelled by glider. In *MARKET-GARDEN* 20,190 men landed by parachute and 13,781 by glider. At Arnhem three battalions (7/King's Own Scottish Borderers; 1/Border Regiment; 2/South Staffordshires) landed from gliders, as did three eight-gun batteries of 1/Airlanding Light Regiment, RA with their 75mm pack howitzers, which fired 14-pound shells to a maximum range of 9,500 yards. Gliders also brought in a number of 6-pounder anti-tank guns and some jeeps.

The workhorse of the glider fleet was the Airspeed Horsa, an all-wood craft with a wing-span of 88 feet and an operational load of 3.1 tons. With two pilots a Horsa could transport twenty-five men or a jeep and trailer. About one in ten of the gliders used at Arnhem was a larger Hamilcar, capable of carrying forty men or (although none were taken on that occasion) a light tank or two bren-gun carriers.

The advantage of gliders, apart from their ability to transport heavy equipment, was that they could land a tactical sub-unit, a platoon, in the same place whereas twenty-five parachutists might be widely scattered on landing. Nevertheless parachutists much preferred their own method of transport, one of them commenting, 'To lumber clumsily earthwards in such a flimsy ply-wood box had always seemed not only frightening but also lacking in the compensating pleasures to be found in parachuting'. It is very true that gliders were especially vulnerable to anti-aircraft fire and could, with bad luck, be destroyed by such landing obstacles as trees.

The members of the Glider Pilot Regiment, none of them less than sergeants, had a dual function. Having landed and unloaded their craft they converted themselves into infantrymen and, at Arnhem, played a notable part in the defence of the landing grounds and of the final perimeter.

NIJMEGEN AND GROESBEEK

THE importance of Nijmegen bridge in the plan to send tanks straight through to Arnhem is obvious. In the event, the bridge proved less of a stumbling block than the main road on its causeway to the north of the river. Many believed the bridge should have been the first objective when 82nd US Airborne Division landed in the area on D-Day. The divisional commander, Major-General Gavin, certainly held this view but orders from Browning, his corps commander, gave priority to securing the high ground near Groesbeek, eight miles to the south east of the bridge. This was the nearest point to German soil and an obvious place for the Germans to launch counter-attacks on the flank of the advance. Ideally both objectives should have been captured on D-Day but with the limited air-lift a choice had to be made. Probably Browning was right in ensuring the advance had adequate flank protection, and wrong in insisting on taking his corps headquarters across on D-Day to establish them near Groesbeek. There he was unable to exert any useful control of the battle but the move had required thirty-eight gliders, sufficient to move a battalion which could have been invaluable at either Arnhem or Nijmegen.

Gavin allocated the covering of Nijmegen and the open flank to 508 Infantry Regiment (Colonel Roy E. Linquist) and these three battalions did all and more than could have been expected of them. They secured the Groesbeek heights without difficulty but on the following day, when the reserve glider-borne regiment was due to land to the west of them, the Germans attacked from the east. Fortunately the weather had delayed the reserves and, before they could be landed, a well-timed counter-attack cleared the landing ground. Meanwhile the regiment had sent fighting patrols into Nijmegen and sounded out the powerful opposition there. One of these patrols was cut off in the town. Besieged in an empty warehouse, the men defended themselves until the Guards Armoured Division arrived and relieved them.

DP   DP   *Lt-Col. John Frost.*   RU

THE BLOCKING OF ARNHEM BRIDGE

Immediately following the 21/Independent Parachute Company, whose task was to mark the landing zone and guide in the bulk of 1st Airborne Division, came the gliders of the Reconnaissance Squadron with heavily armed jeeps. It had been hoped they would sweep round Arnhem and take the bridge from the north before any resistance was organized. Unfortunately the squadron was scattered on landing, and the first force gathered for the raid on the bridge was ambushed on the way.

1 Parachute Brigade landed on Ginkel Heath at 2 pm and within an hour was setting out to march the seven miles to the bridge. It is just possible that they might have made the distance had Field Marshal Model not been in a position to watch them drop at short range. There is nothing like an active field marshal for getting things done in a hurry and as soon as he had convinced himself that the landing was not an attempt to abduct him, he quickly galvanized the local commanders into defensive action and, by telephoning to von Rundstedt, his immediate superior, ensured that reinforcements were rushed to the area. Thus before the parachute battalions could start their march an improvised line had been formed to oppose them. 1/Para, moving on the left, north of the railway, found the main road to Ede patrolled by armoured cars and picketed by infantry. This meant that they had to detach a company to guard their flank and, when the main body of the battalion continued their march, they were brought to a stand by infantry and machine guns around the hamlet of Johanna Hoeve and the woods beyond. On their right 3/Para reached the western outskirts of Oosterbeek but suffered from damaging fire into their left rear from a post of the Bilderberg rise which they failed to dislodge before dark. They did, however, manage to slip one company round the south of Oosterbeek and this succeeded in reaching the bridge during the night. It is possible that, had the brigade radio not been in such a parlous condition, more troops could have reached the objective by this route.

Only close to the river did the Germans fail to create some kind of defensive line; Lieutenant-Colonel John Frost's 2/Para, though failing to secure the railway bridge before it was blown, reached the road bridge with astonishingly little trouble - barring an enemy post on the rise known as Den Brink (where the Post Office Tower is now). This they managed to circumvent by fire and movement. It was growing dark as they reached the bridge. Fortunately the Germans were showing that disinclination to fight in the dark which was one of the Wehrmacht's few weaknesses in the Second World War. This enabled 2/Para to establish themselves in the buildings (now rebuilt in different places) from which vantage point they could control the northern end of the bridge. During the night they were joined by most of brigade headquarters (less Brigadier Lathbury wounded with 3/Para), the detached company from 3/Para, part of the Recce Squadron, some sappers and a platoon of RASC who brought with them a captured truck loaded with ammunition. They had no communication with any other part of the division and no prospect of seizing the whole length of the bridge.

Once the RAF had ruled out the prospect of landing troops at the southern end, it became impossible to take the whole bridge without crossing the railway bridge but this the enemy had been quick to demolish. All 2/Para could do was to cling on to their tenuous and basically untenable position at the northern end, hoping that Guards Armoured could come and relieve them from the south. They had no way of knowing how slowly the tanks were advancing.

2/Para held their position and denied the bridge to the Germans until the early hours of 21 September. Then, with John Frost wounded in both legs as well as in the stomach, the survivors, almost out of ammunition, surrendered; the alternative would have been to allow their wounded, more than two hundred of them, to be burned in the houses where they sheltered. Meanwhile the rest of the division exhausted its strength trying to fight a way through to them.

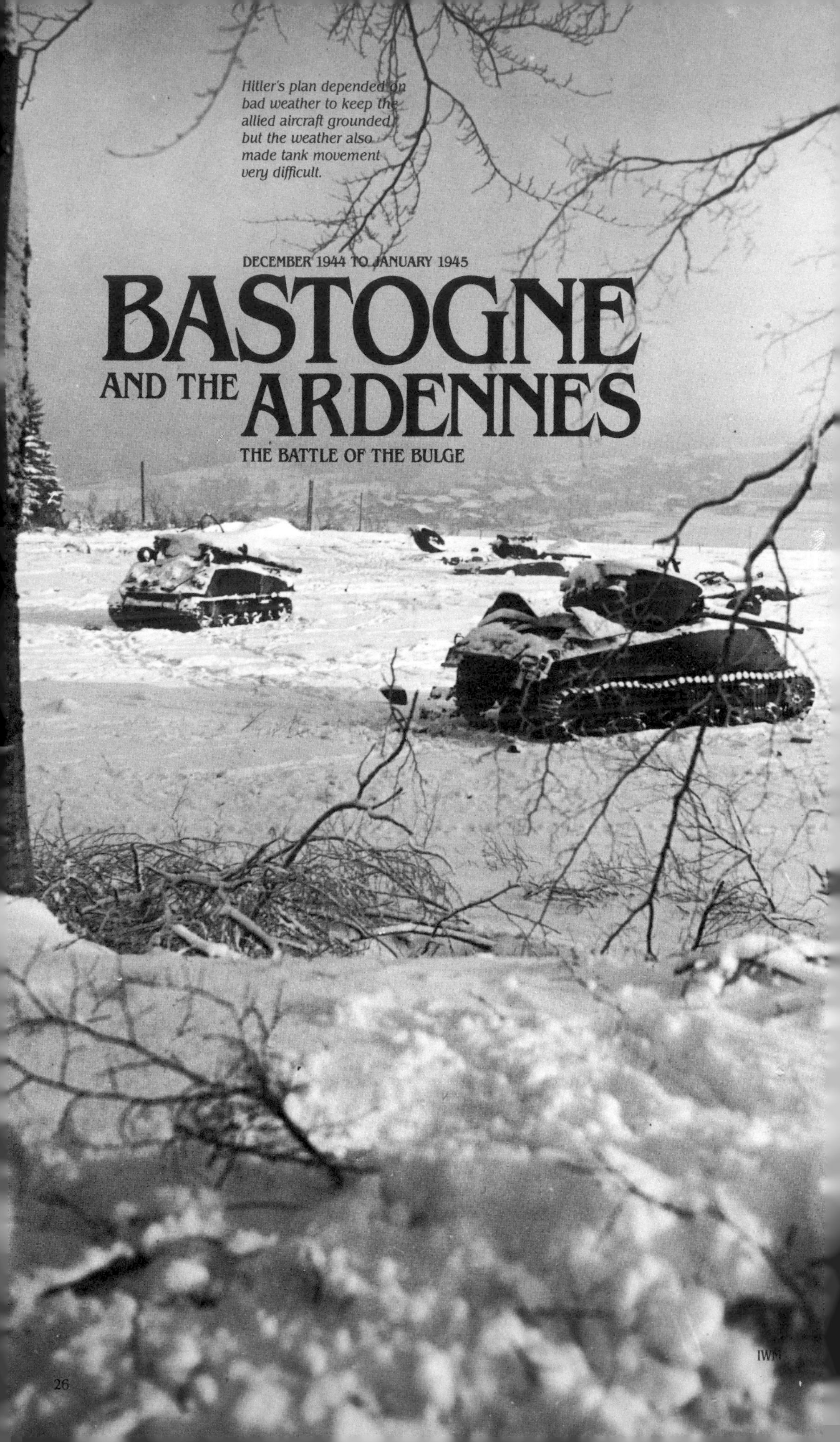

Hitler's plan depended on
bad weather to keep the
allied aircraft grounded,
but the weather also
made tank movement
very difficult.

DECEMBER 1944 TO JANUARY 1945

BASTOGNE
AND THE ARDENNES
THE BATTLE OF THE BULGE

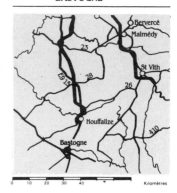

TWO DAYS BEFORE THE FINAL CLOSING of the Falaise Gap which marked the end of the German débâcle in Normandy, Hitler issued orders to 'prepare to take the offensive in November.' On 16 September, which was the day before the Arnhem operation was launched, he declared, 'I have just made a momentous decision. I shall go over to the counter-attack out of the Ardennes with the objective - Antwerp'. With a vast Russian army pressing in from the east and a triumphant Anglo-American force beginning to move fast against the western frontier of the Reich this was a desperate plan but Hitler saw that it represented his only chance to snatch victory from a war many thought already lost. His stated aim was to 'drive a wedge between the British and United States armies' and to pen the British and Canadian armies, which he knew to be irreplaceable, north of Antwerp where they could be forced to surrender. If that happened, he believed the United States would have neither the skill nor the will to continue the war alone. Then he could turn his whole strength against the Russians.

As a piece of political thinking such a plan was plausible but only total success could justify taking the risk. Huge resources of material and trained manpower would be required and even they could not succeed without a great share of luck and the co-operation of that least reliable of allies, the weather. The operation was planned for November in the hope of overcast skies since, in fine weather, the Luftwaffe could not hope to cope with the overwhelming allied air forces. His own generals were more than doubtful about the chances. Field Marshal von Rundstedt, reinstated as Commander-in-Chief, West, believed that 'all, absolutely all conditions for the possible success of such an offensive are lacking'. Field Marshal Model, Hitler's favourite soldier and now commanding Army Group B which would carry out the attack, declared that 'it has not a leg to stand on'. Not that either of these marshals were allowed to influence the planning which was done, under Hitler's personal direction, by Colonel-General Jodl. When the process was complete, the orders were endorsed 'No alterations permitted', written in the Führer's own hand though, thanks to his injuries in the July bomb plot, writing was difficult for him. One alteration was in fact permitted since the start had to be postponed until December so that the preparations could be completed.

The Hitler/Jodl scheme (which has unfairly become known as the Rundstedt Plan) called for an attack on a sixty-mile front between Monschau and Echternach. On the right Sixth Panzer Army (Sepp Dietrich) would make its main break through the Losheim Gap, cross the Meuse south of Liège and turn north for Antwerp. Beside them Fifth Panzer Army (von Manteuffel) would cross the Meuse south of Namur and wheel north to the west of Brussels, their left being covered by the infantry of Seventh Army who would establish a defensive flank from Echternacht to Givet on the Meuse. Other formations would be in reserve and large numbers of fighter aircraft were to be withdrawn from home defence to give air cover. The operation was given the code-name WACHT AM RHEIN* (Watch on the Rhine). This was to give credibility to the elaborate cover plan which aimed, successfully, to conceal the preparations for the attack under the guise of concentrating a mobile reserve to deal with allied thrusts over the border into Germany.

* The code-name was changed to HERBSTNEBEL (Autumn Mist) on 2 December.

The Ardennes, in Belgium, is a beautiful woodland area full of deep valleys and sheer escarpments, and dotted with medieval towns and villages.

Heavy air bombardment in 1944 destroyed much of St Vith and Malmédy, towns that were of prime importance in the Battle of the Bulge; the Bastogne Museum on Mardasson Hill in Bastogne records the events in a multi-vision show, including an ampitheatre with a moving display. The museum can be found next to the Mardasson Memorial dedicated to the American soldiers and is open: June-August from 8.30am-6.30pm; Feb-May (and Sept) 9am-6pm; Oct-Nov 10am-5pm.

Weapons and exhibits related to the battle can also be seen in the Au Pays d'Ardenne Original Museum in Rue de Neufchâteau, Bastogne.

An interesting drive would be to follow the road from Bastogne to Malmédy and then south again to St Vith. This should include a visit to the site of the massacre at the Baugnez crossroads, (south-east of Malmédy on the N62) where the rebuilt Café Bodarwé stands; there is a monument to those who died on the other side of the road.

Despite the German breakthrough there in 1940, the Ardennes was not considered as being good country for armoured warfare, particularly in mid-winter. The area is mountainous, some crests rising to more than 2,700 feet, and heavily wooded while the roads and railways leading through it follow deep, steep-sided valleys. The nearest thing to a clear way through is the Losheim Gap which cuts through by Malmédy to the Amblève river and Liège. Both sides regarded the eastern side of the Ardennes

All mention of *WACHT AM RHEIN* being forbidden in radio communication, the *ULTRA* watchers at Bletchley Park had little chance of discovering what was intended but, as early as September, *MAGIC* (the Japanese equivalent of *ULTRA)* intercepted a message from the Japanese ambassador in Berlin which foretold a large-scale attack in November. Late in that month a similar message reported that the offensive had been postponed rather than cancelled. *ULTRA* did manage to glean some indiscretions from *Luftwaffe* signals arranging air cover over the troop and supply concentrations in the Eifel Mountains, the easterly continuation of the Ardennes. They also discovered some references to a *Jägeraufmarsch* which was rightly interpreted as being an assembly of fighter planes for a planned operation. Other Intelligence sources identified Sixth Panzer Army as being stationed north of the Ruhr while Fifth Army, which had last been placed as opposite the Lorraine front, was found to have reappeared to the east of Aachen. The *Führer Begleit* Brigade, the armoured regiment forming part of Hitler's bodyguard, which had never been committed to battle, was identified at Kochem on the Moselle.

The indications were insufficient to be taken seriously by allied Intelligence which, like the senior commanders, had convinced itself that the German army was too weak at that time to attack on a large scale. Just as the Germans had intended, the concentrations were held to be blocking forces which were meant for use against allied thrusts.

Some other explanation ought perhaps to have been sought for the requests made to the *Luftwaffe* between 3 and 14 December for air photographs of the road centre at Ciney, south east of Namur, and of the Meuse crossings which lay between Maastricht and Givet. The allied command however, when not planning its own offensives, was busy contemplating Christmas festivities and only one senior Intelligence officer, known as an alarmist, raised the likelihood of a German attack - although even he did not allow his forebodings to interfere with his departure on leave to Paris.

Weary but determined: A trooper of the Panzer SS going into action.

IWM

as a quiet sector where tired troops could be rested and inexperienced divisions given their first taste of the front line. North of the Losheim Gap the Americans had stationed 99th Division (V Corps), which had no experience of action other than a month in that sector. South of that was Major-General Troy Middleton's VIII Corps which deployed three infantry divisions in the front line, from north to south, 106th, (just arrived in Europe) and 28th and 4th - both of which were recuperating from heavy losses in the desperate fighting in the Hürtgen forest not far to the north. Middleton's reserve was 9th Armoured Division, also new to the front. The Losheim Gap itself, the route through which Rommel's 7th Panzer Division had forced itself into Belgium in 1940, was guarded by less than five hundred men of a mechanized light cavalry regiment supported by a few anti-tank guns. The inadequacy of the screen in front of the Ardennes, with divisions holding fifteen or more miles, was well known to the Germans; the north of the area, the Eupen-Malmédy district, had been awarded to Belgium after the

US Army

The River Our on the Luxembourg-German frontier. This was the way forward for Fifth Panzer Army.

Treaty of Versailles and contained a high proportion of ethnic Germans, some of whom were prepared to act as informers for their Fatherland. The thinness of the screen had also worried Eisenhower. He had spoken of it to Omar Bradley, commanding Twelfth Army Group, who replied that VIII Corps could, if necessary, give ground to ride any possible blow. Bradley had drawn a map to show how far the corps could safely retreat but it is doubtful if he appreciated the effect of an armoured attack on a vast scale upon troops who were either new to battle or recovering from a traumatic experience at Hürtgen. The Supreme Commander allowed himself to be reassured but commented to Montgomery that the situation had all the makings of a 'nasty little Kasserine.'*

---

* The battle of Kasserine (Tunisia) in February 1943 may have been the prototype for the Ardennes offensive, albeit on a much smaller scale. In it Rommel tried to cut off the US forces in the south of Tunisia and to get between the British (in the north) and the sea. Before the attack was repulsed US forces suffered very heavy losses in men and material.

The Ardennes countryside is heavily wooded and sliced through by numerous steep valleys. The battle was fought in winter, during heavy snow. Throughout their advance the Germans made excellent use of the cover of the forests, and added to the element of surprise by moving across the 'grain' of the terrain.

Malmédy from Spa Road.

DP

Town centre of Malmédy.

DP

Sherman tank in Market Square of Bastogne

DP

US Memorial at Bastogne.

DP

Neufchâteau

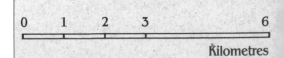

0	1	2	3	6

Kilometres

Houffalize

Noville

Bourcy

Longchamps

Foy

Longvilly

Hemroulle

Bizory

Neffe

BASTOGNE

Wardin

Senonchamps

Marvie

Sibret

Assenois

Road to Arlon

Vaux-les-Rosières

31

In the early morning of 16 December the weather over the battle front was everything that Hitler could have wished. Air support was impossible and, after a heavy artillery preparation, both Panzer Armies (with eight armoured divisions under command) went forward. Most of the American troops held their positions but they were so scattered that there was plenty of room between them for the Germans to go forward in strength. At Losheim a parachute division blasted its way through the cavalrymen allowing a *Kampfgruppe* (battle group) from Sixth Panzer Army to force its way through the valleys. By the morning of 17 December this group had reached the Stavelot bridge over the Amblève, though they failed to find two vast dumps of petrol near their advance.

Shermans of 3rd (US) Armoured moving south to cut off the German spearheads.

IWM

IWM

Men of 53rd (Welsh) Division who were brought down in order to reinforce the line on the Meuse river.

To the south Fifth Panzer Army, advancing on a front of thirty miles, threw seven divisions, four of them armoured, against three American regiments (brigades). Aided by some American command failures, the Germans inevitably broke through but not without difficulty, while behind the American lines there were scenes of chaos as rearward units were hurriedly ordered back to safety and were joined by a number of deserters. This chaos was deceptive - it even deceived a number of American commanders - since, with rare exceptions, VIII Corps was fighting well, holding defiles and blowing crucial bridges, while making the enemy pay for every mile of his advance.

The leading *Kampfgruppe* of Sixth Army reached Soumont but, pushing beyond, was driven back to it and found the Stavelot bridge retaken behind it. To the south of it, St Vith, though under heavy attack, still held out. At the northern end of the front a firm defensive line was being formed on Malmédy and Monschau with the forbidding Hohe Venn ridge behind it. Things went rather better in the south. The spearheads of the Fifth Panzer Army reached the River Ourthe near Hotten and at Orthenville but already a critical shortage of petrol was making itself felt.

Not only had the Germans failed to reach their objective for 17 December - the Meuse crossings - but the main attacking army, the Sixth, was stalled. The American resistance was tougher than had been anticipated and no large quantities of petrol, a vital factor in the planning, had been captured. The weather too was proving an equivocal ally. It continued to hamper the allied air forces, though 1,200 sorties were flown on 17 December, but the weather did not affect only flying. It made the country, always difficult, impassable once off the roads so that any minor obstruction - caused by accident or the Americans - became a major obstacle. There were too few roads for the volume of traffic and too many of the roads, major or minor, led through just two nodal points, St Vith and Bastogne. St Vith fell eventually on 21 December but by that time the main drive of the attack, the *Schwerpunkt*, had been switched from Sixth Army to Fifth Army in the south. From then on Bastogne was all important.

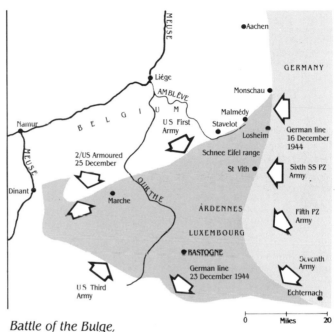

Battle of the Bulge,
16 December 1944 - 16 January 1945

Bradley's plan for VIII Corps to give ground if heavily attacked was unrealistic since they were over-extended on the roughly straight line they had originally held; thus they were bound to be even more so when falling back into a curved position which was twice as long as the original front line. Moreover they had suffered heavy losses and most of 106th Division had been surrounded on the Schnee Eifel, south of Losheim, where, after a most creditable defence, they were forced to surrender. To hold Bradley's line of 'Maximum Permissible Penetration' there must be troops and his own Twelfth Army Group, undertaking an offensive north of the Ardennes and about to launch another to the south, had no reserves. All that could immediately be spared was an armoured division each from north and south. Anything else had to come from Eisenhower's strategic reserve and his contribution could be only two US Airborne divisions which were stationed near Reims, followed by another two from England and an armoured division from Normandy. From British Twenty-first Army Group a corps was despatched to act as long stop on the Meuse crossings. 101st US Airborne Division was directed to move, by land, to Bastogne.

Many allied staff officers were still under the impression that the Germans were attempting nothing more than spoiling attacks to embarrass the American offensives so that Eisenhower's promptness in ordering up reserves may well have saved the campaign but the fact is that for several days no one had more than the vaguest idea of what was going on as divisions, regiments and battalions became fragmented and lost touch with each other. The confusion was heightened when thick fog periodically blanketed parts of the battlefield. Although the Americans did not realize it at the time, the Germans were in almost equal confusion and all their movements were hampered by appalling traffic jams caused by huge quantities of traffic, tracked and wheeled, trying to manoeuvre on a small and inadequate network of roads. On 17 December Model and Manteuffel, the men on whom the whole operation was supposed to depend, met quite by chance when both men had had to abandon their blocked staff cars and make their way forward on foot. Above all, the German commanders were tied hand and foot by an inflexible plan, foisted on them from above, which forced them to press on for the Meuse irrespective of any other considerations.

It was this determination to press on westward that saved Bastogne. This market town, a place of about four thousand inhabitants, stood at a height of some 1,500 feet above sea-level surrounded, unlike most Ardennes towns, with rolling pastureland and small woods. The headquarters of Middleton's VIII Corps were there when the battle opened but, being twenty miles behind the front line, had no garrison. By 19 December the headquarters were pulling out and Bastogne's defence rested on a number of small task forces, known as teams, formed from a Combat Command from 10th Armoured Division, sent north by Third Army, and the remains of a Combat Command from 9th Armoured. None of these teams was big enough to resist a full-bloodied German attack but they had been deployed as blocking forces on the roads leading into the town from the east. One such team, named after its commander, Major Desobry, was sent out in the dark and without a map to hold the village of Noville, four miles north east of Bastogne on the road to Houffalize. There were, all told, about four hundred men, including fifteen Sherman tanks, a company of 'armoured' infantry (travelling in half-tracks) and some sappers.

They had no idea who was in front of them and, wisely, Desobry sent out detachments to picket the roads leading into the village. At 4.30 am, a number of half-tracks was heard approaching on the side road from Bourcy. Such was the darkness and confusion that, when they were found to be German, the two sides were so close together that a quick skirmish was fought with lobbed hand grenades before the intruders withdrew. Two hours later tanks were heard coming down the main Houffalize road and this time the Germans were not surprised, knocking out two Shermans before they were identified as enemies. This convinced Desobry that only Germans would be approaching from the east so he withdrew his outposts and concentrated his force in the village. Scarcely had he done so when two Mark IV tanks, escorted by *Panzergrenadieren* (lorried infantry) approached him. They were greeted by heavy fire from

Bastogne today - reverted once again to a modest market town.

DP

IWM

St Vith from the air as light bombers of USAAF attack it on Christmas Day 1944.

Shermans and bazookas backed by machine guns, whereupon the infantry decamped and both tanks burst into flames. At about 10.30 am, when fortunately a platoon of tank destroyers (76mm guns mounted on a tank chassis) arrived from Bastogne, the fog suddenly lifted to reveal a battalion of German tanks deployed on the high ground beyond while about fifteen tanks, some of them Panthers, were approaching the village in a widely spaced line. They were supported by some markedly unenthusiastic *Panzergrenadieren*. In the ensuing armoured duel the Germans lost a further seventeen tanks while Team Desobry lost a single tank destroyer. The Germans set about destroying the buildings of Noville by long-range fire.

Similar fights, not all so favourable to the defence, were being waged by all the teams on the approaches to Bastogne from the east and south east but, during the night, the leading elements of 101st Airborne had arrived by truck to a point just to the west of the town. Their acting commander, Brigadier-General McAuliffe, had preceded them and it was arranged to send parachute battalions forward to the outlying teams. One battalion of 506 Parachute Infantry joined Team Desobry and made an unsuccessful attempt to clear the high ground beyond Noville. They did, however, help in beating off another tank attack on the place but that evening a shell struck the team's headquarters, killing the Parachutists' commanding officer and seriously wounding Desobry. By this time McAuliffe had decided that Noville was untenable and so he telephoned Middleton, now at Neufchâteau, seventeen miles to the south west, for permission to withdraw Team Desobry. The corps commander replied, *'If we are going to hold Bastogne, you cannot keep falling back.'* The team and the parachutists therefore did their best and McAuliffe reinforced them with five more tank destroyers, stationing another parachute battalion to support them in a position slightly short of the intermediate village of Foy.

At dawn on 20 December German tanks actually broke into Noville and were driven out (losing two of their number) only by desperate work with a bazooka and a damaged Sherman. It was now as clear as anything could be in the fog which had once more descended that there were Germans between Noville and Foy, and McAuliffe, disregarding Middleton's order, told Team Desobry to fight its way back to Bastogne. This, despite an ambush at the northern outskirts of Foy, they succeeded in doing, arriving in the town with all their wounded in the dark. The cost of holding Noville had been, including the parachutists, more than four hundred men, eleven tanks and five tank-

Noville, where Team Desobry fatally delayed the German advance to the Meuse.

ers. It was a heavy price to pay but it had been worth it. The outlying teams had bought time for the 101st Airborne to reach Bastogne and to form a defensive perimeter. Not only had they inflicted heavy losses on 2nd Panzer division, including about thirty tanks, but they had delayed them for more than forty-eight hours on the way to the Meuse.

The problem for 2nd Panzer was that they had no business with Bastogne. Their task was to press on westward and to skirt the town if they found it held, leaving the following infantry to capture it. It was their attempt to bypass the town that brought them to Noville. If they had driven for Bastogne directly, before the airborne division was deployed, instead of trying to fight round it they might well have taken the place. They sought permission to attempt this but Manteuffel would not risk Hitler's wrath by allowing them to stray from the rigid plan. He replied, '*Leave Bastogne and go for the Meuse*', arranging for an infantry division and a *Panzergrenadier* regiment from Panzer Lehr Division to attack the town. By the evening of 20 December these had surrounded the town but they did not have the strength to break into it.

DP

The bust of Brigadier-General Anthony (NUTS!) McAuliffe in Bastogne.

DP

Panther tank after capture by US parachute troops. With its 75mm gun this was probably the best tank of the war.

US Army

General George Patton commanding the Third US Army.

Shell cases beside the position of a US field battery near Elsenborn on the northern shoulder of the bulge.

US Army

US Army

US Army

Damaged American tanks awaiting recovery.

75mm pack howitzers of the parachutists. There was, however, no reserve of ammunition and supplies soon began to run very short.

McAuliffe's hopes were pinned on two things; an improvement in the weather, to allow air supply, and a relief column said to be on its way from Patton's Third Army to the south. This was spearheaded by 4th Armoured Division; by the 20 December one of its Combat Commands had reached Vaux-les-Rosières, a dozen miles from Bastogne on the Neufchâteau road, even sending a small force into the town itself. At this stage the commander of 4th Armoured, Major-General Gaffey, complained to Patton that this Combat Command had moved without his permission and, with the Army Commander's consent, withdrew it - and the men who had entered Bastogne - to a position on the Arlon road; from here a formal attack up to the besieged town was to be mounted. It was this blunder apparently motivated by pique on the part of both Gaffey and Patton, that enabled the Germans to besiege Bastogne. It was to cost Gaffey's men dear since, before he was able to launch his formal attack, the Germans had brought up a parachute division to block it. Fortunately on 23 December the skies cleared and that morning 241 aircraft, many of them the large C47 transport planes, dropped 144 tons of supplies (much of it ammunition and medical stores) by parachute into Bastogne. The town was thus momentarily secure, the more so since strike aircraft were able at last to make life intolerable for the Germans, whose every movement showed clearly against the snow and whose camouflage in the woods was burned away with napalm. There was a further supply drop, and a German air raid, on 24 December but on Christmas Day the weather closed in again and the last great effort to take Bastogne was made.

Once again the Germans could not commit enough troops to assure success but at 3 am a regiment of *Panzergrenadieren* with eighteen tanks (some of them Panthers) and two regiments of self-propelled guns struck at the north-western sector of Bastogne's defences, men and vehicles being camouflaged white to merge with the snow. They broke through the defences of 502 Parachute and 327 Glider Infantry and eleven tanks reached Hemrolle, little more than a mile from the centre of Bastogne, where they were met with such a storm of fire from tank destroyers, tanks, field guns and bazookas that every tank was put out of action. Another attack before dawn turned out to be a spiritless affair as if the troops advancing knew that once again the German command had used too little too late. The original perimeter was soon restored.

Although to the east Neffe and Bizory had been lost, the perimeter was able to anchor itself on the villages of Longchamps, Marvie, Senorchamps and Rolle. Being for the most part on favourable ground, it was reasonably strong but the airborne troops were very thin on the ground and could scarcely be expected to withstand a solid German attack. This never came as the Führer's orders were so rigid that sufficient troops could not be made available. Even when, on 21 December, von Rundstedt gave definite orders to take Bastogne he made it a condition that the operation must not be allowed to interfere with the advance to the Meuse. Their chief hope must be that, under the siege now imposed, the Americans would run out of artillery ammunition. Much of the defence's strength lay in their 130 guns - ranging from 150mm medium guns to the

Shortly before 5 pm on the afternoon of 26 December three American tanks reached the southern perimeter near the railway line that led to Neufchâteau. On the initiative of a junior officer they had bypassed the strong German position around Assenois on which the main body of 4th Armoured Division was unimaginatively butting its head with heavy casualties. Bastogne was relieved although for some time its lifeline was no more than a narrow corridor to the south, constantly assaulted from the flanks. It was, however, enough to bring in supplies and to evacuate the many wounded who had accumulated in the makeshift dressing stations in the town. The cost of holding the town had been about 3,000 casualties. Almost 1,500 more were incurred by 4th Armoured; most of these could have been avoided had Gaffey been prepared to exploit the ready-made breakthrough achieved almost a week earlier at Vaux-les-Rosières.

On 28 December Hitler authorized Model to stop the attempt to reach the Meuse but ordered him to consolidate the ground already captured, to prepare for a fresh onslaught and, at all costs, to take the Bastogne. He may still have believed a breakthrough was yet within his grasp but every one of his generals knew that it was hopeless. They believed that the best that could be done was to withdraw from the tip of the salient they had driven and to make a defensible line on the strongest ground they could find. They were ordered to contest the captured area inch by inch so that it was the end of January before they were back on approximately the line they had held in mid-December. By that time the Allies had lost 76,890 men,* of whom 8,700 were dead and 21,000 missing, mostly taken prisoner. There is no way of accurately assessing the German casualties. 50,000 were taken prisoner and at least 12,500 killed. The total loss may have been as high as 91,000, a blood-letting the Reich could not afford. Both sides lost about 800 tanks and the *Luftwaffe* sacrificed about 1,000 aircraft against the Allies' 647, of which a third were British. The United States could make up their material losses in a matter of weeks; for Germany these tanks and aircraft represented a high proportion of their dwindling reserves.

* Of these, 1,408 were British.

Though less precipitous than most of the Ardennes, the country around Bastogne (FAR LEFT) presents considerable difficulties to military operations, not least in its close-grown woods.
DP

MASSACRE

AT Arnhem the men of the 9th SS Panzer earned tributes from their prisoners for their humanity and consideration but some of their colleagues who fought with 1st SS Panzer in the Ardennes were cast in a different mould. Their attack on 16 December was spearheaded by the *Kampfgruppe* who were commanded by Joachim Peiper, a brave and ruthless soldier who held the Knight's Cross, a decoration not lightly awarded, and spoke excellent English. He and his men had fought for a long time in Russia where atrocities were common on both sides and he later admitted that he was pre-pared to condone the shooting of prisoners *'where local conditions made it necessary'*. This was in line with American practice as laid down by Dr Francis Lieber in General Order No 100 of 1863 during the Civil War - the modern origin of all Laws of War: *'a commander is per-mitted to direct his troops to give no quarter, in great straits, when his own salvation make it* impossible *to give quarter'*.

On 17 December *Kampfgruppe Peiper* was advancing from Thirimont on Malmédy when they caught in the open a battery of 285/Field Artillery Observation Battalion near the little village of Baugnez. The SS men were somewhat trigger-happy, shooting up several trucks which they could well have used themselves and mak-ing threats to their prisoners. When Peiper arrived on the scene he rapidly restored order among his men and started sending the prison-ers to the rear before passing on to direct his battle. At that stage there were about 130 pris-oners still to be sent back since, apart from the artillerymen, there were the crews of two ambu-lances, some engineers, infantrymen (including two medical officers) and military policemen. They were formed into a tight-packed body some eight deep and made to stand in a field two hundred yards south of the café at the Baugnez crossroads. A relatively junior SS offi-cer, Werner Pötschke, called up two passing tanks and ordered them to fire their machine guns into the massed Americans. This they did, other nearby Germans joining in with small arms. The firing went on for a quarter of an hour and there was then a pause of about two hours before a company of SS engineers arrived and proceeded to shoot any who appeared to be alive. Astonishingly, a number of the prisoners survived, though most were wounded, and after the engineers had withdrawn, several made a break for freedom. A few ran to the café where-upon Germans burned it down and shot the fugitives as they tried to escape. In all eighty-six prisoners died and forty-three survived.

At a trial in May 1946 seventy-three SS men were found guilty of these murders. Forty-three (including Peiper) were sentenced to death, twenty-two (including Sepp Dietrich, comman-der of Sixth Panzer Army) to life imprisonment, and the rest to lesser terms in prison. These sentences may have been excessive and it is certain that dubious means were employed

Peiper commanded the Kampfgruppe named after him.

during the interro-gations that preceded them. In fact, before any of the death sen-tences had actually been carried out, a long-lasting and bitter *furore* broke out - first in the United States, later in West Germany. And in Washington a senator who was at that time virtually unknown, Joseph R. McCarthy, used this protest against poss-ible injustice as a first step in making himself a less than savoury name in American politics. Eventually the death sentences were reduced to life imprisonment; Pötschke had died before the end of the war, and many of the defendants were paroled. Peiper, who was almost certainly not guilty as charged and had treated prisoners well at other places in the Ardennes, was even-tually released in December 1957. He lived anonymously in Alsace for almost twenty years until his whereabouts were revealed by the Communist newspaper *L'Humanité*. Not long afterwards his house was destroyed by fire-bombs and he died in the blaze.

IWM

Civilian hostages shot at Bandes as a reprisal for Belgian guerilla activities.

American bodies found in
the snow near Baugnez
after the massacre.

US Army

DP

DP

US Army

General Patton talking to
Col. Chappius (centre)
and Gen. McAuliffe (left).

WHITE FLAG

AT midday on 22 December a party of four Germans carrying a white flag approached the American perimeter where the Arlon road runs into Bastogne. One of the two officers in the party (a lieutenant from the Panzer Lehr Division who spoke passable English) asked to see the American commander, so they were taken blindfold to the nearest company commander. Here they handed over a typed note from General Freiherr von Lüttwitz, commanding XL Panzer Corps. This demanded the surrender of the garrison on honourable terms, failing which the town and its inhabitants - military and civilian - would be annihilated by the German artillery. The note was taken back to Brigadier-General McAuliffe whose immediate reaction was to remark, 'Aw, Nuts!' He set about writing a formal refusal but found the correct words hard to find and it was suggested by one of his staff that his first comment might serve his purpose. His reply therefore read:

To the German Commander,
NUTS!
From the American Commander

This message was taken to the Germans, whose English-speaking spokesman found the colloquialism beyond his linguistic powers and had to ask whether the reply was 'affirmative or negative?' To which he received the reply 'It is certainly not affirmative. In plain English it means the same as "Go to hell."' The Germans saluted and, once more blindfolded, were driven back to the American outposts.

US Army

Prisoner of war taken on 26 December 1944, showing the SS insignia on his lapel.

US Army

An infiltrator in US uniform arrested by military police near Malmédy.

IWM

Three of the infiltrators being executed by firing squad after their court-martial.

IWM

THE FURTHEST PENETRATION

IN an attempt to create confusion behind the lines in December 1944 Hitler arranged for parachutists to be landed behind the American lines but the few that were actually dropped were quickly rounded up. He also put a weak brigade under Oberststurmbannführer (Lt-Col) Otto Skorzeny - the man who had liberated Mussolini - with orders that they should be given American uniforms and equipment and launched in front of the advancing panzers so as to create what havoc they could and, if possible, to seize the Meuse bridges. Despite Skorzeny's undoubted skill and daring the scheme went wrong well before the offensive started. An indiscreet order calling for English-speaking volunteers fell into American hands and alerted them to the danger - while raising few suitable men. The uniforms with which they were issued turned out to be British and had hurriedly to be replaced by American tunics - and even these had black patches in the back, being intended for prisoners-of-war. About thirty jeeps were provided but only one mobile Sherman so that the tank strength had to be made up with Panthers painted - inevitably unconvincingly - to look like Shermans.

As soon as it became clear that the breakthrough had not been achieved most of Skorzeny's men were used in ordinary roles but on 17 December he despatched seven jeeps, each containing four men, in various directions. Little was achieved, beyond cutting telephone cables and reversing signposts, by six of these jeeps; one was stopped by military police within half an hour of setting out, the occupants being shot as spies that evening. The seventh jeep got further and drove fast across the bridge at Dinant which was being guarded by men of 3/Royal Tank Regiment - one of the units Montgomery had sent to defend the Meuse crossings. It was no surprise to the British to see Americans driving jeeps at excessive speeds but the fact that this jeep refused to stop meant that its occupants could not be warned that a necklace of anti-tank mines had been drawn across the western end of the bridge. All four men were killed instantly and 3/RTR were greatly relieved to find that, under their American greatcoats, all of them wore German uniforms.

Those four men were the only German soldiers to obey Hitler's order to cross the Meuse but a more formidable body penetrated nearly as far when a *Kampfgruppe* from 2nd Panzer Division managed to reach Celles, five miles east of Dinant, on 24 December. Their commander, realizing they were very short of fuel, sent his reconnaissance unit forward to probe the river defences. 3/RTR was thin on the ground, being also responsible for the bridges at Namur, but they had sent forward single tanks to the high ground west of the river to warn them of the enemy's approach.

The sergeant commanding the tank on the Celles road heard tracked vehicles approaching just as dawn broke on Christmas Eve and, as the light increased, saw a long column approaching. His first shot missed the leading tank but hit the third vehicle, a truck loaded with ammunition. This exploded, setting fire to the next one behind, which contained the last of the unit's precious petrol. There was a pause before a Panther started to work its way past the two flaming vehicles whereupon the British sergeant prudently withdrew behind the ridge. The German commander, however, anticipated that the crossing was strongly held and retired his *Kampfgruppe* to the village of Foy-Notre-Dame where they were joined by a detachment from Panzer Lehr Division and the whole force settled down to await the arrival of supplies of fuel. These never arrived - they were destroyed in an air strike - but on Christmas Day 2nd US Armoured Division swooped down on them from the north. Nearly a thousand German bodies were found with eighty-two tanks and eighty-three guns. 1,200 prisoners were taken and some 600 Germans escaped on foot.

MAY AND JUNE 1940

AND CALAIS DUNKIRK

It could be argued that Calais and Dunkirk
have no place in this guide as traces of the
fighting there are hard to find on the ground
but since some two million motorists leaving
Britain for the Continent pass through the two
ports it would seem pedantic to omit them.

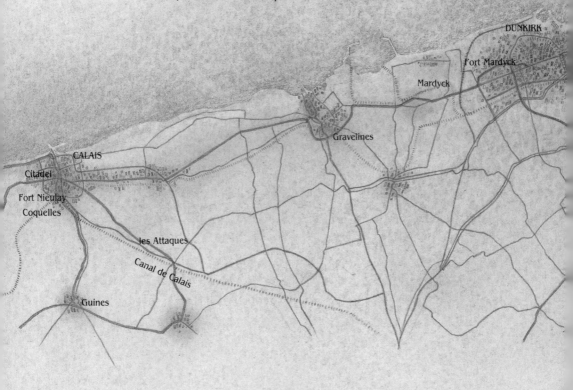

DUNKIRK

Fort Mardyck

Mardyck

Gravelines

CALAIS

Citadel

Fort Nieulay

Coquelles

les Attaques

Canal de Calais

Guines

0 1 2 3   6
Kilometres

Between the Calais ferry-port and the town are the remains of German fortifications. Much of Calais was destroyed in World War II including its medieval square and most of the area near the docks - except for the old church of Notre Dame and Vauban's dominating 16th-century citadel (now a sports stadium). In the centre is the Place du Soldat Inconnu and the famous statues by Rodin of the Burghers of Calais. Fort Nieulay, a Vauban fortification defended by a company of the Queen Victoria Rifles, lies on the road to Boulogne.

Dunkirk was virtually wiped out in 1940, suffering 80 per cent destruction. The long sandy beaches where the embarkation rescue took place lie opposite the resorts of Malo-les-Bains, Bray Dunes and la Panne to the east of the harbour area. A memorial stone commemorates the 345,000 allied soldiers evacuated here. There is an interesting museum to visit and the port, which is a little way to the west of Dunkirk town, can be toured by taking a boat from the Quai des Hollandais. Follow the coast road along to Leffrinckoucke where there is a French cemetery and bunkers enclosed by barbed wire. Unexploded mines are still strewn about the sand dunes. Continue along this road to Zuydcoote where the sanatorium (now a military hospital) is very close to the beach. There are more bunkers in the sand dunes here.

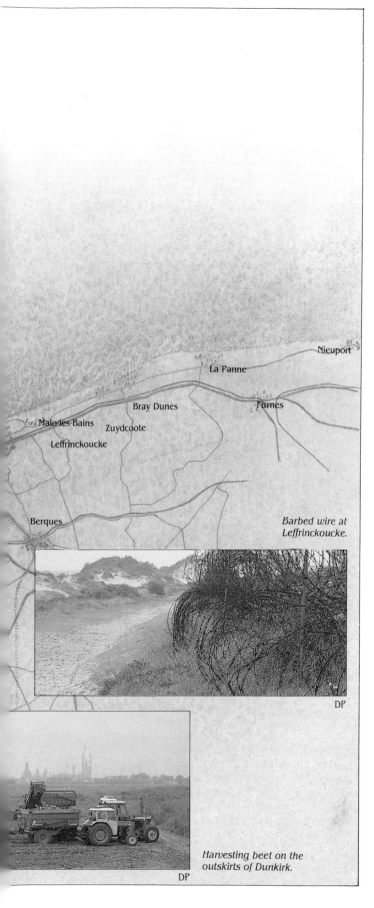

Barbed wire at Leffrinckoucke.

DP

Harvesting beet on the outskirts of Dunkirk.

DP

IT HAS OFTEN BEEN SAID that in 1939 France and Britain went to war against Germany, prepared for the fighting of 1914-18. The fact is that at the outset of the Second World War the only hope of the western allies was to be able to withstand siege warfare of the type experienced in the earlier war; this would apply for two or three years until they had built up enough offensive potential to engage in mobile warfare. Despite the fact that in 1940 they had more tanks, and in some case better tanks, than the Germans, they had no chance of using them so long as Belgium remained obstinately neutral. Neither side could hope to break through on the common Franco-German border and, since neither Britain nor France could, after the events of 1914, contemplate violating Belgian soil uninvited, any decisive operations had to be initiated by Germany. Thus the allies were bound to start the war tied to a strict defensive policy, a scheme which matched the thinking, military and civilian, of France, the overwhelmingly predominant partner on land.

Overshadowing all French military thought between 1919 and 1940 was the memory of 1,315,000 dead from Metropolitan France alone, the great majority of these losses due to a policy of taking the offensive in and out of season between 1914 and 1918. The natural reaction demanded a policy of defence *à l'outrance* and in the 1920s a Minister for War, André Maginot, remembering his experiences at Verdun (see page 195), initiated the line of fortifications which were to bear his name. The Maginot Line was probably impregnable but it covered only the

common frontier, the approach the Germans were least likely to employ, and it was inordinately expensive, costing 87,000,000 francs. On the north-eastern frontier, France, with naïvety and misplaced economy, relied on the sanctity of Belgian neutrality. The theory was that Germany would batter herself to exhaustion on the Maginot Line while France built up her offensive strength in order to deliver the *coup de grâce* after three or four years of war. These ideas had led to an initial neglect of armoured forces. France had built the excellent Somua tank and the 'Char B', admitted by Guderian

IWM

The French 'Char B', which Guderian considered to be the best tank of the 1940 campaign. It mounted a 75mm and a 47mm gun and had a speed of 25 mph but a range of only 60 miles.

to be the best tank of 1940, but she did not create her first two armoured divisions until January 1940, two years after Britain had organized her first. France wanted, from herself and her ally, an army, strong in artillery and infantry, able to hold a previously prepared position.

Britain was in no position to dispute such a policy since her contribution to the land battle was so small numerically that her opinions counted for nothing in the French High Command. It was late in 1938 before Britain contemplated her army undertaking any operations against a European enemy - beyond skirmishing with Italians in the Egyptian-Libyan desert. They were so short of money that they went to war with the artillery of 1918, some of it modified but some still with the iron-shod wooden wheels of earlier wars. The country had seen a ferment of military thought between the wars. The most eminent thinkers, led by Liddell Hart and J.F.C. Fuller, had postulated a war of movement dominated by fast, lightly armoured tanks acting like battle cruisers (ships which had proved markedly vulnerable). The result was that when the British armoured division was finally committed to battle - too late to affect the main issue - it did not contain a single battle-worthy tank.* While France started the war in 1939 with ninety-four divisions, Britain contributed four - to be increased to ten by the following May.

* *The only adequate British tank in 1940 was the Matilda (Infantry Tank Mark II) of which there were sixteen. This was precisely the type of tank of which the Eminent Military Thinkers disapproved since its prime task was to support the infantry rather than career about in the enemy's rear areas.*

The result of this derisory British contribution was that all strategic decisions had to be left to the French, in effect to General Gamelin, their commander-in-chief. A timorous commander, he might have been expected to embrace the French policy of defence at all costs and, had he insisted on standing firm on the French frontiers (including the Belgian frontier) it is possible that he might have staved off the German attack. He was, however, subject to great political pressure since the French government was anxious to preserve intact the great industrial complex around Lille, near the Belgian border, and both the allied governments, with their memories of 1914, believed that their troops must go to the help of Belgium should she be invaded. Gamelin therefore proposed a limited advance into that country, going as far as Ghent, the line of the Escaut (Scheldt) river, with ten French divisions and the BEF. The officer designated to command this advance, General Georges, protested that this was an unwise move:

We should not allow ourselves to commit the bulk of our reserves to this part of the theatre.... It might well be that if a powerful attack came in our centre, between the Meuse and the Moselle, we should be left without the forces necessary for a counter-attack.

Gamelin not only overruled him but decided first to make an even deeper incursion, to the line of Namur and Antwerp, and then, in a final burst of uncharacteristic optimism, to create a new army on his left and send it to link up with the Dutch at Breda. The creation of this additional army drew deeply on the exiguous central reserves of the French army - and these were further depleted since, in a return to his habitual timidity, the generalissimo insisted on heavily weighting his right flank to guard against a highly improbable German attack through Switzerland. The French army, trained and equipped to fight a defensive war, was, together with the BEF, to be committed to an encounter battle.

When, on 10 May 1940, the Germans invaded Belgium, Holland and Luxembourg the whole of the allied left wing, nineteen French and nine British divisions, swept forward into Belgium and by 15 May the BEF was established on the Dyle river between Louvain and Wavre, having met no opposition. On the previous day General Georges' fears had been fully justified since seven panzer divisions had struck through the Ardennes and began crossing the Meuse at and below Sedan. Since Gamelin had deployed so many of his troops on his flanks, his centre was lightly held, the more so since he had decided, in the teeth of French information, that the Ardennes were impassable to armoured columns. The opposition to this great panzer thrust comprised ten divisions, nine of them of inferior troops, strung out on a front of a hundred miles - and the Germans went straight through them, heading for the sea. This they reached, near Abbeville, on the night of 20/21 May after brushing aside a single British Territorial division, under-armed and barely trained, which had been thrown piecemeal in its path. This thrust not only isolated the Anglo-French armies in Belgium but overran or made untenable all the airfields on which they counted for support.

On the day the Germans reached Abbeville, Gamelin was displaced in favour of the veteran General Weygand who had been flown home hurriedly from Syria. His first, if belated orders were for the northern armies to strike south so as to cut the corridor made by the panzers and to join hands with a new French army attacking northwards across the Somme. For this plan two things were essential - a French army on the Somme and supplies for the northern armies. There were no French troops on the Somme, though while they were being gathered as fast as possible from southern France, Weygand mendaciously claimed that they had recaptured Amiens, Péronne and Albert.

The Maginot Line

The Maginot Line was built to cover the Franco-German border but went no further north. It proved wholly useless and its enormous cost would have been better spent on modernizing the French army.

Dunkirk Operation, 25-28 May 1940
The Shrinking Beachhead

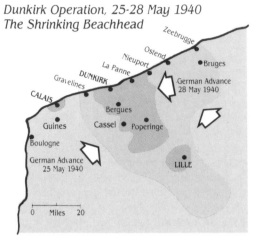

Moreover General Georges had succeeded in getting the three French armoured divisions now formed either destroyed or dispersed. In the event the only attempt to attack northward over the Somme was made by elements of the British armoured division which had just landed in western France.

The task of supplying the trapped northern armies was inevitably largely a British responsibility and was hampered by an almost total ignorance of what was happening on the far side of the Straits of Dover. The operation therefore proceeded on two understandable but unfortunate misapprehensions - that only light mobile German forces were in the Pas de Calais and that the French were in the area in considerable strength. It was decided therefore that what was required was a blocking force at Boulogne and mobile units at Calais which could escort supply convoys from the port to the armies in Belgium. To the first were sent two raw battalions of Guards, to the latter, the last trained infantry left in England - 2/King's Royal Rifle Corps (60th Rifles) and 1/Rifle Brigade, both motorized battalions - supported by 3/Royal Tank Regiment and 1/Queen Victoria Rifles - a Territorial motorcycle battalion who were deprived of their mobility when, by a piece of incompetence, the embarkation staff refused to load their motorcycles. The whole was denominated 30 Brigade and was commanded by Brigadier Claude Nicholson. The existing

garrison of Calais (who had not been warned of 30 Brigade's arrival) consisted of some search-light and anti-aircraft gunners and a single platoon of Highlanders. What no one in London or, at that time, in Calais realized was that when Nicholson's force started to land on 22 May there were three panzer divisions in the neighbourhood of the port. More immediately troublesome was the Adjutant-General of the BEF, Lieutenant-General Brownrigg, who had been given the task of embarking 'useless mouths' from the rear areas and gave orders for the tank regiment to move off southward to relieve the Guards at Boulogne. Before the tanks could be unloaded from the ships, conflicting orders arrived from Lord Gort telling the force to move south east to secure the canal crossings near St Omer. When Nicholson arrived on 23 May he found 3/RTC engaged in an unsuccessful battle with superior forces on the approaches to Guines (scene of the Field of the Cloth of Gold in 1520). With Boulogne having been evacuated on the previous night, it was clear to the Brigadier that the most his brigade could attempt to do was to hold Calais, already coming under attack. Despite reiterated orders from Brownrigg, he deployed his two motor battalions for this purpose under cover of the anti-aircraft and searchlight troops and QVR who were defending the outlying villages and hamlets. His chosen position was the line of ramparts and bastions built in the nineteenth century (and now largely vanished) which followed roughly the line of the railway to Gravelines on the south of the town. (Some of the bastions of this line can still be seen at both seaward ends.) With the Canal de Calais as a dividing line the Rifle Brigade manned the eastern side and the Sixtieth the western, while the QVR and others acted as reinforcements and reserves as they retired or were driven in. Hardly were the troops deployed when mandatory orders arrived from London to strike out due west and escort a convoy carrying 350,000 rations to the BEF through Gravelines. This was attempted during the night 23/24 May and, as might have been expected, failed - although four tanks miraculously reached Gravelines.

1944 bunkers near the
Hoverport.

DP

DP

The tidal harbour, Calais.

DP

DP

The Mardyck Canal in
Dunkirk town.

The beach at Calais.

DP

French sailors on coast defence duties during the bombardment.

Winston Churchill on a visit to France early in 1940 with (left to right) Generals Ironside, Gamelin, Gort and Georges.

ECPA

RHL

Meanwhile London was in a frenzy of indecision. On 23 May they sent the commander of the Canadian Division to Calais to advise on whether Calais could be held and embarked a Canadian brigade to reinforce the place. Without waiting for his report they changed their minds and signalled Nicholson that evacuation had been decided 'in principle'. This order induced the Brigadier to fall back from the ramparts to an inner line north of the Hotel de Ville, marked by a line of canals and harbour basins, a move which was achieved quietly and successfully on the night of 24/25 May and which had scarcely been completed when a further message arrived from London saying that there would be no evacuation, although Calais was 'a harbour of no importance ... for the sake of Allied solidarity'. This volte-face was the result of vehement, and quite unjustified French protests at the evacuation of Boulogne.

The Greenjackets made the Germans pay dearly for Calais as they fought to the end to try to prove to the French that Britain did not intend to desert her. Three battalions and some detachments fought off the whole weight of 10th Panzer Division and (as German records prove) inflicted heavy casualties in men, tanks and vehicles. Of course it was a hopeless struggle. Under constant artillery fire interspersed with dive bombing, the defenders were forced back slowly from house to house, the canal line useless to them since they were unable to blow up the road bridges for want of detonators. One of the reasons why the inner perimeter they defended cannot be seen today is that many of the buildings they defended

were burned over their heads. In the still surviving citadel Nicholson received a summons to surrender. The Germans noted his reply to this in English in their War Diary, '*The answer is no, as it is the British Army's duty to fight as well as it is the German.*' There was no surrender at Calais. The survivors were eventually broken up into small groups and either killed or captured. By the night of 26/27 May the town was quiet when HM Yacht *Gulzar* crept into the harbour mouth and, under machine-gun fire, lifted forty-seven survivors off the end of the pier.

While the firing was dying away at Calais the Flag Officer Dover, Vice-Admiral Sir Bertram Ramsay, gave the order '*Operation DYNAMO* is to commence'.

* The naval operation to evacuate the BEF off the coast from Dunkirk eastward was code-named DYNAMO. This was because Admiral Ramsay's operation room in Dover Castle was one in which electric generators had been installed in the 1914-18 war.

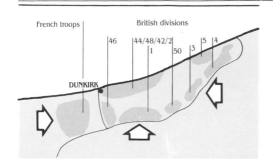

French troops | British divisions

46 | 44/48/42/2 | 5 | 4
1 | 50 | 3

DUNKIRK

Dunkirk Operation
29-31 May 1940

General Weygand visiting French naval headquarters at Dunkirk on 21 May 1940, the day after his appointment as Commander-in-Chief.

ECPA

ECPA

Refugees from Dunkirk starting on their long journey.

Ten days earlier, on hearing of the German breakthrough on the Meuse, the Northern Group of Armies had started to withdraw from their advanced position in Belgium and by 26 May their position resembled a peninsula stretching sixty-five miles south from the coast to the River Scarpe around Marchiennes. The southern tip of this peninsula was held by the bulk of French First Army and to the north of them was the BEF facing east against the German Army Group B and west against Army Group A which contained most and was soon to contain all the panzer divisions. The eastern flank north of Ypres was continued by the Belgian army, overextended, exhausted and increasingly demoralized, while the western flank from north of Cassel to Gravelines was held by an improvised French corps.

By this time the commanders of the French and British armies were in disagreement. Weygand continued to believe that the situation should and could be remedied by the Northern Armies breaking out to the south and joining hands with other French forces striking north across the Somme. If the worst came to the worst he proposed establishing a permanent bridgehead which should be based on, in his own words, '*Calais, St. Omer, Douai, Valenciennes, Roubaix, Courtrai* (Kortrijk), *the course of the Lys and Ostend - a space containing at least 3,000 square kilometres.*'

When this order was given on 25 May every one of the towns named (except Roubaix, Ostend and a small fragment of Calais) were already in German hands. Lord Gort, who had remained wholly loyal to his French military chiefs, believed this plan to be unrealistic not least because it would be impossible to supply more than half a million men through the single port available - Dunkirk - which the crushing German superiority in the air would inevitably soon make unworkable.

He realized that the only chance of saving at least part of the allied armies lay in getting them north to the coast and leaving it to the Royal Navy to do what they could. He had plans prepared for this eventuality from 19 May onwards but was still prepared to allocate his only two reserve divisions to take part in the offensive towards the Somme. Weygand had no faith in an evacuation by sea, having been advised by the head of the French navy, Admiral Darlan, that such a move was 'impossible'.

The situation changed on 25 May when it became clear that the southerly flank of the Belgian army, fought to a standstill, was giving way north of Ypres, and Gort unhesitatingly switched the two reserve divisions to fill the resulting gap in the allied line. Weygand remonstrated vehemently against this disruption of the southern attack which he had ordered but to the British it was clear that if the flanks of the 'peninsula' could not be held the French and British armies would be split up into groups and forced to surrender. 5th and 50th Divisions fought magnificent actions to halt the Germans on the Belgian flank while on the western front 2nd, 44th and 48th Divisions sacrificed themselves to keep back the German armour. The French were unconvinced and the bulk of their First Army stayed obstinately around Lille where, after an epic defence, they had to surrender.

Fear of French accusations of desertion made the British government most reluctant to approve Gort's plan of falling back to the sea although they had sanctioned preliminary planning for such an eventuality since most of the preparations coincided with those necessary for bringing supplies for the army into Dunkirk. By 26 May 28,000 men, who no longer had a function with the field force, had been repatriated in the empty cargo ships. On that day however, the evidence that a breakout from the north was impossible became incontrovertible and steps were taken to obtain French consent to evacuation of both armies. Weygand, however, did not pass the order to evacuate French troops until three days later and the French navy was correspondingly slow to send assistance.

At this stage no high hopes were entertained about the success of DYNAMO. Gort's view was that 'the greatest part of the B.E.F. and its equipment must be lost' and the government's orders to Ramsay

ECPA

ECPA

British 3.7 inch anti-aircraft guns abandoned near Fort des Dunes. The barrels have been blown open to make them useless. The rangefinder (LOWER PICTURE) has also been destroyed.

Firing rifles at German aircraft over the Dunkirk beaches, a practice more calculated to sustain morale than to damage the enemy.

IWM

ECPA

ECPA

IWM

(ABOVE) Some of the British who did not return from Dunkirk.

(ABOVE RIGHT) RAF photograph of Dunkirk burning. To the right are some of the inner harbour basins. At the top left are the marshalling yards, already heavily bombed by the Luftwaffe.

The last sight of Dunkirk burning: A picture taken before it became too dangerous to sail in daylight.

referred to 'lifting up to 45,000 (men) within two days' after which it was thought that embarkation would become impossible. Ramsay, however had planned carefully and had available a substantial number of cross-channel steamers. It was unfortunate that just as the operation was authorized Calais was lost, giving the German artillery command over the shortest sea passage to Dunkirk (39 sea miles). The early rescue ships had to follow a roundabout northerly route (87 miles) until an intermediate channel (55 miles) could be buoyed through the shoals and sandbanks.

Meanwhile a perimeter was being formed around Dunkirk and manned by such troops as were immediately available. It was fortunate that this defensive position could, for the most part, be based on water obstacles (whose course can still be traced). It was anchored on Nieuport on the east and then followed canals to Furnes (Veurne) and Bergues. From Bergues to Gravelines it was less well marked and on 27 May the French were driven in by a heavy attack on the western flank although they managed to hold fast on the line of the Old Mardyk Canal, a firm enough line but one which left Dunkirk harbour under fire from German field guns. By the end of 30 May all the survivors from the BEF and such of the French First Army as had been induced to escape from Lille (about two corps) was within the perimeter and no German attacks succeeded in penetrating it - thanks largely to some degree of confusion in the German command.

IWM

By dawn on 1 June, 194,620 men had been evacuated and Lord Gort was ordered to return to England, leaving the command of the British to Major-General the Hon. Harold Alexander (later Field Marshal the Earl Alexander of Tunis). On his first day in command Alexander pulled back the eastern flank of the beached to the line of the Franco-Belgian frontier (where some fortifications already existed) in order to reduce the number of men needed to guard it. By the night of 2/3 June all the remaining British had been embarked and he made a final tour of the beaches in a motor boat in the early hours of 3 June and, finding no one waiting for embarkation, sailed for Dover. Ships returned to Dunkirk the following night and embarked a further 29,989 French soldiers as well as six British stragglers.

'The Miracle of Dunkirk', the snatching of 338,226 men from under the noses of both a victorious army and an overwhelming airforce, inevitably bred a flourishing mythology particularly because it happened at a time when the British were desperately in need of good news of any kind. The newspapers and radio reports of the time told of impeccable discipline by the men on the beaches while they waited for the 'little ships' to pick them up, while overhead the RAF won a great victory over the *Luftwaffe*, and the French army disintegrated around the beachhead. Such a picture has a large measure of truth but is far from the whole story.

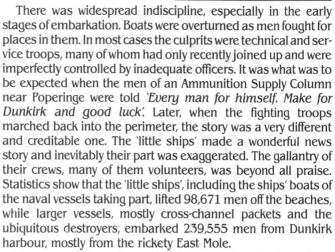

Hudson of RAF Coastal Command flying low over the beaches. The pall of smoke comes from the great oil tanks, some of which were hit by German bombs and shells and the rest were fired by the French to stop them falling into German hands.

There was widespread indiscipline, especially in the early stages of embarkation. Boats were overturned as men fought for places in them. In most cases the culprits were technical and service troops, many of whom had only recently joined up and were imperfectly controlled by inadequate officers. It was what was to be expected when the men of an Ammunition Supply Column near Poperinge were told *Every man for himself. Make for Dunkirk and good luck'.* Later, when the fighting troops marched back into the perimeter, the story was a very different and creditable one. The 'little ships' made a wonderful news story and inevitably their part was exaggerated. The gallantry of their crews, many of them volunteers, was beyond all praise. Statistics show that the 'little ships', including the ships' boats of the naval vessels taking part, lifted 98,671 men off the beaches, while larger vessels, mostly cross-channel packets and the ubiquitous destroyers, embarked 239,555 men from Dunkirk harbour, mostly from the rickety East Mole.

The story of the RAF's great victory over Dunkirk stems from Churchill's laudable and necessary attempt to silence the bitter complaints from the army at the absence of air support. It was based on contemporary reports that 262 German aircraft had been shot down for a loss of 145 RAF machines (and a few from the Fleet Air Arm). The actual loss to the *Luftwaffe* was 132 planes and there is no doubt that some of these fell to the anti-aircraft guns of the destroyers, the navy claiming thirty-five kills up to 1 June. In strictly numerical terms, the RAF suffered something of a defeat over Dunkirk and their victory, such as it was, lay in frustrating Göring's boast that the *Luftwaffe* alone could prevent embarkation - a boast which, even at the time, the German army found unconvincing.

Inevitably the British underrated the French contribution to the embarkation of the BEF. The town of Dunkirk was inundated by French stragglers and deserters, many drunk and unarmed, who refused to do anything to help in the defence or even to board the ships. These were the Frenchmen whom the British saw, but behind them was a solid, tenacious rearguard who fought to the last and earned the admiration of their German opponents. 40,000 French prisoners were taken when the fighting eventually ceased and probably two-thirds of these were still under command of their officers. Behind these determined men, the BEF, 124,000 Frenchmen and 16,000 Dutch and Belgian soldiers were able to escape. Whether so many Frenchmen need have been left behind is another matter. If Weygand had sanctioned embarkation before 29 May and if the French navy had started to collect ships earlier, more French soldiers could have been saved. Earlier notice might have helped them muddle through to a more effective beach-control system; the British evolved theirs through hard experience. As it was there were occasions when empty ships waited throughout the hours of darkness as no French soldiers could be found to board them. The French are right to claim that the British escaped behind a screen of their allies but it was largely the fault of the French that it happened that way.

Despite the imperfections and misrepresentations, the success of Operation *DYNAMO* was justifiably regarded as a miracle; certainly it must rank as the most remarkable improvisation in military history. To assemble 1,765 British vessels within two weeks, to man, provision and use them to rescue more than a third of a million men from a far superior army and air force was an unparalleled feat and one that altered the history of the world.

The memorial to the dead of two world wars at Gravelines.

DP

CALAIS - DUNKIRK

THE attempt to run a convoy of rations from Calais to Dunkirk on the night of 24/25 May was spearheaded by a troop of tanks, one cruiser and three light, commanded by Major Reeves, Royal Tank Regiment. They had the advantage of a full moon but immediately lost wireless touch with the main body behind them. They passed two unmanned road blocks but then found parked beside the road a large number of tanks and some artillery. The commander of the leading light tank, called to them in French, assuming that to be their native language. Realizing that they were Germans, the convoy simply drove on, whereupon the German waved to them and gave the thumbs-up sign. Somewhat later a motor cyclist rode up behind the rear tank and tried to read the number plate with a torch. The next hazard was a string of mines across the road but these they managed to tow away despite the presence of some German infantry who, once again, assumed they were friendly. The troop reached Gravelines, still in French hands, just before dawn and joined the main body of the BEF.

ON THE BEACH

WHEN the BEF advanced into Belgium the guns of 58/Medium Regiment, a Territorial artillery unit from East Anglia, were sent forward by rail since, having wooden wheels, they were capable of only four and a half miles per hour on the road. By some mischance they were misrouted but, with remarkable skill and determination, four of them were retrieved and put more or less into working order. As a fighting unit 58/Medium were thenceforward of only marginal value and so it was decided to evacuate them. As one of their second lieutenants remembered, 'We drove to our final destination, a village about 13 miles from the sea and were ordered to destroy everything - our beautiful brand-new Scammel towers and our four broken down guns - blowing them up and throwing the breach-blocks into a canal. We were allowed to take only what we could carry with our revolvers or rifles. Then we were sorted out into groups of thirty, each with a junior officer, who was told to get them home and stay with them till they got there. We were pretty tired but I put on my British warm and marched off. After about three miles we went over a slight rise and I caught sight of the sea, ten miles off. At dusk we arrived in the sand dunes behind La Panne. Absolute confusion reigned. No one knew anything.*

We slept among the dunes and next morning I discovered two very drunk R.A.S.C. men with a truck. I put them under arrest and opened the truck to find it contained rum, sugar and butter. Getting hold of some 4-gallon containers, I started a Cumberland rum butter factory. It was very good and sustaining if you had not eaten for 24-36 hours. Each man got a large spoonful and I must have fed several hundred before it ran out.

Then we went forward to the dunes beside the sea and were given a number which was supposed to be our embarkation number but there were very few ships at the time. We spent most of the time there and were strafed from the air once or twice but nothing serious. Dunkirk was visible to the west under a huge pall of smoke drifting our way. The sea was blue and calm. It was Sunday and we heard the B.B.C. news on someone's portable radio. It was disconcerting to find the King was leading the nation in prayer for our deliverance. It was the first time we realised how serious it had become because we thought we were holding the perimeter fairly easily and that only useless bodies such as ourselves were being evacuated.

IWM

Next day we marched down the beach for a mile or two to Bray Dunes where we were told we might find a boat but no luck and, as the beach was getting very crowded, we marched back again. Next day it was cloudy and the sea a bit rougher. No boats came till late that afternoon when H.M.S. Kellett, a sloop of 1926 vintage arrived off the beach. She sent a boat ashore and one of our officers waded out to persuade it to stay and take people off. We quickly formed up in two long lines made up of our regiment and others. My group got a posiion near the water's edge with about two hundred yards of people in front of us. Shortly afterwards I drew my revolver for the first time in anger. Discipline on this part of the beach was excellent but there were a few odd stragglers or deserters who made a nuisance of themselves by trying to jump the queues and I told one that if he tried again I would shoot him without hesitation. He melted away. Gradually we worked our way into the water and I felt lucky to be tall. Everyone was very tired, some on their beam ends and up to their chins in water but fortunately it was dead calm. We made everyone throw everything away, including their rifles. It was a desperately slow job as there were only four boats working, each rather dangerously taking about thirty men, but after three and a half hours, about 11 pm, our turn came and I got my party aboard with some difficulty and got myself in by 11.45.

Kellett sailed about midnight with about twenty officers asleep on the wardroom floor, rolling about like logs as the ship moved. I felt quite safe and confident of getting home when, about 1 am, there was a terrific explosion and the whole ship rattled like a gong. I thought we had been hit but the captain, Lord Stanley of Alderley, a perfectly splendid chap, appeared and said we were alright but that a destroyer, H.M.S. Grafton, had been torpedoed about a quarter of a mile away.

We arrived at Ramsgate about 6.30 am.

IWM

(TOP) Walking wounded at Dover waiting for transport. 185 trains (from all over England) made 565 journeys to get the evacuated soldiers away from the channel ports.

(BOTTOM) A destroyer crowded with troops entering harbour. In the background is Dover Castle under which Vice-Admiral Ramsay directed the evacuation from the DYNAMO room.

MOBILITY

It was the vehicles of the BEF that made its escape possible but they had all to be immobilized and left on or near the beaches. Near the shore is a stranded Thames sailing barge, and further out lies the wreck of a personnel ship.

T HE 1940 campaign which culminated at Dunkirk cost Britain 63,879 vehicles; only 4,739 were saved. As the ten divisions of the BEF were very short of tanks and had not even begun to receive the excellent artillery by then designed for them, it is amazing that it had almost 70,000 vehicles in France. It was in fact the only one of the armies engaged that did not rely at all on the horse. In the pre-war period Britain had been plastered with recruiting posters declaring, ITS A MECHANISED ARMY NOW.

B

Dunkirk industrial area from the beach.

DP

This slogan gave rise to much derision when the German armoured divisions carved their way through the allied infantry. Nevertheless it was the mechanization of the British army which saved it on the retreat to Dunkirk. Not only did the British infantry ride most of the way from their forward positions to within easy marching distance of the beaches but it was the trucks of the Troop Carrying Companies, RASC, which made it possible for 5th and 50th Divisions to be switched from Arras to Ypres when, on 25/26 May, the Belgian flank gave way. The Germans who made this breakthrough were dependent almost wholly on horse-drawn transport and could not hope to compete for speed with the mechanized British infantry.

Not the least serious error of the German High Command, one seldom referred to, was the decision to withdraw the three panzer divisions that had begun the campaign with Army Group B and transfer them to the west on 16 May. If they had left even one of these formations in the east it is very doubtful if the divisions that filled the gap caused by the Belgian defeat could have held the line and stopped the German tanks coming between the main body of the BEF and the sea. As it was, the plentiful supply of trucks made it possible to fill the gap and, when the time came to withdraw, enabled the British to move cleanly away from the plodding German infantry. The unromantic three-ton truck was one of the factors which made the Dunkirk evacuation possible.

The British cemetery at Zuydcoote and two views of the Sanatorium, of which only the older centre block is as it was in 1940. The blockhouse in the foreground of the right-hand picture is part of the German fortifications dated from 1942-4.

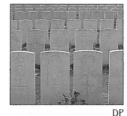

DP

DP

DP

B

IWM

Wounded 'poilu' landed at Dover.

One of the reasons why the Germans bombed Zuydcoote hospital: The nearby French coastal battery mounting four 194mm guns which came from a cruiser. These could be, and were, swung round to fire inland.

ZUYDCOOTE

IN 1940 the beaches east of Dunkirk were lined with smallish holiday villas, most of which have now been swept away and replaced by larger buildings and tower blocks, but to the west of Bray Dunes, the sanitorium of Zuydcoote retains the central block which was a feature of the beaches in 1940. Before the war it had been a hospital for tubercular children but, as soon as Belgium was invaded, it was taken over and used for sick and wounded soldiers, becoming the base hospital for First French Army as soon as the armies started to fall back to the coast. The staff of all the surviving field hospitals and dressing stations were assisted by the civilian staff and nuns and, although designed for only five hundred children, ten thousand wounded - French, British, Belgian and German - were cared for there between 22 May and 5 June. Eight improvised operating theatres worked round the clock with shifts of surgeons. The lightly wounded were quickly sent down to the ships, priority being given to those with Jewish names. One thousand men died in Zuydcoote in those difficult days. Some died of their wounds - more perhaps than need have done due to a scarcity of medical supplies - but most died from shelling and bombing, especially those who were accommodated in tents within the grounds. The hospital was clearly marked with the Red Cross but the Germans could claim that batteries of artillery were in the near vicinity - an inevitable consequence of the smallness of the beach-head. One or two hits might therefore have been unavoidable errors but the fact that seventy shells, to say nothing of bombs, fell on or close to the hospital suggests that either the German gunnery was very poor or that the Red Cross was being ignored.

EACH YEAR ON 20 NOVEMBER the Royal Tank Regiment celebrates Cambrai Day, the anniversary of the first full-scale demonstration of what tanks could do in battle. Not unnaturally they make little mention of the limitations in the capabilities of contemporary tanks which the battle showed only too clearly. Cambrai was a battle which opened in a blaze of glory sufficient to set the church bells ringing in England and closed on the brink of disaster among a plethora of official inquiries.

DP

20 NOVEMBER 1917

CAMBRAI

The motives for launching an attack were mixed. The decision had its basis in a desire to divert German reserves from the Third Battle of Ypres but before enough divisions could be made available for Cambrai, Passchendaele had been taken and the Ypres offensive discontinued. On to that scheme was grafted the desire of the Tank Corps to show what it could do in open country which had not been ravaged by constant bombardment. Lieutenant-Colonel J.F.C. Fuller advocated a raid in strength: *'Advance, Hit, Retire'*, with no specific strategic aim in mind. Proposals for attacks near Lille and St Quentin were discussed and discarded and the Cambrai front was chosen largely because Fuller's scheme found favour with General Byng, the meticulous planner of the attack on Vimy Ridge (see page 164), who commanded Third Army on that front and had been ordered to plan a diversionary attack.

Haig approved the general idea of a tank and infantry attack near Cambrai. Not only was he in favour of keeping pressure on the Germans lest they launch offensives of their own but he was a convinced supporter of tanks as an *'adjunct to the infantry's attack'*. Immediately after their first action at Flers (see page 164) he had asked for a thousand tanks of an improved model and he was delighted with their performance at St Julian, near Ypres, on 19 August 1917, when he wrote, *'All objectives taken, 12 infantry casualties and 14 men of Tanks hit. Without Tanks we would have lost 600'!* He ordered Byng to plan the combined attack near Cambrai, stressing the importance of stengthening the army's front for the winter and in particular the advantages of seizing Bourlon Ridge, possession of which would greatly hamper German use of Cambrai as a nodal point in their railway communications.

Byng's ideas were more grandiose. In addition to seizing Bourlon Ridge he planned to strike eastward and pass the Cavalry Corps round the far side of Cambrai, linking up with infantry pushing north from Bourlon and encircling several German divisions. Since Byng was a hussar by early training, it has been suggested that this ambitious scheme stemmed from his over-estimate of the capabilities of cavalry. Since at Vimy he had noticeably failed to try to use cavalry for exploitation, it seems more probable that the senior officers of the Tank Corps had so persuaded him of the powers of their machines as to convince him that the horsemen really could be launched into open, undefended country behind the German trench lines. As is quoted elsewhere, *'the difficulty was to find something that the tank-men would admit that a tank would not do'.*

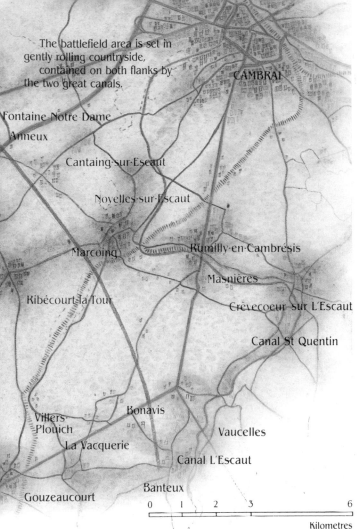

The battlefield area is set in gently rolling countryside, contained on both flanks by the two great canals.

CAMBRAI

Fontaine Notre Dame

Anneux

Cantaing-sur-Escaut

Noyelles-sur-Escaut

Marcoing   Rumilly-en-Cambrésis

Masnières

Ribécourt-la-Tour   Crèvecoeur-sur-L'Escaut

Canal St Quentin

Bonavis

Villers-Plouich   Vaucelles

La Vacquerie

Canal L'Escaut

Banteux

Gouzeaucourt

0   1   2   3   6

Kilometres

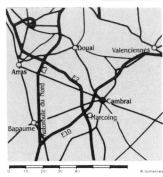

Cambrai, occupied by the Germans from 1914-18, lies between Lille and St Quentin, to the east of the Canal du Nord and L'Escaut (St Quentin) Canal. It is a bustling market town just east of the A2 and A26 autoroutes at a point where many roads converge. If coming from Albert, follow the signposts to Arras and Cambrai. Remains of ramparts designed by Vauban are in The Jardin Public and ruins of an old fortress and barracks lie at the north end of Boulevard Faidherbe. The Cambrai Memorial (to those with no known graves who fell in the Battle of Cambrai) is to the west near Louveral on the N30 crossroads.

To the south-east, via Hermies and crossing the motorway, is the central part of the battle area, alongside the A2 motorway and near to the village and wood of Havrincourt. When the main attack on the Hindenburg Line began, this area was fortified with concrete bunkers, ruins of which remain in the meadows and woods. The Château was used as a German HQ; it was captured by the 62nd West Yorkshire Division whose memorial is on the edge of the village by the wood. Take the road from Havrincourt to Flesquières (a major German defensive position) to the battle area where 400 tanks advanced in a 9-mile (15km) front across the open fields from Havrincourt Wood on 20 November 1917.

The fact was that the tanks of 1917 were somewhat limited and primitive weapons. The Mark IV model of 1917 was an improvement, but not a great one, on those in use on the Somme in the previous year. It was certainly not a machine with which to exploit a break-through, having a maximum speed on the road of 3.7 miles per hour and a theoretical mileage, without refuelling, of thirty-five miles. Over rough country it was unlikely to manage much more than half a mile per hour for as much as twenty miles.

Visibility was extremely limited and manoeuvring difficult since three men were required to steer. The driver operated a gearbox which gave two forward speeds and reverse but steering was done by two subsidiary gearboxes, one for each track, operated by its own gearsman who, since speech was impossible with the engine running, had to watch the driver for visual signals. The driver had a footbrake but there was also an additional braking system, working through the subsidiary gearboxes, operated by the crew commander.

Cut-away view of a Mark IV male tank. The driver and commander sit front. There are two gunners on either side and, in the rear, the two gearsmen.

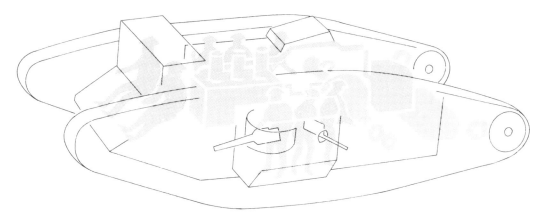

The armament consisted either of two six-pounder guns and four Lewis guns (in the twenty-eight ton 'male' tanks) or six Lewis guns (in the twenty-seven ton 'females'). In both models the guns were mounted in sponsons on either side. The crew of eight, one of them an officer, suffered intolerable conditions, there being neither ventilation nor extractor fans so that the temperature could rise to 120 degrees Fahrenheit and their discomfort was increased by the need to wear helmets and chainmail face masks as a precaution against splinters driven off the inside of the armour by enemy bullets. At its thickest the armour was only twelve millimetres thick and on the roof and belly no more than six millimetres.

TM

Tanks could not go everywhere. An early (Mark I) model, used as a supply tank, ditched in a trench.

The front that was chosen for the attack would have been ideal for a raid since it was naturally limited. On the eastern side the Escaut (Scheldt) Canal - also known as the St Quentin Canal - runs on a generally southerly course from Cambrai to the village of Marcoing where it loops to the east for more than three miles until, at Crèvecoeur, it turns south again and enters a more marked valley which, after the village of Banteux, becomes distinctly sharp-sided. The Canal de l'Escaut was a formidable obstacle tapering from a width of sixty feet at the top to thirty feet at the bottom where it was under six feet of water. The only places where tanks could hope to cross were the substantial bridges at Masnieres, Marcoing and Noyelles. On the west flank is the Canal du Nord, then incomplete and waterless, which runs southward to the east of Moeuvres village and the west of Havrincourt, where it runs in a ninety-foot cutting, and swings sharply westward before resuming its southerly course. The two canals thus marked out a corridor five miles wide running northward from Marcoing and Havrincourt, a line marked by an open valley, magniloquently known as Grand Ravin, having a shallow drainage ditch at its bottom. At the northern end this corridor is blocked by the village and wooded ridge of Bourlon.

The Hindenburg Line (Siegfried Stellung) had been built diagonally across the corridor. The forward defensive system ran almost north and south of Moeuvres to Havrincourt and then swung more easterly to Banteux. It consisted of two lines of trenches, each at least seven feet deep (with a firing step to enable the defenders to use their weapons), tapering from twelve feet wide at the surface to three feet, and well supplied with dug-outs. It was covered by a zone of barbed wire comprising four belts, each twelve yards deep and three feet high, giving an almost continuous zone of wire a hundred yards deep. In front of this was an outpost line consisting of small posts rather than a continuous line, lightly wired and including strong posts in the fortified village of La Vacquerie and, on the west bank of the Canal du Nord, an entrenched spoilheap sixty feet high and four hundred feet long. Behind the forward system was another double line of trenches, the support system, which included Moeuvres and covered Graincourt, Flesquières and Marcoing before reaching the Canal de l'Escaut between Lateau Wood and the village of Vaucelles. Between the front and support systems the village of Ribécourt was strongly fortified. A third defended line, far from complete, defended Bourlon, Noyelles and, on the east bank, Rumilly and Crèvecoeur. Three divisions garrisoned this part of the line, the excellent if tired 54th Division held the centre between Havrincourt and La Vacquerie, having on its right 20th Landwehr, a low-quality formation, and on its left, 9th Reserve.

Early wireless set mounted in a tank. It could not be used with the engine running.

Thanks to the attrition of the fighting round Ypres, only eleven (rather tired) infantry and five cavalry divisions, were available apart from 1,003 guns (319 of them heavies), 289 aircraft, of which only twelve were bombers, and three brigades of tanks. The latter included 324 battle tanks, the remainder were reserves (54), supply tanks (54) and specialist machines including bridge carriers, cable layers and nine which were fitted with wireless although their sets could not, owing to the noise, be used when the tank was in motion. All the battle tanks were fitted with fascines since the twelve-foot trenches were too wide for the Mark IVs to cross without support. These fascines were bundles of brushwood, ten feet long and four feet six inches in diameter, being bound with chains tightened by two tanks pulling in opposite directions. Their construction required four hundred tons of wood - each fascine weighing nearly two tons - and twelve thousand feet of chain. They were constructed by 51/Chinese Labour Company and mounted on top of the tank (where they obstructed the forward periscope) and could be released from inside the tank so that they toppled forward into a trench.

The essential ingredient of Byng's plan was surprise. Aided by low cloud which kept the German aircraft away from the front, the tanks and additional infantry were smuggled into their concealed forming-up positions and the guns forbidden to register their targets. All the additional guns were to fire by prediction, only the guns normally on the front were permitted to fire an average number of rounds from known positions. No attempt was made to cut the wire by gunfire, it being assumed that the tanks would crush it, and the infantry had been carefully rehearsed in a drill designed to get them through the gaps and into the trenches beyond (see pages 74-75).

The decision to rely on surprise and pass the cavalry across the Canal de l'Escaut on the first day made its own problems, since three horsed divisions had to be sandwiched between the two assault corps of infantry and the reserve corps. As the front was narrow and crossed by only two substantial roads, the inevitable result

IWM

DP

(TOP) *Early but effective anti-tank obstacles. Trees felled by the Germans near Havrincourt.*

(BOTTOM) *'The Green Fields Beyond'. The gently rolling country south west of Marcoing.*

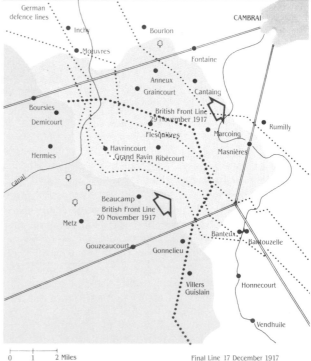

The Battle of Cambrai, November 1917

German defence lines

CAMBRAI

Inchy
Bourlon
Mœuvres
Fontaine
Anneux
Graincourt
Cantaing
Boursies
British Front Line 29 November 1917
Demicourt
Rumilly
Flesquières
Marcoing
Havrincourt
Masnières
Hermies
Grand Ravin Ribécourt
Canal
Beaucamp
British Front Line 20 November 1917
Metz
Banteux
Bantouzelle
Gouzeaucourt
Gonnelieu
Villers Guislain
Honnecourt
Vendhuile

0   1   2 Miles

Final Line 17 December 1917

was that if the initial attack was not completely successful it would be difficult to bring the reserve corps forward quickly to strengthen the onslaught. As it was, success or failure was to be dependent on the tanks and seven infantry divisions. On the right Lieutenant-General Sir William Pulteney's III Corps with 12th, 20th and 6th Divisions attacking and 29th in reserve were to attack from Ribécourt eastward, aiming to capture the canal crossings at Marcoing and Masnières and then break through the third

increase the garrison by two further eastern formations. The movements of these divisions had been detected by the British but Haig's Chief of Intelligence, General Charteris, refused to admit the fact, replying to the officer who had reported the move, *You are mistaken. This is just a bluff put up by the Germans. I am sure the units you mention are still on the Russian front; they are not to be shown on our Intelligence map'.*

Belts of barbed wire in front of the Hindenburg Line.

IWM

defensive system whereupon the two leading cavalry divisions would be passed through for their swinging ride round Cambrai. On the left IV Corps (under Lieutenant-General Sir Charles Wollcombe) was to aim for Bourlon situated astride the Canal du Nord. On the east bank would be 51st and 62nd Divisions and on the west 36th and 56th, the latter being little more than a flankguard in the early stages. 1st Cavalry Division was under command but the corps had no reserve.

The Germans were in total ignorance of the blow that was about to strike them. Some hints came from prisoners that an offensive *'possibly supported by tanks'* might be in the offing but the absence of any preliminary bombardment assured them that the danger was not imminent. It was the purest mischance that on 19 November a division released from the eastern front, as a consequence of the Russian Revolution, began to arrive at Cambrai for the routine relief of 20th Lanwehr Division. In fact the High Command, knowing that that part of the front was lightly held, was planning to

A few minutes after 6 am on 20 November a solitary British aircraft flew low across the front and, under cover of its noise, the engines of the tanks were started and they nosed forward to their start line. Zero Hour was at 6.20 am, just as it started to grow light; at that moment the whole weight of the artillery fell on the outpost zone and the forward trenches. It was a misty morning and as the guns made their first pre-arranged lift and the Germans scrambled to man their parapets they saw, looming through the murk, a seemingly endless line of tanks lumbering towards them. It must have been a terrifying sight.

III Corps on the right, having the shorter stretch of no man's land to cross, were first in action, and by 11.30 am were across both the forward and support systems, many Germans surrendering willingly and others fleeing in panic to the rear. There were isolated points of strong resistance, notably at Lateau Wood, and also behind La Vacquerie where a company of 12/KRRC lost all its officers but captured its objective under the leadership of the company runner, Rifleman A.E. Sheppard, who also found time to rush a machine-gun post singlehanded - a feat which won him the Victoria Cross. The tanks were delayed crossing the Grand Ravin and the infantry, forging ahead, were repulsed at Ribécourt but the arrival of the tanks decided the enemy withdrawal.

On IV Corps front there were more difficulties. Astride the canal, 62nd Division was held up in front of Havrincourt until the six-pounders on the tanks made the buildings untenable and 36th took the spoilheap, both divisions being through the support system by 10.30 am. On the right of the corps front, 51st (Highland) Division overran the Grand Ravin without any problems but was soon in difficulties beyond. The Tank Corps were inclined to blame most of the trouble on the divisional commander, Major-General G.M. Harper, whose ideas of infantry/tank co-operation deviated slightly from that generally adopted. The real trouble seems to have been the situation of the village of Flesquières which lies behind the crest of a ridge and was strongly held. Its garrison consisted of more than two battalions, two machine-gun companies and plenty of artillery - including a battery newly arrived from the eastern front. Moreover most of these gunners had, unusually, been specially trained in anti-tank work (see page 74).

They were ideally sited for this role since, as the tanks crawled over the crest, they exposed their lightly armoured bellies to the guns. Twenty-eight of them were knocked out and, in the ensuing check, the barrage, true to its timetable, rolled on ahead, leaving the infantry with no artillery support and thick belts of wire which, since the tanks could not move forward, was uncut.

Throughout the afternoon the attack on Flesquières continued, with yet more tanks being brought forward. These however had not been trained with the Highlanders and co-ordination was very defective. Nor could any satisfactory co-operation be established with 6th Division (III Corps) on their right who had taken Premy Chapel, little more than a mile in the right rear of Flesquières. From here they were able to capture or drive away some of the guns which had plagued the tanks. Co-operation was made no easier by General Harper's decision to keep his headquarters in its initial position behind the original start line now five miles behind the fighting troops. At about four o'clock half a dozen tanks managed to plough through the wire and enter the village. Some of 1/6th Seaforth Highlanders followed them into the streets but, owing to some misunderstanding, the tanks withdrew before the place could be consolidated and the infantry were forced back. At nightfall Flesquières was still firmly in the hands of the Germans. Its position, however, was severely threatened since 186 Brigade (62nd Division) commanded by Brigadier-General R.B. Bradford VC - at twenty-five the youngest brigadier in the army - had taken Graincourt. Although repulsed from Anneux, the brigade had succeeded in pushing the line forward right across the Cambrai-Bapaume road.

DP

The gates of Havrincourt Château. Many of the attacking tanks formed up under cover of the surrounding wood.

On III Corps front, tanks were in Marcoing before 11 am - and a Tank Corps officer managed to cut the electric leads which the Germans hoped would detonate the demolition charge they had laid under the railway bridge. Nevertheless it was not immediately possible to move troops across. At Masnières a demolition charge damaged the road bridge without destroying it and, although 11/Rifle Brigade occupied Les Rues Vertes on the south side of the canal, they could emplace only small detachments on to the far bank, where they were pinned down by fire.

At this stage 29th Division, the reserve to III Corps, was sent forward to continue the advance. Two companies of 4/Worcesters slipped across the canal at a lock half a mile east of Masnières (just before the eastward bend in the canal) and were joined by some 2/Hampshires but no progress could be made against the third defensive system, here close to the canal, though a gap was cut in the wire. 1/Essex managed to gain a toehold in the village itself but when a tank attempted to cross the damaged bridge, the whole structure collapsed and the crew, looking horrific in their chainmail masks, had to swim back to the bank. During the afternoon some infantry, followed by two tanks, crossed the Marcoing railway bridge but were held up in front of the German trenches.

According to the plan the cavalry should by now have begun their long ride and a start had, indeed, been made. A squadron of the Fort Garry Horse of Canada succeeded in improvising a bridge on top of the lock used by the Worcesters. Pushing eastward through the gap in the wire they charged and took a German battery, although their squadron commander was killed in the process. They penetrated more than a thousand yards to the east of Rumilly before they were held up by machine-gun fire. By this time the infantry and cavalry commanders on the south bank had relapsed into caution. Deciding that the bridge over the lock was insufficient to support a large advance and culpably ignorant of another bridge (which was marked on their maps) half a mile further east, they decided to hold back the rest of the cavalry and sent orders to call back the Fort Garry men. This order never reached them but, finding themselves unsupported, the thirty-three survivors waited until dark and then withdrew on foot, bringing nine prisoners with them. Their acting commander, Lieutenant Strachan was awarded the VC.

With the cavalry advance halted before it had begun, the acquisition of Bourlon Ridge became, as it had always been to Haig, the overriding objective of the attack. The urgent need therefore was more infantry, the more so since Flesquières still held out, but IV Corps had no reserve division and Third Army reserve, V Corps, was separated from the fighting by most of three cavalry divisions who had no role to play and were merely blocking the way forward. To make matters worse Army Headquarters (and those of lower formations) were largely ignorant of what was going on in the firing line. Messages from the Royal Flying Corps were frequently misleading - at one stage they reported that Flesquières had been captured - and other means of communication were largely ineffective. Elaborate plans had been made to run telephone lines forward behind the advancing troops but those laid on the ground had, for the most part, been cut by the tracks of tanks or by the limbers of field artillery going forward, while the cables raised on poles had been ripped down by the fascines on top of the tanks. As had so often been the case in attacking battles, the most effective means of communication was the runner but, although this task was safer at Cambrai than at the Somme or Ypres, the distances involved, five miles and more, ensured that messages moved very slowly.

Spoils of War: A Mark IV tank being used to tow in a captured 5.9 inch naval gun on 20 November 1917.

IWM

Female tank caught by a flame-thrower. Petrol-driven tanks were particularly vulnerable to fire.

By nightfall it was clear that Third Army had made an advance which was longer than any made by either side in a single day since 1914. On the left the line was not too far short of Moeuvres, Graincourt was held and, beyond unsubdued Flesquières, so was Nine Wood on the spur north of Marcoing. A small bridgehead covering Marcoing and part of Masnières was in British hands and on the right the front line had been pushed up to the Canal de l'Escaut as far south as Banteux.

RHL

Destroying enemy wire was the thing that tanks did best - but sometimes the wire won!

A combination of ignorance at Byng's headquarters and the hyperbole of the press caused the day's work to be hailed in all the allied countries as a great victory. Unfortunately it was nothing of the kind. Neither of the main objectives had been achieved. The Cavalry Corps had not been launched into open country and Bourlon Ridge had not even been attacked. The only people with some cause for satisfaction were the Tank Corps who had set their hearts on showing what they could do. They could point to having, with the support of infantry, broken into the most powerful trench system that had ever been devised.

What they had failed to do was to break out the far side - and to achieve even this partial success they had lost 179 tanks, almost half the strength of their fighting echelon. Nor was this the most significant weakness shown. Despite the heavy casualties in front of Flesquières, only 65 tanks, 38 per cent of the total loss, actually fell to enemy action. Of the remainder, 71 had broken down and 43 had been ditched. Many of the remaining machines needed mechanical attention and the crews were, for the most part, exhausted.

Haig, who had said that he would break off the attack unless success had been achieved, was in a dilemma. Partial success had been won and had been represented as victory.

RHL

The next morning the Germans counter-attacked from north and east. On Bourlon Ridge an epic stand by 2nd, 47th and 56th Divisions held the Germans back from all but the smallest gains and inflicted crippling loss. It was very different on the east. Here the main German thrust, assembled and launched in a thick mist, was directed up the Banteux Ravine, the re-entrant (now bridged by the A26) which runs westward from the Canal de l'Escaut towards Gouzeaucourt. This ravine was the boundary between Pulteney's III Corps, whose attention was still fixed to the north, and Sir Thomas Snow's VII Corps which had not been involved in the offensive and held the line in the strength that could be expected in a quiet sector. Snow had heard of preparations for a German attack and warned both III Corps and Third Army of the impending blow but both ignored the warning. Thus VII Corps, though thin on the ground, was standing by for the on-slaught but III Corps was caught unprepared and the first German attack captured La Vacquerie, Gonnelieu, Gouzeaucourt and Villers-Guislain. That they failed to take their final objective, Metz-en-Couture, and cut off the salient that Third Army had driven was due to a thin screen of hastily collected infantry, cavalry and pioneers, the few remaining tanks and, above all, to a magnificent counter-attack by 1 Guards Brigade which succeeded in recovering Gouzeaucourt.

On that day alone the British lost six thousand prisoners. The Germans continued to attack for the next five days, making no progress. After 5 December the battle died away but the salient the Germans had driven into Third Army's salient made the advanced British positions too dangerous to retain. Over the next two days the British withdrew successfully to a line covering Flesquières, Ribécourt, Villers Plourch and Gouzeaucourt and there the front settled down for the winter. The battle had cost the British 47,000 casualties, of whom 5,000 died - and the Germans about 55,000. The net gain of ground to the British was roughly balanced by their loss on the eastern flank. Public opinion on 30 November and three inquiries, one of them presided over by General Smuts, were set up to discover the cause of the set-back. Rather surprisingly it was found that 'no one down to and including corps commanders was to blame' though the training of everyone else, from major-general to private soldier came in for much, not undeserved, criticism.

Cambrai undoubtedly pointed the way to the warfare of the future but that warfare was further in the future than was anticipated. The Tank Corps could talk of 'Through mud and blood to the green fields beyond' but the tanks of World War I would have broken down before they reached the green fields and if they had not done so they would have run out of petrol! Moreover the Germans were already developing techniques for dealing with them, techniques which the British and French disastrously neglected in 1940.

Vickers machine guns of 11/Leicesters in a captured second-line trench near Ribécourt, 20 November 1917.

RHL

IWM

Towards a war of movement: Tank advancing through shellfire and the wreckage of a trenchline.

DP

For a total of four thousand British casualties, less than the number of prisoners taken, two trench systems had been overrun giving an advance of three to four miles on a six-mile front and a hundred guns had been captured. It seemed to be enough of a success to merit reinforcing and Haig, encouraged by the German evacuation of Flesquières during the night 20/21 November, authorized Byng to continue the attack, once more laying stress on the importance of capturing the Bourlon Ridge. Scarce as they were, he sent reinforcements to Third Army but the Germans, partially with the divisions coming from the eastern front, could reinforce faster. Moreover the Tank Corps was a spent force. Reduced to ninety-two machines by 23 November they had to be pulled back to Havrincourt Wood a few days later.

Meanwhile the offensive continued, largely as an old-fashioned infantry and artillery battle. By 29 November a footing had been gained on the ridge but there were insufficient reinforcements and that day the attack had to be halted.

THE DEMON GUNNER OF FLESQUIÈRES

IN his despatch on the Cambrai battle Sir Douglas Haig wrote that *'Many of the hits upon our Tanks at Flesquières were obtained by a German artillery officer who, remaining alone in his battery, served a field gun until killed at his gun. The great bravery of this officer aroused the admiration of all ranks.'* This striking tribute to an enemy in a public document reflected many stories of this gallant gunner, most of them crediting him with hitting sixteen tanks though some cut his score to eight. No bodies of German officers were actually found beside guns but the body of a major wearing the Iron Cross was, for a time, thought to be the one referred to. It was later discovered to be the body of an infantryman, severely wounded near Flesquières château. He had been abandoned by the stretcher bearers when found to be dead.

It is curious that there do not appear to be any contemporary German accounts of this hero, though it might be thought to be an excellent news story to boost morale in Germany. In 1937, however, an artillery officer who was present and had read Haig's tribute, named the man as *Unter-Offizier* (warrant officer) Krüger of 8th Battery 108/Field Artillery Regiment and places his gun some eight hundred yards east of Flesquières. Unfortunately other authorities deny that Krüger was present on this occasion. The probability is that no one gun, let alone one gunner, actually caused the heavy loss ascribed to him by British accounts at the time.

Certainly the tanks attacking Flesquières were very unlucky, not least in being ordered to make a frontal attack on a particularly well-defended strongpoint from an angle which exposed their bellies. They were moreover opposed by gunners who had been specially trained in anti-tank work.

CO-OPERATION BETWEEN TANKS AND INFANTRY

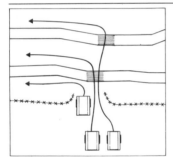  

The Tank Unit of attack will be a Section of 3 Tanks which will work together, one acting as the Advanced Tank and two as the Main Body Tanks.... The object of the Tanks is to break the enemy's line and then assist the Infantry to envelop the unbroken portions of it.

Normally Infantry will only follow the Main Body Tanks.... In most cases it will not be advisable to allot more than one platoon (30 to 40 men) to follow immediately each Tank, as the path crushed down through the wire by the two tracks of the Tank will only permit of men moving along them in single file, and any crowding at the point of penetration may result in unnecessary casualties.... Hurried crossings must be avoided for, if the leading men catch their foot in the crushed down wire and pull it up, delay to those in the rear will result.

DP

IWM

The defenders: German machine-gun detachment on the Cambrai battlefield.

The commander of 54th Division, Major General Freiherr von Watter (not to be confused with the general by the same name and title who commanded XIII Corps on the Cambrai front) was himself a gunner and had received firsthand accounts of the capabilities of tanks from his brother, also an artilleryman, who had encountered them at their début at Flers in 1916 (see page 164). He had therefore trained his divisional batteries to haul their guns out of their pits to give them plenty of traverse on the approach of tanks and had made them practise against moving dummies, which were hauled on cables, at ranges of up to one thousand yards. Moreover they had also had some practical experience against French tanks during the Nivelle offensive earlier in 1917.

EXTRACTS FROM THIRD ARMY TRAINING NOTE, 30 OCTOBER 1917

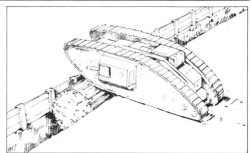

The Infantry, for each Trench Objective should be organised in three waves or lines:
1. Trench clearers
2. Trench stops
3. Supports
Their duties will be as follows: 1. To operate with the Tanks and clear the trenches. 2. To form 'Stops' in the trenches at various points and to improve paths through the wire. To mark these paths by means of flags so that those following may see where gaps exist. To place ladders in the captured trenches, or prepare the parados (the parapet at the rear of a trench) for rapid exit. 3. To support (1) and (2) and form an Infantry advanced Guard on the further side of the trench to protect the advance of the next echelon.

The Advanced Tanks will cross straight over the enemy's wire and swing to the left and move along the enemy's trench close to the parapet. They will not cross the trench until the Main Body Tanks and the Infantry are over.

The Main Body Tanks will traverse the enemy's trench at the same spot, so as to economise in the use of fascines. One will move down the fire trench and the other proceed forward to the support trench where, if necessary, it will cast its fascine and cross over, then turn and work down the support trench to the left.

Once the Infantry have been well placed in the enemy's trenches by the Tanks, they must depend on themselves to do all minor cleaning-up work, as the number of Tanks available will seldom permit of

Tanks remaining with them throughout an entire operation. Should a Tank break down, the Infantry must press on by themselves: their security will depend on so doing.

Tanks working in threes should cross the wire at the same spot, or if this is not feasible, at intervals of not less than 100 yards. The reason for this is that it has been found that if two Tanks cross the wire at a less interval, the second Tank crossing sometimes loosens the wire crushed down by the first and partially closes the gap made.

Infantry should keep from 25 to 50 paces behind the Tank as it enters the wire, so as not to get entangled in any trailing strands. Crowding around the Tank must be guarded against.

DP

(ABOVE) American Chapel
at Belleau Wood.
(RIGHT) German cemetery
at Belleau Wood.
(BELOW) The Marne at
Château-Thierry.

DP

DP

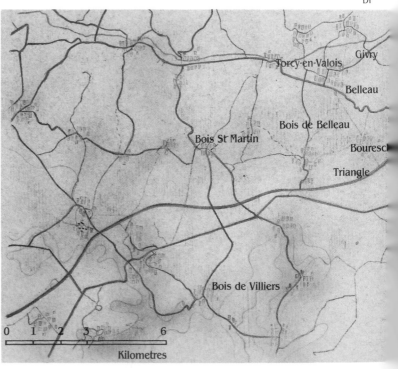

Roses on approach to American cemetery.

DP

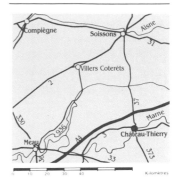

JUNE 1918
CHATEAU THIERRY

The terrain consists of a heavily wooded plateau, through which the Marne and its tributaries have cut their way to form deep valleys.

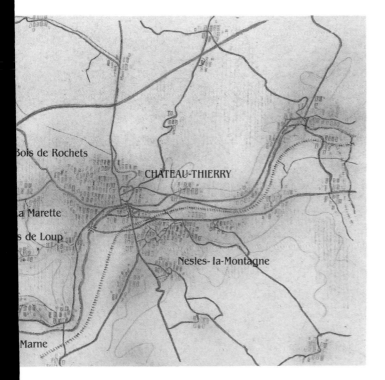

Château-Thierry, on the River Marne, lies between Paris and Reims in lovely wooded countryside and is dominated by the ramparts of an ancient fort. Just over a mile (2km) away, immediately off the N3 west, is Hill 204; a great monument commemorates its capture by the American 2nd Division and the French 39th Division in July 1918 (car parking here). Look down over the landscape to the town and the river.

The scene of the American victory at Belleau Wood lies 5 miles (8km) west of the town, near the quiet village of Belleau. Opposite the village green are gates leading to an American cemetery with over 2,000 graves. (Car parks concealed behind buildings flanking the drive.) Climb into the woods behind the chapel for a pleasant walk with glimpses back to the chapel and arc of gravestones below. (Immaculate visitors' rooms and toilets available here.) Returning to the road, turn left out of the gates to visit the German cemetery; alternatively turn right and then right again up a narrow road for Belleau Wood where abandoned guns can still be seen lying close to the road.

Just east of Compiègnes on the N31, approaching by the Carrefour de l'Armistice, is a replica of the railway carriage in which was signed the Armistice of 1918 and the surrender of the French in the Second World War.

WHEN THE UNITED STATES declared war on Germany in April 1917 and made herself not an ally but an Associated Power of the Western Allies, France and Britain saw a chance of boosting their dwindling numbers. Unfortunately the regular American army consisted of only 135,000 men, poorly armed and without training for war against an enemy with a major army. The highest peacetime rank was Major-General and an act of Congress as late as 1916 had limited the General Staff to fifty-five officers. Nor did the coming of war produce any rush of volunteers and in the first three weeks only 32,000 men came forward so that conscription had to be introduced in May. The first American troops, 14,000 soldiers and marines, landed in France on 28 June 1917. However two-thirds of them were recruits and they were in need of intensive training before they could be sent into action and much of this training had to be entrusted to the British and French armies. Before the war ended in November 1918 twenty-nine US divisions had seen service in France and each of these divisions was more than twice the size of the British, French or German divisions.

US artillery survey party checking the fall of shot on Belleau Wood.

US Army

Château-Thierry, 4-25 June 1918

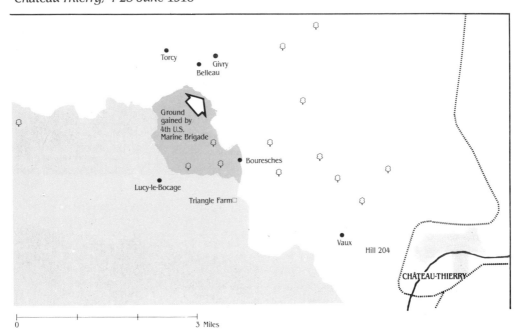

The fact that the two allies were training American troops led them to propose that they should also commit them to action, that they should incorporate them into the French and British armies, a suggestion made more plausible because they were having to supply them with most of their equipment. Most naturally the Americans resisted this idea of subordination and insisted on having their own identifiable group of armies even if it meant a substantial delay in their active involvement. In practice the First US Army was not formed and ready for action until 10 August 1918.

No one was more determined to preserve the identity of the American Expeditionary Force than its commander, General John J. Pershing, fifty-seven year-old veteran of wars against the Apache and Sioux Indians, the Spaniards (in Cuba), the Moros in the Philippines, and Pancho Villa in Mexico. One of his two, contradictory, sets of orders (one from the Secretary for War, one from the Chief of Staff) laid down that 'the forces of the United States are a separate and distinct component of the combined forces, the identity of which must be preserved'. He had every intention of obeying this injunction.

Circumstances, however, can alter cases and the great German offensive which opened on 21 March 1918 drove the British back towards the English Channel and looked as if it might decide the war by splitting the two allied armies. Near Amiens the line was held but a succession of further German blows still threatened disaster and Pershing offered Marshal Foch, newly appointed Supreme Commander, the use of the American troops, declaring:

A detachment of 7/US Machine Gun Battalion in action in the ruins of the town of Château-Thierry, 1 June 1918.

US ARMY

DP

'At this moment there are no other questions but of fighting'. Surprisingly little advantage was taken of this generous offer until late in May when another German onslaught drove an Anglo-French force off the ridge of Chemin des Dames, a supposedly strong position. As it happened this attack had been intended as a feint to draw French reserves southward but its success, unexpected by both sides, induced the Germans to reinforce success and the French to believe that the offensive's aim was to overrun Reims and continue to Paris.

As the Germans approached the River Marne at Château-Thierry, Foch asked Pershing to provide the 2nd and 3rd Divisions to plug the gap in the line. Although assured by the retreating and demoralized French that they were too late, some of the infantry of 3rd Division moved into the town of Château-Thierry and they succeeded in holding the river line. Meanwhile a section of 7th Machine Gun Battalion (taking two Hotchkiss guns), under Lieutenant John T. Bissell, actually crossed the river and fought on the far side.

The blown bridge over the Marne at Château-Thierry, showing the buildings held by 3rd US Infantry Division.

US ARMY

Although the French blew the bridges behind them, Bissell and his men fought for two days in their isolated position before extricating themselves, less one man, over the skeleton of the railway bridge.

To their left came 2nd US Division, 26,665 strong, under Major-General Omar Bundy whose third set of orders within twenty-four hours had put the division as a reserve to French XXI Corps under General Degoutte. This was holding a section of the line where no natural obstacle opposed the German advance and where the defenders were elderly and dispirited French troops, most of whom were in flight to the rear. On the night of 2-3 June, as the American infantry was beginning to arrive, the Germans seized Belleau Wood but were stopped by 2nd Division on a line running through Lucy-le-Bocage. It was clear that, far from being in reserve, Bundy's men were the only force to hold the Germans.

Worse than that, Degoutte was a passionate believer in improvised counter-attacks to recover lost ground, a theory with which Pershing had some sympathy since he believed that the French and British were too committed to trench warfare while he wished the Americans to train for fighting in open country.

There had to be a short pause while the American artillery was brought forward but at dawn on 6 June, 4 Marine Brigade advanced from the line Lucy-le-Bocage - Triangle Farm to recapture Belleau Wood. They had no trench mortars, no hand grenades and no signal pistols but, led by Brigadier-General James G. Harbord, who two weeks earlier had been Pershing's chief of staff, they went forward fearlessly and as if on parade - with five yards between each man and twenty yards between each of the four ranks. They were scythed down by the German machine guns but, incredibly, they took the village of Bouresches even if they gained only a small foothold in the wood itself. They suffered 1,087 casualties and were lucky that the Germans did not manage to mount their own counter-attack until 8 June.

DP

Relief on US Memorial.

For a week vicious German onslaughts continued and although fifty German dead (mostly from Alsace) were found in the streets of Bouresches, the Marines held. On 19 June the brigade was relieved by some green infantry but after forty-eight hours they had to return since the infantry, having mounted two unsuccessful attacks, was in chaos and one battalion had disintegrated - a circumstance which was fortunately not appreciated by the enemy.

More attacks followed until, after a fourteen-hour bombardment, the Marines cleared the whole of the wood, behind a rolling barrage, on the morning of 26 June. It was a tactical feature of very dubious value but it cost them 5,200 casualties, which was more than half their original strength.

As a tribute to their courage the French government decreed that the wood should be renamed 'Bois de la Brigade de Marine' but it is noticeable that modern maps still refer to it as Bois de Belleau. A more lasting tribute came from the German corps commander opposing the Marines:

2nd American Division must be considered a very good one.... The moral effect of our gunfire cannot seriously impede the advance of American infantry. Their nerves are not yet worn out.

DP   *Belleau Wood today.*

US observation officer directing from a balloon 3,000 feet above Château-Thierry.

US ARMY

DISORIENTATION

WHEN the first American prisoners were taken in Belleau Wood, the Germans were astonished to find that even the sergeants had no idea where they were. The Intelligence officer who interrogated them reported that 'They are kept in complete ignorance'.

The truth was that this ignorance was unintentional and due to the swift change in the orders that 2nd Division received from the French. They had been fully briefed on their first intended destination but when they eventually reached the Château-Thierry area even brigade commanders had little idea of their whereabouts and maps were almost unobtainable. They had been transported in small covered French trucks with seventy-five trucks to a battalion of rather more than a thousand men, and with each man carrying his weapons and a pack weighing 172 pounds, they were scarcely able to move, far less observe the passing signposts. At one of their halts those with keener noses thought they smelled spirits and one of the better-informed soldiers suggested, 'If there is a brandy distillery here, this could be La Ferté-sous-Jouarre'.

THE MARINES ATTACK ON 6 JUNE

FOR the last few minutes before five the fire was terrible. At exactly five there was silence ... then the guns were directed to the fields beyond Belleau Wood to prevent the Germans from bringing up reinforcements. We could see the long white lines of explosions, but we did not watch that for long.... There were some yells to our left towards Lucy-le-Bocage. We saw the long lines of Marines leap from somewhere and start across the wheatfields toward the woods. Those lines were straight and moved steadily, a few paces in front of each its officer leading, not driving. The attackers went up the gentle slope and, as the first wave disappeared over the crest we heard the opening clatter of machine guns that sprayed the advancing lines. Then we heard some shrieks that made our blood run cold. High above the roar of the artillery and the clatter of machine guns we heard the war cries of the Marines. The lines continued to go over the crest and, as the last disappeared a machine gun would go out of action. This meant that the Marines were either shooting the gunners or crawling up and bayonetting the crews.... How long this took I do not know, but it seemed less than half an hour before all the machine guns had stopped firing.

American troops with a German 'Minenwerfer' (mortar) captured in Belleau Wood.

US ARMY

THE SINEWS OF WAR

I N World War II the United States was called 'the arsenal of democracy' but this was far from the case in 1917-18. There were only 285,000 Springfield rifles (the standard infantry weapon) in the whole USA and they were found to be so difficult to mass-produce that most GIs were armed with Lee Enfields, which were already being manufactured in America for the British, with the bore reduced to .30. During the war ten million tons of war stores were purchased in Europe compared to seven million tons shipped from the USA and, conspicuously, the American troops wore British steel helmets. In the air the US army possessed a single squadron of elderly reconnaissance aircraft belonging to the Signal Corps and although 4,089 combat aircraft were produced before the armistice, most of the Air Corps work had to be done in allied aircraft. Since the army had only 450 field guns, all obsolete, it was decided to use French artillery and of the 3,499 guns used by the AEF only 130 of them were US made. American artillery fired 8,875,000 rounds in action but only 8,400 of them came from the far side of the Atlantic.

LIAISON 1918

W HEN 4 Marine Brigade neared the line, Brigadier-General Harbord was met by a French divisional commander whom he asked for information about the position of the Germans, of the French holding the line and of the general's headquarters. He replied, 'Je ne sais pas, mon Géneral'. Together they studied the only map they had which was on a small scale and the 'hachures gave no real information as to the physical features of the ground'. According to French information Belleau Wood was not occupied by the Germans bar for an entrenched line across the north-east corner but it turned out that there were three lines of trenches. The foremost of these was just inside the edge of the wood and all three were wired, while the many large boulders with which the ground is scattered also gave excellent machine-gun positions.

After their abortive meeting with the French general, 'who did not look underfed, and there was a slight overhang that shadowed the buckle of his belt', Harbord's interpreter asked him where he was going. 'A happy smile lighted up the General's stern face as he replied, "La soupe!"'

Azincourt and Tramecourt villages were surrounded by woods with an open space between them which widened to the north west. This 'funnel' was closed at the narrowest part by the wooden stakes of the British archers.

CRÉCY AND AGINCOURT

The English occupied the low ridge between Crécy and Wadicourt, with their backs to the evening sun. The French advance from Marcheville took them across the Maye, into the Vallée des Clercs.

Wadicourt

River Maye

Crécy-en-Ponthieu

Estrées-les-Crécy

Forêt Domaniale de Crécy

Marcheville

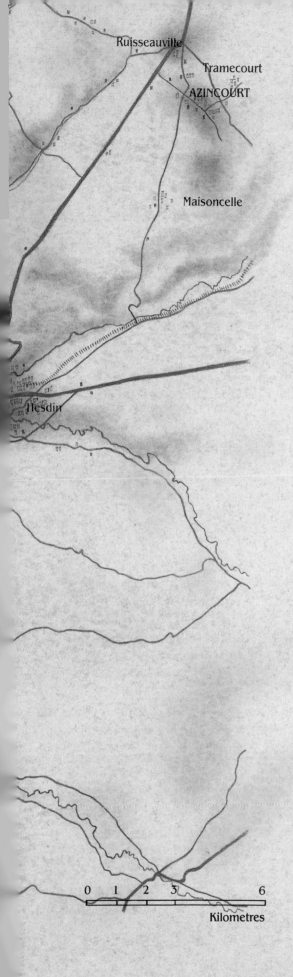

Ruisseauville

Tramecourt

AZINCOURT

Maisoncelle

Hesdin

0 1 2 3   6

Kilometres

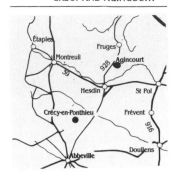

Étaples

Fruges

Montreuil

Agincourt

Hesdin

St Pol

Crécy-en-Ponthieu

Prévent

Abbeville

Doullens

The attractive old town of Hesdin, with its old walls, cobbled streets and pleasant market-place makes a convenient base for visiting the sites of both Crécy and Agincourt.

The village of Crécy-en-Ponthieu lies some 13 miles (21km) south of Hesdin. The site of the battlefield is ½ mile (1km) north of the village on the Wadicourt road. The site of the windmill where King Edward stationed himself is on the right-hand side of the road, and the view-tower provides a fine panorama of the field of battle.

The site of the Agincourt battlefield lies about 7 miles (12km) north of Hesdin, just off the D928 near the village of Azincourt which has a museum, café and bar. The road from here to Tramecourt marks the line of the English army and the area of the battlefield has changed very little. Notice boards placed at strategic points indicate the plan of events so it is relatively easy to trace the course of the battle. A simple cross marks the French communal grave. During July and August a museum exploring the history of the battle can be visited (open by appointment only during the rest of the year).

The nearby village of Maisoncelle is where Henry V made his famous St Crispin's Eve speech. (If travelling via Le Havre it might also be opportune to visit the remains of the old ramparts at Harfleur, scene of Henry's siege.)

IN 1328 CHARLES IV OF FRANCE died and with him the long line of kings of the House of Capet. He was succeeded by his cousin Philip de Valois, known as Philip VI. There was a nearer heir, the son of the late king's sister, but he was excluded on the reasonable ground that he was King Edward III of England, a neighbouring but constantly hostile realm. While making it clear that he had a better title, Edward did not press his claim and no one at the time raised the question of whether the French crown could pass in the female line. It was to be some years before the somewhat suspect 'Salic Law' came to be mentioned.

The Hundred Years War started as a trade dispute. England and Flanders were economically dependent upon each other · England produced wool which Flanders turned into cloth but Flanders was a French county whose aristocracy was loyal to Philip VI and constantly interfered with the wool trade until, determined to bring matters to a head, Edward placed an embargo on the export of wool. The rich burghers of Flanders, their prosperity threatened, replied by driving out their Francophil count and called on England for help which was readily given since the French had imprisoned Englishmen. There were, however, Flemings who had qualms about taking part in a revolt against their lawful sovereign and, to quiet their scruples, Edward declared that, by right of inheritance, he was the lawful king of France. The Kings of England therefore adopted the title of King of France from 1337 to 1802.

The war in Flanders was indecisive since the Flemings with their neighbours and allies, the Hainaulters and Brabaçons showed themselves less than keen on serious fighting but the Anglo-French struggle became widespread notably in Gascony, where the English crown still had large possessions, and in Brittany, where a disputed succession to the dukedom found the French supporting one candidate and the English another. English intervention in all these theatres was made easier by their overwhelming naval victory at Sluys (24 June 1340) on a site which is now substantially inland in Holland. There was also a prophetic victory won by the English against impossible odds at Morlaix (30 September 1342) which retrieved an almost impossible situation for the pro-English party in Brittany.

On the face of it England, with a population of less than four million and involved in almost continual warfare on her Scottish frontier, was in a poor position to challenge France, culturally and militarily the first power in Europe with a population of ten million. England's chance lay in her more advanced military organization. The disastrous caperings of the knights of Edward II at Bannockburn (1314) had shown the weakness of an army based on feudal knight service and a reluctant militia; in its place Edward III created a more permanent force, regularly paid and serving under contract (indenture). At the same time he turned away from the idea that battles should be decided by heavily armoured horsemen bashing away at each other with lances, swords or maces. Such hand-to-hand combat was always most likely to end in favour of the larger army and, in any continental war, the English army was almost certain to be the smaller one. Edward preferred to deal with his enemies before they were able to get into close combat and this could best be achieved by employing archers who were armed with the longbow, a weapon which was first brought to prominence by the Welsh but, by the fourteenth century, was entirely in English hands - the Welsh having by then been relegated to the role of spearmen.

The six-foot longbow was the most effective weapon of war to be used before the second half of the nineteenth century. A trained archer could fire up to a dozen aimed arrows a minute to an effective range (meaning that it would go through chainmail and well into the body) of two hundred and fifty yards. By contrast the muskets used at Waterloo would fire three to four aimed rounds a minute to an effective range of less than a hundred yards. The yard-long arrows were, in the fourteenth century, fitted

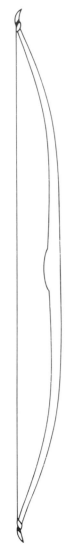

The six-foot longbow was the most effective weapon of war devised before the middle of the 19th century. It could fire twelve arrows a minute and penetrate chain-mail at 250 yards, but it required a supremely fit archer.

MC

Ferdinand Sere del.

with a barbed point so that the most effective way of extracting them from a wound was to push them on through the body. It had two drawbacks. The first was ammunition supply. An archer could carry about three dozen arrows and, though reserves were carried in the baggage train, these were not readily available in the heat of battle and, during any lull in the fighting the archers would have to dash forward and wrench arrows already fired from the bodies of the dead and wounded. The second drawback was the difficulty of shooting with a bow which required a seventy-pound pull, so that the strength and stamina of the archer were under constant strain.

It had been found, and proved at Morlaix, that the best way of deploying archers was to form them into hollow wedges, *herces*, projecting forward from the main line of battle which was formed by men-at-arms (armoured swordsmen) who, in Edward's army, usually fought dismounted. Any assault on this line would find itself taken in flank by the *herces*. To give mobility Edward had instituted mounted archers and their value can be assessed by the fact that they were paid sixpence ($2\frac{1}{2}$p) a day while spearmen had twopence (1p) and even earls received only six shillings and eightpence (33p).

While the English were pinning their faith to missile tactics, the French clung to the old-fashioned shock tactics of trying to beat a hole through the enemy's line by charging it with a mass of armoured knights supported by mercenaries and a large, ill-trained and partially armed militia. They too had their missile troops in the form of Genoese mercenaries armed with the cross-bow. While this could out-range the longbow and fired a heavier missile - a four-sided dart known as a quarrel - it was less accurate and so slow to load that three rounds in two minutes would be a good rate of fire. It was also cumbersome, weighing twenty pounds.

MEPL

Edward III, King of England, quartering the arms of both England and France on the surcoat worn over his armour.

87

Apart from the Genoese, who were hardened professional troops, the chief want of the French army was discipline, the knights being notably independently minded and, as French sources noted, the army plundered its own country more thoroughly than the invading English.

For 1346 Edward planned a concentric attack on Paris with one thrust being launched, largely by the allies, from Flanders and the other from the coast of Normandy. This last was to be executed by an English army, with Welsh and Irish mercenaries, of about 15,000 men including 4,000 men-at-arms and 6,000 archers. A well-prepared cover plan gave the French, and the troops themselves, the idea that the expeditionary force was to land in Gascony and, despite contrary winds which held fleet and army weather-bound at Portsmouth through May and June, complete surprise was achieved when they landed at St Vaast on the east side of the Cotentin peninsula (about twelve miles north of the right flank of what was to be *UTAH* beach on 6 June 1944) on 12 July. From there they marched to Caen, which they stormed on 27 July, and then headed for Paris. By this time the French were alerted and King Philip had a large army at Rouen on 2 August, on which day Edward was at Lisieux.

The attack on Caen, 27 July 1346.

BNSP

The other attack from Flanders proved disappointing, so the idea of marching on Paris had to be dropped and the English problem became how to join the Flemish allies despite a greatly superior army and two major river lines barring their way. The first obstacle, the Seine, proved well defended at all crossing points so that Edward had to move as far east as Poissy, now almost a suburb of the capital, and draw off the French by a demonstration against Paris. The Seine safely crossed, the English raced for the Somme only to find Philip and his army in Amiens before them. Attempts to find a crossing downstream from that city were just as unsuccessful as those at the same bridges by the Queen's Bays on 24 May 1940; the situation would have been desperate had not a French traitor, Gobin Agache, revealed the existence of a way across the Somme, then uncanalized and tidal, from the village of Saigneville below Abbeville.* To commit the whole army to a ford, knee-deep even at dead low tide and two thousand yards long, was a desperate venture but, with a large part of the French army pursuing them and having reached Airanes, there was no alternative. On 24 August the army started to cross as soon as the tide fell sufficiently, the vanguard of archers being able to advance on a front of eleven men. A French detachment of cross-bowmen and men-at-arms held the north bank and the Genoese inflicted losses on the archers who were not able to open fire until almost clear of the water for fear of wetting their bowstrings. Once they could shoot they quickly overcame the defensive fire of the cross-bows and then opened their ranks to allow men-at-arms to splash forward and engage the French horsemen, with the waters of the Somme up to the bellies of the horses. The defenders were shepherded away towards Abbeville and the whole English army crossed. The main French force arrived in time to capture a few baggage wagons but found the tide rising again. They fell back to Abbeville.

The ford was known at the time and referred to by historians as Blanchetaque but this name does not appear on modern French maps. There is a track leading north from Saigneville which coincides with another beyond the Canal Maritime D'Abbeville and reaches the railway about a mile north west of Port-le-Grand. This may well represent the line of the ford.

The clearing at Agincourt.

The Campaign of Edward III

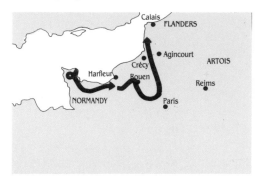

Meanwhile Edward pushed on northward to the south side of the Forest of Crécy and it seems to have been then, with his retreat secure, that he decided to offer battle. His confidence had been greatly restored by the miraculous forcing of the Somme and his army, disheartened by their long retreat, were as anxious to fight as, centuries later, Moore's men were on their weary road to Corunna. On the north side of the forest Edward found an ideal defensive position just beyond the little River Maye, and on 25 August the army marched there, spending the night near the little village of Crécy-en-Ponthieu.

The main road from Abbeville to Hesdin (D928) then ran further west than it now does, passing through Marcheville and almost midway between the villages of Crécy and Estrées. After crossing the Maye on this line there is on the left a re-entrant, now disfigured by a factory at the southern end, known as the Vallée des Clercs. To the west is a ridge which joins the villages of Crécy and Wadicourt and it was on this ridge that Edward deployed his army. it gave a front of about two thousand yards, rather long for the twelve or thirteen thousand men available but it is broken in the centre for about 350 yards by three terraces, one behind the other. These terraces, almost certainly strip lynchets *(raidillons)*, would be impassable to armoured horsemen and could be guarded by some Welsh spearmen. On either side of them were deployed one of the army's three divisions (battles), that on the right being commanded by the Prince of Wales (who may or may not have worn black armour*); that on the left by the Constable, the Earl of Northampton. The third 'battle' was in reserve behind the Crécy-Wadicourt road under command of the king. Edward stationed himself by a windmill on the spur above Crécy village. (The site of this windmill is now marked by a concrete transformer hut.) The two formed 'battles' were flanked by *herces* of archers.

The army was in line by dawn but for many hours there was no sign of the French who initially had been under the impression that the English were seeking to re-embark at Le Crotoy at the mouth of the Somme. It was not until well after they had eaten a cooked midday meal and endured a heavy shower of rain that, at about 4 pm, the watchers by the windmill saw the French vanguard, the Genoese cross-bowmen, start to appear on the road from Marcheville. These probably did not see the English until they were across the Maye and at that stage Philip very wisely gave the order to halt. His army was probably about forty thousand strong but he was faced with the tricky problem of getting the long column across the river and deployed through an angle of ninety degrees to face the enemy. To do this required planning and precise orders but French discipline was not equal to the occasion. The Genoese duly halted but the men-at-arms behind them insisted on pushing to the front and propelled the cross-bowmen forward. Seeing no alternative, the Genoese set out to attack the Prince of Wales' division, firing a few quarrels as they advanced. They got to within a hundred and fifty yards of their enemy who made no response until, on the order being given, the archers of

* The nickname 'Black Prince' is almost certainly of later date and was not used in writing until 1569.

The Battle of Crécy

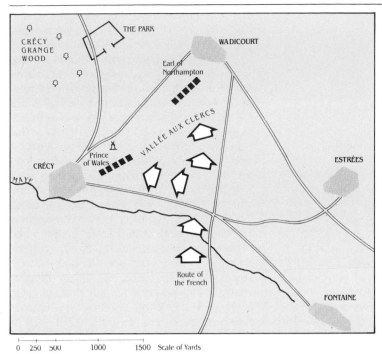

CRÉCY GRANGE WOOD

THE PARK

WADICOURT

Earl of Northampton

VALLÉÉ AUX CLERCS

Prince of Wales

CRÉCY

MAYE

ESTRÉES

Route of the French

FONTAINE

0   250   500   1000   1500   Scale of Yards

the English right, some two thousand of them, opened fire. At even a moderate rate of fire the Genoese would have had to endure about twelve thousand arrows fired at short range in the first minute. To complete the discomfiture of their enemies, the English shot at them with their secret weapons, three new cannon, the first to be used in the field (see page 98). It is no discredit to the Genoese that they broke and ran - only to find behind them the leading division of mounted men-at-arms led by the Conte d'Alençon who, convinced that they were shamefully deserting, attacked them, receiving a few quarrels in exchange. D'Alençon then pressed on to attack the Prince of Wales' line. Outflanked by the archers, who disabled horses and riders, they suffered terrible losses and failed to get to grips with the English men-at-arms who, interspersed with spearmen, were fighting on foot. The dispersal of the Genoese gave the English the monopoly of missile weapons and for the rest of the battle the French had to do their best to manoeuvre into hand-to-hand combat with one or both of the English 'battles'. Despite some fifteen charges, all pressed with the utmost bravery, they failed though at times the margin was narrow. At one stage Sir Godfrey Harcourt, right-hand man to the Prince of Wales, was so concerned at the danger to that division that he sent to the king and to the constable for reinforcements. The latter obliged with a limited counter-attack across the front of the strip lynchets but the king, believing the situation was in hand, replied immortally, 'Let the boy win his spurs'. He nevertheless sent down a small body of knights led by that battling prelate, the Bishop of Durham. Night fell but the French continued their onslaughts by moonlight. Nothing could stop the fire of the archers and finally the spirit of the attackers gave way and the remains of the French army drifted off, most making for their homes. They had given everything and failed. Very wisely Edward forbade pursuit there was no solid body to pursue - and his army slept where they had fought and without supper. In the days that followed, the corpses of 1,542 French knights and men-at-arms were counted and buried. No one bothered to count the bodies of the mercenaries and militiamen but the total number of French dead may have been as many as ten thousand. English casualties were trifling, though (as with the French) no reliable figure can be found. The army went on to besiege Calais which stood an eleven-month siege before surrendering to become, for two centuries, an English town.

A cross-bowman drawing his bow, a time-wasting performance which put the Genoese cross-bowmen at a fatal disadvantage to the English archers.

Ten years after Crécy, on 19 September 1356, the Prince of Wales again thrashed a French army, this time at Poitiers, capturing two thousand French knights and King John of France. After King Edward had raided up to the gates of Paris, peace was made under which England obtained a vast extension to her *Gascon possession*, Calais and the county of Ponthieu, which included Crécy. She had, in fact, grabbed too much of France and exhausted herself in doing so. Over the next fifty years, aided by the incompetence of Richard II and the Black Death, she lost most of it.

The Anglo-French war, however, rambled on until in 1412, there came to the throne an energetic young king of twenty-five, Henry V. Though a far less sympathetic character than William Shakespeare depicted him, Henry was a born leader and saw that the best way of making his subjects forget the murky and divisive character of their history since the accession of Richard II was a successful invasion of France. Although Edward had specifically renounced his claim to the French crown, Henry reasserted it and landed an army with two thousand men-at-arms, eight thousand archers and sixty-five gunners near Harfleur on 14 August. He took the port on 22 September after a bombardment which drove the garrison to capitulate. By that time an epidemic of dysentry had reduced the army's strength and, after leaving a garrison for Harfleur, the seven thousand men available for the field army were insufficient for a march on Paris. A council of war recommended that the army should be shipped home for the winter, but Henry decided to march on Calais, using the same ford across the Somme that had been found by Edward III. It was a bold, possibly foolhardy decision since the French, although in some confusion, could produce a very large army of brave men who had learned much from Crécy and Poitiers. In fact they had already massed a large force, perhaps fourteen thousand men, at Rouen where they would be on the flank of Henry's march.

Certainly the French had learned about the ford at Saigneville and when the English approached it on 13 October it was strongly held. The army therefore moved eastward, spending the night of 13-14 October at Hangest where, on 5 June 1940, Rommel was to get his tanks across the river. Henry, however, was not so fortunate as to find a bridge that was both intact and unguarded, as Rommel was to do, and it was not until the army had passed both

Amiens and Péronne that he found a possible crossing place near the village of Voyennes, east of Nesle. On the way they learned from prisoners that the French horsemen were planning to make their main attack against the archers and, on Henry's orders, each archer cut himself a hefty six-foot stake which he sharpened at each end so that an instant barricade against cavalry could be formed.

Once across the River Somme, the army was approached by three French heralds, one of whom, like Shakespeare's herald, was called Mountjoye. They enquired which road Henry was intending to take so that their army could 'meet thee to fight thee, and be revenged for thy conduct'. The king replied, 'Straight to Calais, and if our enemies try to disturb us in our journey, it will not be without the utmost peril'. He then dismissed them with a purse containing a hundred gold crowns apiece. The army then circled round the east of Péronne and marched across the Somme battlefields of 1916 to Albert. For some unaccountable reason the French, who had been across their route, fell back on Bapaume and even then did not, as Henry feared, attempt an attack from the flank. The English, dispirited and with sickness increasing in the army, plodded on, short of food and weary; they were kept going mainly by their confidence in the king. No one obstructed their march as they skirted Doullens, went through Frévent and reached the village of Maisoncelle, north east of Hesdin. As they were bivouacking, their scouts found the enemy 'a terrible multitude' across their path between the villages of Tramecourt and Agincourt.* It was 24 October, the eve of the Feast of Saint Crispin.

* So spelled at the time. The modern version as Azincourt evolved later.

The Campaign of Henry V

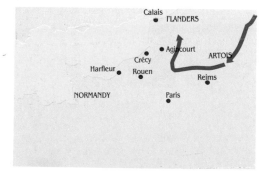

Henry V, King of England, a hard and unromantic character but a born leader.

Phase 1

Dawn 25 October 1415. Opposing armies line up. The French do not advance. The English move within bow-shot. When the bowmen open fire, the French cavalry attacks but is halted by arrows.

Phase 2

The mass of French Infantry moves forward. With the onslaught of the English arrows their formation becomes crowded and disorganized. English archers advance on the flanks. English men at arms fight the French to a halt.

Phase 3

With the collision of the two forces the French are jammed together with no room to wield their weapons. They are killed by English arrows or fall in their heavy armour and suffocate in the press.

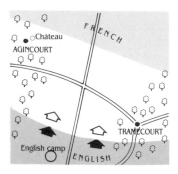
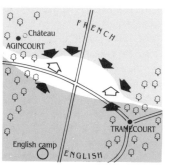
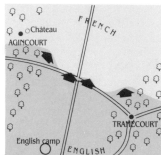

The Battle of Agincourt

Armoured cavalry were excellent against an unsteady enemy but the horse at best was vulnerable and a fallen knight could not get to his feet unaided.

The French had learned something from Crécy and Poitiers but they had still to learn discipline. They had chosen a fine defensive position and their commanders intended to hold it and let the English try to force a way through. They had no need to move since it was the English who needed to extricate themselves from an impossible position. As it happened, King Henry spent much of the night sending messages through heralds in an attempt to buy his way out, even offering to give up Harfleur.

Both Tramecourt and Agincourt were, and still are, hidden in woods but between these woods is an open space, then newly sewn with wheat, about 950 yards across. Through this ran the road to Calais, now the minor road to Ruisseauville. At the northern end the woods open out to form a funnel and it was across the mouth of this funnel, about 1,200 yards wide, that the French army, which probably numbered about 25,000 men*, was drawn up. They were deployed into three lines, each about three deep but greatly disordered, the first two lines being dismounted men-at-arms, the third line being on horseback. Bodies of cavalry were on each flank and there were a few cannon and some archers and cross-bowmen fitted in where space could be found, mostly between the second and third lines.

The English army, about six thousand strong of whom over four thousand were archers, formed up in a single line across the southern end of the clearing. The men-at-arms, dismounted, were in three divisions, the king commanding in the centre. There were *herces* of archers on the flanks of each division. On the extreme ends of the line were additional bodies of archers, each about nine hundred strong whose outer flanks were echeloned forward. There were too few men to allow a reserve.

Soon after dawn on 25 October both armies were formed for battle about a thousand yards apart but for four hours nothing

* At this period all calculation of the strength of armies is largely guesswork. The French army at Agincourt has been variously estimated at between 5 and 200,000. 25,000 seems to be a reasonable estimate.

Phase 4

A small French force attack the English camp. This threat from front and rear leads Henry to order the execution of all prisoners. However, this attack proves to be shortlived and soon the French, defeated, leave the field.

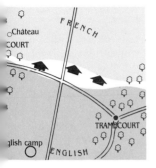

happened - except in the French lines where more and more men-at-arms tried to force their way into the front rank, resulting in much jostling and overcrowding. At last King Henry saw that he must make the first move and gave the order *'Advance Banner!'* whereupon his army moved forward slowly, crossed the Tramecourt-Agincourt track and halted some two hundred yards beyond. Then the archers drove their pointed stakes into the ground to form a hedge pointing at an angle of 45 degrees towards the enemy and started a slow fire of arrows towards the French. It was at a range of about three hundred yards, beyond their most effective range but it was enough to stir the enemy into action.

The mounted squadrons on the French wings came forward and tried to ride down the flanking archers. Those who escaped the arrows found that their horses would not face the *abatis* of stakes and as they turned away, goaded by arrows, they rode into and through the first line of men-at-arms who were advancing behind them. These were moving very slowly since they were wearing plate-armour (much heavier than the chainmail of Crécy) and were increasingly getting in each others' way. The French line, which had been drawn up on a front of 1,200 yards and had already been swollen by eager aspirants from the rear lines, was trying to force itself into a width of 900 yards and the crush was so great that the men-at-arms could scarcely wield their swords. Not that they had much opportunity to do so since, apart from the storm of arrows, each man had difficulty in keeping his feet. A heavy storm overnight had made the ground treacherous for heavily armoured infantrymen and when a man fell he was unable to regain his feet without assistance which, in the circumstances, was not forthcoming.

Soon the ground was littered with armoured figures, dead, wounded or merely unable to rise, and many of the archers dashed forward to recover their arrows and, with their swords and daggers, to finish off, or merely wrench the armour from the fallen. Into this scene of confusion stumbled the second French line, meeting the same fate as their predecessors when the English men-at-arms, led by the king, came forward to deal with them over the bodies of the first line. After half an hour's fighting the English were protected by a barrier of bodies so substantial that the third, mounted, French line saw that there was no object to be gained by charging. The English set about disentangling the live prisoners from the corpses and securing them in the hope of ransom.

In this very short time the French had been totally defeated - with minimal loss, a few hundred, to the English. The most prominent loss was that of the king's uncle, the Duke of York, who died, unwounded, when he tripped over and fell, only to be suffocated by several fully armoured French knights falling on top of him.

There was a short and tragic epilogue to the battle. The Duke of Brabant, who had been attending a christening party, arrived late for the battle with a small band of followers. Finding the third French line standing by contemplating the wreck of the first two lines, he urged them forward and led them into a futile, hopeless attack but, by coincidence, three French knights and some peasants simultaneously fell on the lightly guarded baggage train in the English rear and killed the escort. Faced thus with a mounted attack in front and an onslaught of unknown strength behind, King Henry felt obliged to order the killing of the prisoners and many were cut down in cold blood before the situation on both fronts was stabilized. Contemporary French writers condemned Brabant's attack and the cowardly assault on the baggage but for a long time afterwards Frenchmen referred to Henry V as 'Cut-throat'.

The total French loss at Agincourt cannot be established; it is known that 5,800 bodies were buried in three large pits but this was far short of the total casualty figure. The survivors of the French army disbanded themselves as they had done after Crécy. The English army, much encumbered with booty despite the king's orders, marched on to Calais.

THE PRINCE OF WALES' FEATHERS

ABOUT a mile from the *Vallée des Clercs* a cross on a modern plinth stands beside the road from Crécy to Fontaine. It is dedicated to the memory of King John of Bohemia, a son of the Count of Luxembourg, who had married the heiress to the Bohemian throne and was crowned king in 1311. He had been a notably successful general both in the Hapsburg lands and in Italy and, his wife having died, married a sister of Philip V. Despite becoming blind in 1337 he led a contingent of Luxembourgeois soldiers in the campaign of 1346. Tradition has it that he insisted on charging at Crécy, his horse being led into battle by four of his knights and that the bodies of all five horses and riders were found roped together after the battle was over. If this is true he cannot have died, as is alleged, at the site of the cross; this was well beyond arrow range and King Edward permitted no pursuit after the battle. He was buried with full honours in the presence of King Edward and the Prince of Wales adopted his crest of three ostrich feathers which has been borne by the Prince of Wales ever since. While the ostrich is generally thought of as a South African bird and thus unlikely to occur in medieval Europe, it is still to be found in Tunisia, Algeria and the Sudan. Ostriches had been imported from Mauretania for many centuries and there is a record of one being seen walking about Rome in the year 200 BC.

Edward, Prince of Wales (known later as the Black Prince) shown in effigy. His magnificent armour would have been used in jousting rather than in battle.

The skill of the English longbowmen was unparalleled in western Europe.

BM

THE MASSACRE OF THE PRISONERS

MANY later accounts castigate Henry for his orders to kill the prisoners but at the time even the French recognized that the order was dictated by military necessity and placed the blame on the Duke of Brabant since, futile as his attack was, his force still outnumbered the English army.

The laws of war, as they had been most recently formulated (1387) by a French abbot, Honoré Bonet, laid down that, *'If a knight, captain or champion takes another in battle, he may freely kill him, but if he were to lead him to his house and then, without further reason, kill him, I consider that he would have to answer for it before judgment.'*

There were recent precedents for killing prisoners on grounds of military necessity. In 1396 a French-commanded Franco-Hungarian army had killed a thousand Turkish and Bulgarian prisoners since they had insufficient men to guard them during the imminent battle of Nicopolis with Sultan Bajazet's Turkish army. Eleven years before that, English mercenaries were fighting for King João I of Portugal at the battle of Aljubarotta. One Spanish assault had been repulsed but when a second threatened, João ordered the prisoners to be killed rather than have to spare guards for them. The order was obeyed but only with the greatest reluctance and murmurs of *'So perish four hundred thousand francs'.*

That, of course, was the point. No doubt there were humanitarian objections to killing prisoners but there were financial reasons for sparing them. The very fact that, under the new military system, the soldiers were entitled to the share of *Gaignes de Guerre* (see page 99) meant that they, and above all the king who took the largest share, would be thoroughly opposed to killing a rich source of income. Moreover the number of prisoners killed must have been exaggerated since 1,500 prisoners survived the battle. Many of them were released on the spot on, according to Froissart, *'their own undertaking to come to Bordeaux with their ransom money before Christmas'.* There were also a number of knights taken at Harfleur who were riding with the English army while their ransoms were arranged. On the night before the battle they were released on the understanding that, in the unlikely event of the English winning, they would return to pay their dues, which they did.

The important prisoners who passed into the king's custody, Marshal Boucicault and the Dukes of Bourbon and Orleans, proved a sad disappointment since their ransoms were placed so high that France, which was still recovering from the 1.6 million gold crowns paid to recover King John after Poitiers, was quite unable to find the money. Boucicault and Bourbon died in England and Orleans was eventually sent back to France on giving his word never to serve against England again. In the meantime he had lived in great luxury at the king's expense for twenty-one years.

THE GUNS OF CRÉCY

THERE is a good deal of evidence, though not conclusive, that the English had cannon at Crécy. This would be the first use of field guns as opposed to siege weapons as there is little doubt that the latter were used by both sides when Tournai was besieged in 1340. Certainly Edward III had ordered guns to be prepared in 1339 and ordered more, together with metal shot for them, for the 1346 expedition. Cannon-balls, both of iron and stone, have been found on the battlefield which does not seem

to have been fought over at any other time. They varied between 3-inch and 3.6-inch in calibre and weighed between $1\frac{1}{4}$ and $1\frac{3}{4}$ pounds.

Such early cannon were made by welding together strips of iron and binding them by shrinking white-hot iron hoops over them. A breech was made by hollowing out an iron casting which fitted over the end of the composite tube. Recoil was prevented, or at least minimized, by erecting a wall of stout wooden planks behind the breech. The muzzle was supported on wedges and the whole was transported on a cart. It seems probable that such a contraption would be at least as dangerous to its own gunners as to the enemy but it might have had some value in frightening the horses, especially as the English habitually fought dismounted.

A contemporary recipe for gunpowder, rediscovered in the West about 1320, laid down:

12 pounds of live sulphur, 2 pounds of willow charcoal, 6 pounds of saltpetre, if they be well ground on a slab of marble, then sift the powder through a fine kerchief.

Henry V took cannon with him on the expedition of 1415 but, intending to travel light to Calais, left them with the garrison of Harfleur. At Agincourt the French discharged a few pieces, ineffectively, early in the battle but their undisciplined advance obscured the field of fire and they were not fired again.

THE HELMET OF HENRY V

ABOVE the tomb of Edward the Confessor in Westminster Abbey hang the helmet and sword that Henry V used at Agincourt. Strictly, it is a bascinet rather than a helmet since helmets had crests on the top and were used only for jousting. At Agincourt it was surrounded by a crown - actually more of a coronet - to identify the king. A party of eighteen French knights, led by Brunelet de Masiguehen and Ganiot de Bournoville, vowed that they would fight their way to the king and strike the crown from his head. All died in the attempt but one got close enough to slice a fleuron from the circlet and, as can still be seen, to dent the top of the helmet.

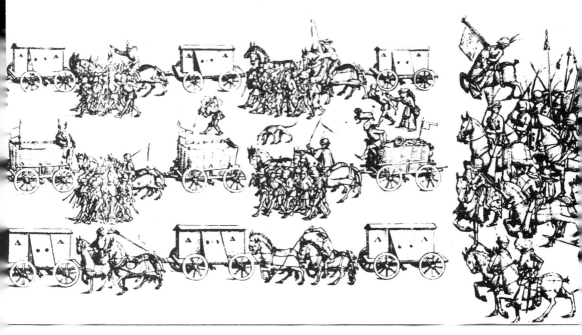

A fifteenth-century army on the move.

RAISING AN ARMY

THE English success at Crécy, Poitiers and Agincourt derived partly from better leadership but more from military professionalism. They had learned that feudal duty, however punctiliously performed, was no substitute for good order and military discipline. Henry V and Edward III both formed their expeditionary forces from men who, whatever their rank, served under contract for a settled period and a fixed rate of pay. Men-at-arms, often wrongly equated with knights, received a shilling (5p) a day, twice as much as a mounted archer, but they had out of that to support at least one horse, as well as a page who helped them into their armour and was expected to be available to hoist them back on to their horses, or to their feet, if they fell over. The Bishop of Durham was given the same pay as an earl but barons received only four shillings (20p) a day while the Prince of Wales was paid a full pound. This was not the whole of the possible income of a soldier. The English kings were unfashionably strict about loot, especially if it came from churches, but they acknowledged that there was legitimate booty to be had - *Gaignes de Guerre* - and they contracted to receive one third of 'all gold, silver and jewels exceeding the value of ten marks' (1 mark = 6s 8d or 33p) from each of their captains, just as the captains received one third of the value of the booty from each of their subordinates. Greatest profit came from prisoners, especially if they were rich. If poor they might, if

they were lucky, be turned loose because the maintenance of a prisoner was traditionally the responsibility of his captor. The ransom of a knight was calculated as a year of his usual income. Archers were £2 a head. When Geoffrey Chaucer was captured in 1359 while acting as secretary to the Duke of Clarence he cost his employer £15 to reclaim. As with the valuables, one third of all such ransoms went to the king.

A different system applied for very important prisoners. In one contract made by Henry V a special clause dealt with the capture of, 'The Adversary of France* or any of his sons, nephews, uncles or cousins-germans, or any King of any Kingdom;** or his lieutenant, or other chieftain, having command from the said Adversary of France'.

In such cases the prisoner reverted to the king's custody and the king made 'reasonable arrangement' with the captor. When David II of Scotland was captured at Neville's Cross, Edward obtained a ransom of £66,000. The captor, John Coupland, received promotion to knight-banneret and an annuity of £500.

---

* Since Henry claimed to be King of France himself, he had to use this clumsy title to describe the actual incumbent of the French throne.

** At Crécy there had been in the French army not only the King of Bohemia but the exiled King David II of Scotland and Charles the Bad, King of Navarre.

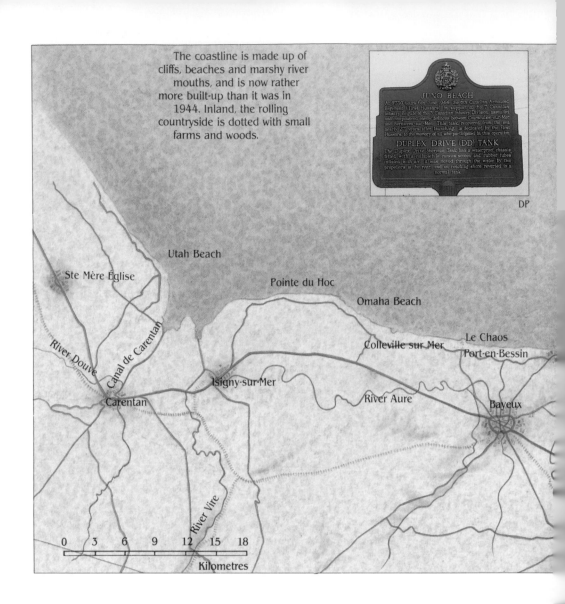

The coastline is made up of cliffs, beaches and marshy river mouths, and is now rather more built-up than it was in 1944. Inland, the rolling countryside is dotted with small farms and woods.

JUNO BEACH

At 0750 hours 6th June 1944, the 6th Canadian Armoured Regiment (First Hussars) in support of the 7 Canadian Infantry Brigade of the 3rd Canadian Infantry Division assaulted and overpowered enemy defences between Courseulles-sur-Mer and Bernieres-sur-Mer. This tank, recovered from the sea nearly 27 years after launching, is dedicated by the First Hussars to the memory of all who participated in this operation.

DUPLEX DRIVE (DD) TANK

The Duplex Drive Sherman Tank had a waterproof chassis fitted with a collapsible canvas screen and rubber tubes inflated with air. It was moved through the water by two propellers at the rear and on reaching shore reverted to a normal tank.

DP

Utah Beach
Ste Mère Église
Pointe du Hoc
Omaha Beach
River Douve
Canal de Carentan
Le Chaos
Colleville sur Mer
Port-en-Bessin
Isigny-sur-Mer
River Aure
Carentan
Bayeux
River Vire

0   3   6   9   12   15   18
Kilometres

NORM

(RIGHT) UTAH beach today.

(FAR RIGHT) The harbour at Grandcamp-Maisy, near Pointe du Hoc.

DP

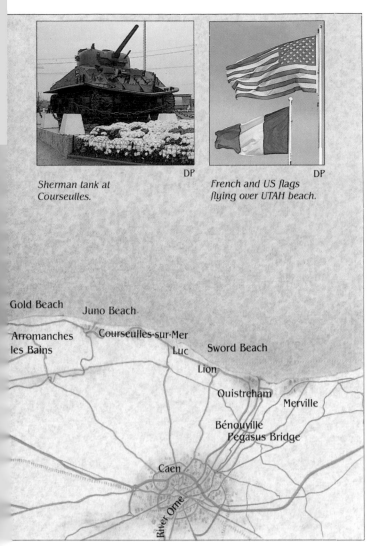

Sherman tank at
Courseulles.

French and US flags
flying over UTAH beach.

Gold Beach
Juno Beach
Arromanches
les Bains
Courseulles-sur-Mer
Luc
Sword Beach
Lion
Ouistreham
Merville
Bénouville
Pegasus Bridge
Caen
River Orne

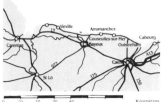

To the west is Ste Mère
Église, the first French
town liberated by
Americans in 1944. Visit
the Airborne Museum and
nearby dunes of Utah
Beach strewn with half-
submerged guns and
tanks. The N13 can be
followed towards Caen but
the D514 coast road is a
better route.

The atmosphere of war is
still strong at Pointe du
Hoc where German
bunkers may be visited
(car parking, café and
toilets) and at desolate
Omaha beach, best
viewed from the American
cemetery at Colleville-sur-
Mer (good museum, café
and toilets). Nearby the
D517 follows a stream
that served as one exit
from the beach.

East of Port-en-Bessin the
D104 leads to the German
battery, Le Chaos; gun
emplacements still house
original guns. Mulberry B
harbour can be seen at
Arromanches as well as a
panorama of the landings
and the excellent Invasion
Museum (open 9.30-11.30
and 14.00-17.30). Above
and to the east on the
D514 is a bunker with a
panorama of the beaches.

At Bayeux the British
Military Cemetery is
opposite the superb
Museum of the Battle of
Normandy. (Allow 2 hours
if you wish to visit the
Bayeux Tapestry Museum.)

Tanks, armoured cars and
anti-aircraft guns can be
seen at Courseulles-sur-
Mer and St Aubin-sur-Mer.
Pegasus Bridge, the café
Gondrée and a museum
lie south of Ouistreham.

ANDY
AND OPERATION NEPTUNE

THE BRITISH HAD PLANNED TO RETURN to the mainland continent of Europe ever since the evacuations from Dunkirk,
Cherbourg and Brest in 1940 but their lack of resources had
meant that this could be only long-term planning. The entry of
the United States into the war made such a return more feasible
and, thanks to US strategic thinking, more urgent. Nevertheless,
the disaster at Dieppe and the fact that a safe line of communication across the Atlantic was not secured until the summer of
1943 ensured that the invasion could not be mounted before
1944. Serious planning began in April 1943 and was entrusted
to an Anglo-American staff headed by Lieutenant-General F.E.
Morgan, and the simplest part of their job was deciding where
the landing should be made. The choice was limited by the effective range of the Spitfire fighter, an essential weapon in the
provision of air cover; this meant that the beaches would have to
be somewhere in between the Scheldt estuary on the east and
the Cotentin peninsula on the west. Within this arc the choice
quickly narrowed itself to two stretches of coast, the area around
Calais and Boulogne and the coast of Normandy west of the
River Orne. The first had the advantage of a shorter sea trip and
more Spitfire flying time overhead but, as well as seeming too
obvious, it had difficult beaches and no major ports within reach.
In fact, preliminary studies had opted for Normandy as early as
1942 and Morgan and his staff reaffirmed the choice.

DP

DP

*Evidence of the solidity of
the Atlantic Wall can still
be seen. These
fortifications are at Port-
en-Bessin (TOP) and east
of Arromanches (BOTTOM)*

The contribution of Morgan and his planners to the success of
NEPTUNE* can scarcely be overrated but they suffered severe
disadvantages, notably that the Combined Chiefs of Staff
insisted that they plan for no more than three divisions landing
from the sea in the first wave and two airborne divisions. This
restriction was dictated by the shortage of landing craft, a shortage largely caused by American insistence that a simultaneous
landing (Operation ANVIL) be made in the south of France. The
result was that the planners had to exclude landing on the east
coast of the Cotentin peninsula, an attack which would greatly
have facilitated the speedy capture of the supposedly vital port
of Cherbourg.

Morgan was only a planner and had no power to take execu-
tive decisions and it was unfortunate that the commanders were
not (for political reasons) appointed until December 1943,
taking up their posts in January. When Dwight D. Eisenhower was
appointed Supreme Commander and Sir Bernard Montgomery
commander of the land forces in the opening phase, both
instantly came to the conclusion that the landing force was too
small, Montgomery forthrightly declaring that it was 'not a
sound operation of war'. Both men had recently lived through
the trauma of the invasion of Sicily where the assault by seven
seaborne and two airborne divisions had barely proved sufficient to overcome German opposition on a scale far smaller
than was to be expected in Normandy. Both insisted that the
initial landing should have not less than five seaborne and three
airborne divisions and that the east coast of the Cotentin should
be included from the start. On 25 February this was eventually
agreed and entailed finding 263 additional landing craft, to say
nothing of an additional naval task force, resulting in the postponement of D-Day from early May to early June and a
three-month delay in mounting ANVIL (renamed DRAGOON).

---

* NEPTUNE was the code-word for the assault on Normandy,
ending officially on 30 June. The more commonly used OVERLORD
referred to the whole allied attack on north-west Europe.

Allied Landings, 6 June 1944

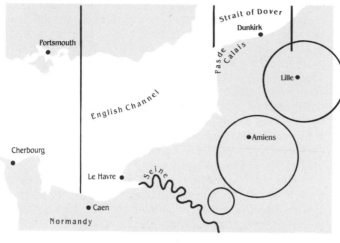

Intended landing areas (weaker in defence than Pas de Calais). Also, main embarkation ports in England further away from German spy-plane activity.

Allies intent on misleading Germans that invasion will occur in this area

Areas heavily bombed by allies prior to 6 June 1944

DP   DP

Since Eisenhower was heavily committed to *ANVIL* as a simultaneous operation, it was Montgomery who should have the main credit for the vital strengthening of *NEPTUNE*. His handling of the whole Normandy battle has been the target of much criticism but it is extremely doubtful if any other allied commander could have won that campaign. Without his strengthening of the initial assault, the securing of the first lodgement would probably have failed and, if he made mistakes in the subsequent fighting, they were few and nugatory. His errors were in speech and writing and, for a man with a genius for public relations, it is astonishing how frequently he managed to say the wrong thing. Not only did he succeed in antagonizing every American commander by his arrogance, he earned the lasting hatred of all the allied air commanders by deliberately misleading them in the planning stage. He assured them that he could quickly capture the airfields south of Caen (which they considered badly needed) although he knew that there was scant chance of this happening. This was done because he realized that the airmen would never agree to his plan unless he made this promise; he believed, rightly as it turned out, that they would be able to provide air cover mainly based in England.

On all 20th-century battlefields, danger still lurks. This warning sign is close to the memorial at Pointe du Hoc.

His basic plan, from which he never departed, was to hold the main German strength with the British army in the east, the side from which reinforcements had to come, so as to allow the Americans to break out in the west. Though he may not have realized it, he was adopting the scheme of one of Marlborough's battles, based on the idea that, rightly or wrongly, it was the British troops that the enemy most feared. At Ramilles (1706) Marlborough had concentrated all his redcoats on his right, drawing the main French strength to that flank. The allies were thus able to break through on the left and centre. Montgomery's plan was (with the flanks reversed) identical, as he had made clear from the start. As early as January 1944 he had written, *The British Army will operate to the south to prevent any interference with the American Army from the east'*. In the final orders for *NEPTUNE* he gave the British task as *'to protect the eastern flank of the First US Army'*. The success of this gambit is shown by the fact that, even when all the German reserves had joined the battle, there were always three times as many German tanks opposing the British as faced the Americans.

Montgomery's other great contribution to the mounting of the assault was the confidence he exuded and communicated to the troops. Others were less certain. Churchill had spoken privately of *'Channel tides running red with Allied blood'*. The US Deputy Commander (Air) considered the invasion plan as a *'highly dubious operation'*; even Sir Alan Brooke, Montgomery's friend and patron, wrote in his diary, *'It may be the most ghastly disaster of the whole war.... A sudden storm might wreck it all'*. With an operation of such complexity, a storm or even relatively few misjudgements might easily throw everything into chaos but, even more serious, was the fact (fortunately not widely realized on the Allied side) that the German tanks were markedly superior to those of the invaders. The Sherman, workhorse of the American, Canadian and British armies, was scarcely a match for the German Mark IV which was the lightest of all their battle tanks. Against the German Panthers and Tigers, the only possible opponents were the comparatively few 17-pounder Shermans known as Fireflies and even these were badly under-armoured. If the Germans could get their armoured divisions in among the beachheads at an early stage the issue would be very doubtful indeed. This last danger was averted by faults of the German command structure. In supreme command was Hitler who believed that every inch of coastline must be guarded and fought for - while insisting that no reserves could be committed to the battle without his consent. Marshal von Rundstedt, whose command covered France and Belgium, wished to have no more than a thin screen of coastal defence and massive reserves held centrally to counter-attack the landing forces when their landfall had been determined. Marshal Rommel, whose Army Group B was responsible for the north coast of France, agreed with Hitler to the extent that he believed the invasion must be smashed on the beaches but he wished the main strength available to be concentrated behind the most likely beaches and the panzer divisions to be kept well forward. His experience in Africa had shown him that, with overwhelming allied air superiority, it would be a long and difficult task to move armoured formations to the point where they were needed for an immediate counter-blow. He did gain permission to station one panzer division, 21st, near Caen but the remaining seven in France (and two in the Low Countries) were all out of reach of Normandy and could not be moved without Hitler's permission. This was the less likely

IWM

The British defiance of German aggression was depicted in this cartoon of Churchill, printed in the 'Daily Express' on 8 June 1940.

MARS

SV

PPL

RHL

Hitler, in this picture being advised by Göring, kept a very tight control on the preparations for resisting any invasion.

to be granted since, along with Rundstedt and Rommel, Hitler was convinced that the main invasion would come across the Straits of Dover and that any assault elsewhere would be a diversion. This German *idée fixe* was brilliantly nourished by a deception plan, Operation *FORTITUDE*, which led the High Command to believe that, some six weeks after the landing in Normandy, there would be a huge assault on the Pas de Calais and a smaller operation against Norway. So well was this idea fostered that Hitler, Rundstedt and Rommel all clung to it for a month after the allies were ashore in Normandy.

Nor were German forces abundant in France. It is only a slight exaggeration to say that the battle for Normandy was won on the steppes of Russia where the Germans had already suffered two million casualties. On the eastern front they had 179 divisions, while in France there were 58, of which 32 were low-grade formations suitable only for static duties In coast defence. The *Luftwaffe* had 1,700 bombers and 2,420 fighters engaged with the Russians; in France they had only 890 aircraft of all types, of which only 497 were operational on 6 June.

The German command was fatally divided. Von Rundstedt (RIGHT) was a solid, conservative soldier but his subordinate, Rommel (LEFT) was a brilliant opportunist with recent experience of fighting the allies. This dichotomy largely nullified the German advantages of superior tanks and a prepared position.

In its final form the plan for *NEPTUNE* called for five landing areas code-named, from west to east, *UTAH* (at the eastern base of the Cotentin peninsula), *OMAHA, GOLD, JUNO* and, close to the west bank of the Orne estuary, *SWORD*. This gave a total length of fifty miles of coast to be attacked and the first flight would consist of five brigade groups (or regimental combat teams), two each on *OMAHA, GOLD* and *JUNO*, one each at *UTAH* and *SWORD*.

The Allied Assault on Normandy

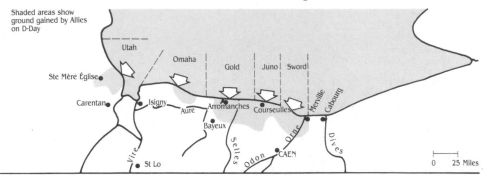

The first flight of each would consist of two battalions, preceded by amphibious (DD) tanks and assault engineers who, in the British sectors, would land in their special armoured vehicles (see page 116). This flight would be quickly followed by a third infantry battalion, tanks, artillery and, in some cases, commandos or Rangers. By the end of D-Day it was hoped to have more than ten divisions landed from the sea. In addition, the flanks were to be secured by dropping two US airborne divisions at the base of the Cotentin peninsula and 6th British Airborne on the eastern bank of the Orne north of Caen.

To get all these troops to Normandy in a single day and to supply and reinforce them once they were there required prodigious efforts from the other services. For bombardment, transport, escort, covering operations and servicing facilities, the allied navies deployed 6,939 ships. Of these 1,213 were warships*, ranging from 7 battleships and 23 cruisers to 2 midget submarines (to act as beacons for the run-in to shore). There were 4,126

IWM

Invasion forces moving off to the embarkation ports in southern England.

landing vessels of all types, including 837 tank-landing craft and 236 tank-landing ships, as well as 864 merchant ships. Apart from 14 rescue tugs, 216 other tugs were needed and there were 6 vessels for laying cross-channel cables.

* *79% of these warships were British or Canadian, 16½% American and the remainder French, Norwegian, Dutch, Polish or Greek.*

American bombers and US Army
fighter planes awaiting
their servicing prior
to flight.

IWM   IWM

The allied airforces supported the landings with 11,590 aircraft which flew 14,674 sorties on D-Day alone. This, however, was only the tip of the iceberg. In the nine weeks previously 197,000 sorties (at a cost of 1,251 aircraft and some 12,000 aircrew) had been flown and 195,000 tons of bombs dropped on targets connected with the invasion, care being taken not to indicate to the enemy where the blow was to fall. The railway system of northern France was utterly dislocated, in particular by a series of raids by Ninth US Air Force which destroyed or made impassable every one of the twenty-four bridges over the Seine between Paris and the sea. According to a *Luftwaffe* report, the German railway authorities 'are seriously considering whether it is not useless to attempt further repair work'. Northern France had, in effect, been cut in half and (as pointed out by von Rundstedt) this could presage invasion on either side of the Seine.

At 4.30 am on Monday 6 June, twenty-four hours later than he had hoped (see page 119), General Eisenhower gave the order which set the whole gigantic operation in motion. From every port and loading beach - from Milford Haven to Harwich - vessels of all sizes put to sea and headed towards the strip of coast that contained *UTAH, OMAHA, GOLD, JUNO* and *SWORD*. During the night 1,267 Lancasters, Halifaxes and Mosquitoes flew to deliver 5,267 tons of bombs on the coastal batteries behind the beaches and on other defences; meanwhile 17,000 airborne troops embarked in 1,795 aircraft and 867 gliders to start their flanking missions, led by a glider-borne party which was to seize the vital bridges north of Caen (see page 118). At 5.50 am on 6 June the great guns of the allied fleets opened on the beach defences, the destruction they wrought being added to by the 1,600 bombers of Eighth and Ninth US Airforces. As that bombardment came to an end the eight assault waves approached their allotted beaches.

Awaiting them, though largely unsuspecting, were two German infantry divisions, three coast-defence divisions and 21st Panzer; also, counting all those that could be brought to bear, there were twenty-four coastal batteries. These last, to some extent, epitomized the confusion of the German command system since most of them were manned by sailors who, when firing out to sea, were subject to naval control but came under the army when shooting on the beaches. Likewise most of the anti-aircraft guns, which were used in an anti-tank role, were subject to the *Luftwaffe*, as were a regiment of parachute troops who were in the western sector. All these troops and their weapons were in well-prepared positions. Rundstedt described the much-publicized 'Atlantic Wall' as *'largely a fake'* but, thanks to Rommel, it was formidable enough. All the batteries (coastal and field) were in concrete emplacements, heavily protected with mines and barbed wire, as were many of the infantry and machine-gun posts. The beaches had been thickly sown with obstacles designed to sink, cripple or explode landing craft, and the exits from the beaches had been so fortified that to leave the foreshore would be as difficult as to reach it. Von Rundstedt described the coast-defence divisions as being *'equipped with a hotch-potch of foreign artillery and filled with personnel from older age groups and low physical categories, plus thousands of Russians* who were a menace and a nuisance'*, but most of them, if they survived the preliminary bombardment, were prepared to fight and die where they stood. No German soldier is a pushover.

(BELOW) Concrete emplacement for heavy artillery.
(BELOW RIGHT) Pillbox camouflaged as a house.

B

B

NORMANDY
WESTERN TASK FORCE
UTAH AND OMAHA

On the extreme right of the allied onslaught everything started badly and turned out well. 82nd US Airborne Division had been ordered to secure the important road junction of Ste Mère Église and to establish a defensive front on the River Merderet. 101st Airborne had orders to take the line of the River Douve and exploit to the south to prepare for the junction through Carentan with troops on *OMAHA*. Both divisions had had to be flown in across the Cotentin peninsula and German anti-aircraft fire had somewhat dispersed the transport aircraft so that the parachutists dropped much scattered. This was an area in which special precautions had been taken against airborne landings but the wide dispersion of the parachutists caused so many alarms to be raised among the defenders that little concerted action could be taken against them until late in the day. By that time 82nd Division had a firm hold on Ste Mère Église, La Fière and Chef-du-Pont and even had isolated groups on the west bank of the Merderet. Separated from them by a German pocket in the Fauville-Turqueville area, 101st (although only 1,100 out of 6,600 had reached the rallying points) held Les Forges and Hiesville and, quite as importantly, the airborne landings had cleared the inland ends of the causeways through the flooded areas behind the *UTAH* beaches, facilitating a link-up with those coming from the sea.

* Of von Rundstedt's 850,000 men, 7% were men who had been taken prisoner by the Germans on the eastern front. All had volunteered - some willingly, some under pressure - to serve in the German army.

IWM

UTAH saw the easiest of all the eight landings made from the sea although it started in chaos. An uncharted minefield cost the naval escort one of the navigational control vessels and another had engine failure. These losses and the strong southward set of the current meant that the two leading battalions of 8 RCT (4th Division) landed a mile further south than their target, the beach below St Martin de Varreville.

(ABOVE) American troops coming back ashore at UTAH beach.
(BELOW LEFT) Heavy naval gun used as coastal artillery in Normandy.
(BELOW RIGHT) Observation cupola at Pointe du Hoc.

SV

B

As it happened this was a much more lightly defended sector and, with twenty-eight of their amphibious tanks swimming safely to shore, the operation went smoothly.

By nightfall 4th Division was safely ashore, holding the coast from Hamel-de-Cruttes in the north to Pouppeville in the south, and was in contact with the airborne divisions.

Things were very different on *OMAHA* where two RCT's were to land (116 RCT from 29th Division and 16 RCT from 1st). With the beaches closely overlooked by high ground, these two formations struck the most heavily defended sector of any of the landings. To increase their difficulties, three serious errors had been made in the planning of the *OMAHA* operation. The transfer from ships to landing craft took place eleven miles out to sea (the British transferred seven miles out); apart from the increased discomfort for the troops on the long run-in, the very choppy sea swamped at least eleven of the infantry assault craft. The artillery suffered even greater losses as it was decided to bring them ashore in DUKWs which, in the sea conditions,

were overloaded, twenty-two of the thirty guns being lost. Similarly thirty-two amphibious tanks were launched six thousand yards from the shore; only three came safely to land.

The second error was the shortness of the naval bombardment. The US Navy decided to restrict the shelling to forty minutes - the British fired for two hours - and the results were unsatisfactory. At *UTAH* this was of no great moment but, as Rear-Admiral J.L. Hall, who commanded the task force at *OMAHA*, reported, 'the time available for the pre-landing bombardment was not sufficient for the destruction of the beach defense targets'.

In addition the defenders had excellent fire discipline and did not shoot until the landing craft touched the beach. Thus until the last moment, the assaulting infantry imagined that surprise had been achieved. Tensions relaxed until, as the boats touched ground a torrent of fire burst on them from weapons of all calibres.

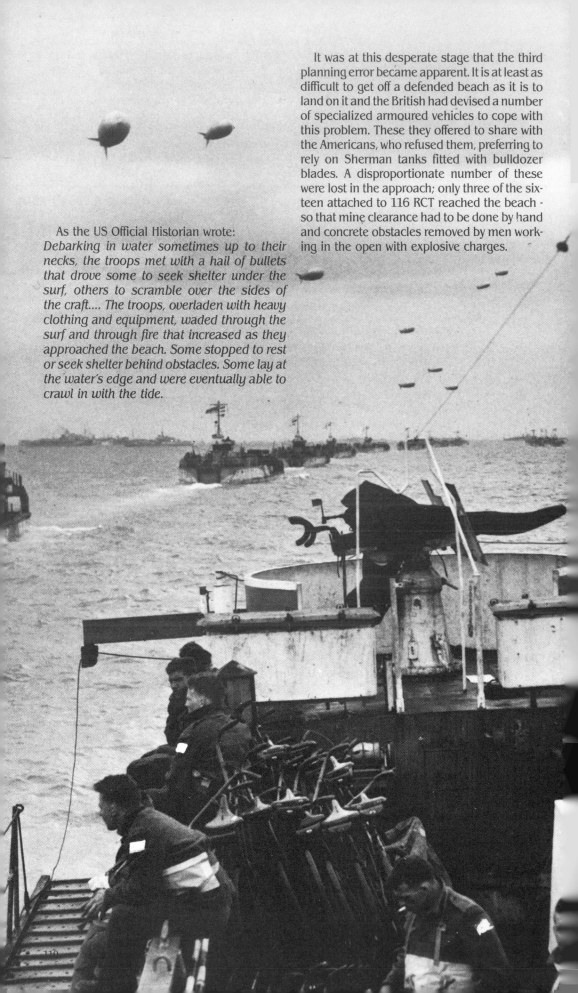

It was at this desperate stage that the third planning error became apparent. It is at least as difficult to get off a defended beach as it is to land on it and the British had devised a number of specialized armoured vehicles to cope with this problem. These they offered to share with the Americans, who refused them, preferring to rely on Sherman tanks fitted with bulldozer blades. A disproportionate number of these were lost in the approach; only three of the sixteen attached to 116 RCT reached the beach - so that mine clearance had to be done by hand and concrete obstacles removed by men working in the open with explosive charges.

As the US Official Historian wrote:
Debarking in water sometimes up to their necks, the troops met with a hail of bullets that drove some to seek shelter under the surf, others to scramble over the sides of the craft.... The troops, overladen with heavy clothing and equipment, waded through the surf and through fire that increased as they approached the beach. Some stopped to rest or seek shelter behind obstacles. Some lay at the water's edge and were eventually able to crawl in with the tide.

29th Division landed in front of Vierville-sur-Mer and 1st Division to the east of St Laurent and, for four hours, both were deadlocked on the beach behind the high dunes.

Succeeding waves of landing craft brought in more men who added to the crowding and casualties. General Omar Bradley, commanding First US Army, began seriously to consider evacuating *OMAHA*, and the German defenders reported that they had brought the landing to a halt. They were wrong. More naval fire support was brought up and at one stage eleven American and British destroyers were pounding the defences at short range. At the same time intrepid engineers were cutting ways through the wire and lifting mines while gallant officers were rallying the infantry, notably Colonel George A. Taylor who strode fearlessly down the beach calling, *'Two kinds of people are going to stay on this beach, the dead and those about to die. Now let's get the hell out of here!'* It was about 9.30 am that the men of the 1st Division stormed up the hill and into Colleville. It was a desperate battle but by dark Vierville, St Laurent, most of Colleville and parts of Grand Hameau were in American hands. 33,000 men were ashore on the beaches; the position was safe against anything but a major counter-attack, which by then the Germans were too committed to mount. Four miles to the west of Vierville the *OMAHA* landing scored its most spectacular triumph.

Rangers under siege at
Pointe du Hoc. The flag is
to warn off allied aircraft.

P

Three companies of 2/Ranger (Commando) Battalion were detailed to assault the coastal battery on Pointe du Hoc. They struck from the sea, climbing the rugged cliff with scaling ladders and grappling irons - only to find that, under pressure of the naval and air bombardments, the guns had been withdrawn; they were now resited to the rear of the concrete emplacements in order to fire on the *OMAHA* beaches. The guns were duly destroyed but the Rangers were then besieged for forty-eight hours on the cliff top, surviving largely because of the accurate supporting fire of two destroyers, USS *Satterly* and HMS *Tallybont*.

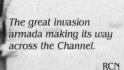

*The great invasion
armada making its way
across the Channel.*

RCN

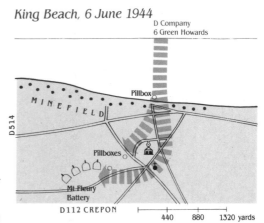

King Beach, 6 June 1944

NORMANDY
EASTERN TASK FORCE
GOLD JUNO SWORD

While the landings of the five British and Canadian brigade groups went more smoothly than those of the Americans they equally did not achieve the objective set for them - roughly a line from the River Dives on the east to Caen in the south and Bayeux in the west. This objective, like all the 'phase lines' Montgomery laid down (or suggested) has been the subject of much controversy. To have achieved this D-Day line would have required a combination of luck and skill which would have been remarkable even if the Germans had been weaker and more surprised than they actually were. Montgomery must have realized this but the objective was laid down as a target to strive for, an ideal to overcome the inertia which had marked, or appeared to mark, the landings at Gallipoli and Anzio. The efforts of commanders and soldiers had so long been focused on the immediate problem of getting safely ashore that the chance of exploitation tended to be overshadowed, so that it was necessary to set more distant targets.

The two beaches on *GOLD* were the responsibility of 50th (Northumbrian) Division attacking with 231 Brigade Group on the right and 69 Brigade on the left. From the latter 6/Green Howards landed, behind their engineer tanks, exactly on time (7.30 am) at a spot immediately below the village of Mont Fleury, their final objective being the village of St Leger, ten miles inland on the Caen-Bayeux road. Between their beach and that village there were intermediate objectives in the form of the battery by Mont Fleury and a supposed rocket site (actually a headquarters) near Meuvaines. Four pillboxes at Hable de Heurtot were quickly overcome with the help of engineer tanks firing petards (see page 116) and a breakthrough was made over the wall by two tanks. Immediately ahead of them was the Mont Fleury ridge with a road leading straight up to it and passing, on the right, a house with a circular drive - which is still identifiable.* This house was familiar to the men of the Green Howards as they had been shown air photographs on their briefing. This road was the vital exit road from the beach and, shortly before D-Day, it had been noticed that a large crater had been blown in the road short of the crest. It is an indication of the meticulous planning of *NEPTUNE* that a tank had been detailed to drop a fascine of exactly the right size into this crater to make it passable. Meanwhile, as the flanking battalion, 5/East Yorks, cleared La Rivière, the Green

---

* The houses to the right have been built since the war. The battery lay behind them.

The way ahead. British tanks moving off GOLD beach on the road opened by the Green Howards' attack.

IWM

DP

Green Howards

CSM
Stan Hollis VC

IWM

Howards stormed up the slope, took the house with the circular drive and, after Sergeant Major Stan Hollis disabled two pillboxes (and became the only man to win the Victoria Cross on 6 June), went on to seize the battery. This was found not to have fired a shot that day, the crew being so demoralized by the bombardment that they were more than anxious to surrender. By dark the battalion was only a mile short of its objective, St Leger, having been assisted forward by a squadron of 4/7/Dragoon Guards.

The experience of the Green Howards was typical of much of the British front (although easier now to identify on the ground than most). On their right 231 Brigade had a hard struggle to overcome resistance at Le Hamel but had reached Arromanches as the light faded at about 9 pm. Beyond them 47/RM Commando, having bypassed the great battery at Longues (Le Chaos) was close to Port-en-Bessin where the junction with troops from OMAHA was due to be made. On the east of 50th Division contact was made with the Canadians from JUNO who had driven inland as far as Villons-les-Buissons and Le Fresne-Camilly, though the enemy still held Tahon. A detachment of Canadian tanks had succeeded in penetrating to the outskirts of Caen but, unsupported, had been forced to pull back. On the Canadian left their 8 Brigade had run into trouble clearing the beach exits at Bernières and 48/RM Commando, which was due to pass through them, had a difficult and

dangerous landing. They managed to seize Langrune but were unable to capture Luc-sur-Mer. Meanwhile, two miles to the east, 41/RM Commando, landing on SWORD, had an equally tricky landing and, despite the assistance of a company of 1/South Lancs, could not make its way into the powerful defences of Lion-sur-Mer. Thus, at the end of the day, there was a gap in the British beachhead.

Things had started very well on SWORD with 8/Brigade taking Hermanville and Colleville-sur-Orne without too much difficulty, while a start was made in reducing the garrison of Ouistreham. Problems arose when moving from Colleville towards Bénouville where there were two strongpoints astride the road. The more easterly, code-named MORRIS, had been powerfully affected by the bombardment and was taken by 1/Suffolks but when they turned their attention to the other (HILLMAN) things were different. This was a very powerful complex of interconnected concrete bunkers which had been so well camouflaged that its strength had been underestimated in the Intelligence assessment and it was scarcely damaged from the sea or the air. Its occupants, moreover, fought in a more determined style than most of the Germans in the British sector and the Suffolks' first attack failed with considerable loss. It was difficult to bypass HILLMAN as the 1/Norfolks discovered to their cost when they tried to slip past it and suffered 150 casualties. It was late in the day before HILLMAN was taken with the assistance of two squadrons of tanks from the Staffordshire Yeomanry - tanks which should have been working in support of 2/King's Own Shropshire Light Infantry who, for want of them, were held up at Biéville and Beuville on their way to Caen.

MARS

SV

It had been foreseen that the greatest danger to the British beach-heads would come from the reconstituted 21st Panzer Division which was known to be south of Caen. Its power had been exaggerated since it was believed to have 240 tanks and 40 self-propelled guns, some of the tanks being Panthers and possibly Tigers. In fact, apart from the SP guns, it had only 127 Mark IV tanks but it was nevertheless a dangerous threat and, on Rommel's orders, had practised immediate counter-attacks to push invaders into the sea before they could secure a firm foothold. Their effectiveness had been reduced since some of their *panzer grenadieren* (lorried infantry) had been dispersed in defensive roles and their anti-aircraft guns had been deployed forward to protect their advance to the coast. Their commander, Lieutenant-General Edgar Feuchtinger, spent a very frustrating morning while control of his division was passed from Army Group B to Seventh Army and thence to LXXXIV Corps and none of these organizations would give him any clear instructions. Finally, as he had decided to attack 6th Airborne on his own initiative he was told to advance to the west of Caen. This meant that he had to retreat to Caen and cross the Orne within the city, suffering loss from air attack in the process. It was late in the afternoon before he was able to send two task forces forward. One, with about forty tanks, moved quickly on Biéville - to be met, and repulsed, by the anti-tank guns of the KOSLI and two troops of Firefly Shermans of the Staffordshire Yeomanry. Trying to work round a flank the task force met another troop of Fireflies and was driven back, losing fourteen tanks. The other force advanced further to the west and raced down the corridor between 3rd British and 3rd Canadian Divisions. They reached the sea at Lion-sur-Mer and were in a position to do great damage when a huge aerial armada passed overhead, landing gliders and supply parachutes near St Aubin d'Arquenay. In reality, this was 6 Air Landing Brigade arriving to reinforce 6th Airborne but to the tank commander, who must have been in a highly nervous state, it seemed some devilish British plot had been laid to frustrate him. To fly such a force from England and land it close to him must have taken at least six hours and, six hours earlier, he had been the other side of Caen. It was enough to convince him his mission was doomed; he fell back to join Feuchtinger and the rest of the division, now only seventy tanks strong, on the approaches to Caen.

(ABOVE LEFT) German infantry going into a counter-attack.

(ABOVE) Panzer Grenadier with Spandau machine gun.

DP

Gorget patch of SS Totenkopf division.

By midnight, 6/7 June more than 132,000 allied troops were ashore at a cost of some 9,000 casualties. They had not taken all their objectives but, although *OMAHA* still gave rise to concern, they had seized the beachhead. The German command on land was only beginning to get a grip on the situation, the *Luftwaffe* had been totally ineffective and the *Kriegsmarine* had contributed by sinking only one Norwegian destroyer. Hitler and Rommel, despite advocating different methods, had agreed that the invasion must be smashed on the beaches but, by dawn on 7 June, it was clear that the allies were on shore to stay.

The battle for Normandy inevitably involved civilian casualties: a young victim is treated by American medics.

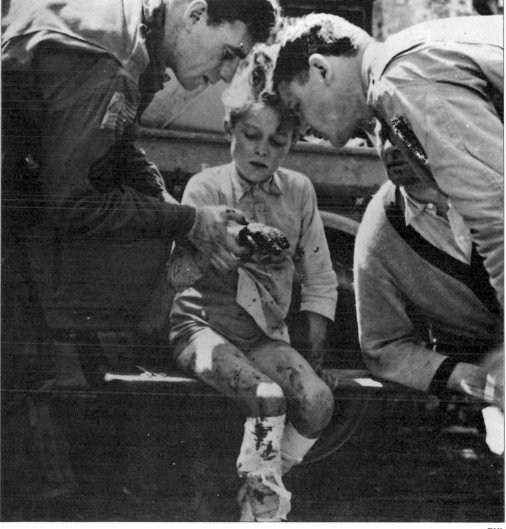

(TOP) A DD (double duplex) tank: a Sherman fitted with propellers and a canvas 'skirt' which enabled it to 'swim' ashore.
(BOTTOM) The ARK (armoured ramp carrier): built on a Churchill chassis, this could make a way for other tanks to cross obstacles such as sea walls.

IWM

IWM

IWM

Major-General Percy Hobart, the deviser of special purpose tanks - the Funnies.

THE FUNNIES

APART from being Montgomery's brother-in-law, Major-General Percy Hobart had been a brilliant but difficult officer. He had created what became 7th Armoured Division but he offended too many people and was retired in 1940. He had, nevertheless, a number of ingenious ideas for specialized uses of tanks and, with Churchill's backing was re-employed to develop them and to command them in 79th Armoured Division. These unorthodox vehicles, known as 'Funnies', played a vital part in the landing, especially for the British, on 6 June.

The type which were most used were the amphibious tanks - known as Duplex Drive (DD) since they had both tracks and propellers; these were Shermans with collapsible canvas screens around the upper part of the hull, which enabled them to float. The Americans used DD tanks and at *UTAH,* where they were launched three thousand yards from the beach, all twenty-eight got ashore. At *OMAHA,* where sea conditions were much worse, thirty-two were launched more than three miles out to sea and all but three foundered. At *GOLD* and *JUNO* the waves seemed so choppy that most were launched either close to the shore or actually on the beach but, in the calmer water of *SWORD,* thirty-two out of thirty-four 'swam' successfully ashore. In each case when they arrived with or shortly after the infantry, their 75mm guns were able to give invaluable and, at the time, irreplaceable support.

The Sherman also provided the basis for the Flail (or Crab) when it was fitted with a giant roller, driven by the engine, at the rear. On this roller were a number of heavy chains which flailed the ground, exploding mines and cutting wire as it progressed - backwards. Less common was the Crocodile; this was a Churchill tank mounting a flamethrower. It was fed from a nine-ton trailer which gave enough 'ammunition' for one hundred bursts of a second each. It was exceedingly effective against pillboxes up to a range of a hundred yards.

AVRE (Armoured Vehicles Royal Engineers) came in many forms with several functions. One type, also based on a Churchill, carried a petard or short-range mortar which threw a forty-pound bomb to a range of eighty yards and proved invaluable against all forms of concrete fortifications. Other types, utilizing several kinds of obsolete tank chassis, were designed for laying short bridges, dropping fascines in craters and ditches, or laying carpets of heavy canvas to enable vehicles to cross stretches of mud or soft clay.

(LEFT) Remnants of the MULBERRY harbour off Arromanches.
(BOTTOM LEFT) MULBERRY in action: 3-5 inch anti-aircraft guns mounted on the gigantic concrete caissons (PHOENIXES) after they had been sunk into position.
(BOTTOM RIGHT) More remaining sections of the Arromanches MULBERRY.

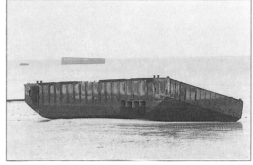

P   DP

MULBERRY

DIEPPE had vividly demonstrated the difficulties involved in capturing a harbour and experience at Naples had shown what German demolition experts could do to a harbour if it were captured. Churchill had been considering this problem even before Dieppe and, some three months earlier, had in fact urged Combined Operations Headquarters to develop 'Piers for use on open beaches'. It was not until August 1943 that the final designs were completed for a harbour which could be imported with the invasion forces. This left very little time available for manufacturing the enormous number of components that would be needed to build a MULBERRY.

The requirement was for two movable ports, each with the capacity of Dover harbour. They must be capable of accepting merchant ships (which when loaded drew twenty-six feet of water) and they would have to be moved to sites on the invasion coast where there was a difference of twenty-three feet between low and high tide. The basis was to be a line of blockships - such an instant breakwater was established on each of the five landing areas. This breakwater would be extended with concrete caissons (PHOENIXES) which would also give lateral protection at either end. Over two hundred PHOENIXES of different sizes were constructed, the largest weighing 6,000 tons and measuring 200 feet long and 60 feet high. Their building required 213,000,000 tons of concrete and 70,000 tons of steel reinforcement. Inside the shelter thus provided would be piers which

adjusted themselves to the rise and fall of the tides and which were linked to the land by steel pontoon bridges.

The first of the sixty-four blockships, code-named GOOSEBERRIES, were sunk precisely into position on 7 June; on the following day the PHOENIXES began to arrive for both the British harbour off Arromanches and the American off St Laurent. By 19 June both were in sight of completion. On that day the worst Channel storm for forty Junes broke and destroyed the American MULBERRY, washing away twenty-five out of the thirty-five caissons which had been put in place. The British harbour, which had some shelter from offshore rocks, survived, sheltering five hundred vessels. It can still be seen, in parts, today.

It had been assumed for administrative planning that Cherbourg would be captured within seventeen days and the great ports of Brittany and the Loire within forty. In practice Cherbourg, though occupied on 26 June, could not accept any cargoes until 16 July (D + 40) while Brest, Lorient and St Nazaire were still in German hands on D + 90. All of the stores (less petrol) for the British and Canadian armies were at that time still being landed through MULBERRY. Ninety days was, as it happened, the design life of these artificial harbours but that at Arromanches had many weeks' work ahead of it.

*Major John Howard,
Oxfordshire and
Buckinghamshire Light
Infantry.*

JH

PEGASUS BRIDGE

THE task of the 6th Airborne Division was to secure the eastern flank of the landing by seizing the high ground between the Orne and Dives rivers and it was vital that the Orne crossing near Bénouville, the only crossing north of Caen, should be seized intact. The job of doing so was entrusted to D Company, 2/Oxfordshire and Buckinghamshire Light Infantry, com-

Cabourg (Proust's Balbec), the tow being slipped at 5,000 feet. Sixteen minutes after midnight, Howard's glider landed with its nose in the wire surrounding the pillbox and only forty-seven feet from it. It was a bumpy landing and for a moment Howard thought he had been blinded, only to realize that his steel helmet had been pushed over his eyes. The other two gliders landed very close but not before Howard's men had disabled the pillbox with grenades and rushed the far end of the bridge, clearing the nearby German trenches. Only one of the three gliders landed close to the river bridge, one going far astray, but surprise had been achieved and, here again there was complete success.

At 1 am, 7 Parachute Brigade landed to the east of them but before they could arrive to relieve the OBLI two tracked vehicles were heard approaching from Bénouville. The only anti-tank weapon available was a PIAT (see

DP

IWM

manded by Major John Howard and reinforced to six platoons with a field troop of Royal Engineers – 180 men in all. They were to travel in six Horsa gliders (see page 114), giving each a load of one platoon and five sappers.

Part of Howard's problem was that two crossings had to be seized, that over the Caen Canal and, five hundred yards away, another across the Orne itself. His Intelligence briefing, which was both detailed and accurate, told him that the guard on these bridges consisted of a weak company - fifty men, billeted in Bénouville. He was allocated two landing zones - both between the two waterways - one immediately south of the canal bridge, the other just to the north of the river bridge. He allocated three gliders to each, giving the first priority to neutralizing the demolition charges known to have been laid at each place. The firing gear for the canal bridge charges was assumed to be in a pillbox at its south-eastern end.

Towed by Halifax bombers, the gliders took off at 10.56 am on 5 June and were taken through a known gap in the German flak over

page 17), a difficult contraption to operate and one slow to reload. It was clear that everything depended on the first round.

Eventually it was possible to see in the darkness two half-track reconnaissance vehicles coming towards them and the PIAT was fired at a range of about fifty yards. The leading half-track was hit and, being loaded with explosives, it blew up in a series of spectacular blasts. The other withdrew.

Contact was made soon afterwards with the parachutists and until midday they were troubled only by snipers and sporadic mortaring. The original landing force did, however, manage to disable two armed boats making their way down the Caen Canal, capturing the crews, before the post was taken over by commandos who had landed on *SWORD*. The total loss to Howard's party was two killed and fourteen wounded.

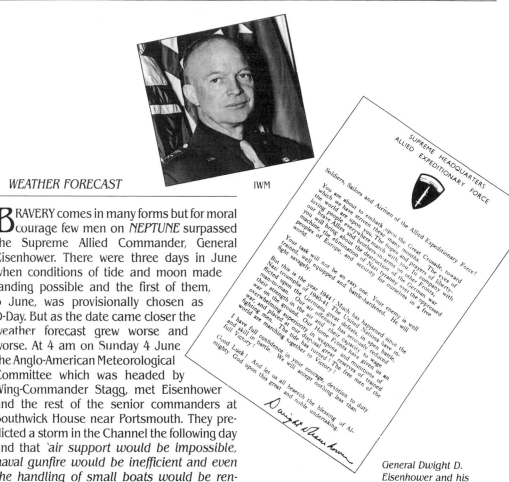

IWM

WEATHER FORECAST

BRAVERY comes in many forms but for moral courage few men on *NEPTUNE* surpassed the Supreme Allied Commander, General Eisenhower. There were three days in June when conditions of tide and moon made landing possible and the first of them, 5 June, was provisionally chosen as D-Day. But as the date came closer the weather forecast grew worse and worse. At 4 am on Sunday 4 June the Anglo-American Meteorological Committee which was headed by Wing-Commander Stagg, met Eisenhower and the rest of the senior commanders at Southwick House near Portsmouth. They predicted a storm in the Channel the following day and that 'air support would be impossible, naval gunfire would be inefficient and even the handling of small boats would be rendered difficult'. The air and sea commanders advised postponement and only Montgomery, despite his reputation for caution, recommended making the attempt. Eisenhower decided to postpone the landings for twenty-four hours. The storm duly arrived and, judging from conditions outside the house, that decision had been right. Stagg could not offer any hope of better weather.

At 4.30 am on 5 June the meeting was reconvened but the storm was still raging outside. Stagg, however, said that 'by the following morning a period of relatively good weather would ensue, lasting probably thirty-six hours'. No forecast beyond that time was possible. The air commanders were still opposed to taking the risk. Montgomery, however, still favoured going ahead and Admiral Ramsay (of Dunkirk fame) who was commanding the fleets, believed that the landings would be possible. He added that a decision would have to be taken within half-an-hour.

Eisenhower was in a terrible dilemma. Meteorologists are far from infallible and, if the storm continued, a landing on 6 June would turn out to be a disaster. Conversely, another postponement might mean that the whole

General Dwight D. Eisenhower and his General Order for D-Day in Normandy.

elaborate scheme would have to be mounted again (should that be possible) in July, within-calculable effects on security and morale - to say nothing of the imminent threat of German 'V' weapons whose power was overestimated.

No commander in history has ever had to make so gigantic a decision at such short notice. If he ordered the invasion to start and the meteorologists were wrong he would be responsible for a holocaust which would overshadow the first day of the Somme in 1916. He might well, if he delayed, extend the war into another year and thus be responsible for even more deaths. He reflected for a few moments and then said quietly, 'I am quite positive we must give the order ... I don't see how we can possibly do anything else'. He then retired to his office to draft a Communiqué which would be issued if he proved wrong and the invasion failed. It was to have ended, 'If any blame or fault attaches to the attempt, it is mine alone'.

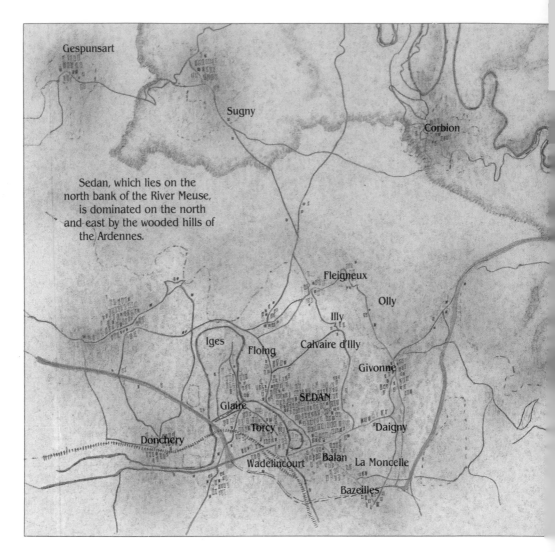

Sedan, which lies on the north bank of the River Meuse, is dominated on the north and east by the wooded hills of the Ardennes.

SEDAN

HISTORY USUALLY ATTRIBUTES the Franco-Prussian war of 1870-71 to the deep schemes of the Prussian chancellor, Bismarck. A fairer view would be that the war sprang from a centuries-old national rivalry between France and Prussia which was bound to lead to war sooner or later but which was brilliantly manipulated by Bismarck so that France was shown to the world as an unreasonable aggressor.

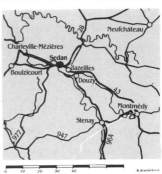

Monument to Chasseurs d'Afrique in the square of Floing

DP

The house in Bazeilles where the French Marines made their last stand.

DP

0 1 2 3   6

Kilometres

The Meuse at Sedan.

DP

Sedan in the Ardennes Forest, a beautiful area, lies on the right bank of the River Meuse. It is near to the Belgian and Luxembourg borders, 12 miles (19km) east of Charleville-Mézières. The town is dominated by a fortress claimed to be the largest in Europe, the Château Fort; this houses a military museum (open daily, April to September, 10.00-18.00 hours).

If you enter Floing from Sedan, the Monument du Chêne Brise is seen before reaching the town square where signposts guide the traveller not only to the Memorial des Chasseurs d'Afrique and the 1870 cemetery, but also to the French cemetery of the Second World War.

Leave Sedan on the Bouillon road, and after climbing out of the city you will reach the plateau on which the battle took place. Mass graves marked with black iron railings are a moving testimony to the dead.

At Bazeilles, just outside Sedan on the N43 to Montmédy, it is possible to visit the Musée de la Maison de la Dernière Cartouche (Last Cartridge) where the French marine unit fought their heroic battle against the Germans in 1870 (open every day except Friday, 8.30-12.00 and 13.30-18.00 hours); at Novion-Porcien the Musée de la Bataille des Ardennes, which has a section on the 1870 action, is open every day from 9.00-20.00 hours.

When the Second Empire was proclaimed in 1852 under Napoleon III, putative nephew of the great Bonaparte, the re-establishment of French military glory was a principal plank of the regime's policy along with an ineffective liberalism. The army succeeded in winning victories, even if not very convincing victories, in the Crimea and in northern Italy with the battles of Solferino and Magenta, and this was sufficient to give the regulars a very high opinion of their irresistability. Moreover they had, or thought they had, advantages other than the professionalism and *élan* which they valued so highly. They had the *Chassepot*, the first really effective breech-loading rifle, and the *Mitrailleuse*,

Chassepot rifle. The best rifle on either side in 1870.

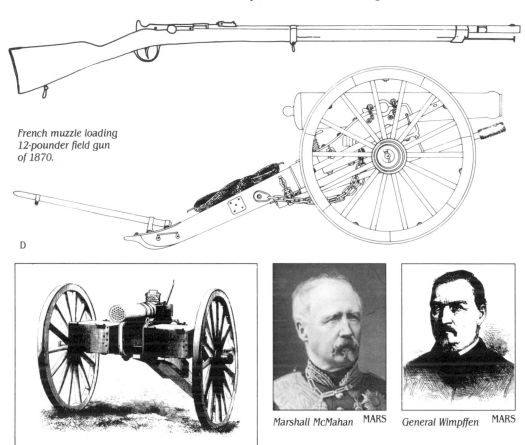

French muzzle loading 12-pounder field gun of 1870.

D

Marshall McMahan MARS

General Wimpffen MARS

an early type of machine gun with 215 barrels and a rate of fire of 150 rounds a minute. These advantages proved to be overrated. The *Chassepot* was not sufficiently superior to the Prussian needle gun, though the former was supposed to be effective at 1,600 yards compared with 600 yards for the needle gun, and the *Mitrailleuse*, which had the drawback of being as conspicuous as an upright piano on the battlefield, had been kept so secret that no one knew how to use it. Both these weapons were outclassed by the superiority of the Krupp breech-loading artillery over the French muzzle-loaders.

Far more decisive than any of their weapons was the Prussian staff work. The *Generalstab* (the General Staff) was the sum of the élite of the Staff College graduates carefully selected and schooled by General Helmut von Moltke so that every field commander had at his side a staff officer who would react according to a common doctrine whatever situation arose.

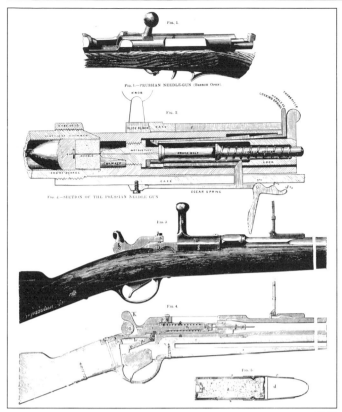

MARS

MARS

General von Moltke, the creator of and inspiration behind the Prussian General Staff.

Moreover, the refinement of the system of mobilization meant that Prussia and her satellite states could bring their full strength to bear on the enemy in an unprecedentedly short time. This operation was greatly helped by intelligent use of a railway system which was operated and, to a great extent, constructed to meet military ends. While it was calculated in Paris that Prussia would be able to have eight army corps ready to invade France seven weeks after mobilization was started, ten corps were actually ready on the frontier within eighteen days.

By contrast French mobilization was chaotic, many of the reservists never reaching their parent units - while the trains which carried them turned out to be the same as those required to supply the troops already facing the enemy.

The French calculation was that, at the outbreak of war, she would have a temporary superiority in numbers so that her wisest course would be to launch an immediate offensive aimed to disrupt the enemy concentration. While this was agreed, no decision had been taken as to where the attack should be made. It was not until the troops were on the frontier and ready to attack that it was realized that no arrangements had been made to supply them once they were inside Germany. In the event six divisions advanced, as if on parade, against three German companies, who inflicted eighty-eight casualties, and induced them to retire from a hill overlooking Saarbrücken. Then they halted while the generals tried to decide what to do next.

This French dithering was as distressing to the Prussian command as it was to Napoleon's troops who had been trained almost exclusively for the offensive. Von Moltke had hoped that his enemy would drive deep into the Saarland so that he would be able to encircle them. Instead he was forced to improvise an advance to surround them and it proved to be a rather expensive exercise - thanks largely to General von Steinmetz, who was commanding First Prussian Army; his early service had been under Blücher and he had no time for tactical subtleties relying on headlong frontal attacks. The result was that the French were driven back rather than encircled, the larger part of their army under Marshal Bazaine retreating to Metz while three corps under Marshal MacMahon headed for Châlons-sur-Marne.

Bazaine reached the powerful fortress of Metz by 9 August, only one week after the tentative advance towards Saarbrücken, and once there he sank into a lethargy so complete that he allowed the Prussian to move round and cut his communications with Paris. There followed a series of battles of which the most serious was that of Gravelotte - St Privat (18 August) where, had Bazaine had the energy to command his army, there should have been a major French victory. Instead it ended with the Germans (who lost more than 20,000 men) being able to besiege 154,481 French regulars in Metz. The peacetime strength of the French army had been only 150,000!

BPK

Staff of a Prussian Infantry Regiment on the advance to Sedan.

If France was to survive the war Metz had to be relieved but MacMahon, at Châlons-sur-Marne, believed this to be impossible. Bazaine, he said, 'cannot be rescued. He has neither supplies nor ammunition. He will have surrendered long before he reached him.' In fact Metz held out until 27 October but MacMahon was right in thinking that the rescue operation was beyond his strength.

He had 130,000 men and 423 obsolete guns but three-quarters of his men had been demoralized by their defeats on the Saarland frontier and the consequent retreat. The other quarter included a division of recruits, one of marines, some regulars rushed up from the Pyrenees and eighteen battalions of Parisian *Garde Mobiles* who were mutinous and untrained. The wise course would have been to retreat and fight in and around Paris but from the Ministry of War came mandatory orders to relieve Metz.

Sedan today

DP

DP

The Meuse at Sedan.

To make matters worse for the unfortunate marshal, Napoleon III insisted on joining the Army of Châlons though he was a sick man who, at the best of times, had difficulty in making up his mind and sticking to any decision he eventually reached.

By 20 August, with no firm decisions taken, German cavalry was reported within twenty-five miles of Châlons and MacMahon moved his army to Reims while the debate about the next move continued. On 21 August the decision to move towards Paris was taken - only to be reversed a few hours later when a two-day-old message from Bazaine was smuggled through the enemy lines. This announced that the troops in Metz were to break out to the northwest in the direction of Montmédy so as to join hands with the Army of Châlons. On 23 August MacMahon marched off north east to help him.

There were plenty of French stores at Reims but there was no one authorized to issue them and the army set off without rations, plundering the countryside until MacMahon ordered them to switch their route to the north to re-establish their contact with the railway at Rethel. When they reached it there were still too few provisions and no word from Bazaine who, it became clear, was making no serious attempt to break out of Metz.

Once more MacMahon decided to make for Paris and once more he was told unequivocably by the government to march on Metz. On 30 August one wing of his army was surprised near Beaumont, east of Montmédy, and driven north in disorder. Von Moltke had now reorganized the German order of battle, disposing of von Steinmetz, and had sent Third Army and the Army of the Meuse swinging north against the flank of the French march towards Montmédy. MacMahon did the only thing left to him and ordered his army north to the old fortress town of Sedan, hoping that he would be able to slip westward through Mezières. In fact he was pinned against the frontier of neutral Belgium and, as one of his officers remarked, 'Nous sommes dans un pot de chambre et nous y serons emmerdés.'

MacMahon realized neither the strength of the German army nor the speed at which they were advancing. His orders for 1 September, issued the previous evening, read, 'The whole army will rest today.' He intended to spend the day in reconnaissance and reorganization. Sedan, although its fortifications had long been dismantled, offered definite advantages as a defensive position. The River Meuse covered the approaches from west and south and a triangle of ridges, largely covered by Garenne Wood, an extension of the vast Ardennes forest, protected the north and east. It was on this triangle that he disposed his troops with VII Corps (Douay) holding the front from Floing to the apex at the Calvaire d'Illy. The eastern front, above the villages of Givonne, Daigny and La Moncelle, were manned by I Corps (Ducrot) and XII Corps (Lebrun), the latter having its right flank at Bazeilles which was garrisoned by the Marine Brigade. In reserve were the remains of V Corps, which had suffered heavily at Beaumont. In command was General Emmanuel Wimpffen who had been sent specially on 31 August from Paris; he held, though he did not disclose the fact, a dormant commission to command the Army of Châlons should MacMahon be incapacitated. He detached some of his troops to hold the crucial stronghold of the Calvaire d'Illy.

Von Moltke planned to encircle the French army where it stood. The Army of the Meuse was to move against the east flank of the French position, interposing itself between Sedan and the Belgian frontier. Third Army was to swing to the west and cut off any possibility of retreat. Before dark on 31 August the road bridge at Donchéry and the railway bridge south of Bazeilles had both been seized intact. As Moltke remarked to the King of Prussia, 'We have them in a mousetrap.'

Before dawn on 1 September the battle opened when the Bavarians (Third Army) attacked Bazeilles which was staunchly defended by the Marines. Soon, to their north, the Saxons (Army of the Meuse) advanced against the ridge - only to be checked by a force of Zouaves sent forward to delay them at Daigny where they held till 10 am. By this time almost the whole of the French line was under fire from the excellent German artillery and one of their victims was MacMahon, disabled by a wound in the leg. He assigned command of the army to the capable and realistic Ducrot, who was in no doubt that the only hope was an immediate breakout to he west, a move for which he immediately gave orders. Before they could be executed he was confronted by Wimpffen flourishing his dormant commission and insisting that the orders to retreat be cancelled. It was an absurd situation but irrelevant, since before midday the two German armies had joined hands at Olly Farm north of Sedan.

The French army was encircled with a ring of artillery and the infantry, exposed on the crest of the ridges, suffered greatly and became increasingly demoralized. Wimpffen tried to muster troops for a counter-attack but only a few would follow him and the defenders of the Calvaire abandoned their position. Only Douay, who had entrenched his men above Floing, was substantially holding the German advance, and it was Ducrot who devised the last desperate fling to try to break out to the west. The whole of the French cavalry was concentrated near Cazal and was to charge downhill towards Floing to force a gap in the German ring through which the infantry could escape. It was the same insensate belief in the power of cavalry that had ruined the horsemen of Napoleon I at Waterloo - and the *Cuirassiers* of Napoleon III had less chance against the breech-loading rifles of the

The Battle of Sedan at (LEFT) 9am and (RIGHT) 2pm.

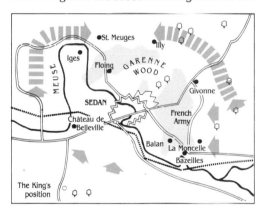
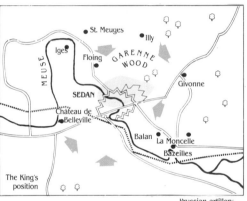

Prussian artillery bombarding French positions from all directions

Prussians than their grandfathers had had against Wellington's smoothbore muskets in 1815. The bravery was the same and so was the result. The cavalry swept over the German skirmishers but could make no impression on the solid mass of the infantry. Those who survived were rallied and even charged a second time, moving the King of Prussia to murmur, 'Ah! Les braves gens! ' and those words are inscribed in the monument to them which has been erected on the slopes above Floing.

By mid-afternoon the Prussian Guard corps had encircled the Garenne Wood and captured some 20,000 demoralized fugitives within, and before long the remnants of the French army were penned inside Sedan. General Wimpffen tried to rally enough men to make a strike at Bazeilles - which the Marines had at last lost - but no one would follow him and towards evening General Reille set off with a white flag, carrying a letter from the French emperor to the Prussian king.

*My Brother,
Having failed to be killed in the midst of my troops, there is nothing left for me to do but to place my sword in the hands of your Majesty. Je suis de votre Majesté le bon frère.*

Just a few French soldiers, chiefly from the cavalry, managed to escape to the west but the Germans took 104,000 prisoners. Their own loss was no more than 9,000 men.

Wreckage in Sedan 1940.

IWM

THE BIRTH OF THE ATROCITY STORY

THE Franco-Prussian war was (apart from the Crimea, which was fought well away from a populous countryside) the very first European campaign to be attended by large numbers of newspaper men. Atrocities are an inevitable result of war, especially of hard-fought actions, but it was at Sedan that war correspondents found that, by drawing attention to atrocities, in the name of humanity, they could boost the sales of their papers.

The hardest fighting of the day was in the village of Bazeilles which the French brigade of Marines defended against the Bavarians. Initially the defenders had the advantage since they were established in solidly built stone houses, impervious to rifle-fire. Shellfire, however, soon set houses alight, driving out the Marines and allowing the attackers more freedom to advance under cover of smoke. Thereafter both sides deliberately set fire to houses both to dispossess their opponents and to provide cover. During the bitter fighting the inhabitants of Bazeilles gave help to their compatriots by carrying ammunition and, in many cases, taking up discarded rifles and shooting at the enemy.

The rules of war, as formulated in the eighteenth century, forbade any warlike acts by non-combatants and these rules could still be thought to be valid, despite the inroads made into them by such bodies as the guerillas in the Peninsular war. Technically therefore the Bavarians were within their rights summarily to execute civilians found with arms in their hands. In fact, there can be little doubt that in the heat of the moment they did more than this. In addition there were cases where men, women and children were found suffocated in cellars when the house above burned over their heads, an occurrence which in most cases was purely fortuitous.

Such misfortunes were pounced upon by the war correspondents. The *Daily News* reported that, *'We were told that many persons were dragged from the cellars where they had taken refuge and shot; others were fastened down and left to the flames. The sick and infirm were bayonetted in their beds. Two infants were thrown out of the windows by the Bavarians, and then thrown back again previous to the house being fired.'*

The Germans replied with atrocity stories of their own, and the correspondent of the *Frankforter Zeitung*, who was in Bazeilles at the time, wrote, *'A wild cry, more like that of an animal than of a human being, rang in my ears. I looked towards the place whence the sound came, and saw a peasant dragging a wounded Bavarian, who was lying on the ground, towards a burning house. A woman was ... kicking the poor creature in the side with her heavy shoes.*

The heart-rending cry of the wretched man had drawn three of his comrades to the spot. Two shots rang out - the peasant dropped. The woman laughed and, before the soldiers had gone three steps forward, she stood once more beside her victim. One blow cleft her skull. I stooped down to the ill-used soldier. He was dead.'

Panzer Mk III of Guderian's Panzer Korps 1940.

IWM

ROUT IN 1940

LATE on 12 May 1940, two days after they had invaded Belgium, the tanks of Guderian's XIX Panzer Korps emerged from the Ardennes and drove unopposed into the town of Sedan. From the west bank of the Meuse French artillery observers could clearly see large concentrations of German tanks but, although there were large dumps of ammunition in the neighbourhood, the local corps commander, General Grandsart, would allow his guns to fire only thirty rounds a day. He believed that in *'four to six days'* the Germans would attempt a river crossing when all available ammunition would be needed.

As it happened, the Germans crossed the river on the following morning, 13 May. The infantry of 10th Panzer Division crossed south of Sedan at Wadelincourt, that of 1st Panzer opposite Floing and of 2nd Panzer at Donchéry - where the infantry of Third Army had crossed, in the opposite direction seventy years earlier.

The defenders, mostly elderly French territorials, had first been demoralized by heavy and unopposed divebombing attacks. As one French officer wrote, *'Riflemen and machine-gunners got up and fled, carrying off in their flight such artillerymen who had not beaten them to it, mixed up with fugitives from the neighbouring sectors.... By two o'clock in the afternoon everyone had gone.'*

Massed defections there undoubtedly were but a number of brave men stood their ground and would have imposed large delays on the Germans had it not been for the withdrawal of their supporting artillery; two gunner colonels withdrew their guns on the unconfirmed report that German tanks were close to their positions. The tanks were, in fact, French.

The commander of the Rifle Regiment of 1st Panzer Division at this action was Colonel Herman Balck, whose great grandfather had served on Wellington's staff in the Peninsula and whose grandfather had been an officer in the Argyll and Sutherland Highlanders.

A TEST FOR PRUSSIAN STAFFWORK

THE Crown Prince of Prussia, in command of the Third Army, described the scene when General Reille arrived at headquarters with a letter from Napoleon to the King of Prussia:

In all haste the Cavalry Guard of the Staff was drawn up behind the King; before these all present formed a wide half-circle behind the King and myself at his side standing out alone in front of it. Prince Karl, Prince Luitpold of Bavaria, the Grand Duke of Saxe-Weimar, the Duke of Saxe Coburg, the Hereditary Grand Dukes of Saxe-Weimar, Mecklenburg-Schwerin and Mecklenburg-Strelitz, Prince Wilhelm of Württemberg, the Hereditary Prince zu Hohenzollern, Duke Friedrich zu Schleswig-Holstein-Augustenburg, together with Count Bismarck, General von Moltke and the War Minister, von Roon. There appeared Comte Reille, accompanied by Captain von Winterfeld ... and a Prussian trumpeter. Directly he came in sight of the King, he dismounted, quickly adjusted something about his riding-breeches, and then took off his red cap and strode up to the King, a heavy stick in his hand, eyes downcast ... but yet by no means without some dignity, and with a few words presented Napoleon's letter.

The King of Prussia read this and having consulted Bismarck and Moltke, prepared to reply. During the campaign his army's staffwork had been notably efficient but now neither the General Staff nor the assembled princes and grand dukes could produce what was necessary. As the Crown Prince recalled:

It was not easy to see where we were to find the necessary materials. Of course no chair could be found anywhere near. A couple of straw-bottomed chairs fetched from a peasant's cottage were put together to form a sort of stand, my Orderly Officer, Lieutenant von Gustedt, laid his sabretache across them for a table-top. I produced my writing paper and eagle signet from my holster, the Grand Duke of Saxe-Weimar supplied pen and ink, and thus our victorious King wrote his reply to the vanquished adversary.

'Someday there will be two spots on the French coast sacred to the British and their Allies. One will be Dunkirk, where Britain was saved because a beaten army would not surrender. The other will be Dieppe, where brave men died without hope for the sake of proving that there is a wrong way to invade. They will have their share of glory when the right way is tried.'

The New York Times,
19 August 1943

DIEPPE

19 AUGUST 1942

DIEPPE

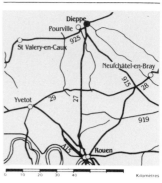

Dieppe is a pleasant seaside town with its old quarter and fishing harbour. Visit the sea front which now has a new casino overlooking the town beaches. When viewed from the beaches (or from the sea) the sheer cliff face, topped by Dieppe Castle, appears insurmountable and one has a chilling impression of how the Canadian soldiers must have felt before the raid.

In the town centre, just behind the dilapidated church of St Rémy, is a stone inscribed *Two Canadians fell here on 19 August 1942*, a reminder of the thousand or so who actually lost their lives on this narrow strip of coastline. There are many such plaques dotted about the town commemorating the fall of the individual as well as the soldiers *en masse*. The scars of shells and bullets disfigure the north-western corner of the church of St Jacques.

A museum specific to the 1942 Dieppe Raid, complete with tanks, can be visited at Pourville. This is open every day except Mondays, from Easter until 30 Sept: 10am - noon; 2pm - 6pm.

The fishermen's chapel of Notre Dame de Bon Secours on the East Headland, the 15th-century castle on the West Headland and the site of the coastal battery at Le Mesnil near Varengeville-sur-Mer are all interesting to visit and offer good viewpoints.

PAC

131

BEFORE THE FIRST WORLD WAR the 'Blue Water School' of strategists, of whom Admiral Sir John Fisher was the most vociferous advocate, maintained that the British Army should not be sent to fight beside its allies on the continent of Europe but used as a 'projectile' to be fired by the Royal Navy at vulnerable points behind the enemy's front in a series of raids. This doctrine was a long time in dying but at no stage did the Navy apply themselves seriously to the problem of how to put an army ashore on a hostile coast, it being generally assumed that they could be rowed to the beach in the boats of the warships. Nor was there much precedent to guide those who would undertake such a landing.

DP

Considering how long Britain had enjoyed her naval supremacy, the number of opposed landings undertaken had been very small - the classic example being the assault on the French in Egypt in the year 1800 when the plan had been worked out by Captain Alexander Cochrane RN and Major-General John Moore. This worked so well that the same scheme was utilized when the army, fortunately unopposed, landed fifty-four years later in the Crimea. No great changes were made for the only other major landing made subsequently, that at Gallipoli in 1915.

In 1940 the question became urgent. With the coastline of Europe, from the Pyrenees northward, in enemy hands, only a large-scale landing could get Britain back into the war with any chance of winning. Almost immediately, spurred on by Churchill, raids were started and it was found that, given a fair measure of luck, small temporary lodgements could be made but, with Britain's tiny military resources, nothing larger could be attempted. The acquisition of allies, while improving the long-term chances of victory, made the need for a successful landing technique even more urgent. The Soviet Union, bearing the whole weight of the onslaught of the Wehrmacht, was crying out for a *Second Front Now* (as, indeed, was Lord Beaverbrook's *Daily Express*), while the United States, dragged into the fighting by the raid on Pearl Harbour, was determined that the war in Europe should be over as soon as possible;

DM

Britain's Army, Navy, and Airforce demand for a second front on the Continent is reflected in this Daily Mail *cartoon of 1942.*

With a fine disregard for logistic reality the Americans were proposing an invasion of the Continent in 1942 and demanding one by April 1943. The British, although seriously underestimating the difficulties, realized that any premature attempt must lead to disaster but they were forced into making a gesture which would contribute invaluable experience for invasion when at last the time was ripe.

Various schemes were discussed, including the capture of Alderney, Le Havre and Cherbourg, while one madcap scheme for the landing of an armoured division to make a raid on Paris was firmly put down by Churchill. Eventually, early in April 1942, it was decided to stage a raid on Dieppe with the aim of 'illuminating' the problems involved in securing the capture of a port.

Dieppe today.
The eastern end of
Dieppe beach where the
Essex Scottish landed.

DP

DP

DP

Two major misconceptions underlay the scheme. The first was that no invasion could succeed without the early acquisition of a major harbour. The second, evolved from the success of commando raids, was that it was possible to gain a foothold on the hostile coast under cover of surprise rather than preparatory bombardment.

Dieppe, rather a minor port, was considered suitable for such an experiment as it was believed to be lightly held and, since it was only sixty-seven miles from Newhaven, within the range of fighter aircraft from England. Its disadvantage was that the coastline on either side consisted of unscalable cliffs broken only by smallish beaches. At Dieppe itself there is a mile-long shingle beach but one that is dominated by headlands at either end. A mile to the east of Puys is a small beach which leads to a defile in the cliffs while, two and a half miles west, near Pourville, is a modest size beach divided by the mouth of the Scie river. Further afield there are a few small landing places in front of gaps in the cliffs. Air photographs had identified the building of pillboxes and, as well as one inland near Arques-la-Bataille, two major coastal batteries, each about five miles from the port. It was clear that these threats must be neutralized if shipping was to be safe off the beaches.

If the batteries could be dealt with, there were two ways of capturing Dieppe, by frontal attack or by landing on the flanks - at Puys and Pourville - and moving in on the town; frontal attacks are deservedly frowned upon by tacticians but at Dieppe there were special circumstances. It was important to deny the Germans time to demolish the harbour installations and, since the whole operation had to be complete in one day, there was insufficient time to work from the flanks. The planners at Combined Operations Headquarters reluctantly decided to make the main attack frontally and to precede it with flanking attacks half an hour earlier. This decision was emphatically endorsed by the General who carried overall responsibility, Bernard Montgomery. In the original plan there was to be a raid by three hundred heavy bombers during the night before the landing and the Admiralty was asked to provide a heavy unit, probably an elderly battleship, to give fire support. This request was firmly declined but arrangements were made for airborne troops to land and destroy the coastal batteries.

German examining a stranded landing ship on Dieppe beach after the raid.

B

The outline plan was complete by 25 April. No troops had yet been allocated to the operation, code-named *RUTTER,* but in England a large Canadian army was amounting, by mid-summer 1942, to four divisions. A brigade group had landed briefly in France in June 1940 and been hastily re-embarked, but the Canadians had seen no action and were becoming increasingly restive. When Montgomery suggested that they undertake the raid, their commanders warmly embraced the idea and approved the plan, even though they had had no part in its making. Major-General J.H. Roberts, GOC 2nd Canadian Division, was nominated as land forces commander; two of his brigades and a tank regiment were moved to the Isle of Wight to undergo intensive training in amphibious operations. A rehearsal exercise on the Dorset coast ended in chaos but after a rerun Montgomery stated: *'I am satisfied that the operation as planned is possible and has a good chance of success given a) favourable weather, b) average luck, c) that the Navy can put us ashore in roughly the right place, and at the right time.... The Canadians are 1st class chaps; if anyone can pull this off, they will'.*

At the same time Lieutenant-General H.G.D. Crerar, commanding the Canadian Corps, wrote that, *'The plan is sound, and most carefully worked out, I should have no hesitation in tackling it, if in Roberts' place'.* By this time a major change had been made in the plan. It had been decided to dispense with the raid by heavy bombers. Air Marshal Harris, A.O.C. Bomber Command, always reluctant to employ his machines except according to his own ideas, had pointed out that nothing approaching accuracy could be guaranteed, that a raid might well have the effect of alerting the enemy and that such a heavy raid on a small target might well reduce Dieppe to an impassable wreck. General Roberts accepted this view and the decision has been debated ever since. On the one hand it deprived the landing of its only substantial support once the Navy had refused to commit a capital ship. On the other, the subsequent experience at Cassino and Caen showed that heavy air attack on a small town usually created more problems than it solved.

RUTTER was scheduled for 4 July and on the two previous days the troops were embarked at Yarmouth, Isle of Wight, and, once aboard, were fully briefed. Then the weather deteriorated and the start was postponed from day to day until, on 7 July, four German aircraft attacked the shipping in Yarmouth Roads and disabled two assault ships (converted channel steamers) although causing only minor casualties. Since the last favourable tide suitable for such an operation was due on the following day, *RUTTER* was cancelled and the troops sent back to the mainland.

That was not the end of the operation. The Russians and the Americans continued to press for an attack on the French coast; Lord Louis Mountbatten, the head of Combined Operations, was still anxious to make his experiment of capturing a port and the Canadian commanders were still very willing to continue with the raid. By 14 July, with its code-name changed to *JUBILEE,* the Dieppe attack was reinstated and timed for August. Further changes were made to the plan. A wholly Canadian chain of command was established (Montgomery having, in any case, left for Cairo); commando attacks had been substituted for the airborne landings (since it had been wind rather than sea conditions that had caused the cancellation of *RUTTER);* it was decided that three battalions should travel the whole distance in assault craft rather than transferring to them from larger ships ten miles off the French coast. This last enabled the assembly in England to be spread over Newhaven and Shoreham rather than concentrating in the Solent ports.

Lord Louis Mountbatten, head of Combined Operations, needed to have practical experience of the problems which would be involved in the capture of a defended fort.

RHL

B

Germans erecting beach obstacles in 1944.

There was obviously an element of risk in reinstating an operation for which the participants, down to private soldiers, had been briefed and then dispersed a month earlier and there is clear evidence that many people knew the destination of *JUBILEE* before it set out. It is, however, certain that no word of this reached the Germans. Unfortunately they were quite capable of dealing with the attack without prior warning. Hitler had rightly divined that Russian pressure would force the western allies to undertake some kind of attack - possibly even a full-scale invasion - during the summer and the Germans were perfectly capable of calculating both the range of fighter cover from Britain and the periods during which the tides would be suitable for a landing. Thus they regularly alerted their defences in the area of air cover when the tides were favourable. The reception the Canadians received would have been the same whether they had attacked in June, July, August or September - or if they had attacked another port.

Detail of the Canadian Memorial.

DP

The quay of Dieppe harbour.

DP

The coastline consists largely of cliffs, the only major exceptions being Dieppe beach itself and the smaller beach at Pourville. The gap in the cliff at Puys is very small.

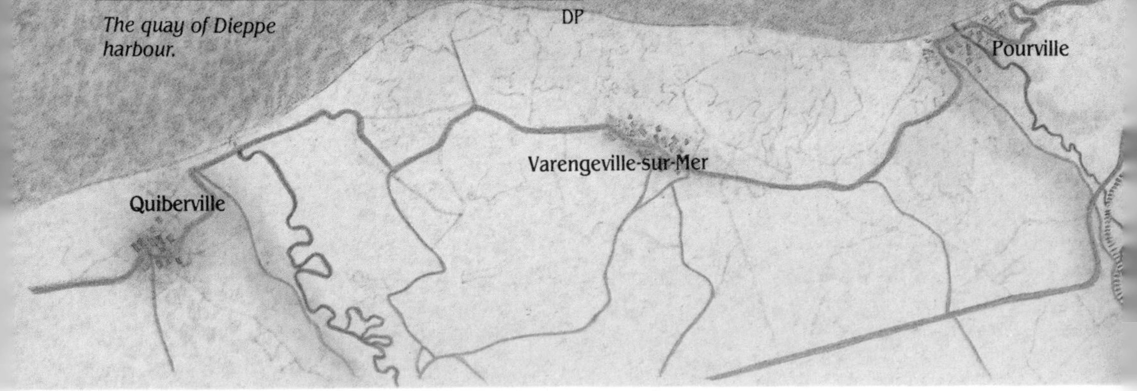

Pourville

Varengeville-sur-Mer

Quiberville

In addition the German strength at Dieppe had been seriously underestimated. In May the garrison, apart from the crews of the coastal guns, had been assessed at two companies. A slightly later estimate put the strength at 1,400 men and 'technical detachments, with no reinforcements within eight hours call'. In practice there was a regiment (brigade) at Dieppe with two battalions in the town and its two headlands and a third in reserve at Ouville-la-Rivière, six miles to the south west. There were four four-gun batteries of field guns in or close to the town, apart from three anti-aircraft batteries manned by the *Luftwaffe.* At least eight further battalions, a company of tanks and some mobile artillery were within eight hours' call and elements of an armoured division were not much further away. In addition the town had been designated a *stützpunkt-gruppe* (group of strong points) and so had many pillboxes and prepared positions while the whole town and its surrounding areas had been encircled with barbed wire.

Dieppe town from harbour.

DP

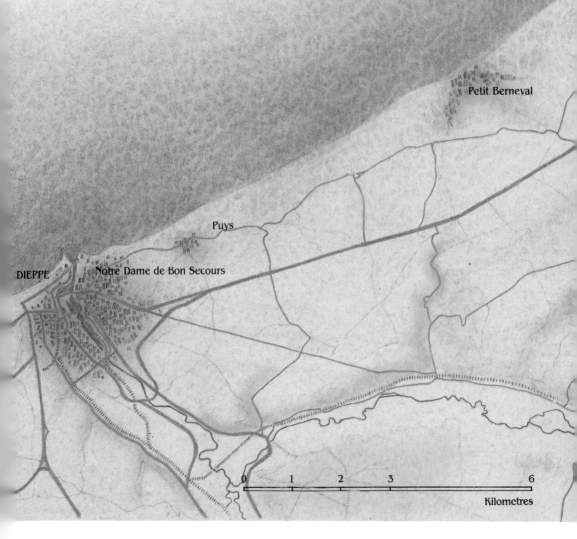

Petit Berneval

Puys

DIEPPE

Notre Dame de Bon Secours

0   1   2   3   6

Kilometres

The raiding force put to sea on the evening of 18 August. 6,100 soldiers and marines were embarked, of whom 4,963 were Canadians, and - apart from three Commando units - there were fifty men of the US Rangers, being sent to gain battle experience, and a detachment of 10/(International) Commando including native speakers of French and German. The convoys were preceded by sixteen minesweepers and consisted of 327 ships and craft including eight destroyers, two of them fitted as headquarters ships, and a gunboat. Seventy squadrons, eight of them from RCAF were allocated for air support. Sixty-one of these were fighters, two were equipped for smoke-laying and only two were bombers (Bostons with a bomb load of four thousand pounds).

While it is probable that nothing could have made *JUBILEE* a success, it had more than its share of bad luck. A German coastal convoy, five small ships escorted by a minesweeper and two submarine chasers, happened to be moving down the coast. Its movement was charted by radar from England and information sent to the British escort. Due to the first of the day's many radio failures, this information failed to reach the warships on the left flank of the convoy and at 3.45 am there was a clash, unexpected on both sides, between the steam gunboat escorting twenty-three assault craft and the submarine chasers. Both sides suffered damage, one German escort being sunk, before the Germans turned away. The firing was heard on shore but

PAC

Hunt class destroyers and landing craft approaching the beach.

PAC

it seems that most of the defenders almost certainly agreed with German naval headquarters in ascribing the incident to routine action against coastal shipping.

The seriousness of this short fight was that it irreparably scattered the assault craft carrying 3/Commando, whose task was to storm the battery at Berneval, and only seven of the twenty-three Landing Craft (Personnel) reached the beach. Most of these, in all carrying 120 men, landed at Petit Berneval (Berneval-sur-Mer) and were immediately pinned down by fire from the defenders who very soon outnumbered them. In a hopeless position, the survivors fought on until 10 am when eighty-two of them surrendered.

The attack on Berneval, however, did not fail. Three officers and seventeen men under Major Peter Young, subsequently a distinguished military historian, in a single craft landed about a mile to the east of the others and found an unguarded beach leading to a narrow cleft in the cliffs. They reached the top, marched to Berneval-le-Grand and approached the battery, midway between the cliffs and the village, from the rear. At a range of about two hundred yards they proceeded to harass the gunners with small-arms fire to such an extent that one of the guns was

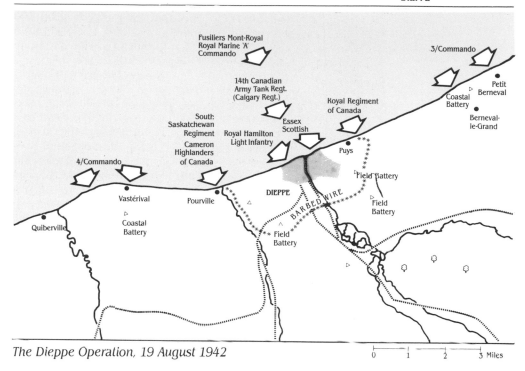

The Dieppe Operation, 19 August 1942

0   1   2   3 Miles

swung round to shoot ineffectively at them. By German accounts it is clear that not a single round was fired out to sea between 5.10 and 7.45 am. After two and a half hours of sniping, Young found opposition building up against him and led his party back to the beach where they successfully re-embarked.

On the right flank there was total success. Lord Lovat's 3/Commando had carefully planned and rehearsed their operation and carried it out impeccably. The battery, containing six 150mm guns, was situated immediately south of the Pourville-Quiberville road north of Vasterival and it was at the last-named hamlet that eighty-eight men under Major D. Mills Roberts came ashore and, having blown a gap through the German wire with Bangalore torpedoes,* reached a point within three hundred yards of the guns. These they engaged with weapons no larger than the 2-inch mortar which fired only two-and-a-half pound bombs. Meanwhile Lovat with the other 164 men landed beside the mouth of the River Saane and moved quickly to the rear of the battery which was already firing out to sea. By an extraordinary piece of luck one of the tiny mortar bombs exploded the ready-use ammunition beside the guns and the blast wrecked one gun and stopped the rest firing. Then Lovat's men charged the rear of the emplacement. They were met with heavy fire from machine guns but they persisted until the commandos could move in among the gunners with the bayonet. In a short bitter fight thirty Germans were killed and thirty more wounded. All the guns were then blow up and by 7.30 am, 4/Commando with four prisoners, had re-embarked. They had suffered forty-five casualties, of whom twelve died.

---

* Bangalore torpedo - a length of jointed steel piping with explosives, which could be pushed forward under a barbed-wire entanglement and then detonated.

*Lt-Col. C.C.I. Merritt, VC
South Saskatchewan
Regiment.*

PAC

Two and a half miles east of 4/Commando the South Saskatchewan Regiment landed near Pourville. At their scheduled time of 4.50 am they came ashore in a single wave but owing to the poor light they landed, not as intended astride the mouth of the Scie river, but all on the west bank. Their objectives were on the hill between Pourville and Dieppe but the landing error meant they had to force a river crossing before they could launch their attack; this delay gave the Germans enough time to recover from their surprise. Led by their commanding officer, Lieutenant-Colonel C.C.I. Merritt (who was to earn a VC before the morning was over) they crossed Pourville bridge and made a number of gallant but costly and unsuccessful thrusts up the slope. Meanwhile the Cameron Highlanders of Canada landed successfully astride the river mouth, again in a single wave, at 5.30 am. Although their colonel was killed on the beach, their left-hand companies went to help the South Saskatchewans, while those on the right pushed up the river and tried to cross at Appeville. By now the Germans were fully alerted and men of their reserve regiment at Ouville began appearing on the Camerons' rear. They were finding their position untenable when orders to retire came over the air. The re-embarkation, made possible by the most gallant handling of the boats, was an expensive business as the Germans held the high ground dominating the beach. Each battalion had about 350 casualties but, by Canadian standards, they got away lightly.

Concrete bunkers near Dieppe harbour.

DP

The eastern headland and the harbour of Dieppe. The Essex Scottish landed on the beach to the right. The harbour itself is dominated by cliffs and was exposed to heavy fire, forcing the withdrawal of Royal Marine Commando A. To the left the cliffs continue unbroken to Puys where they are cut by a narrow gully which leads up from a small point. Here 97 of the attackers survived unwounded to be taken prisoner. There were 554 casualties.

which the new Churchill tanks had been engaged and, although they were somewhat undergunned, their armour showed itself proof against anything that the Germans, who had no 88mm guns present, could fire at them.

The infantry were not able to make much progress. RHLI who had already lost one company from casualties before they crossed the beach, managed to seize the Casino (which stands forward on the promenade) after an hour of fighting but could make only small and temporary intrusions into the town beyond. The Essex Scottish, who had nothing to correspond with the Casino as an intermediate objective, were faced with the wide open space of the promenade before they could gain the cover of houses. They made repeated attempts to cross this killing zone but only one small party managed to get across and establish itself in the buildings on the Boulevard de Verdun.

Under cover of smoke laid by the RAF, two battalions made the frontal attack on Dieppe, with the Royal Hamilton Light Infantry on the right and the Essex Scottish on the left. Their approach was covered by the guns of four destroyers and, at the last moment, by eight squadrons of rocket-firing Hurricanes. It was not enough and both units had suffered heavily before they crossed the beach and gained the cover of the seawall. To make matters worse, the nine leading tanks of the Calgary Regiment,

In his headquarters ship, HMS *Calpe*, General Roberts was receiving very little information. Moreover such messages as did reach

Notre Dame de Bonsecours.

DP

delayed by a navigational error, landed fifteen minutes late and missed the cover of the naval barrage and the air attack. One of them was drowned when it left the landing craft too early, four more failed to make it across the beach and only four reached the promenade. Two more waves of tanks, twenty more machines, were landed in succession and of these, eleven reached the promenade. Even then they were unable to break into the town since the Germans had barricaded all the roads with concrete obstacles. This was the first action in

him were, for the most part, incomplete and misleading; in particular a message received from the Essex Scottish, reading, '*Twelve of our men are in the buildings. Have not heard from them for some time*', reached him as saying that the battalion had taken the houses on the Boulevard de Verdun. This led him to reinforce them with his floating reserve, *Les Fusiliers de Mont-Royal.*

At about 7 am, the *Fusiliers* in twenty-six unarmoured landing craft approached the beach, fire being opened on them ten minutes before the first boat touched the shingle. In consequence they suffered heavy casualties and were scattered all along the beach; in fact some were able to reinforce RHLI in the Casino and make one more temporary penetration into the town. Hearing this in yet another exaggerated form, Roberts sent in Royal Marine Commando A (later 40/RM Commando) which had accompanied the force with the task of cutting out vessels, including invasion barges believed to be in the harbour. They went forward into a storm of fire which was so intense that

Maj-Gen J.H. Roberts GOC 2nd Canadian Division, was in charge of the land forces at Dieppe. Unfairly his career suffered from the inevitable failure of the raid.

PAC

their commander, Lieutenant-Colonel J. Picton Phillips, realized that they could achieve nothing. He climbed on to the raised part of the deck and waved a signal for the boats to reverse course and put out to sea. He was mortally wounded but his bravery saved most of his men although three of the craft failed to see his signal and landed.

By 9 am, it was clear that the attack had failed and the few toeholds that the Canadians had gained were being saturated by artillery, mortars and machine-gun fire. General Roberts

German medical orderly treating a wounded Canadian. The prisoners were, at that time, well treated by their captors.

RHL

UBB

The townspeople of Dieppe sweeping the debris after the raid.

resolved to pull out the remaining men as soon as a new air-support plan could be agreed. Under cover of nine squadrons of fighters and a smoke screen, the landing craft began to return to the beach at 11 am. It was a desperate attempt and, out of one group of eight craft, six were lost. An hour after it started the re-embarkation had to be suspended. Not more than four hundred men, the remnant of three battalions, two squadrons of tanks and various detachments, were taken off Dieppe beach. Worst of all was the attack on Puys. Here the beach is very narrow as is the gully that leads up from it to the top of the cliffs. In view of this the Royal Regiment of Canada (which had been reinforced by three platoons of the Black Watch of Canada) was due to land in three waves. Since surprise gave the only chance of getting ashore on such an unpromising landing place, the attack had been timed for 4.50 am, when the light would be sufficiently poor to protect them from the defenders. As it happened the assault craft became confused in forming up and the first wave arrived incomplete and twenty minutes late, in plain daylight. The defenders here consisted of only two platoons, one of them from the *Luftwaffe*, but they were enough. The beach was outflanked by a house and pillbox on the rising ground to the east and even such of the Royals as could reach the seawall could find no cover. The survivors, nine officers and eighty-eight unwounded men, surrendered at 8.30 am. Of their 554 casualties, 227 were dead. The only members of the battalion to return to England were two officers and sixty-three men on a landing craft which had broken down.

On the face of it *JUBILEE* was an unmitigated disaster. There were 4,259 casualties in all three services of whom one in three lost their lives. In addition 1 destroyer, 5 tank-landing craft, 27 other landing craft and 106 aeroplanes were lost, at least 5 of the aircraft being shot down by the anti-aircraft guns of the navy. The Germans lost a battery of coastal guns, a submarine chaser with her crew of 46, and 591 men on shore - as well as the 37 prisoners brought back to England. The RAF and RCAF, claimed to have shot down 91 aircraft and damaged twice as many. It was eventually discovered that they had destroyed 48 and damaged 24. The Germans admitted to 127 damaged and to only 31 losses. Nevertheless the British airforces did win a considerable victory since, at no stage, was the *Luftwaffe* able seriously to affect the operation.

After the Flanders campaign of 1794-95, in which he served as a lieutenant-colonel, the future Duke of Wellington remarked that '*I learned what not to do, and that is always something*'. Although it can be only a small consolation to the 1,900 Canadians who spent the next three years in German prison camps, the lessons of Dieppe taught the western allies '*what not to do*'. The difficulties and dangers of trying to capture a port led to the invention of the Mulberry harbour which enabled them to take their port with them. It was established that substantial landings cannot be secured without the support of gigantic fire-power from both the sea and the air. Close co-operation

The Casino after the battle with, beyond it, the open area which the Essex Scottish had to try and cross.

B

between all three services began to be practised and many 'gimmicks' in the way of specialized engineer tanks and other methods of clearing beach obstacles were developed. It is no exaggeration to say that without the lessons of Dieppe, the invasion of Normandy could well have been undertaken too early and proved a bloody fiasco.

While the western allies absorbed the hard-won but salutary lessons of Dieppe and profited thereby, the Germans misinterpreted them. Hitler especially became convinced that *JUBILEE* had shown that the best way to stop an invasion was to break it on the beaches. The result was that too many of the available resources were devoted to the building of a thin but powerful belt of fortifications all around their long-occupied coastline; meanwhile the powerful forces, essential for counter-attacks, were neglected.

UBB

The beginning of the long march to a three-year captivity for men of 2nd Canadian Division.

Canadian prisoners, including those slightly wounded, under guard on the beach.

IWM

B

THE GERMAN VIEW

FROM the report of 302nd Infantry Division (responsible for the coast between the Somme and Veules-les Roses):

The main attack at Dieppe, Puys and Pourville was carried out by 2nd Canadian Division with great energy. That the enemy gained no ground at all in Puys, and in Dieppe could only take parts of the beach, not including the west mole and the western end of the beach, and this only for a short time, was not the result of lack of courage, but of the concentrated defensive fire of our artillery and infantry heavy weapons. His tank crews did not lack spirit although they could not penetrate the anti-tank walls which barred the ways into the town.... At Puys the efforts made by the enemy, in spite of heavy machine-gun fire, to surmount the wire obstacles on the first beach terrace showed a good offensive spirit. The large number of prisoners was the result of the hopelessness of the situation of the men who landed and were caught under our machine-gun, rifle and mortar fire between the cliffs and the sea on a beach which offered no cover.

At Pourville the enemy, immediately after landing, pushed forward into the interior without worrying about flank protection. The operations against the coastal batteries were conducted by Commandos with great dash and skill. With the aid of technical devices of all kinds they succeeded in clambering up the steep cliffs at points which had seemed inaccessible.

From the report of LXXXI Corps (responsible for the coast from the River Somme to the River Orne):

The large number of British prisoners taken might leave the impression that the fighting value of English and Canadian units employed should not be rated too highly. This is not the case. The enemy, almost entirely Canadian soldiers, fought - so far as he was able to fight - well and bravely. The chief reasons for the large number of prisoners and casualties seem to be:-

1. Lack of artillery support

2. The British had underestimated the strength of the defences and therefore, at most of the landing places, found themselves in a hopeless position as soon as they came ashore.

3. The effect of our defensive weapons was superior to that of the weapons employed by the defence.

4. The craft provided for re-embarkation were almost all hit and sunk.

HIGHLAND LAMENT, 1940

TWENTY-SIX months before the Dieppe raid, took place, 51st (Highland) Division (under Major-General Victor Fortune) was defending Dieppe with their left on the sea at Belleville-sur-Mer and most of their line on the Béthune river which reaches the sea in Dieppe harbour. They were part of a French corps commanded by the far-from-dynamic General Ihler. His unrealistic orders from Weygand were to retreat on Rouen although, before the orders were issued, that city was in German hands. The obvious move was difficult since, although the Highlanders were well supplied with trucks, the French infantry had only horse-drawn transport and artillery. As Fortune said to his brigadiers:

I know you would not wish to desert our French comrades. We could be back in Le Havre in two bounds but they have no transport. They have only their feet to carry them. We shall have to fight our way back with them, step by step.

On 9 June the real situation became clear to the division who until that day had had to rely on the French for all information. Gunners trying to manoeuvre their pieces back to Rouen returned to say that the Germans were across the line of retreat, and a naval party, landing from HM Destroyer *Wanderer*, reported that Dieppe harbour had already been blocked and mined. These sailors, who had landed to make arrangements for support from naval guns, did at least give Fortune a way of communicating with London. He immediately suggested to Ihler that the corps should move as fast as possible on Le Havre and that two brigades, one of Highlanders, should go there in the transport available to guard the port. This was agreed and the two brigades arrived at Le Havre just before Rommel's 7th Panzer Division cut that line of retreat by reaching the sea at Les Petites Dalles, midway between Fécamp and St Valery-en-Caux. The last town with its tiny harbour was the only escape route left to the Highland Division and two French divisions.

The Royal Navy had already collected ships and boats for such an evacuation but would not sanction the start of the operation without the agreement of the French admiral at Le Havre who had been told by Weygand that Ihler's corps was now fighting its way eastward toward the Somme.

It was not until the afternoon of 11 June that permission to embark was finally given and it was well into the evening before 4/Camerons were ordered to start a three-hour march into St Valery. They decided to cram themselves into the trucks available.

The journey was unforgettable. The battalion passed blazing cottages and blazing châteaux and in the distance the burning buildings of St Valery lit the sky. It was indeed daylight, so many buildings had been set on fire when the column reached the town and descended the steep streets into the upper square.

There they had to abandon their vehicles and, having destroyed them, marched down to the sea, *'the heat of the burning buildings was so great that it was necessary to march in single file'*. Soon after midnight the little harbour and the beaches were crammed with some twenty thousand troops, French and English and throughout the night the Germans fired artillery and machine-guns on fixed lines into the town. No ships came.

Sixty-seven merchant ships and 140 smaller vessels had been assembled off the coast ready to take off the troops but on the crucial night a thick mist descended. The evacuation from Dunkirk, which had ended only a week earlier, had shown how great were the dangers of collisions between ships of differing sizes manoeuvring in a confined space even under ideal weather conditions - the more so since very few of the vessels were equipped with wireless. At St Valery, the problem was complicated by a very difficult coastline, known at the best of times to be a navigational hazard. Reluctantly the Navy decided that any attempt to lift men off the beaches that night would end in massacre and postponed the operation. The weary troops, soaked to the skin by heavy rain, had to make their way out of the crowded town and beaches and take up what defensive positions they could find. Fortune announced his intention of fighting through the day so that the division could be saved on the following night.

General Ihler would not hear of it and surrendered the whole force to the enemy. There was nothing that the Highlanders could do but comply. Eight thousand British soldiers went into captivity.

Five miles to the east, at Veules-les-Roses, a small evacuation was possible. The beach was under fire and many men had to let themselves down the cliffs on ropes contrived of rifle slings. Under the guns of HMS *Codrington*, 2,137 British and 1,184 French were saved. One enterprising corporal of the East Surrey found a small boat and with his section of eight men spent forty hours rowing back to England.

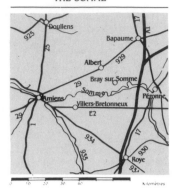

The only prominent features of this rolling countryside are the rivers and the Pozières ridge. This runs through Beaumont-Hamel in the north, is intersected by the River Ancre and continues by Montauban to reach the Somme at Péronne.

The battlefields of the Somme lie between Amiens in the west and the Lille-Paris autoroute in the east. Brown autoroute signs give clear warning 'Champs de Bataille de la Somme' as the area is approached. Take the Bapaume-Cambrai exit in the direction of Amiens to reach the scene of the main hostilities.

Albert is a good centre for touring this area and has several modest hotels and a number of restaurants. There are few facilities elsewhere as this is an area of quiet villages. From the Australian Memorial, $\frac{1}{2}$ mile out of Pozières on the Bapaume road, a full appreciation of the battle terrain may be had. From Albert a tour (taking $2\frac{1}{2}$ hours) of the 1916 battlefield could include La Boisselle and The Great Mine Crater, Thiepval and Beaumont Hamel, where preserved trenches may be seen.

Flers, south east of le Sars, was the objective of the world's first tank attack. The Tank Corps Memorial is at Courcelette, near Pozières which is on the Albert-Bapaume road and can be found near the Pozières wireless mast. The observation platform of the Australian memorial just north of Villers Bretonneux affords a panoramic view of the whole 1918 battlefield.

THE BATTLE HONOUR 'SOMME 1916' which is borne on the Colours of so many British and Commonwealth regiments is to some extent a misnomer as, in the most notorious part of the battle, no British unit fought within eight miles of the River Somme. They were more likely to be concerned with the Somme's tributary, the Ancre, which divided the British front; the disastrous offensive which opened 'Somme 1916' is properly known as the First Battle of Albert. Its first objective was to capture the ridge east of that town which runs down diagonally from the high ground to the north, near Beaumetz-les-Loges to the Somme near Péronne. Since the Germans had overrun it in 1914 they had had eighteen months in which to establish a strong defensive position dug securely into the chalk.

The white spoil from the German excavations showed the line of their trenches clearly from the British lines but what was not appreciated was the way in which they had provided deep dug-outs which would be proof against anything but a direct hit on the entrance by the heaviest type of shell. The Germans had taken advantage of a long period when it had been a quiet sector of the long western front to do a very thorough job of fortification.

Their forward defensive system (which was based on the villages, all fortified, of Beaumont-Hamel, Thiepval, Ovillers, La Boisselle, Fricourt and Mametz) consisted of at least three lines of trenches, which were liberally supplied with communication trenches and with redoubts and strongpoints at vital tactical positions. Many of these positions were on the forward slope but giving splendid observation over any preparation to attack them. In the rear, roughly following the crest of the ridge - known as the Pozières Ridge from the most prominent village on the main road from Albert to Bapaume - was a second defensive system. This was similar in design to the forward one but this time based on the villages of Grandcourt, Longueval and Maurepas. A third system behind the ridge had been laid out but was far from complete, in places little more than a trace on a map.

(FAR LEFT) *The Ulster Tower at Thiepval.*

(LEFT) *Landscape near Serre.*

DP

DP

THE SOMME

Serre

Bapaume

Beaumont Hamel

Grandcourt

Le Sars

Courcelette

Thiepval

Martinpuich   Flers

Delville Wood

Pozières

Longueval

Contalmaison   Ginchy

La Boisselle

Montauban-de-Picardie

Mametz

Fricourt

ALBERT

Maurepas

Ancre River

Bray-sur-Somme

AMIENS

Hamel   Cerisy

Corbie

Mericourt

Morcourt

SOMME

Villers Bretonneux

Bayonvillers

Lamotte-Warfusée

Harbonnières

Cachy

Guillaucourt

Beaucourt-en-Santerre

Fresnoy en Chausée   Le Quesnel

Hangest-en-Santerre

0   3   6   9   12
Kilometres

Roye

Sir Douglas Haig   IWM

There was, on the face of it, little reason to mount a major offensive across the Pozières Ridge. To the east of it lay nothing of strategic value until, twenty miles away, the railway complex around Cambrai was reached. The reasons for choosing it were largely a matter of inter-allied politics. 1915 had been an unsatisfactory year for both sides and in December it had been decided that the quick defeat of the Central Powers could best be secured by mounting major attacks on them from every available direction. From the south Italy would attack the Austrians in the Trentino; from the east the Russians would launch what turned out to be their last great offensive in Galicia; in the west a joint Franco-British onslaught would try to break the stalemate that had settled on the western front since the winter of 1914-15.

General Joffre   IWM

General Joffre, still commanding the French armies, decided that this attack should take place astride the Somme and he gave as its objective the railway complex (*faisceau*) which lay around Cambrai, Le Cateau and Maubeuge. Thirty French divisions were to be engaged on the British right and the only logical reason for his choice of the Somme front appears to be that this was the area where the flanks of the French and British armies joined. His object was to ensure that the British played their full part for, as in 1940, many of the French believed that their ally was not doing her share in the land war. They could point to the fact that, although the populations of the two countries were much the same, the French had ninety-five divisions in the field at the end of 1915 while the British, including divisions from the Dominions, had less than half this number - and this despite the fact that France had already lost a million dead and missing, while the British had suffered only about a fifth of this loss.

Sir Douglas Haig, who succeeded to the command of the BEF at the end of 1915, was willing enough to do his share in the great offensive but disagreed with Joffre on both the place and the time. He believed that more significant gains could be made in the Ypres area and that his new divisions would be more ready for battle if the attack could be postponed until mid-August by which time he had been promised the arrival of the new and highly secret tanks and an end to the shell-shortage that had plagued his artillery since October 1914. He had, however, no practical alternative to falling in with Joffre's schemes. While there was no supreme allied command, close co-operation was clearly essential and since the French army was so superior in numbers Haig took the view that *'I am not under General Joffre's orders but my intention is to carry out his wishes on strategical matters as if they were orders'*.

At the beginning of 1916 there were over a million British soldiers in France and Belgium and many more were arriving but Haig was acutely aware that his was an improvised army. The small but splendid regular army had expended itself in holding the German onslaught in 1914 and, with the help of the Territorial Force, in holding the line ever since. In the first six months of 1916, when no major operations were undertaken, the British had suffered 125,000 casualties. The main burden of the United Kingdom war effort would have to be borne by the divisions of the army Lord Kitchener had called into being. They contained the finest human material that Britain has ever sent into battle.

Every man was a volunteer and almost all were motivated by the highest kind of patriotism. Their courage was unmatched but their training was sketchy, inevitably so since the instructors to train them were hard to find and, in the early days, they had been short of weapons and equipment. They were, in fact, trained to a rigid system which made them an easy prey to the more professional Germans who had the simpler task of defending well-prepared positions. Few had been taught fieldcraft and those who survived the Somme would have to learn it the hard way. Even their musketry was not of the old standard. On the order 'Rapid Fire', pre-war regulars had been trained to fire a minimum of fifteen aimed rounds a minute. It was observed that even the best of the New Armies could scarcely manage more than twelve. Nor were their commanders experienced in handling large bodies of troops. By mid-1916 there were almost as many army corps in the BEF as there had been infantry brigades in 1914 and more army commanders than there had then been corps commanders. This meant that promotion in the upper reaches (and for that matter the lower) had been very rapid and that senior officers were handling more than six times as many troops as they had been two years earlier and to do so had the

DP

In August 1914 Kitchener asked for 100,000 volunteers; 500,000 men responded to the call.

BBC HPL

assistance of staffs which had been improvised since 1914 when it had been difficult to find sufficient trained officers to staff even four of the six divisions. Inevitably some of the commanders of corps, divisions and brigades were to prove inadequate to command and were to receive scant assistance in doing so.

Even supposing that Joffre had been prepared to give the British army more time to prepare itself, the Germans were not. On 21 February they attacked Verdun, launching the greatest battle the world had ever seen. Their offensive made the attack on the Somme more important and less likely to succeed. The French army was steadily sucked into the defence of Verdun and it became essential to draw off the German reserves to some other part of the front. Nowhere could this be done more quickly than on the Somme, where preparations for the offensive were already under way but the demands of Verdun also meant that the French contribution was reduced from thirty divisions to thirteen. The urgency was reinforced when on 7 June the Germans took Fort Vaux (see page 193), their most menacing gain in the Verdun fighting. Haig undertook to launch his attack before the end of the month.

BBC HPL

Haig had now appointed General Sir Henry Rawlinson, commanding the newly formed Fourth Army, to undertake the detailed planning and to carry out the attack, allocating to him four corps (twelve divisions) and proposing an advance on a thirteen-mile front stretching from Gommecourt in the north to Maricourt where a French corps was to attack on the north bank of the Somme.

Haig and Rawlinson disagreed on a number of points. The latter favoured an advance in a series of carefully prepared steps, disregarding the possibility of a breakthrough. Haig, though he had no high hopes of a clean break into open country, still insisted that some forces should be held in readiness to exploit any gap that might be cleared. So far as artillery preparation was concerned, Haig recommended a short sharp bombardment so as to achieve a measure of surprise while Rawlinson pressed for a lengthy shelling which, he was advised, would pulverize the defences and break the spirit of the garrison.

Haig gave way and agreed to a five-day bombardment which, in the event, was extended to seven since on two days bad weather restricted the accuracy of the firing. As things turned out the short bombardment would probably have been as effective.

Rawlinson was also successful in persuading the Commander-in-Chief to allow him to shorten the front by allocating the attack on Gommecourt to a corps from Third Army on the left and to strengthen Fourth Army on the rest of the front by increasing its force to five corps. Of the fifteen divisions composing them four were predominately composed of regular battalions, although much diluted with recruits, two more were Territorials, again much diluted to replace casualties, and nine were New Army divisions, almost all being committed to battle for the first time though most had some experience in the trenches. In Fourth Army reserve were two more infantry divisions and an Indian cavalry division. A separate cavalry force was held to the west of Albert in case it could be used to exploit

Thiepval Memorial   DP

Village of Aveluy   DP

Serre Cemetery   DP

Bird's-eye view of La Boisselle with MASH Valley and the village of Ovillers beyond.

any breakthrough. Fourth Army Intelligence estimated that the line they were going to attack was held by thirty-two German battalions. This prediction was nearly right since the actual number was thirty-four, meaning that the five assault corps had a superiority of almost six to one.

Rawlinson's orders for the first day's attack looked for the capture of, from north to south, Serre, Pozières, Contalmaison and Montauban, a modest advance on the face of it which would require an advance only half-way up the ridge. This, at the north end of the line, would bring them in touch with the second German defensive systems; more time would be needed to bring forward the lighter guns before the second could be attacked.

The plan for the second day envisaged an advance to the line Grandcourt-Martinpuich-Ginchy. Most corps would advance with two divisions forward and one in reserve. On the left, with 46th (North Midland) and 56th (2nd London) Divisions from Third Army attacking

Gommecourt on their flank, VIII Corps and X Corps were to go up to the second defensive system - having first taken, between them, Beaumont Hamel, Serre and Thiepval. In the centre was III Corps who would be aiming at Pozières and Contalmaison. The right attack consisted of XV Corps, aiming at Fricourt and Mametz, and XIII Corps whose objective was Montauban. Between XIII Corps and the river the French XX Corps looked to take Curlu on the Somme. Three more French corps were to attack south of that river.

Fourth Army had, apart from a hundred French guns on loan, 1,537 guns in support, one third of these being larger than field pieces. In the seven days of the preliminary bombardment they fired daily between 138,118 and 375,760 rounds, a total of more than one and a half million shells. Zero hour was eventually fixed for 7.30 am on 1 July.

Lieutenant-General Sir W.P. Pulteney was an exception among generals in the BEF since he had commanded III Corps since its formation in 1914 and was to continue doing so until the end of 1917. In July 1916 his command consisted of three divisions, 19th and 34th, both New Army formations, and 8th, which had two brigades of regular battalions and one from the New Army. The corps front stretched from the north-eastern edge of Anthuille Wood to the floor of the valley a thousand yards north west of Bécourt, about five thousand yards as the trenches meandered. Their first-day objectives were, on the left, the village of Pozières with the German position north of it and, on the right Contalmaison. The corps attack was to be made with two divisions in front, 8th on the left and 34th (on which this narrative will focus) on the right. 19th Division was in reserve to be ready to continue the advance on 2 July.

THE SOMME

FIRST BATTLE OF THE SOMME
LA BOISSELLE 1 JULY 1916

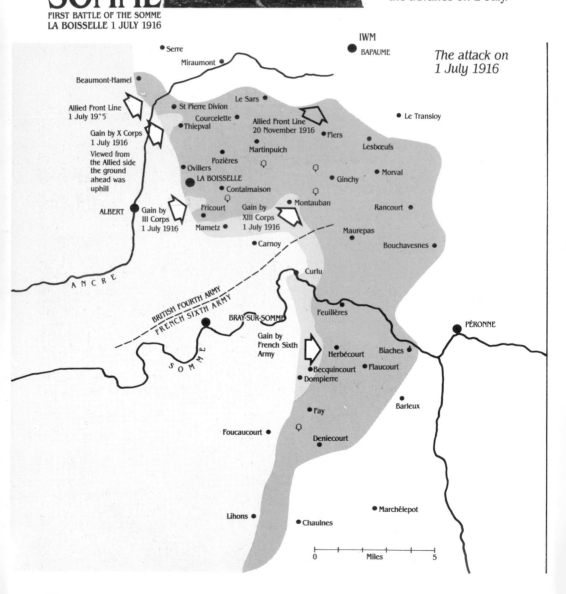

The attack on 1 July 1916

34th Division had been in existence for a year and had reached France in January, thereafter training, rehearsing for the 'Big Push' and spending time in supposedly quiet portions of the line where a single battalion had lost twenty-five killed and ninety-two wounded. Two of the three brigades came from the Newcastle area, 102 Brigade consisting of four battalions of Newcastle Scottish while 103 was made of Newcastle Irish. The third brigade, 101, was more mixed and comprised 15/ and 16/Royal Scots, both raised in the City of Edinburgh (although the senior battalion contained some three hundred Mancunians of Scottish origin), 10/Lincolnshires (known as the Grimsby Pals) and 11/Suffolks, which in practice had been raised in Cambridge. The divisional pioneer battalion was drawn from the Northumberland Fusiliers, which was, in fact, the parent regiment of the eight Tyneside battalions.

The artillery were drawn from Sunderland, Staffordshire, Leicester and Nottingham, the latter city also providing the engineers.

IWM

IWM

DP

Pitiless bombardment. Villages on the Somme front: Serre late in 1916 (TOP) and as it looks today (MIDDLE RIGHT), Gommecourt church when it was finally captured (MIDDLE LEFT), and Contalmaison in September 1916 (BELOW) with the crucifix marking the site of the church.

IWM

Pulteney's orders laid down that they should advance on 1 July in three bounds, the first seizing the fortified village of La Boisselle and its flanking defences. From there the reserve battalions of the assault brigades would go through to the outskirts of Contalmaison. The third bound was to be undertaken by the reserve brigade which would seize the village while keeping its left aligned with 8th Division as it assaulted Pozières. The divisional task was an advance of 3,500 yards on a front of a mile and a quarter through four lines of trenches, studded with redoubts and two heavily defended villages.

Major-General E.C. Ingouville-Williams, commanding 34th Division (he was to be killed on 22 July), seems to have been a capable trainer of troops who was highly respected by his men. He was faced with a very difficult tactical problem but it is hard to believe that he did not solve it the wrong way. His initial objective was the village of La Boisselle which, as can be seen from the road up from Albert, stands just to the south of the main road. It lies on a spur, on the forward slope of which the British front line, known here as the 'Glory Hole', was within fifty yards of the German. With a justified reluctance to undertake a frontal attack, he decided to ignore the village and commit no more than a single company of his pioneer battalion as a garrison to the 'Glory Hole'. His intention was to advance on either side of La Boisselle and pinch the village out. This meant pushing his assault troops up the valleys on either side of it, that to the north being code-named *MASH*, that to the south, *SAUSAGE*. This entailed an advance of six hundred yards to the German front line during which the troops would be exposed not only to the unengaged fire of the village on one flank but to that of the German trenches and redoubts on the other. He thus managed to reproduce on both sides of the village situations strongly reminiscent of the Charge of the Light Brigade - with the disadvantages that 34th Division would not be charging but instead advancing at a steady pace and that their enemy would be plentifully

Lochnager: 60,000 lbs of explosive buried 52 feet deep made a crater 90 yards across and blew a German redoubt into eternity.

DP

supplied with machine guns. He did order that, as the troops passed the village, parties, in all sixty-six men strong, of bombers (that is, men with grenades) should be sent to engage the rear defences of La Boisselle.

The commanders of both the leading brigades and several battalion commanders suggested that their men would be very exposed to flanking fire as they marched up *MASH* and *SAUSAGE* valleys but they were told that the bombardment would have made the German defences untenable and that the garrisons would have been 'wiped out'. It was further pointed out that their advance would be assisted by the explosion of two great mines just before Zero Hour. On the left of the main road, about 350 yards beyond the fork to the village was 'Y Sap', placed at the end of a tunnel cut 1,030 feet into the chalk under a redoubt designed to give flanking fire on an advance up *MASH*. The other, known as Lochnager, was beside the road running south-east from the western end of the village where its crater can still be seen. It was placed to destroy a redoubt known as Schwaben Höhe. It contained 60,000 pounds of ammonal placed in two charges sixty feet apart at a depth of fifty-two feet. Y Sap contained 46,000 pounds of explosive. The attack was to be made in four columns, each comprising half a brigade.

DP

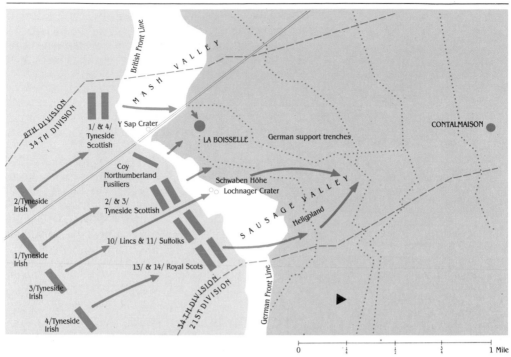

The Advance on La Boisselle, 1 July 1916

One of these columns, consisting of 1/ and 4/Tyneside Scottish, was to advance on the north side of the main road, aiming up *MASH* valley, where the northerly defences were to be attacked by men of 8th Division. South of the road and beyond the 'Glory Hole' were the other two battalions of 102 Brigade, 2/Tyneside Scottish leading. On their right and heading straight up *SAUSAGE*, the Lincolns led the Suffolks and, on the southern slopes of *SAUSAGE* and in particular at a redoubt known as Heligoland, were 13/ and 14/Royal Scots. The reserve brigade, Tyneside Irish, started from the ridge (lying 1,400 yards behind) which separates the La Boisselle ridge from the River Ancre. One Irish battalion was detailed to follow each of the four assaulting columns.

Each battalion advanced on a two-company front with two platoons forward and two behind, the other two companies following in the same formation. Thus each column came forward in eight waves with a hundred yards between each wave and two to three yards between the men in each. Behind each column came another four waves as the Irish backed them up and since they had been instructed to move at the same moment as the assaulting troops, every man from all twelve battalions would appear simultaneously to the enemy.

The pace at which they were to advance was to be regulated at a quarter of a mile in twenty-seven minutes and this was dictated by the speed at which the artillery barrage was to lift. This speed could not be altered without reference to corps headquarters and, in view of the difficulties in communications between the assaulting troops and the rear, it was to all intents and purposes impossible to make such reference. Nor were any batteries left out of this inflexible programme so that they would be available to engage targets that revealed themselves as the advance went forward. In the sector to be attacked by 34th Division was 110 Reserve Regiment which had two of its battalions in the front line and one in reserve.

One of the mines fired on 1 July 1916, shown in four successive pictures. This one contained 18 tons of explosive; about ⅓ the size of the Lochnager mine.

At 7.28 am, on 1 July the two mines were successfully fired, the Lochnager creating a crater ninety yards across, seventy feet deep and throwing up lips fifteen feet high.

DP

It effectively neutralized Schwaben Höhe. Two minutes later platoon commanders blew their whistles and the infantry of three of the four columns scrambled out of the forward trenches and started to march forward. The left centre column (2/ and 3/Tyneside Scottish) was authorized to start five minutes later to avoid possible damage from debris thrown up by the Lochnager mine. This concession turned out to have been unnecessary and cost them dearly. It was soon found that though the bombardment had effectively cut the barbed wire in front of La Boisselle and had demolished the trenches, the defenders, safe in their deep dugouts, were far from 'wiped out'. No one suffered more from this than the four Irish battalions on their long approach march down the forward slope. Their survivors soon found that they were closing up on the assault battalions as the successive waves concertinaed when the leading platoons were held up.

Very soon men in all the waves found themselves part of a confused, milling mass of platoons, companies and battalions scored through by machine-gun fire while a torrent of shrapnel shells burst overhead. Their own barrage went blithely on ahead of them at its steady regulated pace. Fourth Army guns fired 224,221 shells that day but few of them helped the infantry.

IWM

The Tyneside Irish on their long vulnerable approach march across the valley to La Boisselle.

IWM

What happened at Zero Hour is best described as it was seen by a German soldier:

At 7.30 am the hurricane of shells ceased as suddenly as it had begun. Our men at once clambered up the steep shafts leading from the dug-out entrances to daylight and ran singly or in groups to the nearest shell-craters. The machine guns were pulled out of the dug-outs and hurriedly placed in position, their crews dragging the heavy ammunition boxes up the steps and out to the guns. A rough firing line was thus rapidly established. As soon as our men were in position, a series of extended lines of infantry were seen moving forward from the British trenches. The front line appeared to continue without a break from right to left. It was quickly followed by a second line, then a third and fourth. They came on at a steady easy pace as if expecting to find nothing alive in our front trenches. A few moments later, when the leading British line was within a hundred yards, the rattle of machine gun and rifle fire broke out along the whole line of shell holes. Some fired kneeling to get a better target over the broken ground while others, in the excitement of the moment, stood up, regardless of their own safety, to fire into the crowd of men in front of them. Red rockets sped up as a signal to the artillery and immediately a mass of shell from the German batteries tore through the air and burst among the advancing lines.

DP

The advance rapidly crumpled under this hail of shell and bullets. All along the line men could be seen throwing up their arms and collapsing, never to move again. Badly wounded rolled about in their agony and others, less severely wounded, crawled to the nearest shell-hole for shelter. The British soldier, however, has no lack of courage and once his hand is set to the plough he is not turned from his purpose. The extended lines, though badly shaken and with many gaps, now came on in short rushes at the double.... The noise of battle became indescribable. The shouting of orders and the shrill cheers as the British charged could be heard above the violent and intense fusillade of machine guns and rifles and the bursting of grenades, and above the deeper thunderings of the artillery and shell explosions.

Again and again the extended lines of British infantry broke against the German defences like waves against a cliff, only to be beaten back. It was an amazing spectacle of unexampled gallantry, courage and bull-dog determination on both sides.

At the end of the day the Royal Scots, with help from small parties of other regiments including some from the next division on their right, had secured a small lodgement on the extreme right of the division's sector, capturing a redoubt about seven hundred yards behind the German front line. Men of the two centre columns had seized a position in and beyond the great crater of the Lochnager mine. Between these two small but hard-won gains Heligoland redoubt still held out and, on the rest of 34th Division's front, the rest of the German front line was intact. Here and there small intrepid parties had succeeded in making deeper penetrations; Captain Bibby with a few of 2/Tyneside Scottish managed to reach the outskirts of Contalmaison but could not stay there.

No division suffered more heavily on that day than 34th which lost 6,392 men, of whom 1,927 were killed. Of the twelve battalions, seven lost more than 500 men, 4/Tyneside Scottish losing 629 including 19 officers. 16/Royal Scots, although they suffered 'only' 466 casualties had an appalling 333 dead. La Boisselle fell to 19th Division on 5 July and, after a series of murderous attacks, Contalmaison was taken five days later. On that part of the front, at least, contact had been made with the second defensive system.

DP

Serre Road Cemetery: No. 1 resting place of many of Kitchener's New Army.

British casualties for 1 July on the whole front of attack were 57,470 - of whom 19,470 were killed. Even the terrible sacrifice of the Tyneside Scottish was exceeded by that of 4/West Yorkshires (22 officers and 688 other ranks) and 1/Newfoundland Regiment, the only overseas unit in the attack (26 officers and 684 men). The only consolation for 34th Division was that the artillery on their front had succeeded in clearing away the German wire. This was not the case all along the front, notably near Thiepval where the Highland Light Infantry found the wire almost intact and machine guns laid on every existing gap. The only extensive gains occurred on the right of Fourth Army where the village of Mametz, but not its wood, was captured and, further south, where Montauban was taken after an advance of more than two thousand yards. On the extreme right the French attack astride the Somme took the Germans by surprise and gained almost all their objectives, taking four thousand prisoners. The British attack, more than twice as large, took just over two thousand.

1 July was the most costly defeat that the British army has ever suffered. In the whole of the South African War less than half as many men had been killed or died of wounds as it cost to gain a few insignificant acres on Pozières Ridge. The dead and wounded were the best of British manhood, irreplaceable both as soldiers and as civilians after the war. The loss fell most heavily where it could least be afforded, on the regimental officers. It was bad enough that 2,438 of them should be casualties but more than a thousand were lost; 993 of these were killed and 108 went missing and were never afterwards accounted for. Only 12 were taken prisoner.

The ratio of killed to wounded was shatteringly high. In the ranks it was $4:7\frac{1}{2}$ but among the officers $4:5\frac{1}{2}$. Three out of four officers who went into action became casualties. In 34th Division the Tyneside Irish lost one lieutenant-colonel killed, their brigadier and two lieutenant-colonels wounded; fifteen out of sixteen rifle company commanders were wounded. In the Tyneside Scottish all four battalion commanders were killed. 101 Brigade had sixty-two officer casualties but lost no field officers since their brigadier had ordered all battalion commanders, seconds in command and adjutants to remain at their headquarters during the assault, a highly dubious step. The regular officer corps had already been seriously eroded. The Somme made vast inroads into the officers of the New Armies. There were still a number of good officers left but in the future the BEF was going to have to rely very heavily on the divisions being raised by the Dominions in major operations.

IWM

Haig is the usual scapegoat for this vast and unprofitable bloodletting but the responsibility is far more widespread. He was willing enough to undertake a major offensive but the place and time were forced on him by the French. He recognized that a great effort must be made to take the pressure off Verdun but he wanted to make it at Ypres, where the defences were far less developed than they were to be in the following year. Moreover he hoped to break off the Somme attack if it did not attain immediate success and switch the attack elsewhere. French pressure made continuation of the offensive essential. Their agony at Verdun had already lasted 132 days when the Somme attack started and they refused to agree that the British should abandon, or even divert, their effort after one day's disaster. Haig must also bear a share in the responsibility for the pernicious system by which every infantryman was exposed to enemy view from Zero Hour. This was in accordance with the ruling doctrine which laid down that:

IWM

(TOP) Wounded German prisoners being helped to the rear by their guards. (BOTTOM) Evacuating wounded through the trenches on 2 July 1916.

The assaulting columns must go right through above ground to their objectives in succeeding waves.... From the moment when the first line of assaulting troops leaves our front line trenches, a continuous forward flow must always be maintained.

As Commander-in-Chief Sir Douglas Haig must have approved this instruction but, as a former cavalryman, he tended to leave any tactical doctrine for the infantry to be decided by the infantrymen themselves. It can equally be said that no general, British, French or German, had accurately gauged the tactics most suitable against machine guns skilfully used *en masse*.

That erroneous instruction arose from the main cause of the whole débâcle - an overestimate of the capability of artillery. Rawlinson assured his corps commanders that 'Nothing could exist at the conclusion of the bombardment in the area covered by it', and this belief, on which the entire plan was based, turned out to be totally false. Rawlinson spoke it in the presence of his senior artillery officer, Major-General J.F.M. Birch, who did not dispute its truth; indeed it can scarcely be doubted that it was on Birch's advice that the statement was made. It is frequently asserted that the war of 1914-18 was a gunner's war and it is undeniable that, in the end, it was their concentration of artillery and their skill in using it that won them the war.

Unfortunately on 1 July 1916 they had miscalculated and the infantry, who were expected to do little more than advance and occupy the ground, paid the price. The gunners made two serious errors. The first was an underestimate of the amount of artillery necessary to make the enemy positions untenable. They had one gun to every sixteen yards of front. In the first battle in which the preliminary bombardment can be said to have been decisive, the storming of Messines Ridge in 1917, there was a gun to every seven yards of front and a far higher proportion of them were heavy pieces. Nor at the Somme were the available heavy guns (one to every fifty yards) satisfactory for their tasks. Thirty-two of them were obsolete 4.7-inch naval guns dating from the nineteenth century. Most of the twenty 6-inch howitzers dated from 1895 and had a very short range while the sixty-four 8-inch howitzers were improvisations made by shortening the barrels of 6-inch coast-defence guns and boring out the barrel.

DP

Their second error stemmed from the first. Given that the Germans would not put up a defence after the pounding they had received, it may have been logical to have a fixed and unalterable timetable for lifting the barrage, especially as the difficulty in communications made alterations extremely difficult, but there can be no excuse for not allocating some batteries, both field and heavy, to engage targets which had not previously been located or appreciated. As it was the infantry lost all artillery support as soon as they met their first check on the ground.

The Royal Artillery could plead in mitigation that their contribution was, through no fault of their own, less effective than it should have been. In May 1915 David Lloyd George had been appointed Minister of Munitions and, in the year that followed, made his reputation as a war minister by the striking way in which he increased the production of artillery ammunition. Unfortunately this vast increase in quantity was partially purchased by a decrease in quality. There was a deliberate cutting of standards that resulted in much of the ammunition, particularly that for the larger pieces, being defective. As the Official Historian wrote:

The 60-pounders averaged two prematures (that is, explosions which occur either in or close to the barrel) per thousand rounds fired owing to the shrapnel heads becoming detached in the bore.

Defective shells caused one 9.2-inch howitzer to burst on 1 July and another a few days later. Fuse trouble beset the 8-inch howitzers and it was estimated that one third of the rounds fired failed to explode. One officer on the right wing, where the only substantial advance was made, reported 'a dud shell every two or three yards over several acres of ground'.* Even the field artillery was not immune. So many 4.5-inch howitzers burst from prematures that their detachments were known as 'suicide clubs' and representatives of the Ministry of Munitions actually admitted that an eighteen-pounder might burst for every thousand rounds fired.

Despite its ghastly opening the first battle of the Somme ground on until mid-November when the weather made any hope of advance impossible. Every infantry regiment in the British army and half the cavalry regiments took part together with the regiments from Australia, Canada and New Zealand. At Delville Wood the South African Brigade made its own epic, going into action on 14 July with 121 officers and 3,032 men and emerging six days later with 29 officers and 751 men. When the battle ended the British could have claimed to have taken the whole of Pozières Ridge while, on the right, there had been an advance of six miles. The centre and left were, as on 1 July, much more difficult and Thiepval did not fall until 28 September while Beaumont Hamel, another first-day objective, held out until 13 November. By this time those, and a dozen other obscure hamlets, had earned themselves a sad immortality as Battle Honours on the Colours of scores of regiments.

The cost of this agony and glory was 415,000 British casualties and 195,000 for the French who continued to attack on the right. The Germans, who during the battle launched more than 330 attacks and counter-attacks, suffered about 600,000 casualties. By their own admission their army never recovered from the losses at Verdun and the Somme but two more years of blood and sweat were needed before the decline in its powers began seriously to show.

* Such duds still come to the surface occasionally and remain highly dangerous.

DP

Before and after: 1/Lancashire Fusiliers on parade before attacking Beaumont Hamel and answering a roll call on the day after the attack.

IWM

IWM

THIEPVAL

ON top of Thiepval Ridge is the great memorial to the seventy-three thousand British and French soldiers killed near the Somme in 1916-17 who have no known graves. On the other side of the village lies Thiepval Wood from which 36th (Ulster) Division made one of the most remarkable attacks on 1 July. According to the old calender this was the anniversary of the Battle of the Boyne and some of the troops went into action wearing orange sashes over their uniforms. They had the advantage that they could form up under cover of the wood and the leading

DP

The Thiepval Ridge seen from the valley of the Ancre in front of Mesnil.

Sir Edwin Lutyen's memorial to the 73,412 British and French soldiers who went missing forever on the Somme 1916-17. It stands on the site of Thiepval Château which was utterly destroyed.

DP

wave crawled forward into no man's land so that at Zero Hour they were within a hundred yards of the German front line.

As soon as the barrage lifted the two leading battalions, 9/ and 10/ Royal Inniskilling Fusiliers, dashed into the German trenches and seized them before they could be manned. Without a check and keeping close behind the barrage they swarmed on and by 8.30 am, had overcome the powerful Schwaben Redoubt where the divisional memorial, copied from Helen's Tower at Clanboye, County Down, now stands. They had overrun the whole of the first defensive system and had taken more than four hundred prisoners. Unfortunately although 11/Royal Irish Rifles kept pace with them on their left, there was total failure on both their flanks.

Despite orders and counter-orders from corps headquarters the reserve brigade, comprising four more battalions of the Irish Rifles, went through them soon after 10 am, aiming for the second defensive system which ran south from Grandcourt. By some unfortunate misjudgement they moved ahead of the artillery timetable and suffered seriously from their own guns but they took the *Feste Staufen*, known to the British as Stuff Redoubt, half a mile east of the Schwaben, and found it apparently unoccupied although soon Germans in large numbers started emerging from their dug-outs. By this time the enemy had recovered from the surprise and the Ulstermen were under crushing fire from the unsubdued villages of Thiepval on their right and St Pierre Divion on their left. The captured Schwaben Redoubt was subjected to a constant hail of gunfire.

For a fleeting moment there was a chance the division's success might be exploited by putting in part of the corps reserve, 49th (West Riding) Division, but Lieutenant-General Morland, GOC X Corps, having havered for a time, decided to commit the Yorkshiremen to reinforcing the failures on his flanks. Thus the captured positions could not be reinforced, nor could ammunition be brought forward to them. Bit by bit the ground gained was lost to German counter-attacks until, by nightfall, all that could be held was a short section of the German front-line trench by Thiepval Wood. A small party, including some West Yorkshires, managed to hold out for two days in Schwaben Redoubt and then succeeded in returning to the British lines. The division's casualties were 3,949 of whom 53 officers and 1,230 other ranks were killed. It is an indication of the fierceness of the fighting that only 6 Ulstermen were taken prisoner.

Medical orderlies ministering to lightly wounded men in the forward trenches.

IWM

A DOCTOR ON THE SOMME

NEWLY arrived on the Western Front, the Medical Officer of 1/6 Duke of Wellington's found on reaching his battalion on 5 July that his aid post:

...had been dug out from the side of a little secondary valley, at right angles to the main valley of the Ancre; its front was of sandbags with timber balks at intervals supporting the roof which was of sandbags, earth and flints on cross timbers. The entrance had the usual gas curtain of blanket. The ground dropped away in front but had a sort of terrace upon which corpses awaiting burial were put.

My busiest night was 6th July. Casualties poured in. The hurricane lamps on which we depended for light were continually being blown out by the concussions of near bursts. One could not evacuate anyone as the passage of the communication trench was too dangerous to be attempted. The aid post was so full that one had to walk on the stretchers on the floor, avoiding those suspended from the ceiling. The climax came when a shell burst on the roof. Fortunately it was only a three inch and most of the roof held and only light stuff fell on the wounded. This was enough to unnerve some already seriously wounded. The lamps had, of course, all been blown out and we were in darkness except for torches. Secretly I was frightened but managed, I think, to preserve an appearance of calm and cheerfulness.

One man was brought in who had been lying in no-man's land for some days - he had compound fractures of both legs and I had to give chloroform to splint them straight enough to allow the stretcher to get through the communication trench. His wounds were full of maggots. When he came round from the anaesthetic, I gave him tea and tried to give him some brandy before his long journey back to the Field Dressing Station. He rounded fiercely on me, 'How dare you give me that. I've been a teetotaller all my life!'

A NEW FORM OF WARFARE

IT was at Flers, two and a half miles from the Albert-Bapaume road (turn right at Le Sars) that, on 15 September 1916, the first tanks went into action. They had been designed not, as is sometimes stated, as a weapon to exploit a breakthrough but in order to cross trenches. In the words of their military progenitor, Colonel Edward Swinton, the idea was to produce a bullet-proof vehicle *capable of destroying machine guns, of crossing country and trenches, of breaking through entanglements, and of climbing earthworks*. The tanks of 1916 were of very limited capabilities. They weighed twenty-eight tons but had only enough armour to withstand small arms fire. Off the road they could not be counted upon to make more than half a mile, or about one kilometre, an hour. Their 105 horsepower engines were scarcely strong enough for their tasks and subject to frequent breakdown.

Their debut was no more than a qualified success. Of the forty-nine tanks available, seventeen broke down or ditched before reaching the start line. Fourteen more failed to make the distance between the opposing front lines and of the remaining eighteen, a half reached the German trenches *after* the infantry they were supposed to lead. The remaining nine did good work, largely by creating a panic among the enemy who had no warning of the approach of these armoured monsters.

Ten days later a tank put up a rather more impressive performance though once again there were many mechanical failures. Nevertheless, when 64 Brigade seized two bridgeheads in Grid Trench (no longer visible) beyond Thiepval and could not fight their way along the intervening 1,500 yards of well-wired trench, their corps commander reported:

Arrangements were made for a tank to move up ... for an attack next morning. The tank arrived at 6.30 am, and, followed by bombing parties, started moving south eastward along Grid Trench, firing its machine guns.... No difficulties were experienced. The enemy surrendered freely as the tank moved down the trench. They were unable to escape owing to our holding the trench at the southern end. Eight officers and 362 other ranks were made prisoners and a great many killed. Our casualties only amounted to five.

It is said that tanks were used before sufficient numbers of them were available although Haig, who had asked for a hundred and fifty by August could obtain only forty-nine by mid-September, the result of inefficiency in England. It was, in fact, a blessing since, without this practical trial which highlighted the tank's shortcomings, the necessary modifications would not have been made. Nor is it fair to say that, too often, tanks were used for tasks for which they were unsuitable. An infantry officer, who was experienced in co-operating with them, remarked that *the difficulty was to find something that the tank-men would admit that a tank would not do*. The tanks of 1916 were designed to cope with siege conditions in trench warfare. Their potential was only realized more than twenty years later when they were used in open country.

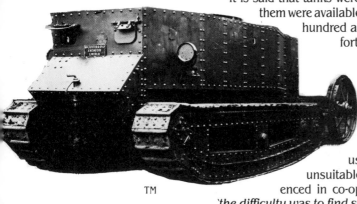

The grandfather of all tanks: 'Little Willie' was the first tank to be built (in 1915) but was never committed to battle.

BY MID-NOVEMBER 1916 when the offensive was finally abandoned, the front line had reached the village of Le Sars, about six miles from Bapaume on the Albert road. Thence it ran eastward to Le Transloy, which remained in German hands, before going south following roughly the line of the N17 road except that Péronne, Chaulnes and Roye were still uncaptured. The long battle had thus taken from the Germans the best defensive position available to them south of Arras. It had also, though this was far from immediately apparent, done irreparable harm to the German army.

Crown Prince Rupprecht of Bavaria, commanding a group of armies, wrote 'What remained of the old first-class, peace-trained German infantry was expended on the battlefield'.

German casualties on the Somme added to those at the parallel bloodbath at Verdun amounted to almost a million - a fact that set the authorities to falsifying their casualty returns - and not even the magnificent German army could withstand the physical and moral effects of such loss. As a regimental history admitted, 'The tragedy of the Somme battle was that the best soldiers, the stoutest hearted men were lost; their numbers could be replaced, their spiritual worth could not'.

There were to be serious repercussions within the German High Command.

THE SOMME 1916-1918

DP

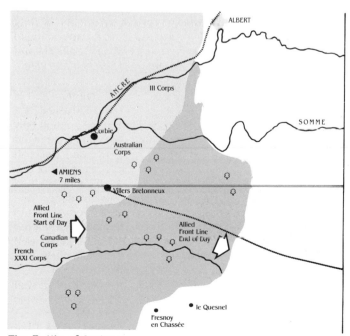

The Battle of Amiens
8 August 1918

Von Falkenhayn, who had planned the Verdun attack and had made the Somme needlessly expensive in lives by his insistence on recapturing all lost ground, was relegated to commanding the successful invasion of Romania and replaced by the tried and trusted combination of Hindenburg and Ludendorff from the eastern front. They took over in August and one of their first moves was to order the construction of a powerful defensive line in the rear. As Ludendorff wrote:

The High Command had to bear in mind that the enemy's great superiority in men and material would be even more painfully felt in 1917 than in 1916. 'They had to face the danger that some fighting would soon break out at various points on our fronts and that even our troops would not be able to withstand such attacks indefinitely, especially if the enemy gave us no time for rest and for the accumulation of material.... If the war lasted our defeat was inevitable'!

The winter of 1916-17 was particularly bitter but throughout it's rigours work was pressed ahead on the new position which, through the inaccurate statement of a prisoner, was known to the British as the Hindenburg Line though the Germans called it the *Siegfriedstellung*. The line was built in a period of tranquillity and became the most formidable trench system constructed by either side in the 1914-18 war. Swinging away from the

IWM

IWM

IWM

The change in the high command. Hindenburg, hero of the eastern front, takes over from the discredited Falkenhayn who was relegated to command in Romania.

(ABOVE RIGHT)
The German retreat 1917. The village of Sars on the Albert-Bapaume road was shelled and deliberately demolished.

existing line south of Arras, it covered Croiselles, Cambrai, St Quentin and La Fère before rejoining the original front near Vailly-sur-Aisne, a few miles east of Soissons. Though originally planned as a stop-line in case there was a breakthrough on the Somme, senior German commanders began over the winter to advocate a voluntary withdrawal to it. The new line would be shorter, requiring twelve fewer divisions as garrison than would the great salient they had driven towards Amiens in 1914, and the withdrawal would yield no ground of value to Germany. There would still be plenty of ground between it and the vital lateral rail link between Metz and Roulers (Rosslare) which enabled them quickly to move reserves from one end of their front to the other. Nor would it release to the allies the use of the line running from Verdun through Reims, Châlons and Amiens which would give them the same facility.

This retreat, finally sanctioned on 4 February, was conducted over some six weeks from February to April, the allied pursuit being staved off by determined rearguards. These, indeed, were scarcely pressed since the allied armies, and especially the British, being trained almost wholly for trench warfare, showed themselves singularly unskilful at manoeuvring in open country. A thousand square miles of French territory were thus liberated but the Germans had taken good care that no advantage should be reaped from it. The countryside was deliberately laid waste, roads and bridges destroyed, houses demolished and even trees felled while the whole area was liberally strewn with mines and booby traps. When an allied front was eventually established facing the Hindenburg Line it had in its rear a desert in which all means of communication had to be developed afresh. For a year the Somme battlefields were quiet.

The wreckage left by the Germans in their 1917 retreat. This village (BELOW RIGHT) was mined to obstruct the allied advance. (BELOW LEFT) The destruction wrought on the Grande Place in Péronne.

IWM

IWM

THE SOMME 1918

VILLERS BRETONNEUX
APRIL - AUGUST 1918

IN 1917 THE WESTERN ALLIES lost one ally and gained another. Torn by revolution, Russia was easing her way out of the war and the Peace of Brest-Litovsk was finally signed on 3 March 1918. Meanwhile the USA was easing her way in. In the short term this gave a great advantage to the Germans as the American army had to be formed from scratch whereas German divisions from the east could be switched quickly to the west. The one hundred French, fifty-nine British, six Belgian and two Portuguese were joined in early 1918 by just seven American divisions*, of which only one was, by March, considered sufficiently trained to take its place in the line. Meanwhile the number of German divisions in the west rose from one hundred and fifty to over two hundred. It was clear to the German High Command that they had a fleeting opportunity to crush the French and British armies before they could be reinforced by the vast, hitherto untapped manpower of America. Their only chance of winning the war lay in a single smashing offensive to decide matters. It was a dream that had haunted their opponents for the first three years of the war.

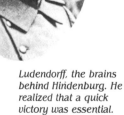

Ludendorff, the brains behind Hindenburg. He realized that a quick victory was essential.

* US divisions were at least twice as large as British, French or German.

They decided to strike at the right flank of the BEF - as Ludendorff said, 'We must beat the British' - where it joined the French, and chose the front between Croiselles and La Fère. The force allocated to this attack was thirty-two divisions with thirty-nine in reserve and the support of 6,473 guns. Since the battles of 1916 and 1917 had claimed so many of the best of the soldiers the High Command resorted to forming the surviving skilled men into élite squads and training them in infiltration tactics. Every assaulting unit would be led by such storm-troopers.

Since November 1917 Field Marshal Haig had been engaged in hostilities with Lloyd George, the Prime Minister, almost as bitter as those with the Germans. The latter was convinced that the way to win the war was to engage in peripheral operations in Italy, Salonika and Palestine while maintaining a strict defensive on the western front until the Americans were ready to win the war. To enforce this policy he pursued a policy of withholding reinforcements from the BEF. More than this, he insisted on reducing the size of each division, cutting the infantry brigades from four battalions to three, a practice which the Dominions wisely refused to follow. There were thus 141 fewer United Kingdom battalions in France and Belgium in 1918 than there had been in the previous year. Even those that remained were under strength since when Haig asked for six-hundred thousand men in drafts to complete the various fighting units, only one-hundred thousand fit men were released to him though many more were available.

The remaining élite of the German army, the storm troops, going into the attack - the last great German offensive.

IWM

Where the German advance stopped. Villers Bretonneux, only 10 miles from Amiens, scene of a vital Australian counter-attack.

DP

Lloyd George may have been justified in trying to restrain Haig from launching major offensives but he had entirely overlooked the possibility that the Germans might do just that. The result was that Haig had a difficult problem in distributing the forces available across a battle front which, on French insistence, now extended as far south as the River Oise near La Fère. Rightly he decided to keep his main strength in the north, where the vital Channel ports were close behind the lines, while spreading his strength more thinly to the south where, if the worst came to the worst, ground could be yielded without disaster. Thus on the extreme right stood Hubert Gough's Fifth Army with a front of forty miles and a strength of fourteen divisions, including reserves, and a promise from Pétain, now French commander-in-chief, that he would help if need be. The German onslaught was to be launched by forty-three divisions (including reserves).

Under a shattering barrage the Germans attacked on the morning of 21 March along the front of Fifth Army and to the right of their neighbours, Third Army. The storm-troopers came forward under the fortuitous cover of a thick mist, reducing the visibility to about fifty yards and masking the machine guns. Most of the forward brigades were overrun.

The experience of a single battalion must stand for all: *About 4.40 am, the enemy bombardment opened, a considerable amount of gas-shells being included. The bombardment included all the back areas which had not previously been shelled since we occupied that sector. From that moment nothing was heard of, or from, our Seventh Battalion.*

By evening the rear party of that battalion reported the day's casualties as 20 officers and 525 other ranks missing. It was later discovered that most of them were dead or wounded. On that day the British army suffered 38,500 casualties, 7,500 dead, the worst single day of the war saving only 1 July 1916.

French and British wounded falling back in the 1918 retreat. The screen behind them is to shield the crossroads from artillery observation.

IWM

'With our backs to the wall...' Four British soldiers who stayed in their positions to the last.

IWM

With the junction between the British and French armies ruptured, Haig called on Pétain for the promised help to sustain his right but was answered by the statement that the first duty of the French army was to protect Paris. It seemed, with Fifth Army in full retreat, that the Germans had succeeded in splitting the allied armies but Haig demanded that a supreme allied commander be appointed. This was a different proposal from that put forward by Lloyd George in 1917 (see page 179) that the British army be subordinated to the French command. This time it was a call for a man who would direct the operations of both Pétain and Haig (and soon of Pershing and his Americans) and who would be responsible to all their governments.

By 26 March, Foch was appointed to this post. He had his limitations as a general - he was given to dangerous flights of optimism - but, unlike Pétain, he realized that the war could be won only if the two main allies held together.

Meanwhile the Germans continued to advance despite the efforts of British, and some French, brigades, battalions, companies and even platoons which fought desperate and isolated rearguard actions where they stood or could find somewhere to stand. These in themselves would not have halted the overwhelming flood of their enemies but the Germans were discovering, as the allies had before them, that to make a breakthrough was one thing - to exploit it was quite another.

Tanks could have been of some use but the Germans had very few apart from a handful of worn-out captured models. Cavalry might have contributed but they had sent almost all their horsemen to the eastern front. As it was they were tied to the pace of the increasingly tired infantrymen who in their turn were reliant on the artillery - and that had to be brought forward through the artificial desert they themselves had created in 1917 and the ravaged lands of the 1916 battle. There are limits to even German endurance.

They gained as much as forty miles in sixteen days of advancing but on 5 April they ground to a halt and Ludendorff, who seems to have had no clear idea of what conditions were like at his spearheads, conceded *The enemy's resistance was beyond our powers ... the High Command was compelled to take the hard decision finally to abandon the attack on Amiens'.* Both sides sustained a quarter of a million casualties, the British share being 178,000, the French 70,000, but it was the Germans who lost most in quality. It was on their picked storm-troopers that the heaviest loss inevitably fell. With the last of their *'old first-class, peace-trained infantry'* gone, they had to fall back on mass formations and, by the end of the advance, British officers were astonished to see German infantry advancing against them in five lines each five deep. Ironically the BEF

Australian memorial at Villers Bretonneux. Almost the whole of the battlefield of 8 August 1918 can be seen from the observation gallery at the top.

DP

eventually gained in strength from their sharp rebuff. The crisis seemed so threatening that Lloyd George was compelled to send over 419,000 fit reinforcements, the Dominions contributing a further 73,000.

The Germans switched their offensive to other parts of the front, thus prompting Haig's famous 'Backs to the Wall' order in which he stressed that *'Victory will belong to the side which holds out longer'* but lesser attacks, designed to pin down allied reserves continued on the Amiens front. On 24 April they captured

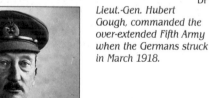

Lieut.-Gen. Hubert Gough, commanded the over-extended Fifth Army when the Germans struck in March 1918.

IWM

the village of Villers Bretonneux which, standing on a rise, gave them a view of the cathedral of Amiens, ten miles away. The main reason for this success was that they threw in their small force of tanks and, since the British had neglected to develop anti-tank weapons, caused a panic among the defenders. By now Gough had been removed from his command and Fifth Army, renumbered Fourth, was under the command of the same General Rawlinson who had commanded it on 1 July 1916. He ordered the immediate recapture of the village. After a two-mile approach march by moonlight, two Australian brigades stormed into Villers Bretonneux and, with the help of 8th British Division, took it in the early morning of 25 March, the third anniversary of

ANZAC Day. On the same day, away to the north, the Germans drove a French corps from Mount Kemmel in the right rear of Ypres but that was their last success in the British sector of the long front.

In the forty days since 21 March they had lost 348,000 men. The British losses were 239,800, the French 110,000. Neither the first Battle of the Somme, nor the struggle at Ypres which led to Passchendaele could show forty such bloody days. Lloyd George must surely have learned that defence could be as expensive as attack.

With both sides exhausted by the fighting of March and April a long pause ensued on the Somme front until, on 4 July, 4th Australian Division - supported by sixty British tanks and, despite a last-minute effort by Pershing to withdraw them, four companies (each 250 strong) of United States infantry - mounted a brilliant little operation against the village of Hamel on its spur (three and a half miles north east of Villers Bretonneux). They captured 1,500 prisoners and suffered only 900 casualties, of

General Arthur Currie - who was in peacetime an insurance agent and part-time soldier - and the Australian Corps (also four divisions) led by John Monash - a Melbourne civil engineer whom Haig considered to be 'a most thorough and capable commander who thinks out every detail of any operation and leaves nothing to chance'.

A British division was in reserve to each of the Dominion corps and in Army reserve three cavalry divisions were detailed to work in uncomfortable alliance with two battalions of Whippet tanks.* On the right was French First Army which, in an unprecedented delegation, Foch had put under Haig's command.

Infantry/tank co-operation. Note the telephone cable which is just about to be cut by the tank.

which 134 were Americans. Meanwhile Haig had told Rawlinson to plan an attack which would 'disengage Amiens and the Paris-Amiens railway' and recapture the old Amiens defence line which ran from Mericourt on the Somme to Hangest, south of the Amiens-Roye road, an advance of some seven miles. British III Corps, now under a new commander, was to attack north of the Somme to clear the flank of the main attack. The striking force was to consist of the splendid Canadian Corps (four divisions) now under a Canadian Lieutenant-

* Designed for exploitation rather than crossing trenches, the Whippet weighed only 14 tons; it could achieve 8mph on a road and had a range of 80 miles. The three-man crew manned four machine guns. Like the battle tanks, the Whippet had 14mm of armour.

The main attack was to be supported by 324 of the new Mark V tanks, the first large tank to be steered by a single driver, with a road speed of 4.6 miles per hour and a range of forty-five miles. In support, either for carrying supplies or in mechanical reserve were 184 more tanks, many of them Mark IVs. The artillery to help the infantry and tanks forward comprised 1,386 field pieces and 684 heavies to cover the eleven-mile front of Fourth Army. Recently developed techniques of sound-ranging and flash spotting, assisted by observation sorties flown by the RAF (formed 1 April 1918), succeeded in pin-pointing almost every German battery position.

This large artillery support was not used before the battle opened, firing being restricted to routine counter-battery tasks. Unlike the opening of the 1916 attack the enemy was not warned of his danger by a heavy preliminary bombardment. The guns were moved secretly into position by night and laid on their targets by calculation rather than by ranging shots. Secrecy was the indispensable precondition of the whole plan and nowhere more so than in the introduction of the Canadians into the line.

The Whippet tank: Designed to exploit a breakthrough and armed only with machine guns. On 8 August they were out-paced by the cavalry, when the cavalry could move at all.

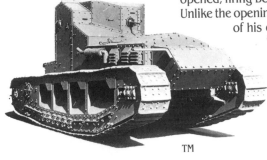

TM

So thorough was the deception plan that 4/Canadian Mounted Rifles (an infantry unit despite their title) were put into the line at Ypres, where the Germans expected to find them. There they advertised their presence by active raiding for a few days before being rushed by train back to Amiens. The whole Canadian Corps was introduced into the line behind a thin screen of Australians and only completed their take-over an hour and a half before Zero Hour.

There were, inevitably, several alarms that the Germans were suspicious of what was coming. On the night of 5/6 August a heavy attack on the north bank of the Somme gained some ground from III Corps and then on the afternoon of 17 August a chance shell in the dead ground behind Villers Bretonneux set light to a supply tank loaded with petrol. The conflagration attracted heavy shelling which destroyed fourteen tanks.

The distant objective: The nearest view that the Germans obtained of Amiens in 1918.

DP

At 4.20 am, on 8 August, just as the first glimmers of light appeared in the eastern sky, the guns opened. The heavies saturated every known German gun position. The field artillery put down a three-minute concentration on the enemy front line and then lifted a hundred yards. As they did so seven divisions rose from their trenches and, with their tanks, went forward. Between the Amiens-Roye road and the railway line to Nesle were three Canadian divisions. On their left two Australian divisions covered the space between the Roye road and the Somme, beyond which there advanced two British formations. South of the river the troops were able to keep close behind the barrage which was timed so that the first hundred yards was covered in three minutes, the second in five minutes, the next eight at three minutes each and thereafter at four minutes for every hundred yards. As during the German attack on 21 March there was heavy mist on the ground but, as things turned out, it was something of a disadvantage to the attackers since their tanks, which at the best of times had very poor visibility, tended to lose their way.

The Germans were utterly surprised. Their infantry hardly put up a struggle and, as the senior gunner officer of Fourth Army reported, 'Hostile artillery fire was insignificant and several enemy batteries were captured with the muzzle covers still on the guns, showing that the detachments had failed to reach their positions'.

Any enemy gun that opened received special treatment from batteries that had been kept out of the preliminary bombardment to engage opportunity targets. By 7 am, the Australians were on their first objective, from Cerisy Gally to the far side of Warfusée Abancourt, an advance of two miles, and their reserve divisions went through to take Morecourt and Harbonnières by 10.30 am. Only on their extreme left did the Australians fail to take Mericourt which held out under the cover of fire from across the Somme - where III Corps (who had lost much of their start line during the German sortie on 5/6 August) failed to make all their objectives.

So shattered were the Germans that the Australians succeeded in winning only one VC that morning. The Canadians had a somewhat harder time, winning four VCs and suffering 3,868 casualties against less than 3,000 casualties for the Australians. The Canadians, however, kept pace on their left with the Australians and made in places a penetration of more than five miles, failing only at Le Quesnel and Fresnoy, where the Germans had had time to recover from their surprise and organize their defence.

The Mark V tank which first went into action on 8 August 1918. In this picture, taken two weeks later, it was accompanied by New Zealand troops.

TM

IWM

The heaviest proportional casualties were suffered by the Tank Corps who lost over a hundred tanks from enemy action and twice as many from breakdown and accident. Even calling on the reserves, only 145 were available for use on the following day. The RAF also had an expensive day, due largely to low cloud which favoured the defenders and to the presence of the Richthofen squadron commanded by Hauptmann Herman Goering.* The 205 sorties flown by the British cost them 44 aircraft lost and 52 substantially damaged. The spoils of battle included 12,435 prisoners and more than 400 guns. Five German divisions were irretrievably ruined.

After the war Ludendorff referred to 8 August 1918 as 'the black day of the German army' and at the time he admitted that 'the warlike spirit of some of the divisions leaves much to be desired'. He offered his resignation but it was not accepted. Nevertheless the Kaiser said on 11 August, 'We have nearly reached the limit of our powers of resistance. The war must be ended'.

* Baron Manfred von Richthofen himself had been shot down on 21 April 1918, either by Captain Roy Brown of the RAF or by Australian machine gunners. His plane hit the ground a few hundred yards outside Corbie across the Somme, north of Villers Bretonneux, on the right-hand side of the road to Bray.

THE FIRST TANK-TO-TANK ACTION

IN the attack which briefly captured Villers Bretonneux on 24 April 1918, the Germans employed their tank force which, apart from some captured British Mark IVs, included a handful of their own tanks, A7Vs, fearsome monsters which crammed a crew of eighteen into a body twenty-four feet long. The armament consisted of a 56mm gun and six machine guns and the frontal armour was thirty millimetres thick, more than twice the armour the British considered necessary.

Having cleared Villers Bretonneux, three A7Vs moved to the south west into the village of Canchy where there were three British Mark IV tanks, one of them a 'male' with two six-pounder guns, and two 'females' armed only with machine guns. The two latter were quickly knocked out but the male, commanded by Lieutenant F. Mitchell, manoeuvred on to the flank of the leading German tank and fired with such effect that, in trying to evade the six-pounder shot, it turned too sharply, found itself on a steep bank and overturned. Mitchell then engaged the other two A7Vs, forcing one to surrender. The other, while trying to escape, was engaged by six guns from 56/Australian Machine Gun battalion. Their bullets could not penetrate the armour but the impact produced so many metal splinters inside the tank that the crew abandoned it.

War is mostly waiting for something to happen. The sentry watches through a box periscope while the Lewis gunners check their weapon.

IWM

General Sir John Monash, commander of the Australian Corps, who did not believe that the job of the infantry was 'to expend itself in heroic physical effort'.

MC

SIR JOHN MONASH (1865-1931)

THE first ever Jewish general in the British Commonwealth was, thanks to his civilian and engineering background, more open-minded in his approach to military problems than were most professional soldiers. Before 8 August 1918 he had been much influenced by Plumer's meticulous preparation for the attack on the Messines Ridge in the previous year (see pages 214-215). He later wrote:

I had formed the theory that the true role of infantry was not to expend itself upon heroic physical effort, nor to wither away under merciless machine-gun fire, nor to impale itself on hostile bayonets, nor to tear itself to pieces on hostile enganglements ... but on the contrary to advance under the maximum possible array of mechanical resources, in the form of guns, machine guns, tanks, mortars and aeroplanes; to advance with as little impediment as possible; to be relieved, as far as possible, of the obligation to fight their way forward; to march resolutely, regardless of the din and tumult of battle, to the appointed goal, and there to hold and defend the territory gained; and to gather, in the form of prisoners, guns and stores, the fruits of victory.

AIR SUPPLY

THROUGHOUT the war both sides found the problem of resupply after an advance almost insuperable. Getting ammunition forward over shell-torn ground under heavy machine-gun fire was at best expensive in lives and at worst impossible. When the Australians and Americans took Hamel on 4 July the RAF set a new pattern in warfare by air-dropping 100,000 rounds of small-arms ammunition which enabled the Australians to stay in action and beat off the German counter-attacks. In October 1918 British and French aircraft dropped thirteen tons of supplies to the troops advancing on Bruges.

Part of 2nd Indian Cavalry Division waiting for a breakthrough which never came.

IWM

MOUNTED ACTION

SO much is heard of the uselessness of cavalry in the First World War that it is pleasant to be able to record a cavalry success. So often had they caused congestion on the supply routes as they marched forward hoping to find the 'G in Gap' only to ride off to the rear when no gap appeared.

On 8 August 1918 they were able to make a useful contribution. The Canadian Cavalry Brigade swept into Beaucourt taking three hundred prisoners although they were unable to penetrate Beaucourt Wood. To their left the Queen's Bays were checked trying to seize Harbonnières but, while the Australians were assaulting that village, 5/Dragoon Guards swung round them and charged, sabres drawn, up to the old Amiens defence line near the railway, an advance of six miles. Half a mile ahead they saw two trains which had been halted by RAF bombs. Two squadrons were sent forward and secured six hundred prisoners and an 11-inch railway gun.

The most spectacular event was the charge of 15/Hussars with 19/Hussars in their right rear. Keeping close behind the Canadians as they cleared Guillaucourt, the 15th formed a line of half squadrons with two squadrons forward and charged two thousand yards at the gallop, the Canadians standing to cheer them as they thundered past. They reached the old trenchline with only a handful of casualties and, sending back their horses, dismounted to hold the line. On the left the railway bridge south of Harbonnières held out until the Germans were scattered by a splendid charge by B Squadron. 19/Hussars took over the trenches on the right and, some time later, the Whippet tanks, which had been completely outpaced by the charging horses, came forward to help consolidate.

One officer of the 15th commented that their charge was 'worth all the years of waiting' and no doubt he also remembered all the occasions when the cavalry had fought so gallantly as infantry.

*The Canadian Memorial:
Standing on Pt 145, the
highest point of Vimy
Ridge and the objective
of 4th Canadian Division.*

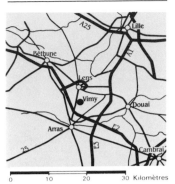

9 APRIL 1917

VIMY RIDGE

1916 HAD BEEN AN UNSATISFACTORY YEAR for both sides. The Germans had tried to grind the French down at Verdun and the British, against Haig's inclination, had tried to do the same to the Germans on the Somme. Both had failed with gigantic losses. It was now clear to the more intelligent commanders that the kind of spectacular breakthrough for which the French in particular had striven since 1914 was not going to be practical. If the war had to be won, and after thirty months of bitter fighting the politicians were in no mood to accept a compromise peace, there was no military alternative to continuing the grinding-down process until one side could resist no longer. Such a conclusion, with its inevitable concomitant of a long casualty list, was distasteful to the allied politicians. While publicly committed to outright victory, they were none the less reluctant to commit themselves to a war of attrition.

Searching for a way round reality, the French prime minister, Aristide Briand, threw his weight behind General Nivelle, who had recently made a great name for himself at Verdun (q.v.), and who was asserting that he had discovered the secret of achieving a decisive breakthrough which would win the war at a blow. Superseding such senior and experienced figures as Pétain and Foch, Nivelle was put at the head of the French army in succession to the overstrained Joffre and told to make good his boast. Lloyd George, newly prime minister in Britain, was attracted to Nivelle not only because of his promise to win the war quickly but, fancying himself as a phrenologist, he was impressed by the shape of the bumps on the French general's head. He sought by subterfuge to subordinate Haig and the British army to Nivelle, introducing the subject without warning either Haig or the Chief of the Imperial General Staff, at an inter-allied conference to discuss transport problems in February 1917. His chicanery was defeated only by Nivelle himself who made demands which no British government could be expected to concede. It was therefore agreed that, for the limited period of Nivelle's 'decisive' offensive, Haig would conform to the French commander's wishes, a course he would have followed in any case.

Vimy Ridge lies 5 miles (8km) north of Arras and left of the road to Lens (N25). The site is marked by an imposing memorial to the 60,000 Canadians who died there. This was one of the scenes of battle visited by Sir Harry Lauder on his 1917 tour, after his son had been killed at the front, an event which inspired his song 'Keep Right on to the End of the Road'. There is a huge car park here. Standing by the memorial one has a vivid impression of the desolate battle scene as the landscape is still scarred with great shell craters. After driving the one-way circuit round the memorial, return to the road, turn left and then turn right again to visit the German and Canadian trenches. Standing in these, one can suddenly appreciate the closeness of the enemy frontlines. Guided tours to the tunnels in which the soldiers lived start from the building next to the trenches' car park.

Arras, virtually on the frontline and almost destroyed in World War I has been sensitively rebuilt to restore its 17th-century Flemish appearance. Near the citadel is a memorial to 200 French Resistance fighters shot in the Second World War. Many World War cemeteries are in this area - including Notre Dame de Lorette, 10 miles (6km) south-west of Lens where there are 34,000 French graves. 40,000 Germans are buried at Neuville-St-Vaast, their graves marked with black crosses.

General Foch   RHL

In 1918, at Haig's suggestion Foch was appointed supreme commander but he was not simultaneously commander-in-chief of the French army. However he was in a position to give orders equally to the commanders of the French, British and American armies and thus responsible to each of the allied governments.

Nivelle asked the British to mount an attack from Arras a short time before his own offensive was launched so as to draw northward the German reserves which would otherwise have opposed him. This Haig was very ready to do since there was an urgent need to push the front line away from the vital rail junction of Arras where it ran almost in the suburbs of the city and indeed through the ground which is now part of the growing town. Haig proposed to attack with three of his five armies with Third

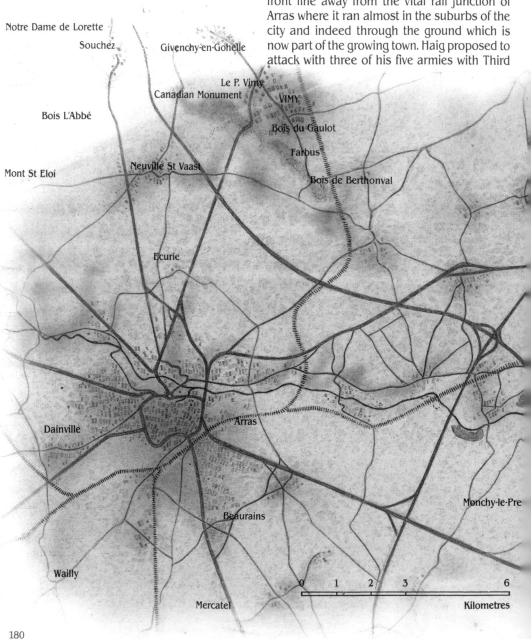

Notre Dame de Lorette

Souchez
Givenchy-en-Gohelle

Le P. Vimy
Canadian Monument
VIMY

Bois L'Abbé
Bois du Gaulot

Farbus

Mont St Eloi
Neuville St Vaast
Bois de Berthonval

Ecurie

Dainville
Arras

Monchy-le-Pre

Beaurains

Wailly

0   1   2   3   6

Mercatel
Kilometres

Army (Allenby) in the centre striking due east from Arras to aim at Monchy le Preux, a valuable bastion standing on high ground about six miles east of the city. On their right Fifth Army (Gough) would attack the salient the Germans had driven around Bapaume. On the left First Army (Horne) would seize Vimy Ridge which menaced the north-western approach to Arras. This last plan was opposed by Nivelle who was reluctant to see troops wasted on an objective, which he believed to be unattainable, so far to the north. He tried to insist that the divisions earmarked for Vimy be used further south but Haig was adamant, regarding the ridge as a vital bastion for his defensive line.

In mid-March, while the question was still undecided, the Germans made a voluntary withdrawal of up to eighteen miles, abandoning the Bapaume salient. The countryside over which they retired was already a wilderness from previous fighting and as they fell back they systematically devastated what remained, reducing it to a landscape through which no army dependent for attacking on its heavy guns could operate until, at the very least, the roads had been rebuilt. Since the object of the German withdrawal was the powerfully fortified Siegfried Stellung (known to the British as the Hindenburg Line) there was nothing effective that Fifth Army could do once they had followed their enemy to his new position and Nivelle grudgingly gave his assent to the Vimy attack as being the only practicable operation which would achieve his purpose of containing the German reserves.

The Germans had seized the ridge in 1914 and in the following year the French made desperate attempts to regain it and even, for a short time, managed to get troops on the crest - only to be driven off. They had succeeded in capturing and retaining only the westerly spur of Notre Dame de Lorette, now crowned by the great cemetery where lie the dead of their 150,000 casualties. Early in 1917 the British front line ran roughly along the course of the A26 Autoroute, to the east of the villages of Souchez and Neuville St Vaast, and was entirely dominated by the enemy positions on the ridge. There the Germans had constructed three lines of trenches on the forward slope which were not only well supplied with deep dug-outs but made use of many old tunnels which they found in the chalk and which they improved and extended so that the defenders could shelter in safety during the preliminary bombardment. Then they would emerge as soon as the rain of shells ceased so that they could man their weapons and mow down the assailants as they toiled up the slope. Behind the ridge, where the escarpment falls steeply to the east, they hid their reserves and installed their batteries in concrete emplacements. With dozens of concrete and steel-protected emplacements for machine guns, Vimy Ridge was probably the most formidable defensive position on the western front.

Vimy Ridge, though not itself a particularly impressive feature, dominates Arras to the south as well as all the low ground to the east.

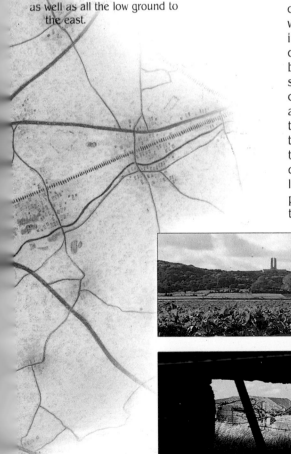

Vimy Ridge and the Canadian Memorial from the east.

DP

German bunker at northern end of the ridge.

DP

181

The task of storming Vimy Ridge was allocated to the four divisions of the Canadian Corps who by this time were, with the possible exception of the Australian and New Zealand divisions, the best infantry in the British army. They were fortunate to be led by Lieutenant-General the Hon. Sir Julian Byng who, although a hussar by origin, had mastered the art of combining the operations of all arms and had the ability, rare in British officers, of being able to lead and inspire Canadian soldiers. He saw to it that his men were meticulously trained for their tasks, that every soldier knew what was intended and what his part in it was to be. Battle drills were devised and practised while junior leaders

Lieut-Gen. Sir Julian Byng, a cavalryman who had learned how to make all elements of the army work together, and secured the confidence of the Canadian Corps.

IWM

were trained to act independently since all too often earlier attacks had bogged down when the unexpected happened and when senior officers became casualties. A large Plasticine model of the ridge was constructed by Captain Oswald Birley (later to be a distinguished portrait painter) and was used for briefing every officer in the attacking troops. Byng recognized, however, that there was a limit to what even the best trained infantry could achieve. Ways had to be found to protect them from the enemy's artillery and machine guns and to enable them to manoeuvre through the barbed wire which was disposed in belts some thirty yards deep in front of each of the German trench lines.

To deal with the enemy artillery, Byng insisted on developing the sound-ranging system being pioneered by William Bragg, which enabled enemy guns to be pin-pointed and neutralized. The gunners had long maintained that barbed wire could be cut by air-bursting shells over it, but if one lesson had been learned at the Somme it was that this was not always true and a start had been made on developing an impact fuse. This was Fuse 106 which, bursting actually among the wire, could be counted on to demolish it.

The second wave of Canadian infantry storming up the ridge on 9 April 1917.

PAC

Supplies were short but Byng succeeded in securing enough for his guns to do the job. To avoid the fire of the German machine guns, the concept of a creeping barrage was developed. As the attack started the guns would increase their range by one hundred yards and thereafter lift another hundred yards every three minutes. The infantry were taught that their lives depended on keeping so close behind the barrage that the Germans would not have time to move from their shelters before the attackers were on them with bayonets and grenades.

The engineers also played their part. Taking advantage of the underlying chalk, they constructed a dozen subways, totalling six miles, the longest of them 1,883 yards in length, through which most of the attackers could move safely forward to the assault trenches. These subways, in which a tall man could stand comfortably, were twenty-five feet below ground and were lit by electricity. Telephone cables were run through them and into their sides were tunnelled chambers to use as battalion headquarters and first-aid stations.

With all four divisions in line, the Canadian Corps was to assault on a front of six thousand yards, their left being to the south of Souchez, their right north of Ecurie. Behind them, packed into every available scrap of cover, was a vast artillery, one heavy gun (sixty-pounders to 15-inch howitzers) to every twenty yards of front and one field piece (eighteen-pounders and 4.5-inch howitzers) to every ten yards. In the preliminary bombardment they fired 1,135,700 rounds, some 50,000 tons of metal, into the narrow area selected for assault, pulverizing the German trench system and, to a great extent, destroying their wire. At 5.30 am on 9 April, Easter Monday, the barrage made its first lift and the seven assaulting brigades* started up the slope behind the creeping line of shells. To help them a sharp wind threw a snowstorm into the faces of the enemy. At the southern end of their line 1st and 2nd Divisions had a relatively easy advance to their objectives from the Commandant's house near Farbus, to the Bois du Goulet, due south of Vimy village. In most cases the Canadians were into the wreck of the German trenches before the defenders had time to man their weapons. All that was needed was to post sentries at the exits to the tunnels to keep the garrison there until supporting troops could arrive to march them away as prisoners. If they gave trouble, a few grenades thrown into the tunnels soon produced quiet. 3rd Division overran La Folie Farm and the wood on the eastern escarpment behind it with less than two thousand casualties - by the standards of the day an astonishingly small loss for such a significant advance.

* 1st, 2nd and 3rd Divisions had two brigades forward and 4th Division had one forward and two back. 2nd Division had an additional British brigade under command.

The Battle of Vimy Ridge, 9 April 1917

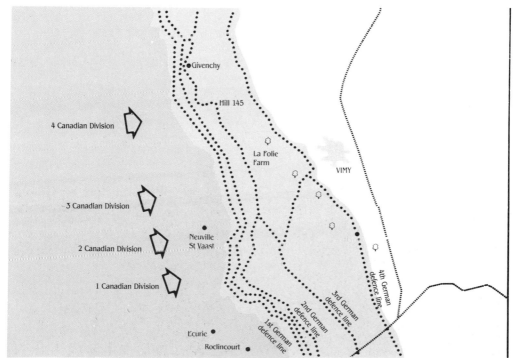

DP

Only at the northern end of the Canadian advance was there any serious trouble. 4th Division's principal objective was the highest point of the ridge, known as Point 145, where the Canadian Memorial now stands. It seems that a German strongpoint which covered the exit from one of the subways had been duly destroyed by the bombardment but, before the day of the attack, patrols reported that it had been re-established. The gunners offered to demolish it once more but some infantry officer, a battalion or brigade commander, ruled that it should be left on the grounds that it would make a useful headquarters. The result was that troops suffered heavy casualties from close-range machine-gun fire as they emerged from the subway and were delayed for so long that they lost the advantage of the barrage. Thus the garrison of Point 145 were able to man their defences which consisted of a double circle of trenches round the height with deep concrete-built dug-outs. They beat off every assault made on them and it was not until the following morning that, behind a new barrage, 44/ (Manitoba) and 50/ (Calgary) battalions made a splendid charge which secured not only the height but also the Hangstellung, the complex of dug-outs built into the steep face of the ridge behind it. German counter-attacks, usually a prompt and effective feature of their defensive system, were few and useless, due partly to the magnificent interdiction of the artillery and partly to mistakes in the German command which kept the reserves too far in the rear, believing the ridge to be impregnable.

DP

The view eastward from the Canadian Memorial. The sight of open unravaged country was a revelation to those who had faced the seemingly impregnable ridge for so many months.

Two days after the capture of Point 145, the 4th Division, again spearheaded by the Manitoba and Calgary battalions, seized the Pimple, the detached height west of Givenchy, which formed the most northerly part of the ridge; to their left 24th British Division secured the Bois en Hache, the spur which linked Vimy Ridge to Notre Dame de Lorette.

The capture of Vimy Ridge was one of the outstanding feats of arms in the whole of the First World War, a triumph both for the Canadians and for Byng's careful planning and preparation. It cost the Canadians 11,000 casualties, of whom 3,598 were killed. They captured more than 4,000 prisoners, 54 guns, 104 mortars and 124 machine guns. It also gave the allies something to cheer about when a few weeks later, Nivelle's much vaunted offensive collapsed in bloody fiasco, leading to widespread mutiny in the French armies. Above all it gave the British an invaluable bastion on which to anchor their line when, a year later, the last great German offensive burst on them.

Aircraft were used to drop messages to forward troops but low flying could be a hazardous business.

IWM

COMMUNICATIONS

IN the First World War the problems of command were almost insuperable. There was no way in which senior commanders could tell what was happening to the forward troops. Wireless was still too primitive and too cumbersome for use in the trenches while the cables of field telephones were too vulnerable to shellfire and the wheels of passing wagons to be reliable. Usually runners, vulnerable though they were, were the best way of getting messages back and occasionally horsemen were used although over heavily shelled ground horses could scarcely move faster than men on foot. At Vimy each of the four divisions was allocated a troop of Canadian Light Horse 'to supplement the motor cycle despatch riders'. In the hope that watchers from the rear might be able to judge the speed of advance the assaulting troops carried divisional battle flags, that of 1st Division being dark blue and yellow, that of 3rd Division black and red. Discs in the same colours were also issued on the scale of two to each assaulting platoon. The orders laid down that 'These discs and flags must be waved and not stuck in the ground.'

At intervals during the advance it was arranged that aircraft fitted with klaxons flew across the front at five hundred feet, a dangerous manoeuvre in view of the number of artillery shells passing over the heads of the troops. When the flying klaxons sounded, the leading troops were told to light recognition flares. If the worst came to the worst there were always pigeons and six were issued to each brigade. 'These pigeons will "home" to Mont St. Eloi (the ruined abbey still visible on the hill behind Neuville St Vaast) where the messages will be transmitted by wire to Divisional Report Centres and thence to brigades'. Unfortunately pigeons were vulnerable to fire and their handlers to human weaknesses. On another part of the front, a corps headquarters were anxiously waiting for news of an attack when 'a carrier pigeon was seen coming back to the loft. Great was the excitement of the staff as the message was carefully unwound, and what they read was, "I'm fed up with carrying this bloody bird".'

ARRAS 1940

THE largest British attack on the Dunkirk campaign formed up in the village of Petit Vimy, below La Folie Farm on the eastern side of the ridge. On 20 May 1940 German tanks destroyed 12th British Division around Amiens and Abbeville, opening their way to the Channel coast and cutting the main Anglo-French striking force in Belgium off from France. It was planned that French and British columns, including tanks, should strike southward to cut a way through the corridor that the panzers had made to the sea. Unfortunately the French force failed to materialize and the British contingent, intended to be two divisions and an army tank brigade, eventually consisted of a single infantry brigade (only two battalions went into action) and seventy-four tanks of which fifty-eight were obsolete.

Major General H. E. Franklin, the commander, planned to advance in two columns moving south from Petit Vimy, swinging round the west of Arras and making for the crossings on the Sensée river, north of Bapaume. In fact a very powerful German force, which included Rommel's 7th Panzer Division, was moving across the south of Arras, intending to swing around the west of Arras and head north so that it would meet Franklin's columns head on. The movement of this German column was known to Intelligence at BEF headquarters but for some reason they failed to tell Franklin about it. It was fortunate that the formation intended for Rommel's right was delayed and the left-hand British column, led by 4/Royal Tank Regiment, was able to break through the German defensive screen whose anti-tank guns could make no impression on the armour of the Matilda tanks. They pressed on through Dainville, shooting up transport and causing considerable panic among the SS *Totenkopf* Division - only to be stopped short of Beaurains by hastily deployed 88mm anti-aircraft guns.

The other column enjoyed less success, largely because wireless touch was lost between tanks and infantry and because, when emerging from Duisans, the tanks took a wrong turning and veered to their left, overrunning the Germans in Wailly before being brought to a stop in front of Mercatel. Their supporting infantry, 8/Durham Light Infantry, were lucky to find help from some stray French tanks and established two companies and battalion headquarters in the village of Warlus after a brisk action. The French tanks then withdrew, promising to return after dark. Before that time, however, the village was surrounded and their tracer bullets set fire to the thatch of the houses. Three despatch riders were sent back for orders but all were lost and eventually the mortar officer struggled through on foot and was able to transmit orders to withdraw.

With the Germans all round their position and, having many wounded, there seemed no way in which the DLI could escape but, to their great credit, the French tanks kept their word and fought their way into Warlus. The wounded were loaded on to the eight remaining bren-gun carriers, the fit soldiers mounted trucks and clung to the outside of the tanks and the column, with French tanks at front and rear, battled its way back to safety.

The Arras counter-attack of 21 May 1941 achieved little except to give a severe shock to the German High Command but the little battle of Warlus deserves to be remembered as one of the rare examples of good Anglo-French cooperation in that unhappy campaign.

DP

(ABOVE) Verdun from the road to Fleury.
(ABOVE RIGHT) The town centre of Verdun.
(BELOW) Verdun: The Citadel.

DP

DP

Flag at half-mast over Fort Vaux.

DP

DP

Bois des Caures

Samogneux

Mort Homme

Fort de Vacherauville

Fort de Marre

Fort de Bois Bourrus

Fort de Choisel

Fort du Chana

Fort des Sartelles

VERDUN

0 1 2 3 6

Kilometres Voie Sacrée

VERDUN

FEBRUARY TO DECEMBER 1916

AFTER THE FAILURE of their 1914 offensive, General Erich von Falkenhayn was appointed to the command of the German army and throughout 1915 he maintained a strict defensive on the western front apart from the minor and experimental attack known as the Second Battle of Ypres (q.v). For 1916, however, he decided that the war could be won by launching a limited offensive at an objective so important to France that she would be bound to defend it to the limit and that in the process the French army would be 'bled white'.

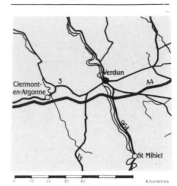

Verdun lies on the River Meuse which runs in a narrow valley and effectively cuts the battlefield in half. The high ground on either side of the river is defended by forts that ring the city.

Fort Douaumont

Tranchée des Baïonettes

Thiaumont

Ossuaire   Fort de Vaux

Memorial de Fleury

Casemate Pamard

ort de Belleville   Monument du Lion de Souville

ort St Michel   Fort de Tavannes

Fort de Moulainville

Fort du Rozelier

Verdun is on the N3, west of Metz. A huge monument to the battle stands in the High Street and beyond the Bishop's Palace is the Cidadel that provided underground sleeping quarters for the exhausted troops. Along the Voie Sacrée milestones capped with soldiers' helmets mark the only road out of range of German artillery and so vital for transportation of reinforcements, supplies and the wounded.

The battlefield sites with their vast monuments and cemeteries are north and north east of the town on the right bank of the River Meuse. To the north west lies Le Mort Homme.

An interesting tour of the battlefields could start at Fort Vaux which lies off the major road (D913) but merits the diversion. *En route* to the main monuments is a museum with models of the trenches; toilets and shops make this a convenient centre but note the *Memorial-Musée* (near Fleury) is closed 1200-1400 hours. Fleury, a village devastated during the war, has a small memorial chapel; plaques mark the site of former buildings and farmhouses.

Visit Fort de Douaumont and the Tranchée des Baïonettes (bayonets protrude from trenches filled in during artillery bombardments), and the Ossuary. (St Mihiel, twenty miles south of Verdun was the scene of the action fought by the 1st American Army in September 1918.)

This aim was not communicated to the German Fifth Army, commanded by the Crown Prince, which was to undertake the attack. The Prince and his army were told the aim was to break through the French line and escape from trench warfare by making a wide manoeuvre round the rear of the Anglo-French army.

Verdun was selected partially because it was well away from the water-logged land of Flanders, and partially because it was an historic symbol of French security and protected by an elaborate system of late nineteenth-century fortifications. It was rightly judged that the French command would use every resource to defend Verdun, and Falkenhayn knew that such a defence would be very costly to the defenders since the official doctrine of the French army was based on *l'attaque à l'outrance*, the offensive at all costs, which entailed immediate and repeated counterattacks, irrespective of casualties, to regain any position lost to the enemy.

Falkenhayn did not care whether Verdun was taken or not. so long as the French bled themselves white defending it. By mid-February 1916 the assault force, 72 battalions, had been concentrated opposite the chosen front, that on the right bank of the Meuse, and in support were 1,220 guns and minethrowers, with vast stocks of ammunition, and 168 aircraft and four zeppelins. Facing them was one French corps with 270 guns, mostly small and short of ammunition. In theory the French had the advantage of three rings of forts and of smaller works (*ouvrages*) which surrounded the city but fortifications had no place in the doctrine of *l'attaque à l'outrance* and the forts at Verdun had been neglected. Many of their guns had been removed and in some cases the forts had been prepared

HPL

*General Robert Nivelle:
He believed he had
the formula for victory.*

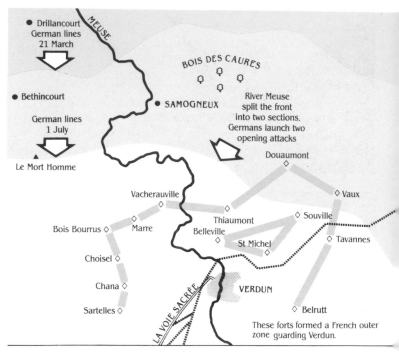

Drillancourt
German lines
21 March

MEUSE

BOIS DES CAURES

Bethincourt

SAMOGNEUX

River Meuse
split the front
into two sections.
Germans launch two
opening attacks

German lines
1 July

Douaumont

Le Mort Homme

Vacherauville

Vaux

Souville

Bois Bourrus   Marre   Thiaumont
                Belleville

St Michel

Tavannes

Choisel

Chana

VERDUN

LA VOIE SACRÉE

Sartelles

Belrutt

These forts formed a French outer
zone guarding Verdun.

The Battle of Verdun

DP

DP

*Fort Vaux: Memorial
plaque.
A mon fils (To my son).
The original was
damaged and has been
duplicated.*

for demolition. Moreover, at French headquarters General Joffre had made up his mind that Verdun would not be attacked and, until the last moment, refused to reinforce the sector. It was the weather that saved Verdun. The Germans had intended to mount their attack on 12 February but driving snow and mist blinded the artillery observers and zero hour had to be postponed for nine days. In that time Joffre had grudgingly parted with two more divisions for the defence.

Early on the morning of 21 February the German barrage, the heaviest the world had ever known, was opened by 380mm naval guns (with a range of twenty miles) firing on the railways in the French rear and on the bridges over the Meuse in Verdun itself. Soon they were joined by the rest of the German guns including thirty 420mm mortars, the true 'Big Berthas', which fired shells weighing a ton each. This pulverizing bombardment fell on the French infantry positions, on their artillery and on their communications. With only one short break, the fire continued until 4 pm when German infantry started probing forward, expecting to find all opposition obliterated. They made some gains but many desperate pockets still resisted them and that night the bombardment was resumed prior to an all-out infantry attack on the morning of 22 February. Much of the French artillery had been destroyed and, since their telephone cables had been cut by the shelling, they were out of touch with the remnants of their infantry. Nevertheless the Germans had two days of heavy fighting before they felt that resistance was crumbling. This was a temporary victory helped by the widespread and novel use of

(TOP) Big Bertha: The German 420mm mortar firing a shell weighing a ton. Thirty of them were used in the preliminary bombardment of Verdun. (BOTTOM) The underground storerooms of Fort Douaumont, the great stronghold which the French forgot to defend.

IWM

IWM

flame-throwers, which caused panic among the defenders, and by the well-meant but ill-directed efforts of the French artillery which, along with several other mistakes, contributed to the driving of the French defenders out of the key village of Samogneux.

The crucial day was 25 February. It was then that the Germans took Fort Douaumont (see page 194) and that General Pétain was put in charge of the defence with orders that 'Verdun is to be defended at all costs'. This was Falkenhayn's chance to bleed France white but Pétain, unlike his colleagues, was not an apostle of *l'attaque à l'outrance* and forbade the suicidal and unsuccessful counter-attacks, which on the previous days had marked every German gain. He rallied the defenders, reorganized the artillery and made his troops believe that he would not waste their lives unnecessarily. By the end of the month the Germans realized that they were not forcing a breakthrough and paused while a secondary offensive was prepared on the left bank of the river. This was launched, with the same kind of artillery preparation, on 6 March, only to bog down on the sinisterly-named ridge *Le Mort Homme*, the Dead Man.

Falkenhayn was well on the way to bleeding France to death but he was being almost as successful with Germany! By the beginning of April France had suffered 89,000 casualties but the Germans had lost more than 81,000. Characteristically each side believed that the other had lost 200,000 men. By the middle of the month the Crown Prince, who was not as stupid as he looked, believed that no breakthrough was possible and recommended that the operation be suspended, only to be overruled by his own chief of staff and by Falkenhayn. The German attacks continued, their greatest success being on 7 June when they took Fort Vaux (see page 193) while on 11 July thirty Germans reached the outer defences of Fort Souville only to be massacred. This, their furthest advance, is marked by the Lion Monument. Since early June the Germans had been using phosgene gas, a poison against which the French gas-masks were not, at first, wholly effective.

By this time the German losses might well have exceeded those of the French but Joffre, dissatisfied with Pétain's comparatively passive style of defence, promoted him to command the local Group of Armies and entrusted the immediate command at Verdun to General Robert Nivelle. Nivelle was fanatically in favour of *l'attaque à l'outrance* and insisted on immediate counter-attacks being made to attempt to regain every German seizure, however unimportant. This lethal policy ensured that overall French losses continued to exceed the German although, late in August, Hindenburg superseded Falkenhayn and ordered that no further attacks should be made at Verdun. The balance of loss at that stage was 281,000 German and 315,000 French. Nivelle had to wait until mid-October before he could accumulate the strength to launch major offensives of his own but between then and Christmas he succeeded in recapturing almost all the ground, devastated though it was, lost since February. The final recapture was not made until 8 November 1918 when 26th United States Division retook the Bois des Caures from a dispirited enemy.

The battle of Verdun, all ten months of it, was probably the bloodiest battle in the history of war. There is no accurate 'butcher's bill' for the fighting. The Germans eventually admitted to about 337,000 casualties and the French Official History admits to 377,231 but both these figures are probably too low. All that can be said for certain is that three-quarters of a million men - killed, wounded or captured - achieved, in military terms, nothing.

DP   DP   DP

Stained-glass windows at
the Verdun Ossuary.

ILS NE PASSERONT PAS

HISTORY has given credit for the successful defence of Verdun to Pétain but at the time the public hero was in fact Nivelle. Pétain held the direct command in the battle for the period 26 February to 19 April, which was only a fifth of its actual course. His part in steadying the shaken troops and organizing the defence cannot be overvalued and was greatly appreciated by the soldiers who relied on him not to squander their lives, but his taciturn, pessimistic personality was not the kind which journalists can present as heroic and the public reserved its devotion for the flamboyant Nivelle who arrived at Verdun declaring '*I have the formula*' and killed thousands of his men in order to prove that he had the secret of victory. It was Nivelle who coined the phrase, usually attributed to Pétain, '*Ils ne passeront pas*' (They shall not pass) which he used in a General Order of 23 June.

While Pétain made no secret of his contempt for politicians, Nivelle was adept at charming them and this facility, joined to the eventual success of his counter-attacks, led to his appointment as commander-in-chief of the French army in succession to Joffre in the December of 1916. For 1917 he planned a great spring offensive, using only French troops which, he asserted, would end the war at a blow: '*Our method has proved itself, Victory is certain*'. Such was his faith in his artillery preparation for this attack that he promised his troops '*You will find no enemy left to oppose you*', the very words that Falkenhayn had used to the German soldiers before the February attacks at Verdun. Nivelle's spring offensive started on the Chemin des Dames on 16 April 1917 and after two days had gained nothing, at a cost of 120,000 casualities. Within three weeks there were widespread mutinies in the French army and by June fifty-four divisions were too unreliable to be sent into the line. Falkenhayn had failed to bleed France white but Nivelle broke the army's spirit.

Plaque at Fort Vaux to
the carrier pigeons killed
in the war.

DP

THE PIGEONS OF FORT VAUX

FORT Vaux was less than half the size of Douaumont and much of its defences and its only remaining gun, had been destroyed before the Germans attacked it on 1 June. Nevertheless Major Sylvain-Eugene Raynal with a garrison of 250, encumbered by almost twice as many wounded and stragglers, made an epic defence. On the first day the outer defences and the surface of the fort was lost but Raynal continued to dispute the underground galleries foot by foot. His only contact with the outside world consisted of four pigeons and these were dispatched one by one with Raynal's report and calls for counter-attacks. The last of them, though suffering severely from gas, was sent off on 4 June bearing the message 'We are still holding ... relief is imperative' and fell dead as it delivered its message in Verdun, becoming the only pigeon to be decorated with the Legion of Honour. Raynal eventually surrendered on 7 June, the last of the water, a gill to each man, having been issued two days earlier.

FORT DOUAUMONT

BUILT in 1885 and modernized three times subsequently, Fort Douaumont in 1916 was the most powerful fortress in the world, one that in 1915 had withstood sixty-two shells, each weighing a ton, from 420mm 'Big Berthas'. Encircled by two belts of barbed wire, each thirty yards deep, to say nothing of an eight-foot iron railing and a dry moat twenty-four feet deep, Douaumont should have been impregnable. Its guns were protected by retractable turrets topped by thirty inches of steel and the whole fort, with underground barracks for a thousand men, was covered by eight feet of concrete below a thick layer of earth. Unfortunately the defence was a chapter of indecision and accidents. Most of the guns had been sent to other parts of the front and, until the last moment, no decision was taken whether or not to defend the place, a decision made more difficult because the forts were under the command of the Governor of Verdun rather than the field commander.

On 25 February the garrison consisted of a sergeant-major with a white beard and fifty-six elderly gunners who manned the one 155mm

Sleeping quarters inside Fort Douaumont.

DP

Cross section of Fort Douaumont.

Gorge bunker with flanking galleries

Barbed wire

Casements

Barracks

Rue de Rampart

and two 75mm guns that remained. An infantry unit had been detailed to cover the front of the fort but its orders had not been delivered.

The details of the German capture of Douaumont read like the scenario of a farce. Four separate detachments, the largest of them not more than fifty strong, found their way independently into the interior of the fort, some of them in the hope of escaping from the fire of their own artillery. The first man in was a sergeant of pioneers, accompanied by two men. He succeeded in stopping the fire of the larger gun and, having lost his companions in the complicated corridors, locked up half the garrison in their underground quarters. He then turned his attention to having a good meal during which his captives escaped, only to be retaken by another German party. It took the French eight months and tens-of-thousands of casualties to regain Douaumont - and when they reached it they found only twenty-eight men cowering in the cellars - but they had succeeded in losing it without firing a single shot in its defence.

LA VOIE SACRÉE

WHEN Pétain took over the command at the end of February not the least of his problems was to supply his troops and, above all, his artillery, since the railway to the east was in German hands and that to the west was made unusable by German artillery. All that remained was the secondary road to Bar-le-Duc, unsurfaced and only wide enough to allow two trucks to pass. There were only seven hundred trucks in the military area, giving a lift of 1,250 tons, barely half the daily requirement of the troops there at the beginning of the battle. By requisitioning 3,500 *camions* from all over France, 25,000 tons were moved into Verdun during the following week despite a sharp thaw which reduced the road to a sea of mud. For the rest of the battle the equivalent of a division of men was constantly employed in keeping the *Voie Sacrée*, the sacred road, open and it is said that three-quarters of a million tons of stone was shovelled on to its surface.

The Chapel at Fleury.

One of the turrets of Fort Vaux.

DP

DP

Concrete shelter
Observation turret
7mm turret
Glacis
Barbed wire

LIFE IN THE BATTLE

FOR those ten months in 1916, more than half a million men at one time fought over the Verdun battlefield (about seventy square miles) and there were very few latrines. In addition there were anything up to 400,000 corpses, many of which had to be left unburied. Even in April, when the weather was wet and mild, the stench was so bad that the German army doubled the tobacco ration. Things were infinitely worse through the torrid summer with water desperately short. One French officer noted 'a man drinking from a green scum-covered marsh where lay, his black face downwards in the water, a dead man lying on his stomach'. Another wrote, 'You find the dead embedded in the walls of the trenches ... the corpse of an infantryman in a blue cap emerges but, a few hours later, he has disappeared and been replaced by a tirailleur in khaki. Other corpses in other uniforms appear successively as the shell which buries one disinters another.

Since 1918 more than 130,000 corpses have been discovered - they are still occasionally emerging - and their bones have been placed in the *Ossuaire*.

AMONG THOSE PRESENT

NO ONE was ever the same after fighting at Verdun and its effect was felt into the Second World War. One man who learned a profitable lesson there was Marshal von Manstein, who went through the whole battle as a staff officer. It was he who devised the plan which enabled the Germans to cut through the French defence in 1940, thus avoiding any repetition of the trench warfare of 1914-18.

Guderian, who carried out the Manstein plan also fought at Verdun, as did von Paulus who, when encircled at Stalingrad, may have felt a twinge of fellow feeling for Pétain and Nivelle. Von Brauschitch and Keitel both fought there but the saddest case was that of General von Stülpnagel, Governor of Paris in 1944. Deeply implicated in the plot against Hitler, he was returning to Germany to face the vengeance of the Gestapo.

On Le Mort Homme, where he had commanded a battalion in 1916, he tried to commit suicide but succeeded only in blinding himself.

On the French side President Lebrun, whom Pétain displaced in the hour of France's defeat, fought at Verdun as a private soldier; the future Marshal de Lattre de Tassigny was also there, as was Admiral Darlan who, as a lieutenant, commanded a 155mm naval gun. Captain Charles de Gaulle was wounded and captured defending Douaumont village. He was serving in the *33me Régiment* which he had asked to join when commissioned from St Cyr - his reason for choosing that unit was his admiration for its commanding officer, Colonel Pétain. The value of the Verdun forts made a lasting impression on another combatant, Sergeant André Maginot.

*Where the village of
Fleury stood.*

DP

Fort Vaux, Verdun, looking north west towards Douaumont. The tower of the Ossuary is on the skyline to the left. The German advance from the right gave them possession of all this ground by 1 July 1916.

(BELOW LEFT) *Hotel de Ville, Verdun.*
(LEFT) *Barbed wire at Fort Vaux.*
(BELOW) *Entrance to Bayonet trenches.*

DP

DP

DP

THERE CAN BE VERY FEW PLACES outside the Commonwealth where there are so many British graves - English, Welsh, Scottish, and Irish; Canadian, Australian, New Zealand and Indian - as the area around Ypres. In 1383 an English army, led by the Bishop of Norwich, unsuccessfully besieged the city and it was triumphantly stormed by a detachment of the New Model Army while Oliver Cromwell, the Lord Protector, lay dying in 1658. Most of the graves, however, date from two and a half centuries later. There are 174 First World War cemetries near Ypres, the largest of them containing 11,908 graves, and the district is dotted with place names that are as well known as any in British military history - Armentières, Ploegsteert, Messines, Hill 60 and, above all, Passchendaele. (It remains a mystery why the British still cling to this complicated spelling of the last named when the simpler, Passendale, is equally acceptable.)

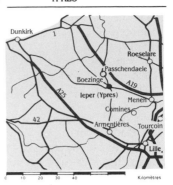

YPRES

Ypres (Ieper) in Belgium, 7 miles (11km) from the French border, is a good centre for touring Flanders battlefields. The replica 13th-century Cloth Hall houses The Salient 1914-18 War Museum. Remains of shelters and gun emplacements mark the line of a trench atop its ramparts. The Menin Gate is engraved with the names of 54,896 missing soldiers. Here, every evening at 8pm, buglers still sound the Last Post.

On the Menin Road, the Potijze/Zillebeke crossroads is the site of Hellfire Corner. The Sanctuary Wood Museum (with café), Hill 62 and the Canadian Memorial are clearly marked on the south side of the Menin Road, the N9. Authentic stretches of trenches are preserved. At Hill 60, farther south of the Menin Road at Zwarte-Leen, there is an interesting small museum (toilets available), with a motley collection of memorabilia; slot machines present views of the battle.

From Ypres to the north-east, the N332 leads to Passchendaele and Zonnebeke. Visit Polygon Wood; turn left out of the cemetery and there is a good café at the end of the road in Zonnebeke. Tyne Cot Cemetery overlooks Passchendaele's field of slaughter and is the largest British war cemetery in the world. Essex Farm Cemetery at Boezinge (where Lieut-Col J.M. Macrae wrote the poem *In Flanders Fields the Poppies Grow*) lies north of Ypres on the N69.

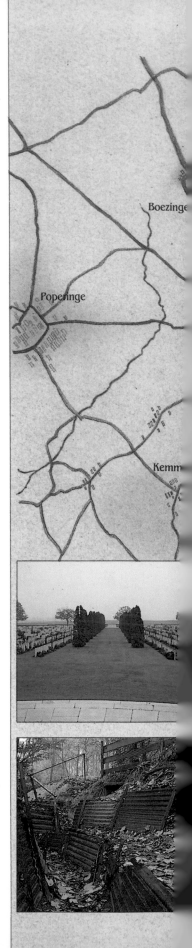

The ridge, which is low but long, runs from the north of Passchendaele southwards through Gheluvelt to the railway by Zwarte-Leen, and then swings away westwards to Kemmel and beyond.

The vast blood-letting around Ypres between 1914 and 1918 is barely explicable in military terms. At the beginning of that war it was a declining town of little consequence to anyone other than its eighteen thousand inhabitants. By 1918 it had been so heavily bombarded that it was said that a man on a horse could see across the town from one side to the other. This misfortune came to it because it is situated squarely between the rivers Lys and Yser and in October 1914 both sides believed that this corridor offered a last chance to break free of the siege warfare which, to the south, had followed the German repulse on the Marne. The allies hoped to outflank the Germans and, by an encircling move, recapture the rich industrial region comprising Lille, Tourcoing and Courtrai. The Germans were intent on driving westward to seize Calais and Boulogne, the key links between France and Britain. The two thrusts met head-on and the Germans were by far the most powerful.

They made valuable gains but, at the cost of Britain's regular army, they failed to take Ypres. Thereafter the city became a symbol which the allies believed they must not lose, the British because they had given so much of their best to save it; the French because their tactical doctrine forbade yielding ground without fighting to the death to retain it; the Belgians because it represented the southern tip of the thin strip of national territory which remained to them. While Ypres could be held to be an outer bastion of the defence of the Channel Ports, it was a singularly inconvenient bastion, one in which all the advantages had been seized by the enemy.

It lies in the Flanders plain where the water table is only a few feet below the ground level even in dry times and where, after prolonged rains even a small crater will fill with water. All that can be said for the ground is that the area between Ypres and the sea is even wetter. To some extent it is a road centre but in 1914 all the roads that met there were narrow, built on meagre foundations and far from suitable for carrying the transport of large armies. On two sides the city is screened by low ridges. To the east is the Passchendaele - Gheluvelt ridge, nowhere higher than 131 feet above the ground at Ypres. At the southern end the ground falls away to the Ypres - Comines railway where stands Hill 60 which is not properly a hill but the spoilheap from the building of the railway cutting. From there westward runs the second ridge, rising first to 195 feet above Ypres at Wytschaete, due south of the city, and further west to, by contrast, the more substantial height of Mont Kemmel.

The first Battle of Ypres (October - November 1914) gave the Germans possession of the whole of the eastern ridge and the Wytschaete-Messines feature on the southern, the allied front line being pushed back to just in front of the villages of, from north to south, Pilckem, St Julien, Frezenberg, Zillebecke, St Eloi, Wulverghem and Ploegsteert. This was an unacceptable position since every observation point, barring the distant Mont Kemmel, was in German hands. The enemy could, therefore, see every allied movement while their own were screened. The situation was not improved when, in April 1915, the Germans launched the Second Battle, originally intended as little more than a diversion, and seized Pilckem and St Julien.

It being politically and morally impossible to fall back to a position where all the advantages did not lie with the Germans, the only practical solution was to recapture the ridges but in 1915 the British had not the strength to attempt it since her army was, in effect, being rebuilt from the ground up and the French were devoting all their main strength elsewhere. When Sir Douglas Haig succeeded to command of the British Expeditionary Force in December 1915 he was determined that the clearing of the Ypres ridges should be the British priority but British strategy had to be subservient at this stage to French, and allied solidarity demanded that he make his first great effort, an unsuccessful one, on the Somme (see page 148).

By 1917 he was in a position to undertake the essential attack on the eastern ridge and he preceded it with a brilliant subsidiary operation which gave him possession of the Wytschaete-Messine feature. The real Third Battle of Ypres started at the end of July and, after a shaky start, had gained the crest of the whole ridge, except its northern tip, in a series of excellently planned and executed limited attacks.

DP

The turning off the Menin Road near Hooge, leading to Sanctuary Wood.

Troops moving up the Menin Road from Ypres in September 1917.

It remained to capture Passchendaele, which would give real security to Ypres; and the attempt to do so, mostly in appalling weather, made that name a symbol of horror. At a frightful cost in lives on both sides, the attack was eventually successful but, in the Spring offensive of the following year, all the gains were lost and even Mont Kemmel fell. By that time, however, it was too late for Germany.

In a book on this scale it is impossible to follow in detail all the fighting around Ypres over three years and it is suggested that the visitor should first visit the Menin Road area, the site of the most critical fighting in 1914, and then work north to Passchendaele. If time allows, a visit to Messines (see page 219) would be rewarding.

IWM

YPRES

WITH THE GERMANS DRIVEN BACK to the Aisne, it was clear by the end of September 1914 that the Schlieffen Plan had miscarried and that the armies were deadlocked on the direct route to Paris. Both sides therefore sought for the only open flank remaining, that between Lille and the English Channel, in the hope of restoring open warfare since the siege conditions developing in the centre and south of the front suited neither side. Von Moltke, who had fumblingly directed the first German offensive, was shuffled aside and his place taken by Erich von Falkenhayn, who retained his position as Minister for War and who decided to 'bring the northern coast of France and therefore control of the English Channel into German hands.' He aimed to do so in the gap between the built-up industrial complex north of Lille and the wetlands stretching south from the coast, using the corridor between the rivers Lys and Yser. Simultaneously the French commander-in-chief, Joseph Joffre, started to move French corps from the south of the front to his left, intending to liberate Lille (lost on 12 October) and turn the German flank. As part of this process he moved the three corps of the BEF to the area of La Bassée, where they were closer to their communications with the Channel Ports, and where they were joined by the improvised IV Corps, a single infantry division and two cavalry brigades.

This had been formed to assist the Belgians in their defence of Antwerp and when that fell on 10 October had marched south to join the main body of the British force. With the remains of the Belgian army holding the coastal strip and French forces being moved into the gap between their right and the British left, Joffre appointed Ferdinand Foch to co-ordinate the operations of the allied army. He was notoriously an aggressive commander but was hampered because he could only advise and could not give orders either to the king of the Belgians or to Sir John French, commanding the BEF. This phase of the war has become known as 'The Race to the Sea' but it was a race that neither competitor wished to win since to reach the coast would spell deadlock and initiate siege warfare from Nieuport to Switzerland. In the event the Germans won a pyrrhic victory since the French were always 'twenty four hours and an Army Corps behind the enemy.' This, however, was not clear in mid-October and optimism was the order of the day. On 15 October, by which time his left flank had been extended as far north as Langemarck, five miles beyond Ypres, Sir John French issued a general order which began, 'It is the intention of the Commander-in-Chief to advance eastward, attacking the enemy wherever met.' On the right III Corps was to advance astride the Lys through Armentières and seize the high ground overlooking Lille from the north. In the centre the understrength IV Corps would move from Ypres to Menin and, as soon as it had arrived from the south, I Corps (Lieutenant-General Sir Douglas Haig) was to march north-east from Ypres 'via Thourout (Torhout) and capture Bruges'.

This grandiose scheme was based on Sir John's belief, shared by Foch, that 'the enemy's strength on the front Ostend-Menin is about one corps, not more.' Even had this been true the advance of III Corps on the right was notably sluggish and they could hardly be induced to reoccupy Armentières when the enemy evacuated the place. The real error in the estimate of German strength was brought home to Henry Rawlinson on 19 October when his III Corps was approaching Menin and:

An airman came in with the startling intelligence that four strong columns of Germans were coming down from the east on my left flank. I had only just time to warn 7th Division when they were attacked, but the warning enabled them to front up to their opponents and we got out of a difficult situation with only 150 casualties.

Canadian stretcher bearers evacuating wounded from Passchendaele, October 1917.

IWM

This new threat did not diminish French's optimism and on the following day I Corps started its advance to the north-east of Ypres and were gaining ground towards their first objective, the village of Passchendaele, when the left flankguard, consisting of French cavalry, was drawn off by a further threat to the north and the British advance had to halt.

The fact was that von Falkenhayn was launching a major assault on the whole front from the Lys to the sea. Since the only troops he had immediately available were those released from the siege of Antwerp, who were plentifully supplied with heavy artillery, he added four newly raised corps of volunteers, many of them students, who made up for their lack of training by their bravery and enthusiasm. By throwing these young men - most of them potential officers - so early into battle, Falkenhayn was mortgaging Germany's military future but, as he said, 'the prize was worth the stake'. He may have been right but in the event, the prize, Calais, was not won.

The Germans were to refer to their attacks as *Kindermord*, the Slaughter of the Innocents, since, too raw to manoeuvre and too brave to turn aside, they attacked in heavy columns and were mown down by the rifles and machine guns of trained regulars.

Nevertheless, they only just failed. One of these new corps attacked down the Menin Road where the 7th Division was strung out on a V-shaped front, their right at Zandvoorde, their centre at the Nieuwe Kruisecke crossroads, a mile in front of Gheluvelt, and their left at Zonnebeke. The defenders, many of them on the forward slope, had inadequate trenches and no means of improving them since their spades had been lost in earlier fighting. Somehow they held but at a terrible cost.

Some battalions were reduced to skeletons, 1/Royal Welch Fusiliers being cut down to six officers and 206 other ranks. The onslaughts continued for a week, new attackers constantly coming forward, and at times it seemed that they must succeed by weight of numbers against the weary and diminished defenders. On 24 October Polygon Wood was captured and a breakthrough was averted only by the Northumberland Yeomanry, the first Territorial Force unit to be heavily engaged. The wood was retaken by a bayonet charge by two battalions from I Corps, 1/Highland Light Infantry and 2/Worcesters, the latter losing six officers and two hundred men. The BEF with few reserves behind it simply could not afford such losses and, as gaps in the line were plugged, battalions, brigades and divisions were becoming increasingly intermingled.

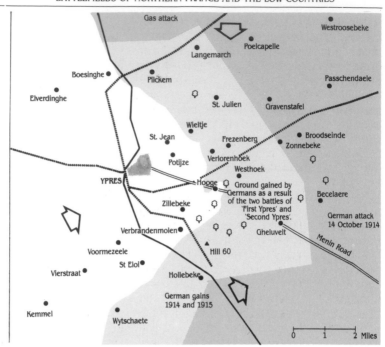

The Ypres Salient 1914-15

On the Menin Road front there was a brief breathing space after the Polygon Wood attack but more was to come and the next attack, delivered largely by more experienced troops from the southern front, was urged on by a general order:

We must and will conquer, settle for ever with the centuries-old struggle, end the war, and strike the decisive blow against our most detested enemy. We will finish the British, Indians, Canadians, Moroccan and other trash, feeble adversaries who surrender in great numbers if ... attacked with vigour.

Quite apart from the underestimate of their opponents' fighting capacity, this exhortation suggests that German Intelligence was as ill-informed as British since no Canadians were yet in France, the first Indian troops were only beginning to come into the line away to the south of Armentières and there were no Moroccans on the Ypres front.*

The short pause had given the BEF time to consolidate its position to some extent. The French took over some ground on the left, allowing I Corps to hold the line north of the Menin Road and allowing the remains of 7th Division to shorten its front so that it was holding only from the Nieuwe Kruisecke crossroads to Zandvoorde Château, about two miles from where the line was taken up by the Cavalry Corps, who were fighting dismounted. The corps boundary between I and IV Corps was at the crossroads where the northern sector was held by 1/Coldstream Guards, reduced to 350 all ranks and supported by two companies of 1/Black Watch. To the south were 1/Grenadier

Guards who were in some very unsatisfactory trenches on the forward slope.

The first of the renewed attacks took place at 5.30 am on 29 October. Led by a fresh division of Bavarian volunteers it was directed against the positions on the north side of the road. Three battalions attacked the Coldstream and Black Watch, scarcely five hundred men in all. Screened by a thick mist until they were within fifty yards of the defenders, the Bavarians came on in column of fours and, at that range, would have presented a superb target had not luck turned against the British. Normally British infantry at rapid fire would achieve fifteen aimed shots a minute and experts could manage thirty but on this particular morning it was discovered that faulty ammunition had been issued so that the spent case would not eject and the bolt of the rifle had to be forced, in some cases - kicked, open. For the same reason, two of the three available machine guns jammed.

---

* There were, however, Zouaves present and the Germans may not have appreciated that, despite their distinctive uniforms, these were French soldiers enlisted in North Africa.

The defenders were overwhelmed and that evening 1/Coldstream mustered only eighty men commanded by the quartermaster. Later in the morning the Grenadiers on the other side of the road were attacked and suffered 470 casualties, reducing them to five officers and less than two hundred men. The crossroads were lost and, although a splendid counter-attack by five battalions drawn from three brigades failed to regain them, the breakthrough was checked, leaving Gheluvelt in the front line.

Next day the main attack fell slightly to the south of the Menin Road, capturing Zandvoorde, destroying two squadrons of Household Cavalry and reducing 1/Royal Welch Fusiliers to eighty-six all ranks but still the Germans could not force a gap through the thin line. 31 October was even more serious as thirteen German battalions, advanced on Gheluvelt. They got as far as the château to the north of the village and although the building and its grounds were cleared by 1/South Wales Borderers there was a yawning gap in the front and, for the first time, the road to Ypres was open to them. It was at just this time that another disaster struck the British. A succession of heavy German shells hit Hooge Château, midway between Gheluvelt and Ypres, where were the headquarters of 1st and 2nd Divisions. One general was killed, the other concussed. Most of their staff officers became casualties, one of the few to escape uninjured was Major the Viscount Gort who, twenty-five years later, was to command another BEF.

The situation was saved through the prompt action of a great-grandson of King William IV, Brigadier General Charles Fitzclarence VC. Realizing that his puny reserve, three companies of 2/Worcesters, was too small to plug the gap, he ordered them to attack the village. They succeeded, aided by the fact that the Germans were relaxing after the capture of the village and were less alert than they should have been. Among them was 16/Bavarian Reserve Regiment in which, as a company runner, was a twenty-five year old Austrian, Adolf Hitler.* Sadly for the future of the world he was not among the killed. That night, on Haig's proposal, Gheluvelt, exposed on its spur, was evacuated and, without German interference, or even knowledge, the British line was brought back to the crest of the main ridge and its reverse slope.

On 11 November came the final German attack of 1914. This time the assault was led by the Prussian Guard Division under General Winkler. As on the previous occasions the attackers came on in heavy columns, their front stretching from south of the road to the south face of Polygon Wood, where the 450 remaining rifles of 1/King's spread over a front of a mile, diverting the attention of the whole of 3/Foot Guard Regiment so that it played no effective part in the advance. On the main road Veldoek was taken but the situation was stabilized when 2/Duke of Wellington's counter-attacked and destroyed a complete battalion of the Fusilier Guard. Only between these points was real progress made when 1/Foot Guard Regiment managed to break through Fitzclarence's 1 (Guards) Brigade, now consisting of 850 men drawn from 2/Scots Guards, 1/Black Watch and 1/Cameron Highlanders. The regiment reached Nonne Bosschen (Nun's Copse) where brigade headquarters was defending itself at short range, the garrison being composed of cooks and clerks.

Once more Fitzclarence saved the situation by rallying units and fractions of units to hold the bulging line until, striking in from Glencorse Wood, came the three hundred bayonets of 2/Oxford and Buckingham Light Infantry. They were supported there by a company of Northamptons, a Field Company of Engineers and two field batteries which resolutely ignored the shell shortage which was rationing British gunners to ten rounds a day. By great good fortune the German guns chose this moment to drop their shells short, among their own troops, and the Guard Regiment fell back having lost ten officers and 310 killed as well as sustaining hundreds of wounded.

Once again the Menin Road was blocked and, after ten days of lessening attacks, Falkenhayn had to admit that he could not break through to Calais by way of Ypres. Sadly one of the last casualties on 11 November had been Brigadier Fitzclarence. His name may be seen today at the top of Panel Number One on the Menin Gate among those thousands of others who have no known grave.

Rudolf Hess served in the same battalion.

Shell-holes and trenches
at Hill 62.

DP

DP

View from Hill 60.
Hill 60 from the ruins of a German bunker.
The path to the left leads to the Queen
Victoria's Rifles Memorial and the village of
Zwarte-Leen is in the centre. It was spoil
from the construction of the railway that
created this artificial hill - which became
known as 'Lovers' Knoll' or 'Côte des Amants'.

On 10 December 1914 German 39th
Division captured the hill from the French
XVI Corps and thus acquired an invaluable
observation post overlooking the British
lines to Ypres. Within three months

operations to regain the hill had begun;
three tunnels were dug and six mines laid
under the German positions. On 17 April
1915 five mines were blown, killing many
of the defenders. Heavy artillery
bombardment followed.

Attack and counter-attack reduced the hill
to an unrecognizable wilderness filled with
shell-holes and soldiers' bodies but by the
night of 18 April, Hill 60 was in British
hands. The Germans, after a series of gas
attacks, took the hill once more in May and
held it until June 1917.

*German gun outside
Menin Road museum.*

*Ypres from the Eastern
Ridge. The spires of the
Cathedral and the Cloth
Hall break the skyline.*

DP

The breakthrough to the Channel Ports had been frustrated but the cost had been terrible. The battles on the Menin Road had formed only a small part of the whole First Battle of Ypres, and Germans, Belgians and French all lost appallingly. To the British the loss was most serious since they had relied on a small volunteer army. They had sent seven infantry divisions to France and their losses at Ypres (58,000 men) was equivalent to the full strength of three of them, and three battalions besides. 614 officers, the establishment for twenty battalions, were killed; 333 more were missing.

The infantry of 7th Division which was taken out of the line on 7 November, had already lost 356 out of 400 officers and 9,664 out of 12,000 others ranks and, unlike the other six divisions, 7th was entirely regulars and not diluted with reservists. As the Official Historian wrote, describing these original BEF battalions, '*there scarcely remained with the colours an average of one officer and thirty men of those who landed in August*'.

Until the New Armies could be raised and trained the British regulars could do little more than provide a covering force.

KRRC Museum

John Dimmer, 60th Rifles, was awarded the Victoria Cross for his part in the defence of Klein Zillebeke in November 1914.

DP

THE MACHINE GUNS OF THE SIXTIETH

IN peacetime few of the officers in the King's Royal Rifle Corps (the Sixtieth Rifles) had risen from the ranks but John Dimmer was an exception, having served as a Rifleman in the South African War and having been promoted to corporal after it. He was commissioned in 1908 and by the time war broke out he was a lieutenant and in command of the second battalion's two machine guns, a command not highly envied by his brother officers. He first came to notice on 31 October, the day on which Gheluvelt was captured from the remnants of the Scots Guards, the Queen's, the South Wales Borderers, the Welch and the Sixtieth, about a thousand men in all, by thirteen German battalions. As the survivors fell back, the Germans were held back by Dimmer's guns. The battalion War Diary wrote:

Although the Germans constantly got within a few yards of his guns, he held them at bay, and inflicted very heavy loss on them, and eventually got back (to Veldhoek) *without losing either gun.*

On 12 November a German attack drove the French out of Zwarte-Leen, near Hill 60, and exposed the British right, held by a few dismounted cavalrymen at Klein Zillebeke. To guard against an enveloping attack, all that could be spared were two platoons of 2/KRRC and their machine guns, a tiny detachment since the whole of the battalion now numbered less than two hundred.

Hardly had they reached Klein Zillebeke when one of the machine guns was destroyed by a direct hit but Dimmer fired the other gun himself, feeding in belt after belt until, with the Germans only a hundred yards away, it jammed. To get it into action again he had to strip it, lying in the open, but he succeeded - only to be hit, almost immediately, by a rifle bullet in the jaw. He continued to fire when another bullet struck his right shoulder and when, a few minutes later, the same shoulder was hit by three fragments of shrapnel. Unable to speak or use his right arm and almost blinded by blood from a wound in his scalp, John Dimmer went on firing until he collapsed while trying to put another belt into the breech. At almost the same moment the German attack was abandoned.

They awarded him the VC; they could hardly do less, and he lived until January 1918 when he was killed whilst serving as a lieutenant-colonel in the Berkshires.

THE RECAPTURE OF GHELUVELT

IN the last days of October 1914 Gheluvelt was the foremost bastion of the British line facing eastward, exposed to fire as it sat forward on the spur pointing to Menin but valuable for the observation it gave over the German lines. Only a thousand men could be found to hold the village and its flanking defences and, on 31 October, after an intense bombardment, the Germans attacked it with thirteen battalions, charging 'with *the greatest enthusiasm cheering and singing; for they had been warned that the Kaiser was present'*. 2/Welch were literally shelled out of their trenches in front of the village and the Germans seized them before turning their attention to the defenders to the south of the road. By 1.30 pm they had cleared a gap a mile wide in the British line and reduced 1/Queen's to a strength of fourteen men and almost destroyed two companies of 2/Sixtieth. A company of 1/Gloucesters counterattacked but failed, their strength being reduced from eighty to thirteen.

To the north of the road the situation was marginally better, as 1/South Wales Borderers held firm in the sunken lane to the south of Gheluvelt Château and their left was secured by the remains of 1/Scots Guards. It was fortunate that the Germans lost the momentum of their advance and did not press on the road to Ypres where the new line being improvised at Veldhoek could scarcely have made effective resistance. Brigadier-General Fitzclarence reported tersely, *'My line is broken,'* and set about restoring the situation. He found that 2/Worcesters had been made available by 2nd Division and had moved to the south-west corner of Polygon Wood, near the place since known as Black Watch Corner. Having lost two hundred men on 24 October, apart from other engagements, it was not a strong battalion but Fitzclarence felt bound to detach one of the four companies to cover the Menin Road at a point some four hundred yards north-west of

DP

Gheluvelt. That left twelve officers and 350 men under Major E.B. Hankey. The brigadier's orders to them were *'to advance without delay against the enemy who are in possession of Gheluvelt and to re-establish our line there'*.

It was possible to cover the first nine hundred yards in comparative safety to reach a small copse, north-east of Veldhoek. Here the companies extended into open order, but the next stage, the 250 yards down to the valley of a small stream, cost them dearly as German shrapnel burst above them. Having reformed,

RTWSF

2/Worcesters under Major E.B. Hankey advancing through the grounds of Gheluvelt Château in their historic counter-attack.

they charged up the slope, joining the SWB in clearing the château. They moved into the north-east side of Gheluvelt, taking their places between the Welshmen's right and the village. For a time they suffered local sniping but their detached company came forward to eject the enemy from the village. The German advance was checked for that day but cost the battalion three officers and 184 men. The Worcesters' recapture of Gheluvelt was a brilliant feat of arms and may well have affected the whole course of the war. The history of one regiment rarely gives undue credit to the feats of another, but the highest tribute to the Worcesters came from another regiment's history, *'This was, perhaps, the most critical moment of the whole war. If the counter-attack had been unsuccessful, an attempt would have been made to establish a new line in front of Ypres, and it is doubtful if any such attempt would have succeeded.'*

A modern historian has written:
It was the last time that such a handful would be
able to produce such an effect - the last flourish of
the British Regular tradition.

DP

Polygon Wood

BLACK WATCH CORNER

Polygon Wood was named after the riding school of the Belgian cavalry which was within the trees and it was from its southern edge that 1/King's poured rapid fire into 3/Prussian Foot Guard Regiment as it tried to pass across their front. Decimated by the rifles of the Liverpool men, the Guard tried to veer away to their left to join their senior regiment which was pushing into Nonne Bosschen - only to be brought up short by a strongpoint which the engineers had completed only an hour before, though it had been started more than two weeks earlier by French sappers. On 11 November 1914 *'It consisted only of a traversed trench inside the four hedges of a cottage garden, which had been converted into an obstacle by a few strands of barbed wire'.*

The garrison, commanded by Lieutenant Francis Anderson, consisted of only forty of the Black Watch but they were enough to divide the Guard Regiment in an attempt, albeit unsuccessful, to envelop their post. As the history of the Prussian Guard wrote *'Among the garden enclosures the leaderless line abandoned the forward movement and drifted to the right. As no reinforcement could be got to the attackers, the assault came to a standstill at the third of the British lines.'*

The so-called third British line consisted of very little more than this Black Watch post in which Anderson, with most of his men, had been wounded, but it held out until the German attack recoiled. Some kind of strongpoint was also defended in a shed behind Verbeek Farm, a few hundred yards to the west. Here the commanding officers of the Black Watch and 1/Cameron Highlanders with a signal sergeant fought off the enemy with pistols; all of them were wounded. That night 1/Black Watch consisted of less than a hundred men with a single officer, Captain Victor Fortune who, twenty-six years later had the melancholy duty of surrendering 51st (Highland) Division at St Valery. Congratulating the survivors after the battle, Sir John French linked their stand with the advances currently being made on the Eastern Front: *'...you, by holding the Germans back, have won great victories as well, since, if you had not done so, the Russians could not have achieved their success'.* When this comment came to the notice of a Perth newspaper, it came out with the banner headline, *HOW THE BLACK WATCH SAVED THE RUSSIAN ARMY.*

To the north of St Julien
is the Canadian Memorial
to victims of the German
gas attack in 1915. The
2,000 mentioned in the
inscription were, in most
cases, victims of
weapons other than gas.

THIS·COLUMN·MARKS·THE
BATTLEFIELD·WHERE·18,000
CANADIANS·ON·THE·BRITISH
LEFT·WITHSTOOD·THE·FIRST
GERMAN·GAS·ATTACKS·THE
22⁻24⁻·OF·APRIL·1915·2,000
FELL·AND·HERE·LIE·BURIED

JG   JG

YPRES
THE SECOND BATTLE

NORTH OF THE CITY and astride the motorway is the line
between Poelcappelle and Streenstraat, on the canal which in
the spring of 1915 was held by two French divisions, one Algerian
and one composed of elderly reservists. On the afternoon of
22 April the Germans released against the French chlorine gas
from cylinders, taking advantage of an ambiguity in the Hague
Convention which forbade only the employment of asphyxiating
gases from 'projectiles'. It was not, as is generally believed, the
first use of poison gas in war since the French had experimented
unsuccessfully with *cartouches suffocantes* in 1914 and, during
the winter of 1914-15, the Germans had fired chlorine gas shells
against the Russians - only to find that the intense cold inhibited
the release of the gas.

This first German use of poison gas in the West was both successful and unsuccessful. It caused less than 650 casualties of
whom only three died but it created a panic among the low-
grade French troops, who were totally unprepared for gas, and,
with few exceptions, fled, leaving a ten-mile gap in the line. The
Germans were insufficiently confident in this new weapon to be
ready to exploit their success immediately.

The French defection had left the flank of the newly arrived
Canadian division on the Ypres-Poelcappelle road completely
in the air. None the less these splendid but untried troops
managed to extend their front to their left rear, to hold a German
attack and, assisted by a scratch force of British troops (hastily
collected from rest camps), to mount a moonlit bayonet attack.
This restored the situation if not the original line. Early
on 24 April a second wave of gas was released against the
Canadians who, although without respirators, managed to
maintain an unbroken line - despite having to give ground as far
as the south side of St Julien. It is no surprise that three VCs were
won by the Canadians in these three days.

By 1917 so much French and British blood had been spilled to maintain a hold on Ypres that a retirement, forced or voluntary, from the city was unthinkable. The tactical situation there was, however, less tolerable than it had been in November 1914. The Second Battle of Ypres and various lesser action had constricted the Salient until the front line ran little more than four thousand yards from the city walls on the north, east and south while all the high ground, meaning all the positions for artillery observation from Passchendaele to Wytschaete, were in German hands (see page 202).

Sir Douglas Haig had always believed that the main British effort should be made in the Ypres area and in 1917 he was under pressure from the Admiralty to neutralize the Belgian ports since they believed (mistakenly, as was later discovered) that it was from Zeebrugge and Ostend that the most dangerous part of the U-boat campaign was mounted. Haig could also believe that he had the support of his government for launching further heavy attacks since the new Prime Minister, David Lloyd George, had declared at an inter-allied conference in May 1917:

Third Ypres, July-November 1917

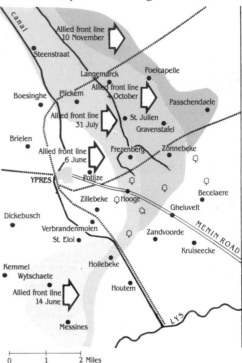

The enemy must not be left in peace for one moment.... We must go on hitting and hitting with all our strength until the Germans end, as they always do, by cracking.

Lloyd George was later to renounce this view in favour of various impractical schemes for winning the war without incurring British casualties but his assertion of it in May reinforced Haig's view that, with both sides equally matched, victory could go only to the side that was most successful in wearing down the enemy. The bald fact was that the conditions of war in 1914-18 gave all the advantages to the defender. By prodigious efforts an attacker could break into the enemy's defensive line but there was no way of breaking out into the open country beyond. Cavalry was at the mercy of every machine gun and susceptible to the lightest of barbed-wire entanglement while the primitive tanks of 1917 were too lightly armoured, had too short a range and insufficient mechanical reliability to exploit a breakthrough. No advance could go faster than the plod of an infantryman and he could plod forward only under cover of massive artillery support; this destroyed the ground to such an extent that it was impossible to move the guns and their vast requirement of ammunition forward to keep pace with the infantryman. All that could be attempted was a series of limited advances which it was hoped would impose such a drain on the enemy that, in the long run, it would be found insupportable. There was no easy way.

Haig's main objective was the eastern (Passchendaele-Gheluvelt) ridge, possession of which would give security to Ypres, observation to the east and, if all went well, a jumping-off point for an advance to the Belgian ports. An essential preliminary was the elimination of the German's own Ypres Salient on the Messines-Wytschaete ridge which sat squarely on the flank of the main attack. The capture of this bastion was entrusted to Second Army under Herbert Plumer, a commander whose suitability for offensive operations Haig had earlier doubted. His attack on the ridge on 7 June 1917 was beyond reproach; it went almost exactly according to plan and achieved its aim with, by contemporary standards, quite moderate casualties.

The great feature of this attack was the explosion of nineteen gigantic mines under the German lines. It was unfortunate that no such aids could be used in the assault on the eastern ridge but mining is a lengthy business; several of the Messines mines had been in construction for two years and the completion of an underground gallery 167 yards long in three months was considered a remarkable feat. (More details of the Messines mines are on page 219.)

The command of the main assault eastward was given to Hubert Gough, the youngest and believed to be the most thrusting of the army commanders. He proved not to have the grasp of organization and insistence on method that characterized Plumer at Messines and in particular he failed to give as much priority to the area of the Menin Road as Haig would have wished. His artillery preparation was, statistically, most impressive. 1,098 field guns, one to every twelve and a half yards of the front of attack, were supported by 324 field howitzers and 752 heavier guns. They fired four million

Lightly wounded British and German soldiers fraternizing near Pilckem Ridge in 1917.

IWM

Prisoner of war: one of the few Germans to survive the defence of Langemarck in September 1917. His less fortunate comrades are buried in the Langemarck cemetery.

JG

IWM

rounds but they were not as effective as at Messines and many of the German batteries were left unscathed. So too were many of the pillboxes which the Germans had constructed of reinforced concrete with walls four feet thick; they were proof against anything short of a direct hit from an 8-inch howitzer or some larger gun.

The attack, launched on 31 July, made immediate gains but German counter-attacks, which at Messines had been broken up by artillery fire, recaptured most of the ground they had lost - and a month's fighting resulted in very small gains, including the remains of the villages of Pilckem, St Julien, Hooge, Westhoek and Langemarck, at a cost of 67,000 casualties. None of the high ground had been taken and the only consolation was that the German losses were scarcely less than the British. The combatants on both sides were plagued by a spell of unseasonable rain which made the going very difficult.

Haig then gave the command to Plumer who asked for, and obtained a much higher propor-

tion of heavy artillery than Gough had used and before the next onslaught (which started on 29 September) 575 heavy and 720 field guns were available on a stretch of front where Gough had used only 282 heavy and 576 field. It is notable that at this stage of the war there were 80 gunners to every 100 infantryman engaged - at Waterloo the proportion had been 10:100; at Mons 33:100.

British 18-pounder field gun bogged down in the mud (August 1917).

IWM

Once more the meticulous planning of Plumer's Second Army paid dividends. In a series of well-calculated but limited attacks, in which I and II Anzac Corps played a prominent part, the crest of the eastern ridge was seized as far north as the level of Zonnebeke, although, isolated on its spur, Gheluvelt remained in German hands; and as a climax 2nd Australian Division took Broodeseinde on 4 October. On their left, 11th (Northern) Division, with the assistance of ten tanks, fought their way into the ruins of Poelcappelle. Only the extreme northern end of the ridge, the area of Passchendaele, remained to be taken, thus depriving the Germans of their last direct observation into Ypres.

On the afternoon of 4 October it started to rain and continued to do so with increasing intensity for the rest of the month. This meant that the British must reap the harvest they had sown. The gigantic bombardment which had enabled the infantry to move forward had churned up the ground which the rain turned into a quagmire. Movement became difficult, in places impossible but this very difficulty made possession of the high ground even more desirable since only there, above the worst of the morass, was it possible to move the essential supplies. Indications from Intelligence, which at this stage tended to be over-optimistic, were

that the Germans were in desperate straits. Indeed the German Army Commander responsible, Crown Prince Rupprecht of Bavaria, was making plans for a voluntary withdrawal. With relief he wrote in his diary for 12 November, 'Most gratifying - rain, our most effective ally.' Three days earlier a British attempt to resume their advance had literally bogged down, with some of the guns sinking up to the barrel into the mud from the force of their recoil.

No decision of Haig's, or possibly of any other general, has been so harshly criticized as his decision to continue the offensive. He believed that success was possible, indeed essential. Nor was he the only man to do so. That greatest of Australian soldiers, Sir John Monash, then commanding 3rd Australian Division wrote:

Great things are possible in the very near future, as the enemy is terribly disorganised. Moreover external pressures urged Haig to continue. The French army was, in large sections, far from reliable after the earlier mutinies and the German reserves had to be kept away from them. October saw the beginning of the Bolshevik revolution which meant that German divisions from the east would soon be available in the west and in Italy there began on 25 October, the Battle of Caporetto in which the Italians were to lose 275,000 prisoners and 2,500 guns and were fortunate to retain Venice.

Only Haig could keep the main German strength occupied. On 12 October, rightly or wrongly, he launched his first direct attack on Passchendaele and once more the Australians bore the brunt. Little progress was made and it was clear the Anzacs were exhausted. Some advance was made by three British divisions on the left, beyond Poelcappelle. The four divisions of the Canadian Corps then came into the line and there was a brief improvement in the weather. The final attack started on 26 October and eleven days later 2nd Canadian Division found themselves in possession of the heap of muddy stones that had been Passchendaele. For four more days they continued to edge forward, gaining a few hundred yards more of the crest of the ridge. On the lower ground the mud became so deep that progress at a yard a minute was the best that could be hoped for on foot. No transport could move. The offensive was halted.

offensive after the weather broke may have been wrong but it would have been even more wrong to abandon the attack.

Like everything else about Third Ypres the casualties incurred have been the subject of bitter argument. The best available figures seem to be 240,000 British casualties of whom 36,000, including 2,000 officers, were killed and 37,000 missing - many if not most of them prisoners of war. To bolster his own view of the battle, Lloyd George inflated the casualty figure to 399,000. The Germans reckoned their casualties in a different way but their official account admits to 217,000 of whom 35,000 were killed. Their returns, however, excluded those (whom the British would have included) '...*wounded whose recovery was to be expected within a reasonable time'*. It is certain that, if the German returns had been made in the same fashion as the British, their total would have exceeded 260,000.

Relics of explosives can still be found and should on no account be touched.

DP

When he was trying to take Quebec in 1759, General Wolfe remarked that 'War *is an option of difficulties'* and no commander has ever faced a more dreadful option than did Haig in October 1917. Few military decisions have ever led to such bitter recriminations. Haig's critics, led by Lloyd George, stooped to shocking lengths to denigrate him, giving rise to a flourishing mythology and the legend that he sacrificed thousands of men to gain a few hundred yards of bloodied mud. He did nothing of the kind. He attacked and eventually gained a vital piece of high ground which secured Ypres and made a huge contribution to exhausting the German army. His decision to continue the

Third Ypres, and in particular the final phase around Passchendaele, was undoubtedly the worst experience of war that Western Europe has ever suffered: '*I died in hell - they called it Passchendaele'* but, despite the myths, it was not a useless hell. A chief of staff to the German army and a future historian of the war, wrote: *Now that we know of the situation in which the French Army found itself during the summer of 1917, there can be no doubt that the stubbornness of the British Army bridged the crisis in France. The French Army gained time to restore itself and the German reserves were drawn to Flanders. The casualties which Britain sustained were not in vain.*

THE ROAD TO PASSCHENDAELE

To the west of Passchendaele village the ground falls away into the valley of the Ravebeek and near where this road runs north from Tyne Cott cemetery stood a number of German pillboxes which were taken by 66th British Division in early October. They were due to be relieved by 11 Australian Brigade. Since there was much doubt about where the British were, one Australian company commander, Lieutenant W.V. Fisher, went forward to find out where he was to take his men.

The slope was littered with dead, both theirs and ours. I got to one pillbox to find it just a mass of dead and so I passed on carefully to the one ahead. Here I found about fifty men alive, of the Manchesters. Never have I seen men so broken or demoralised. They were huddled up close behind the box in the last stages of exhaustion and fear. Fritz had been sniping at them all day and had accounted for fifty-seven that day. The dead and dying lay in piles. The wounded were numerous - unattended and weak, they moaned and groaned all over the place. Some of them had been there for four days already. Finally my company came up, the men done after a fearful struggle through the mud and shell holes, not to speak of the barrage which the Hun put down and which caught numbers. The position was obscure - a dark night, demoralised Tommies and no sign of the enemy. So I pushed out a platoon, ready for anything, and ran into the foe some 80 yards ahead. They put in a few bursts of rapid fire and then fled. We could not pursue as we had to establish the line, which we accomplished about an hour later. I spent the rest of the night in a shell-hole, up to my knees in mud and with the rain teaming down.

Three nights later, when a number of the Manchesters' wounded had still not been evacuated, Fisher (who was unfortunately killed in 1918) wrote:

My two runners were killed as they sat beside me and after I had been blown out of my shell-hole twice, I shifted to an abandoned pillbox. There were twenty-four wounded men inside, two dead Huns on the floor and six outside in various stages of decomposition. The stench was dreadful. We got the wounded away at last as well as two wounded Huns. When day broke I looked over the position. Over forty dead lay within twenty yards of where I stood, and the whole valley was full of them.

Pages from the 'Wipers Times'.

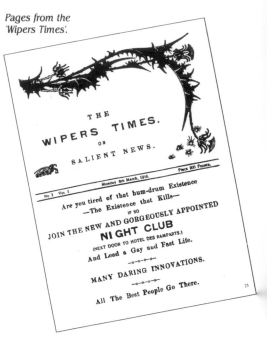

THE BIG BANG

THE assault on the Messines-Wytschaete ridge on 7 July 1917 was heralded by the largest series of explosions ever heard in war before the detonation of the first atomic bomb. Nineteen mines, each containing an average of twenty-one tons of explosives, were fired under the German front line.

Since the days of siege warfare, mining had been neglected as a military art and it was not until trench warfare had established itself along the whole length of the Western front that Britain recruited her first mining company and did so in such a hurry that the men who were landed in France in February 1915 had been building sewers in Liverpool five days earlier. By 1917 there were thirty-two mining companies in the BEF, including units from Australia, Canada and New Zealand. Haig had hoped to attack at Ypres in 1916 and the earliest of the Messines mines had been started in August 1915, several of them having been completed and armed since the summer of 1916.

Each mine was started about a quarter of a mile behind the British front line and was sunk between 50 and 125 feet through the loose and muddy topsoil into the underlying blue clay which was suitable for tunnelling. The longest underground gallery was 2,160 yards long and enormous care had to be taken to dispose of the thousands of tons of soil so as not to arouse the suspicions of the enemy, who were engaged in their own mining and counter-mining operations. In fact the German mining expert on the spot reported that '... a subterranean attack by mine-explosions on a large scale beneath the front line to precede an infantry assault on the Messines Ridge is no longer possible'.

The ridge was bombarded from 26 May to 6 June by 2,266 guns and howitzers which fired three and a half million rounds (at a cost of over seventeen million pounds) but the barrage stopped just before dawn on 7 June and for a brief pause nightingales could be heard among the stumps of Ploegsteert Wood - until the Germans put a shower of gas shells into the wood, causing five hundred casualties among the forming Australians. At 3.10 am the nineteen mines were fired, all detonating within nineteen seconds; a German observer wrote: *Nineteen gigantic roses with carmine petals, or gigantic mushrooms, rose up majestically out of the ground and then split into pieces with a mighty roar, sending up columns of flame mixed with masses of earth and splinters high into the sky.*

The shock, just like that of an earthquake, caused a panic among German troops fifteen miles away at Lille and could be felt in London. The barrage was resumed as the mines exploded and, under its cover, eighty thousand men, nine divisions, left their assault trenches and started to climb the low ridge to find the defenders, where not actually destroyed, in a state of shock. The New Zealanders took the heavily fortified village of Messines and 16th (Irish) Division stormed the fortress that had been the village of Wytschaete. By nightfall the whole ridge from Hill 60 westward was in British hands except for a few isolated strongpoints and a week was spent in mopping up and pushing the front line down the forward slope. It was in this phase that most of the 24,000 casualties, half of them Australians and New Zealanders, were sustained. The German casualties, other than the lightly wounded, were returned as 23,000.

The largest of the craters, the one known as Caterpillar, can be seen at Zwarte-Leen, just across the railway from Hill 60. It contained 70,000 pounds of amonal and when first blown was 260 feet across and 51 feet deep. Another crater, still visible today at St Eloi, had been charged with 96,000 pounds. However, the greatest area of devastation, with utter obliteration of an area 430 feet across, was achieved by the Spanbroekmolen mine, the crater of which is now the Toc H Pool of Peace.

WATERLOO

Lion Monument

Built as a memorial to the Belgian and Dutch troops, the mound now covers the area occupied by the right centre of Wellington's army.

Lion Monument

La Haye Sainte

To Brussels

DP

Hougoumont

La Belle Alliance

Victor Hug
Monumer

Hougoumont

This lay in advance of Wellington's right - and was held by the Guards.
(See page 228.)

DP

To Nivelles

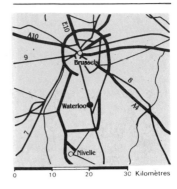

The Lion Monument provides a panoramic view of the battlefield 3 miles (5 km) south of the centre of Waterloo. At the foot of the Lion Hill is a vast circular mural, The Panorama, showing the battlefield at the time of the French cavalry charges. Here also is a museum with a battle plan and various relics; a wax museum shows important battle characters. (Cafés and toilets by the monument.) The Inn of Belle Alliance marks the centre of the French line and houses a room occupied in turn by Napoleon, Blücher and Wellington. Beware of fast-moving traffic here and park with care.

Guided tours of the battlefield can be arranged on request at the Wellington Museum, an old coaching inn in the centre of Waterloo itself, and the Duke's headquarters. It is open daily, April - September and afternoons (except Mondays) October - March. In a garden north of the church a monument commemorates the amputation of Lord Uxbridge's leg!

Le Caillou, $\frac{1}{2}$ mile (3km) south of the battlefield on the Charleroi road, is where Napoleon slept on the eve of the battle and received his senior officers in the morning. Just beyond Mont-St-Jean village is Ferme-St-Jean, used as a dressing station by British troops.

Papelotte

Papelotte
   The farm was in advance of the left of Wellington's position and held by Nassauers

To Wavre

DP

la Belle Alliance
   Napoleon's command post for part of the battle.

DP

Prussian Monument

0   1

Kilometre

IN 1815 EUROPE was starting to enjoy the first peaceful spring, with a single exception, since 1792. Napoleon was supposedly safe on Elba, the diplomats of Europe were struggling at Vienna to hammer out a lasting peace and Britain had settled for a draw in their three-year war with the United States. Then news came that the 'Corsican Ogre' had landed in France and, on 29 March, he returned as emperor to Paris. Very little had been agreed at Vienna but the diplomats were unanimous that Napoleon could not be left in France and from St Petersburg to Lisbon orders were given to remobilize the armies. Millions of men began to march towards the Rhine, the Alps and the Pyrenees but it would take months for the vast armies of Austria and Russia to come into action. Meanwhile Napoleon had, ready to hand, a very powerful army made up not only of serving soldiers but of veterans, many of them bitter from long years in prison camps. He had also a clear objective - Brussels - since even his political opponents believed that Belgium should be a part of France.

Two armies were posted to protect Belgium. In the Rhineland were the Prussians led by the seventy-three year old Blücher while assembling in Belgium itself was a heterogeneous force - British, Hanoverians, Dutch, Belgians, Brunswickers and Nassauers - led by Wellington who was the only general Napoleon's marshals had been unable to defeat - although he had never fought the emperor himself. Neither army was wholly reliable. In the Prussian camp fourteen thousand Saxons had mutinied and had to be sent to the rear. In Wellington's army many of the Hanoverians were raw militia while most of his Belgians had willingly fought for Napoleon before and were believed to be fully prepared to do so again.

Pointing to a British infantryman, who was gawping at the statues in a Brussels park, Wellington remarked, 'It all depends on that article there'. British infantry were at a premium. There were only seventeen thousand of them in Belgium and far too few of them were veterans of Wellington's Peninsular triumphs.

The initiative lay with Napoleon and until he revealed where he would strike with his field army of 123,000 men and 366 guns, the allies had to keep their armies dispersed to guard the long common frontier. Once the campaign started and they had left garrisons for the essential fortresses, the Prussians would field 117,000 men with 296 guns while Wellington could dispose 72,000 and 174 guns.

On 15 June the French struck at Charleroi, aiming at the junction of the two opposing armies, hoping to deal with them separately before they could concentrate their united strength. The first blow fell on Prussian troops and, due to a breakdown in communications, it was well into the afternoon before the first news reached Wellington. In consequence the allies fought separately on 16 June. At Ligny it took the right of the French army all day to drive the Prussians to retreat: at Quatre Bras a mixture of French incompetence and allied tenacity ensured that the French left made no advance. Dawn found Wellington's advance guard still at Quatre Bras but neither he nor Napoleon knew which way the Prussians had retreated, a situation made more difficult because Blücher had been unhorsed and ridden over by cavalry. It was 9 am before Wellington knew that his ally was moving towards Wavre, eighteen miles south-east of Brussels, and by that time Napoleon had fixed upon the idea that the Prussians were retreating eastward, away from Wellington. He despatched Marshal Grouchy with thirty-three thousand men to shepherd him on his supposed way. His main strength he devoted to attacking Wellington who had already started retreating to a sound defensive position near the village of Waterloo, south of the great Forest of Soignes. Apart from a cavalry clash at Genappes, there was no fighting on 17 June.

British infantryman of 1815. His musket and accoutrements weighed about 60lbs and he wore a tight leather stock round his neck to force him to keep his head upright though this made it difficult to aim his musket.

After a night of drenching rain, dawn on 18 June found Wellington's army, amounting after casualties and some detachments to 60,000 men and 154 guns, drawn up astride the Brussels - Charleroi road on the low ridge of Mont St Jean. The army's line was strengthened by a number of buildings on the forward slope, the most notable being the little château of Hougoumont (properly Goumont) on the right and the farm of La Haye Sainte beside the main road. Facing them was a similar ridge on which stood, and stands, the Inn of La Belle Alliance around which was the French army; 72,000 men and 266 guns, many of the latter being heavier than anything in the allied army. It was these heavier guns, twelve-pounders, that opened the battle soon after 11 am by firing a heavy barrage, a somewhat useless procedure since, apart from skirmishers, Wellington's infantry was behind the crest where the roundshot could not reach them. Soon afterwards the French left-wing, led by the emperor's brother, Jerome Bonaparte (whose training had been in the navy), started to attack Hougoumont.

British musket ball (actual size). It weighed 18.9 drams (14½ to the lb) and was slightly larger than that used by the French (20 to the lb).

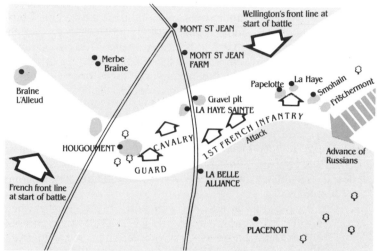

Battle of Waterloo, 13 June 1815

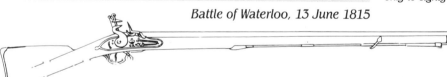

The 'Brown Bess' musket. A flintlock muzzle-loading weapon which could fire about three rounds a minute but was accurate only to eighty yards.

They drove a covering force of Germans from the wood but could make no impression on the buildings or the garden walls which were manned by men of the Coldstream and Third (later Scots) Guards.

The fighting round the château lasted throughout the day and at times the French were near to taking the place (see page 226) but they never quite succeeded. In the event, its principal effect on the battle was that three French brigades were devoted to its assault while Wellington succeeded in defending it with less than two battalions.

The main French attack, sixteen thousand infantry in four divisions, was launched against Wellington's left and centre at about 2 pm. Their left-hand division swept round La Haye Sainte but at all points they were met on the crest by British and regular Hanoverian infantry. Their lethal volleys checked the assault but the French were in overwhelming numbers and, for a few minutes, the issue of the day hung in the balance. Then two brigades of British heavy cavalry charged into the French masses and dispersed them. Unfortunately the horsemen could not be stopped and many of them charged up the opposite ridge and began to sabre the French gunners, a piece of indiscipline which brought devastating reprisals from the French cavalry. The Household and Union Brigades had broken the first great French attack but had reduced their own ranks to remnants.

When the surviving horsemen had regained their own lines there was a slackening in the action, except around Hougoumont, and so Wellington took the opportunity to pull back his infantry (which had advanced to meet the first attack) behind the cover of the ridge.

On the French side this was judged to be the beginning of a general retreat and Marshal Ney, always optimistic and frequently rash, hoped to turn retreat into rout by sending forward eight regiments of *cuirassiers* - a folly which was increased when, without orders, the light cavalry of the Imperial Guard joined the attack. Four thousand magnificent horsemen moved up the slope and found, behind the crest, the allied infantry formed into squares with their artillery in the intervals. Long experience had shown that even the best cavalry could achieve nothing against steady infantry in squares and the *cuirassiers* gained nothing except their own decimation. And worse was to follow. Ney had attacked with twenty-four squadrons but Napoleon compounded his mistake by sending up another thirty-seven squadrons to attempt what had already been shown to be impossible. As a British gunner wrote:

I allowed them to advance unmolested until the head of the column might have been about fifty or sixty yards from us, and then gave the word 'Fire!' The effect was terrible. Nearly the whole leading rank fell at once; the roundshot penetrating the column and carrying confusion throughout its length. The discharge of every gun was followed by a fall of men and horses like that before a mower's scythe.

By this time both commanders were concerned about the movements of the Prussians. Wellington had known since 6 am that at least two of their corps were marching to join him but he had underestimated the difficulties of marching and dragging artillery on the muddy tracks which joined Wavre to Waterloo and the allied army had to endure the full force of the French attack for far longer than had been anticipated. At one time the Duke was heard to murmur *'Night or the Prussians must come'* and one of his officers was reflecting that *'I never heard yet of a battle in which every one was killed; but this seemed likely to be an exception'.*

On the other side Napoleon had decided that Blücher could not possibly play a part in the battle until, at about 1 pm, the Prussian advance guard could be seen away to his right. From that time onwards the French fight became a struggle against time. It was not until about 6 pm that the emperor felt obliged to detach infantry to oppose the Prussian advance but it was just at that time that the French won their only real success against Wellington when Ney took La Haye Sainte from its garrison of Hanoverian regulars who had run out of ammunition. The marshal asked desperately for reinforcements, seeing that a breakthrough

was possible but Napoleon was thinking only of the Prussians and refused for an hour to commit his last reserve, the Imperial Guard. When he did so it was too late and he sent them forward in the wrong place and in the wrong formation. Instead of attacking through La Haye Sainte he ordered five battalions of the *Moyenne Garde* to advance in battalion columns with their left flank close to unsubdued Hougoumont. They aimed at the part of the crest where the Lion Monument now stands and barring their way were two battalions of the First Guards (who that day earned the title Grenadiers) and two companies each of the Coldstream and Third Guards. On their right was Adams' brigade, the most experienced in the army. Napoleon's hesitation had given Wellington the time to reconstruct his defences.

The *Moyenne Garde* came up the hill *'in as correct an order as at a review. As they rose step by step before us and crossed the ridge their red epaulettes and cross-belts put on over their blue great-coats gave them a gigantic appearance which was increased by their high hairy caps'*. The British Guards had been lying in a sunken track, safe from fire, but when the French were within *'fifty or sixty paces'* they were called to their feet and opened fire while Adams' brigade, led by the 52nd Light Infantry, swung on to the French flank and also opened fire. Not even the Imperial Guard could stand such treatment and soon they were streaming away down the slope in total disorder and, seeing this, the rest of the French army, which was beginning to realize that the Prussians were in their right rear, broke and ran for home. Their retreat was covered by two indomitable squares of the Old Guard who bought enough time for the emperor to escape, pursued through a moonlit night by the Prussian cavalry. As Wellington said later, *'Blücher and I met near La Belle Alliance; we were both on horseback; but he embraced me, exclaiming, "Mein liebe Kamerad", and then "quelle affaire!" which was pretty much all that he knew of French'*.

Waterloo was that very rare event, a decisive battle. Napoleon's empire could not recover from such a smashing defeat and afterwards western Europe had comparative peace for almost half a century. In Wellington's army there were 15,000 casualties and the Prussians lost 6,700 men that day. No one was able to make an accurate count of the losses in the French army since so many of his men slipped quietly away to their homes but there can be little doubt that more than 30,000 Frenchmen were killed, wounded or captured.

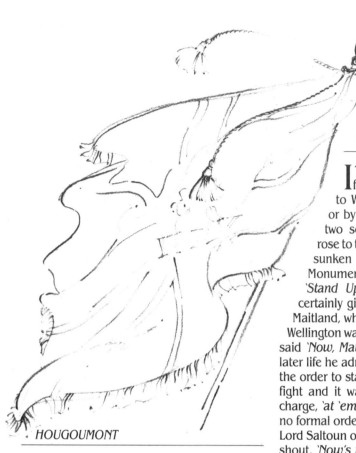

HOUGOUMONT

THE château of Goumont, which was little more than a superior farmhouse with outbuildings, saw the longest and some of the fiercest fighting of the day. Much of the farm looks more or less as it did at the time of the battle and will look even more so when the newly planted orchard reaches maturity. The château itself, which stood on the left of the entrance facing the barn, was burned out and never replaced. The fire reached the surviving chapel at its further end but there burned itself out right at the feet of the wooden figure of the crucified Christ.

The entrance has also changed. In 1815 this was a high and solid wooden gate and, in Wellington's opinion, the fate of the battle depended on whether this gate could be shut. At one stage a party of about a hundred Frenchmen, led by the gigantic Lieutenant Legros, succeeded in forcing a way through but four officers and a sergeant of the Coldstream, under Lieutenant-Colonel James Macdonnel of Glengarry, shut the gate and barred it with a tree-trunk carried by the colonel. The intruders were all shot down except for one drummer boy who was taken prisoner.

UP GUARDS AND AT 'EM

IT is most unlikely that these famous words, usually attributed to Wellington, were spoken by him or by anyone else since they refer to two separate incidents. The Guards rose to their feet from their shelter in the sunken road (now beneath the Lion Monument) in response to the order, 'Stand Up, Guards', which was almost certainly given by Major-General Frederick Maitland, who was the brigade commander. Wellington was with him and is known to have said 'Now, Maitland, now's your time' and in later life he admitted that he might have given the order to stand. There followed a short firefight and it was after that that the order to charge, 'at 'em', would have been given. In fact no formal order seems to have been given but Lord Saltoun of the Third Guards was heard to shout, 'Now's your time, boys!'

Equally apocryphal is the phrase 'La Garde meurt et ne se rend pas (The Guard dies but does not surrender)', which is attributed to General Pierre Jacques Etienne Cambronne when one of the two squares of the Old Guard was summoned to surrender. His actual reply is reputed to be the single word 'Merde' although he later denied this. Cambronne himself surrendered soon afterwards and was mortified when Wellington refused to meet him as he was a rebel to the king of France.

Coldstream badge from Hougoumont

DP

THE WOUNDED

I had to ride twelve miles. The motion of the horse made the blood pump out, and the bones cut the flesh to a jelly.

This officer had two broken ribs and a musket ball was lodged in his liver.

WOUNDED men were still being brought in to Brussels ten days after the battle. There were no anaesthetics but most of the wounded bore their sufferings with astonishing courage. One told how he lay next to a dragoon who was holding his injured arm with his good one while it was amputated. Near him was a wounded Frenchman who was *'bellowing lustily'* as the surgeon probed for a musket ball. *'This seemed to annoy the dragoon and as soon as his arm was off he struck the Frenchman a sharp blow across the head with the severed limb, holding it by the wrist, saying, "Here, take that and stop your damned bellowing".'*

THE COMMANDERS

THE Lion Mound is now the easiest place from which to view the Waterloo battlefield but it was not there in 1815 when there was nowhere from which to take an overall view of the ground. This put a premium on the mobility of the commanders and here Wellington had a distinct advantage since he was in excellent health while Napoleon was suffering the agonies of piles which made riding painful. Wellington's command post, as far as he had one, was by the 'Wellington tree', close to the crossroads above La Haye Sainte. (The present tree is a replacement, the original having been chopped up and sold, many times over, as souvenirs.) In practice he spent little time there, riding continually to whichever part of the line was most threatened. All present agreed that it was a miracle that he was not hit and, on at least two occasions, he was nearly captured by French cavalry.

By contrast Napoleon spent most of the battle outside La Belle Alliance sitting in a wicker chair - from which the seat had been removed on account of his piles. From this position he could see very little - and nothing of Wellington's right. He went forward only towards evening when he led the Imperial Guard down into the valley, where he stayed and, being in dead ground, could have had no idea how his final attack progressed.

The commander who knew least about what was going on was Blücher, struggling to get his army through the muddy lanes between Wavre and Plancenoit. Little information reached him and even that was not all accurate but he urged his men on, crying, *'Forward, boys, I have given my word to Wellington and you will surely not make me break it'.*

LIFE AND DEATH IN THE BATTLE

RIFLEMAN John Lewis of the 95th was employed in skirmishing to the left of the main road near La Haye Sainte and described the fighting in a letter written soon after the battle:

My front rank man was wounded by part of a shell through his foot, and he dropt as we were advancing; I covered the next man I saw, and had not walked twenty steps before a musket-shot came sideways and took his nose clean off; and then I covered another man. Just after that the man that stood next to me on my left had his right arm shot off by a 9-pound shot, just above the elbow, and he turned and caught hold of me with his left hand, and the blood run all over my trousers; we were advancing and he dropt directly.

Boney's cuirassiers, all dressed in armour, made a charge at us; we saw them coming, and we all closed in and formed a square just as they came within ten yards of us.... As I was loading my rifle, one of their shots came and struck it, not two inches above my right hand, as I was ramming down the ball, and bent the barrel so I could not get the ball down. A 9-pounder shot came and cut the serjeant of our company in two; he was not above three file from me, so I threw down my rifle and took his, as it was not hurt at the time.... Seeing we had lost so many men and all our commanding officers, my heart began to fail but, while we was in square, the Duke of Wellington and his staff came up to us in all the fire and saw we had lost all our commanding officers, he himself gave the words of command - '95th, unfix your swords, left face and extend yourselves once more. We shall soon have them over the hill'. Then he rode away to our right, and how he escaped being shot God only knows, for all that time shot was flying like hail-stones.

Napoleon, Emperor of the French. The greatest soldier of his day but at Waterloo, when he was 45, he was past his best and suffering from physical ailments.

Arthur, Duke of Wellington, was, like his opponent, born in 1769. Napoleon said of him that 'in the management of an army, he is full equal to myself, with the advantage of possessing more prudence'.

Gebhardt von Blücher, Prince of Wahlstädt, was twenty-seven years older than Napoleon and Wellington. Known as 'Marshal Forward', he was an indomitable, if unsubtle, commander and a very loyal ally.

MARS

NPG

MARS

Napoleon's view from La Belle Alliance. Only the tip of the Lion Mound (then non-existent) can be seen.

DP

The view from Lion Mound, looking south. The mound was built on the site of Wellington's lines and affords a perspective which was not available to the combatants. The farm of La Haye Sainte is on the extreme left and the road passes La Belle Alliance in the distance. Looking back to the Lion Mound from the middle of the shallow valley between the two farms it becomes clear just how little the French could see of Wellington's forces.

Road number	Total Km	Point to point Km	The Route	Features of interest

1 Arnhem - Operation Market-Garden 1944 Calais to Arnhem 376.5 Km = 234 miles

Road number	Total Km	Point to point Km	The Route	Features of interest
N235	0		ARNHEM .... VVV Offices. Leave by Utrechtstraat	The John Frost Bridge VV Tourist information V
	1	1	....	St Elizabeth's Hospital
	6	5	OOSTERBEEK	**The Hartenstein Airborne Museum** (small entrance fee). Nearby is the new Kleine Hartenstein Restaurant. VVV Oosterbeek has a small office. **Airborne Monument, Lonsdale Church.** Following the green signs, cross over the railway line to the **Commonwealth War Grave Cemetery.**

2 Bastogne and the Ardennes 1944-45 Calais to Bastogne 343.5 Km = 213.5 miles

Road number	Total Km	Point to point Km	The Route	Features of interest
N30	0		BASTOGNE	**Pays d'Ardennes Original Museum** **Bastogne Museum** **Mardasson Memorial**
	17	17	**HOUFFALIZE**	
N89	49	32	Baraque de Fraiture	
N68	61.5	12.5	Salmchâteau	
	64	2.5	Vielsalm	
	77	13	Trois Ponts	
	83	6	**STAVELOT**	
N62	89	6	MALMÉDY................................	Cemetery Air bombardment in December 1944
	93	4	BAUGNEZ...............................	**Site of massacre** at Baugnez crossroads Rebuilt **Café Bodarwé** and **Monument**
	97.5	4.5	Ligneuville	
	114.5	17	ST VITH..................................	Air bombardment December 1944

3 Château-Thierry 1918 (Circular tour) Calais to Château-Thierry 282.5 Km = 175.5 miles

Road number	Total Km	Point to point Km	The Route	Features of interest
N3	0		**CHÂTEAU-THIERRY** Follow signs 'Paris'	
	3.5	3.5	Junction with D9/Unclass. On a corner (care needed) by stone pylons marking entrance to **American Memorial**	
	5	1.5	....	**The American Memorial** on Côte 204 can be visited on either outward or return route
D9	6.5	1.5	Return to the main entrance/exit Junction N3/D9 (care needed) Follow the D9	
	13.5	7	BELLEAU	On the left, entrance to **The Aisne-Marne** **American Cemetery**
	14	0.5		
Unclass	14.5	0.5	Return to Belleau Follow signs 'Château-Thierry' but very	
Unclass			shortly turn right, then turn right again for road to **LUCY-LE-BOCAGE**	
	16.5	2	....	**4th US Marine Brigade Memorial** on right

Road number	Total Km	Point to point Km	The Route	Features of interest
D82			In 1 Km junction with D82	
Unclass	18	1.5	Lucy-le-Bocage	
D1390	19.5	1.5	Bouresches	
N3	22.5	3	Vaux	
			Junction D1390/N3	
			Signs 'Château-Thierry'	
Unclass	23.5	1	Junction N3/D9/Unclass	
			(corner, stone pylons)	
	25	1.5	............................American Memorial	
			Return to	
N3	26.5	1.5	Junction Unclass/N3/D9	
	30	3.5	CHÂTEAU-THIERRY	

---

6 | Crécy 1346 and Agincourt 1415

Calais to Azincourt 73 Km = 45.5 miles
Azincourt to Crécy 37.5 Km = 23.5 miles
Total 110.5 Km = 69 miles

Road number	Total Km	Point to point Km	The Route	Features of interest
N43	0		CALAIS	
A26	23	23	NORDAUSQUES JUNCTION	
D42	37	14	St Omer junction autoroute A26	
D211	39	2	Setques	
D192E	41	2	ESQUERDES	
D928	45.5	4.5	Crehem. Signs 'Hesdin'	
	48.5	3	Cléty	
	49.5	1	Junction D928/D341	
	57	7.5	FAUQUEMBERGUES	
	67.5	10.5	Fruges	
Unclass	71	3.5	RUISSEAUVILLE Take left fork to	
	73	2	AZINCOURT............................Site of **Battle of Agincourt** fought on St Crispin's Day in 1415 when Henry V defeated vastly superior French forces **Museum**. A walking circuit 5 Km	
D71			Follow D71 to	
D928	74	1	junction D71/D928. Signs 'Hesdin'	
	88	14	HESDIN	
	96.5	8.5	Regnauville	
	100.5	4	Labroye (junction with D119)	
	101.5	1	LE BOISLE (junction D224)	
D938	105.5	4	Junction D928/D938	
	110.5	5	CRÉCY EN PONTHIEU	
D111			Direction Wadicourt......................The site of Edward III's famous victory over Philip VI of France on 26 August 1346	

---

6 | Crécy and Agincourt - Return route

Crécy en Ponthieu to Calais 89 Km = 55 miles

Road number	Total Km	Point to point Km	The Route	Features of interest
D938	0		CRÉCY-EN-PONTHIEU	Foret de Crécy on left
	8.5	8.5	Regnière-Ecluse	
N1	10.5	2	Junction D938/N1	
			Signs 'Boulogne'	
	14.5	4	Vron	
	19	4.5	Nampont St Martin	
	21	2	Nempont St Firmin	
	33	12	MONTREUIL	
	35	2	Junction N1/N39	
N1	55	20	BOULOGNE	
			Signs Calais	
	69	14	Marquise	
	89	20	CALAIS	

Road number	Total Km	Point to point Km	The Route	Features of interest

7 | Normandy and Operation Neptune 1944

Normandy beaches - East to West
Calais to Caen 346 Km = 215 miles

Road number	Total Km	Point to point Km	The Route	Features of interest
D515	0		CAEN	
	2	2	Junction with Caen by-pass	
	4	2	Hérouville-St Clair	
D514	9.5	5.5	BÉNOUVILLE	
	10	0.5	....Pegasus Bridge	Gondrée Café Museum
	11.5	1.5	RANVILLE................................Airborne Cemetery and Memorial	Churchyard Site where the gliders landed
			Return to	
	13	1.5	Pegasus Bridge	
	13.5	0.5	Bénouville Signs 'Ouistreham'	
	17.5	4	OUISTREHAM............................ SWORD Beach (The 3rd British	Infantry Division landing)
	21.5	4	Colleville-Montgomery Plage	
	23.5	2	Lion-sur-Mer	
	27.5	4	Luc-sur-Mer	
	28.5	1	Langrune-sur-Mer	
	30.5	2	St Aubin-sur-Mer	
	32.5	2	Bernières-sur-Mer	
	35.5	3	COURSEULLES-SUR-MER ....JUNO Beach (The 3rd Canadian	Division landing) Canadian Cemetery at Beny-sur-Mer 3 Km south
	40.5	5	LA RIVIÈRE ....GOLD Beach (The 50th British Infantry	Division landing)
	48.5	8	ARROMANCHES-LES-BAINS..............The Invasion Museum	(Musée du Debarkquement) Landing beaches The Mulberry Harbour
D104	53.5	5	LONGUES-SUR-MER Keep right D104 for	
	55	1.5	....Le Chaos; German Marine Gun Battery	
			Return to	
D514	56.5	1.5	Longues-sur-Mer	
	61.5	5	Port-en-Bessin	
	66.5	5	Ste Honorine des Pertes	
	70	3.5	COLLEVILLE-SUR-MER Shortly after the village	
Unclass			Unclassified road on right to ....The American Military Cemetery of Colleville-	St Laurent Views of OMAHA Beach (US ISC Infantry Division landing). Visitors' building etc. Just before the entrance to the cemetery there is a track leading to the 5th Engineer Special Brigade Memorial and the Monument erected to the US 1st Infantry Division
	71	1	Return to the main road	
D514	72	1	(Colleville-sur-Mer)	
D517	74.5	2.5	St Laurent Keep right along D517	

Road number	Total Km	Point to point Km	The Route	Features of interest
	75.5	1	LES MOULINS ....*OMAHA* Beach	Monument to the 6th June landings
D514	78.5	3	VIERVILLE-SUR-MER ....Exposition Omaha 6 Juin 1944,	Museum)
	84	5.5	Junction D514/Unclassified road leading to	
D514	85	1	POINTE DU HOC ....The German Battery, eventually stormed by	the US 2nd Rangers who scaled the cliffs
N1	86	1	Return to main road	
	89	3	Junction unclass/D514	
	97	8	Grandcamp-Maisy	
	99	2	Osmanville; Junction D514/N13	
	106	7	ISIGNY-SUR-MER Junction N13/D913	
D913	110	4	CARENTAN	
	113.5	3.5	Junction N13/D913 Follow D913	
	118.5	5	Vierville	
	120.5	2	STE MARIE DU MONT	
	121.5	1	Junction D913/D14	
D421	126	4.5	Continue to coast for .... La Madeleine Monument	*UTAH* Beach (4th US Infantry Division landing) Monument to the American 4th Division and two other monuments American Landing Museum
D421			Follow the coast road D421 Route des Allies	
	130	4	LES DUNES DE VARREVILLE	
	134.5	4.5	Ravenoville-Plage	
D15			Road runs inland	Monument to the French Armoured Division
	137	2.5	Ravenoville (village)	
	141	4	Baudienville	
	144	3	STE MÈRE ÉGLISE .... The Church	Airborne Museum - Le Musée des Troupes Aeroportées is a building constructed in the form of a parachute canopy; one US paratrooper's parachute was caught on the spire of the church

8 | **Sedan 1870** Calais to Sedan 286 Km = 178 miles

Road number	Total Km	Point to point Km	The Route	Features of interest
N43	0		SEDAN.................................Château Fort 15th-17th century A plan of the town is advised	Contains a military museum
			From the junction of Autoroute A203 with N43 follow Avenue de la Marne. Cross railway bridge into Avenue des Martyrs de la Resistance (unclassified)	
Unclass	2	2	TORCY Follow Rue la Breteche	
	2.5	0.5	....Cimetière Militaire:	Sedan-Torcy French National Cemetery
			Return along Rue la Breteche to junction with Boulevard Chanzy. Follow Boulevard Chanzy in direction of 'Hôpital' (Hospital)	

Road number	Total Km	Point to point Km	The Route	Features of interest
	3	0.5	**PONT NEUF** (Bridge over the River Meuse) Cross bridge and at far end follow Boulevard Gambetta	
D5	3.5	0.5	Junction with Avenue de General Margueritte (D5) To the left along D5 is ....Monument du Chêne Brisé 1870 Follow route du Cimetière	
N43	4	0.5	for..Cimetière St Charles (Communal Cemetery) Signposted 'Montmédy'	
	6.5	2.5	BAZEILLES...............................Maison de la Dernière Cartouche Museum of the Franco-Prussian War	

9   Dieppe

Road number	Total Km	Point to point Km	The Route	Features of interest
D925			DIEPPE.....................................Dieppe Castle Commemorative plaques in town Casino; Museum	
	0		Signs for 'Abbeville'	
D54	10	10	Graincourt	
	12	2	**BERNEVAL-LE-GRAND**	
	13	1	**BERNEVAL-SUR-MER** (Petit Berneval)	

To visit Pourville

Road number	Total Km	Point to point Km	The Route	Features of interest
	0			
D75	4.5	4.5	**DIEPPE** Signs 'Pourville' POURVILLE ....Museum, specific to Dieppe raid, with tanks	

10   Battles of the Somme 1916 and 1918   <small>Calais to Bapaume autoroute junction 137 Km = 85 miles</small>

Road number	Total Km	Point to point Km	The Route	Features of interest
D929	0		**BAPAUME JUNCTION** Leave motorway to follow signs 'Albert'	
	1.5	1.5	Bapaume	
	9	7.5	Le Sars	
	14.5	5.5	Pozières	
D50	22	7.5	**ALBERT**	
	24.5	2.5	Go north to Aveluy	
	29.5	5	Hamel	
D163e	31.5	2	Junction with D163e	
	33.5	2	BEAUMONT HAMEL ....British cemetery; Newfoundland Memorial Park and Caribou Memorial; preserved trenches	
D73	37	3.5	Return to the D50 Junction D50/D73 (edge of) Hamel Follow D73	
	39.5	2.5	THIEPVAL..................................Thiepval Memorial to the Missing (73,412 names are recorded)	
D929	43.5	4	POZIÈRES...............................Military Cemetery and Memorial to the Missing of the 5th Army, 14,690 names	
D104	47.5	4	Follow signs 'Albert' LA BOISSELLE.......................... From the village there is an unclassified road which leads to **The Great Mine Crater**. There are also two **Memorials** in the village	
D20	50.5	3	Contalmaison	

Road number	Total Km	Point to point Km	The Route	Features of interest
D197	56	5.5	East to LONGUEVAL	
			....For **Delville Wood Cemetery, Museum** and **Memorial** (South African)	
	61.5	5.5	South to Maricourt	
	68	6.5	Suzanne	
			Continue on D197	
			Junction D197/D1 (Cappy 1 Km)	
D329	70.5	2.5	**BRAY-SUR-SOMME** Continue south to	
	76.5	6	Proyart	
	78	1.5	Junction D329/N29	
			Follow signs 'Amiens'	
N29	85	7	Junction N29/D337	
	87	2	Lamotte-Warfusée	
D23	92	5	**VILLERS BRETONNEUX**	
	94	2	....Australian National Memorial in the **British Military Cemetery** Interesting exhibits in **Franco-Australian Museum**	
	95.5	1.5	North to Fouilloy. Continue on D23	
D23	96	1	(Corbie)	
	98.5	2.5	Bonnay	
D929	101.5	3	Junction D23/D929	
	111.5	10	**ALBERT**	
	119	7.5	Pozières	
	124.5	5.5	Le Sars	
	132	7.5	**BAPAUME**	
A26	133.5	1.5	Bapaume Junction	

11   **Vimy Ridge 1917**   Calais to Arras Nord autoroute junction 104 Km = 64.5 miles

Road number	Total Km	Point to point Km	The Route	Features of interest
N25	0		**ARRAS** Nord Junction	
			Leave motorway to follow	
			signs 'Vimy'	
	2	2	(THÉLUS)	
Unclass	3	1	Junction with unclassified road	
			Follow unclassified road into the	
			BOIS DE VIMY	
	7	4	....Canadian Memorial, Vimy Ridge Commemorating the Canadian Divisions 1914-18, 60,000 lives. On the wall are 11,000 names of those with no known grave. Preserved battlefields and trenches.	

12   **Verdun**   Calais to Verdun 367 Km = 228 miles

Road number	Total Km	Point to point Km	The Route	Features of interest
N3	0		**VERDUN**	
			Go east signs 'Metz'	
D913	5.5	5.5	Junction N3/D913	
D913A	7	1.5	Junction D913/D913A ....Monument Ford de Tavannes (on right)	
	9.5	2.5	**FORT DE VAUX**	22.5 Km up wooded slopes. About halfway
			Return to	along, Memorial to Resistance Workers 1944
D913	12	2.5	Junction D913A/D913	
			Keep right	
	14	2	Carrefour de la Chappelle	
			Ste Fine	

Road number	Total Km	Point to point Km	The Route	Features of interest
	15	1	FLEURY	Memorial de Verdun: Museum
	16.5	1.5	....	Ossuaire (Ossuary) and Cemetery
				(D913B Fort de Douaumont 1 Km smaller road, unclassified, to the Tranchée du Baïonettes 1 Km)
D913B	18.5	2		
D913			Return to D913	
D115	23.5	5	Bras-sur-Meuse	
			Junction D913/D964/D115	
D38	25	1.5	Charny-sur-Meuse	
			Take right fork to	
	29	4	Marre	
	31	2	Junction D38/D123	
	32	1	CHATTANCOURT	Unclassified road to Cimetière Nationale
			Turn right at Junction D38/D38B	
D38B	34	2	LE MORT HOMME	
			Return to	
D38	36	2	Chattancourt	
	37	1	Junction D38/D123	
	39	2	Marre	
D115	43	4	Charny-sur-Meuse	
	44.5	1.5	Bras-sur-Meuse	
D964	51	6.5	VERDUN	

13 Ieper (Ypres) 1914 and 1917 Calais to Ieper 95 Km = 59 miles

Ieper to Sanctuary Wood

Road number	Total Km	Point to point Km	The Route	Features of interest
N9	0		IEPER (YPRES)	
			Menenpoort (Menen Gate)	
	1	1	....	Menen Road South Military Cemetery
Unclass	1.5	0.5	....	Hellfire Corner
			Turn right to follow unclassified local road	
	3	1.5	ZILLEBEKE	
	4.5	1.5	....	Sanctuary Wood
				Hill 62, Canadian Memorial Museum; Preserved trenches

Ieper to Mesen (Messines)

Road number	Total Km	Point to point Km	The Route	Features of interest
N365			IEPER (YPRES)	
	0		Go south, following signs to 'Mesen' (Messines)	
	4.5	4.5	St Elloois	
	7.5	3	Wijtschate (Wytschaete)	
N304	9.5	2	MESEN (MESSINES)	
		0.5	Turn right, follow road towards	
		1	WULVERGEM	
	10		....	Mesen Ridge British Cemetery
	11		....	Ration Farm (La Plus Douve) Annexe
			Unclassified road goes south to PLOEGSTEERT	

Ieper to Passendale (Passchendaele)

Road number	Total Km	Point to point Km	The Route	Features of interest
Unclass			IEPER (YPRES)	
			Menenpoort (Menen Gate)	
			Leave by road for Zonnebeke	
	1.5	1.5	....	Aeroplane Cemetery, Ieper
				Local road to right for Polygon Wood

Road number	Total Km	Point to point Km	The Route	Features of interest
	5.5	4	**ZONNEBEKE**	
	7.5	2	Return to Zonnebeke	
N332	8.5	1	**BROODSEINDE**	
			Signs 'Passendale' (Passchendaele)	
	9.5	1	....Local road left for **Tyne Cot Cemetery** 1Km (11,908 graves) and **Memorial to the Missing**	
	11.5	2	**PASSENDALE (PASSCHENDAELE)**	
			Through the town for ....**Passchendaele New Cemetery**	

14 Waterloo 1815 (By Motorway)

Calais to Waterloo 210 Km = 130.5 miles
Waterloo Motorway Junction to Le Champ de Bataille
9 Km = 5.5 miles

Road number	Total Km	Point to point Km	The Route	Features of interest
A202			**WATERLOO JUNCTION**	
			Follow signs 'Mons'	
	1.5	1.5	Junction for Joli-Bois	
Exit 5	3	1.5	Junction for **MONT-ST JEAN**	
			Leave motorway and follow signs 'Charleroi'	
	4	1	Junction No 5/unclassified (Crossways) for ....**Ferme de la Haie Sainte, Butte du Lion,** and **Ferme de Hougoumont**	
	6	2	**LA SALIÈRE**..............................Road to left for **Caberet de la Belle Alliance, Post D'Observation de Napoleon** and **Plancenoit**	
	8	2	**MAISON DU-ROI**	
	9	1	....**Ferme du Caillou**	

14 Waterloo 1815 (By Main Road)

Calais to Waterloo 210 Km = 130.5 miles
Waterloo to Le Champ de Bataille 9 Km = 5.5 miles

Road number	Total Km	Point to point Km	The Route	Features of interest
Exit 5/6	1		**WATERLOO**	
			Signs 'Charleroi'	
	2.5	1.5	Joli-Bois (Junction with road from Tervuren)	
Exit 5	4	1.5	**MONT ST JEAN**	
	5	1	Junction 5/unclassified (Crossways) ....for **Ferme de la Haie Sainte, Butte du Lion** and **Ferme de Hougoumont**	
	7	2	**LA SALIÈRE**..............................Road to left for **Caberet de la Belle Napoleon** and **Plancenoit**	
	9	22	**MAISON DU-ROI**	
	10	1	....**Ferme du Caillou**	

Alternative route to Ferme de Hougoumont 6.5 Km = 4 miles

Road number	Total Km	Point to point Km	The Route	Features of interest
Exit 5/6	1.5	1.5	**WATERLOO**	
			Signs 'Nivelles'	
			Joli-Bois (Junction with road from Tervuren)	
Exit 5	3	1.5	**MONT ST JEAN**	
	5.5	2.5	Junction with road from Braine l'Alleud (2.5 Km)	
			Leave road at junction 5	
			Unclassified road crosses bridge over motorway	
	6.5	1	into the battle area for..................**Ferme de Hougoumont** (right signposted Goumont)	

General & pre-1900 Battles

Brett-James, Antony
The Hundred Days
Macmillan 1964

Burne, Alfred H.
The Crecy War
Eyre & Spottiswood, 1955
The Agincourt War
Eyre & Spottiswood, 1956

Ffoulks, Charles
Arms and Armament
Harrap, 1945

Frederick III, Emperor
(Ed: A.R. Allinson)
War Diary 1870-71
Stanley Paul, 1927

Glover, Michael
The Velvet Glove
Hodder & Stoughton 1982

Glover, Michael
**Warfare from Waterloo
to Mons**
Cassell 1980

Hibbert, Christopher
Agincourt
Batsford, 1964

Holt, Tonie and Valmai
Holts Battlefield Guides
Leo Cooper
In association with
Secker & Warburg

Horne, Alistair
The Fall of Paris
Macmillan, 1965

Howard, Michael
The Franco-Prussian War
Rupert Hart Davies, 1961

Houssaye, Henri
1815 Waterloo
Perrin, Paris
(42nd Edn) 1902

Naylor, John
Waterloo
Batsford, 1960

Pericoli, Ugo
& Michael Glover
**1815: The Armies at
Waterloo**
Leo Cooper
(Seeley Service) 1973

Siborne, H.T. (Ed)
The Waterloo Letters
Cassell, 1891

World War I 1914-18

Blaxland, Gregory
Amiens 1918
Frederick Muller, 1968

Coppard, George
**With a Machine Gun
to Cambrai**
HMSO, 1969

De Weerd, Harvey A.
President Wilson's War
Macmillan, New York, 1968

Farrar-Hockley, A.H.
The Somme
Batsford, 1964
Ypres, 1914
Arthur Banks, 1967

Falls, Cyril
**History of 36th
(Ulster) Division**
M'Caw, Stephenson
& Orr, 1922

Giles, John
**The Somme:
Then and Now**
Reprinted by After The
Battle, 1986

Harbord, James G.
**The American Army in
France 1917-18**
Little, Brown & Co,
Boston, 1936

Harris, John
**The Somme: Death of
a Generation**
Hodder & Stoughton 1966

Hart, Basil Liddell
The Tanks (Vol 1)
Cassell, 1959

Horne, Alistair
The Price of Glory
Macmillan, 1962

McKee, Alexander
Vimy Ridge
Souvenir Press, 1966

Marshall Cornwall, James
Wars & Rumours of Wars
Leo Cooper, 1984

Middlebrook, Martin
First Day on the Somme
Allen Lane, 1971

Shakespear, John
The Thirty-fourth Division
Wetherby, 1922

Stallings, Laurence
The Doughboys
Harper & Row
New York, 1963

Terraine, John
**The First World War
1914-18**
Hutchinson, 1965
**The Road to
Passchendaele
To Win a War: 1918**
Sidgwick & Jackson
**White Heat: The New
Warfare 1914-18**
Sidgwick & Jackson, 1982

Vandiver, Frank E.
**Black Jack: The Life &
Times of John J. Pershing
(Vol 2)**
Texas A & M University
Press, 1977

Williams, Jeffrey
Byng of Vimy
Leo Cooper, 1983

Woollcombe
**The First Tank Battle:
Cambrai 1917**
Arthur Baker, 1967

Wood, H.F.
Vimy!
Macdonald, 1967

World War II 1939-45

Angus, Tom
Men at Arnhem
Leo Cooper, 1977

Atkin, Ronald
**Dieppe 1942
The Jubilee Disaster**
Macmillan, 1980

Belchem, David
Victory in Normandy
Chatto & Windus, 1981

Belfield, Eversley
& Essame, H.
The Battle for Normandy
Batsford, 1965

Blaxland, Gregory
Destination Dunkirk
William Kimber, 1973

Buckley, Christopher
**Norway, The Commandos,
Dieppe**
HMSO, 1952

D'Este, Carlo
Decision in Normandy
William Collins, 1983

Divine, David
Nine Days of Dunkirk
Faber & Faber, 1959

Eisenhower, Dwight D.
Crusade in Europe
Doubleday,
New York, 1948

Frost, John
A Drop too Far
Buchan & Enright, 1982

Glover, Michael
**The Fight for the
Channel Ports**
Leo Cooper, 1985

Hackett, John
I was a Stranger
Chatto & Windus, 1977

Hamilton, Nigel
**Monty: Master of the
Battlefield**
Hamish Hamilton, 1981

Hastings, Max
**Overlord: D-Day and the
Battle for Normandy**
Michael Joseph, 1984

Horne, Alistair
To Lose a Battle
Macmillan, 1969

Johnson, Garry &
Dunphie, Christopher
Brightly Shone the Dawn
Leo Cooper, 1980

Keegan, John
Six Armies in Normandy
Johathan Cape, 1982

Lamb, Richard
Montgomery in Europe
Buchan & Enright, 1983

Lefevre, Eric
*Dunkerque: La Bataille
des Dunes*
Charles-Lavauzelle
Paris, 1981

Lewin, Ronald
Hitler's Mistakes
Leo Cooper, 1984

Linklater, Eric
The Defence of Calais
HMSO, 1941

Lord, Walter
The Miracle of Dunkirk
Allen Lane, 1982

MacDonald, Charles B.
The Battle of the Bulge
Weidenfeld & Nicholson
1984

Neave, Airey
The Flames of Calais
Hodder & Stoughton 1972

Robinson, Terence
**Dieppe: The Shame
& the Glory**
Hutchinson, 1963

St Croix, Philip de (Ed)
Airborne Operations
Salamander, 1978

Spiedel, Hans
(Tr. Ian Colvin)
We Defended Normandy
Herbert Jenkins, 1951

Thompson, R.W.
Dieppe at Dawn
Hutchinson, 1956

Urquhart, R.E.
Arnhem
Cassell, 1958

Abbeville 47, 88, 90, 187
Airanes 88
Aisne 203
Albert 47, 63, 93, 146, 150
Amblève, river 28, 29, 32
Amiens 47, 79, 88, 167, 171, 173, 177, 187
Ancre, river 146, 155
Anneux 68
Anthuille Wood 152
Antwerp 11, 12, 27, 47, 204, 205
Appeville 140
Ardennes 26-43, 47, 121
Ardennes Forest 126, 129
Arlon road 37, 41
Armentières 204, 206
Arnhem 10-25
Arras 60, 63, 166, 179, 180, 181, 187
Arromanches 101, 113, 117
Assenois 39
Azincourt 85

Bandes 40
Banteaux 65, 71
Banteaux Ravine 72
Bapaume 68, 93, 165, 181, 187
Bar-le-Duc 194
Bastogne 26-43
Baugnez 27, 40, 41
Bayeux 101, 112
Bazeilles 121, 126-8
Beaucourt 177
Beaumont 126
Beaumont Hamel 146, 151, 161
Beaurains 187
Bécourt 152
Belleau Wood 77, 78, 81-3
Bénouville 113, 118
Bergues 53
Berneval 138
Berneval-le-Grand 138
Berneval-sur-Mer 138
Bernières 113
Béthune, river 145
Beuville 113
Biéville 113, 114
Bilderberg 25
Bizory 37
Black Watch Corner 211, 212
Boezinge 199
Bois des Caures 191
Bois du Goulet 183
Bois en Hache 185
Boulogne 45, 48, 50, 102, 200
Bourcy 34
Bouresches 81
Bourlon Ridge 62, 64, 65, 67, 69-73
Bray Dunes 45, 59, 61
Breda 47
Brest 117
Broodseinde 216
Bruges 204
Brussels 11-12, 222 223, 227

Cabourg 118
Caen 88, 101, 103, 106, 107, 112-14
Caen Canal 118
Calais 44-61, 91, 93, 95, 98, 102, 200
Calvaire d'Illy 126
Cambrai 62-75, 148, 166
Canal de Calais 48
Canal de l'Escaut 63-6, 71, 72
Canal du Nord 63-5, 67
Canal Maritime d'Abbeville 88
Carentan 108
Cassel 51
Celles 43
Cerisy Gally 174
Châlons 125, 167
Châlons-sur-Marne 124
Charleroi 221, 222, 223
Charleville-Mézières 121
Château-Thierry 76-83
Chaulnes 165
Chef-du-Pont 108
Chemin des Dames 79, 192
Cherbourg 102, 117
Ciney 28
Colleville-sur-Mer 101, 111
Colleville-sur-Orne 113
Compiègnes 77
Contalmaison 151, 152
Corbie 175
Cotentin 88, 102, 106, 108
Courcelette 146
Courseulles-sur-Mer 101
Courtrai (Kortrijk) 51, 200
Crécy 84-99
Crécy-en-Ponthieu 85, 90
Crécy Forest 90
Crèvecœur 64, 65
Croiselles 166, 168
Curlu 151

Daigny 126
Dainville 187
Delville Wood 161
Den Brink 25
Dieppe 102, 117, 130-45
Dinant 43
Dives, river 112, 118
Dommel 17
Donchéry 126, 129
Douai 51
Douaumont 195 see also Fort de Douaumont
Doullens 93
Douve, river 108
Driel, 19-21
Duisons 187
Dunkirk 44-61, 145, 187
Dyle, river 47

Echternach 27
Ecurie 183
Ede 25
Eifel mountains 28
Eindhoven 11, 14, 15, 17
Eisenborn 37
Elder 11

Elst 11, 21
Escaut (Scheldt) 13-4, 47
Essex Farm cemetery 199
Eupen 28

Farbus 183
Fauville 108
Fécamp 145
Ferme-St-Jean 221
Flanders 86, 88, 199, 217
Flers 164
Flesquières 63, 65, 68-74
Fleury 189
Floing 121, 126, 127, 129
Fontaine 96
Fort de Douaumont 189, 191, 193-4
Fort des Dunes 52
Fort Nieulay 45
Fort Souville 191
Fort Vaux 148, 189, 191, 193
Foy 35, 36
Foy-Notre-Dame 43
Fresnoy 174
Frévent 93
Frezenberg 202
Fricourt 146, 151
Furnes (Veurne) 53

Garenne Wood 126, 127
Genappes 222
Gheluvelt 200, 205, 207, 210, 211, 214, 216
Ghent 47
Ginchy 151
Ginkel Heath 17, 25
Givenchy 185
Givet 27, 28
Givonne 126
Glencorse Wood 207
GOLD 106-7, 112, 116
Gommecourt 150-1
Gonnelieu 72
Goumount see Hougoumount
Gouzeaucourt 72
Graincourt 65, 68, 71
Grandcourt 151, 146, 162
Grand Hameau 111
Grand Ravin 64, 68
Grave 11, 13, 17
Gravelines 48, 51, 53, 58
Gravelotte 124
Groesbeek 17, 24
Guillaucourt 177
Guines 48

Hable de Heurtot 112
Hamel 171
Hamel-de-Cruttes 109
Hangest 93
Hangstellung 184
Harbonnières 174, 177
Harfleur 85, 93, 94, 97, 98
Havrincourt 63-6, 68, 73
Hellfire Corner 199
Hemrolle 37
Hermanville 113
Hermies 63

Hesdin 85, 90, 93
Heuman 17, 19
Hiesville 108
Hill 60 199, 200, 210, 219
Hill 62 199
Hill 204 77
Hindenburg Line (Siegfried Stellung) 63, 67, 181
Hohe Venn Ridge 32
Hooge 202, 207, 215
Hotten 32
Houffalize 34
Hougoumount 223, 225 226
Hürtgen 28, 29

Johanna Hoeve 18, 25
John Frost Bridge 11
JUNO 106-7, 113, 116

Klein Zillebeke 210
Kochem 28

La Bassée 203
La Belle Alliance 221, 223, 227
La Boisselle 146, 154, 155, 156
La Fère 166
La Fiere 108
La Folie Farm 183
La Haye Sainte 223, 225, 227
La Moncelle 126
Langemarck 204, 215
Langrune 113
La Panne 45, 58
La Rivière 112
Lateau Wood 65, 68
La Vacquerie 65, 68, 72
La Voie Sacrée 194
Le Caillou 221
Le Cateau 148
Le Crotoy 90
Leffrinckoucke 45
Le Fresne-Camilly 113
Le Hamel 113
Le Havre 85, 145
Le Mesnil 131
Le Mort Homme 189, 191, 195
Lens 179
Le Quesnel 174
Le Sars 164-6
L'Escaut (Scheldt) Canal see Canal de l'Escaut
Le Transloy 165
Les Forges 108
Les Petites Dalles 145
Les Rues Vertes 69
Liège 27, 28
Ligny 222
Lille 47, 52-3, 63, 200, 203-4, 219
Lion Monument (Lion Mound) 191, 221, 225-7
Lion-sur-Mer 113, 114

Lisieux 88
Lochnager 154, 156, 158
Loire 11, 117
Lommel 13
Longchamps 37
Longues 113
Longueval 146
Lorient 117
Losheim Gap 27, 28 32
Louvain 47
Louveral 63
Luc-sur-Mer 113
Lucy-le-Bocage 81, 82
Lys, river 51, 200, 203, 204, 205

Maas, river 13
Maastricht 28
Maas-Waal Canal 13, 17
Maginot Line 46, 47
Maisoncelles 85, 93
Malmédy 27, 28, 32, 40, 42
Malo-les-Bains 45
Mametz 146
Marcheville 90
Marchiennes 51
Marcoing 64-7, 69
Mardyck Canal, Old 53
Maricourt 150, 171
Marne, river 77, 79
Martinpuich 151
Marvie 37
Masnières 64, 67, 69, 71
Maubeuge 148
Maurepas 146
Maye, river 90
Menin 204, 211
Menin Gate 199
Menin Road 199, 202, 205-8, 211, 215
Mercatel 187
Merderet, river 108
Mericourt, 174
Messines 160, 202, 214, 215, 219
Metz 124-6, 166, 189
Metz-en-Couture 72
Meuse, river 13, 14, 27, 28, 32-4, 36-9, 43, 47, 51, 121, 126, 129, 189, 190
Meuse-Escaut Canal 14
Meuvaines 112
Moeuvres 64-5, 71
Monchy le Preux 181
Monschau 27, 32
Montauban 151
Mont Fleury 103, 112
Mont Kemmel 171, 200, 202
Montmédy 121, 125-6
Mont St Eloi 186
Mont-St-Jean 221
Morecourt 174
Moselle, river 28, 47
MULBERRY harbour 101, 117, 143

Namur 27, 28, 43, 47
Naples 117
Neerpelt 13, 15

Neffe 37
Nesle 93, 174
Neufchâteau 35 37 39
Neuville-St-Vaast 179, 181, 186
Nieuport 53
Nieuwe Kruisecke 205, 206
Nieuwe-Plein 21
Nijmegen 11, 13, 14, 17-20, 24
Nine Wood 71
Nonne Bosschen 207, 212
Normandy 100-19
North Brabant 12
Notre Dame de Lorette 179, 181, 185
Noville 34-6
Novion-Porcien 121
Noyelles 64, 65
Nun's Copse 207, 212

Olly Farm 127
OMAHA 101, 106-9, 111, 113, 115-16
Oosterbeek 11, 17-20, 22
Orne river 102, 106, 114, 118
Orthenville 32
Ostend 51
Ouistreham 101, 113
Our river 29
Ourthe river 32
Ouville-la-Rivière 137, 140
Ovillers 146

Paris 88, 93, 107, 125
Pas de Calais 48, 105
Passchendaele 62, 199, 200, 202, 205, 214, 216-18
Pegasus Bridge 101, 118
Péronne 47, 93, 146, 165, 167
Petit Berneval 138
Petit Vimy 187
Pilckem 202, 215
Plancenoit 227
Ploegsteert 202, 219
Poelcappelle 213, 216, 217
Point 145 184
Pointe du Hoc 101, 103, 111
Poissy 88
Poitiers 93, 94, 97, 99
Polygon Wood 199, 205-7, 211
Ponthieu 93
Poperinge 57
Port-en-Bessin 101, 113
Port-le-Grand 88
Potijze 199
Pouppeville 109
Pourville 130-1, 134, 139, 140, 144
Pozières 146, 148, 154, 151, 161
Premy Chapel 68
Puys 130, 134, 142, 144
Pyrenees 125

Quatre Bras 222
Quiberville 139

Ravebeek 218
Reichswald Forest 17
Reims 33, 125, 167
Rethel 126
Rhine 12, 13, 18
Rhineland 222
Ribécourt 65, 67, 68, 72
Rolle 37
Roubaix 51
Rouen 88, 145
Roulers (Rosslare) 166
Roye 165
Ruhr 12
Ruhrland 12
Ruisseauville 94
Rumilly 65, 69

Saane, river 139
Saarbrucken 124
Saarland 124, 125
Saigneville 88, 93
St Aubin d'Arquenay 114
St Aubin-sur-Mer 101
St Elizabeth Hospital 11, 18
St Eloi 202, 219
St Julien 62, 202, 213, 215
St Laurent 111, 117
St Leger 112, 113
St Malo 11
St Martin-de-Varreville 109
St Mère Église 101, 108
St Mihiel 189
St Nazaire 117
St Oedenrode 17
St Omer 48, 51
St Pierre Divion 162
St Privat 124
St Quentin 63, 64, 166
St Vaast 88
St Valery-en-Caux 145, 212
St Vith 27, 32, 35
Samogneux 191
Sanctuary Wood 199, 202
Scarpe, river 51
Scheld estuary 102
Schnee Eifel 33
Schwaben Höhe 154
Scie, river 134, 140
Sedan 47, 120-29
Seine, river 11, 88, 107
Senonchamps 37
Sensée 187
Serre 151
Siegfried Stellung (Hindenburg Line) 181
Soissons 166
Soignes, Forest of 222
Somme 47, 48, 52, 88, 90, 93, 146-77, 182
Souchez 181, 183
Soument 32
Spanbroekmolen 219
Stavelot 32
Streenstraat 213
SWORD 106-7, 113, 116, 118

Tahon 113
Thiepval 146, 151, 161, 162, 164
Thirimont 40
Toc H Pool of Peace 219
Torhout 204
Tourcoing 200
Tramecourt 85, 93-5
Triangle Farm 81
Turqueville 108
Tyne Cott 218

Uden 20
UTAH 101, 106-9, 116
Utrechtstraat 11

Vailly-sur-Aisne 166
Valenciennes 51
Vallée des Clercs 90, 96
Varengeville-sur-Mer 131
Vasterival 139
Vaucelles 65
Vaux-les-Rosières 37, 39
Veghel 11, 13, 15, 17, 20
Veldoek 207, 211
Verbeek Farm 212
Verdun 11, 149, 159, 161, 165, 167, 179, 188-97
Veules-les-Roses 145
Vierville-sur-Mer 111
Villers Bretonneux 146, 168, 170, 173, 176
Villers-Guislain 72
Villers Plourch 72
Villons-les Buissons 113
Vimy 62, 178-87
Voyennes 93

Waal river 13, 19
Wadelincourt 129
Wadicourt 85, 90
Wailly 187
Walcheren 12
Warfusée Abancourt 174
Warlus 187
Waterloo 220-29
Wavre 47, 222, 224, 227
Wesel 12
Westhoek 215
Wilhelmina Canal 13
Willems Canal 13
Wolfhezen 16
Wulverghem 202
Wytschaete 200, 201, 214, 219

Ypres 52, 60, 62, 65, 159, 171, 198-219
Yser, river 200, 203

Zandvoorde 205-7
Zillebeke 199, 202
Zon 11, 13, 17, 19
Zonnebeke 199, 205, 216
Zwarte-Leen 199, 210, 219
Zuydcoote 45, 61